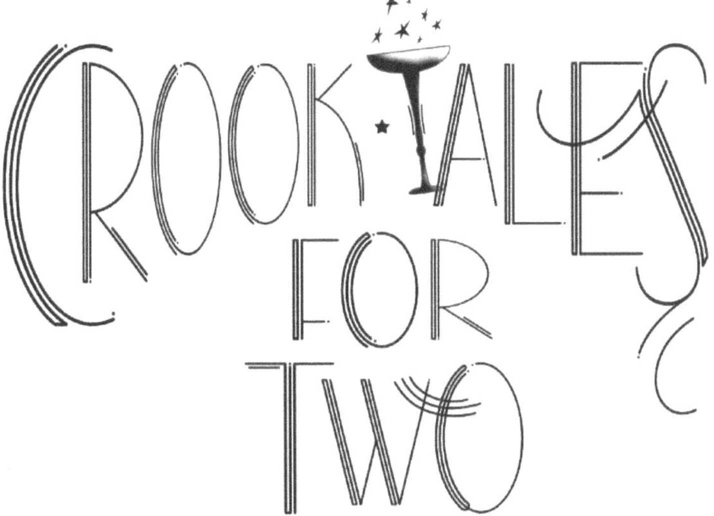

CROOK TALES FOR TWO

Also by Ellen Byerrum

The Crime of Fashion Mysteries
Killer Hair
Designer Knockoff
Hostile Makeover
Raiders of the Lost Corset
Grave Apparel
Armed and Glamorous
Shot Through Velvet
Death on Heels
Veiled Revenge
Lethal Black Dress
The Masque of the Red Dress
The Brief Luminous Flight of the Firefly (a prequel)

Thrillers
The Woman in the Dollhouse

Plays, writing as Eliot Byerrum
Boom Town Blues
Interviewing Techniques for the Self-Conscious
Red She Said
Ghost Dance
A Christmas Cactus
Gumshoe Rendezvous
Father Jeremy's Christmas Jubilee
The Angel of Death Rises Early

Books for younger readers
The Children Didn't See Anything
Sherlocktopus Holmes: Eight Arms of the Law

The Cassidy James Stories
The Last Goodbye of Harris Turner
The End of Summer

Praise for Ellen Byerrum

"Devilishly funny. Lacey is intelligent, insightful and spunky...thoroughly likable." (*The Sun*, Bremerton, WA)

"Laced with wicked wit." (*SouthCoastToday.com*)

"Fun and witty...with a great female sleuth." (*Fresh Fiction*)

"A load of stylish fun." (*Scripps Howard News Service*)

"Always well-written, entertaining, and stylish." (*More Than a Review*)

"Skewers Washington with style." (Agatha winner Elaine Viets)

Killer Hair (also a movie)

"Girlfriends you'd love to have, romance you can't resist, and Beltway-insider insights you've got to read. Adds a crazy twist to the concept of capital murder." (Agatha winner Sarah Strohmeyer)

Designer Knockoff

"Clever wordplay, snappy patter, and intriguing clues make this politics-meets-high-fashion whodunit a cut above the ordinary." (*Romantic Times*)

"A very talented writer with an offbeat sense of humor." (*The Best Reviews*)

Hostile Makeover (also a movie)

"Byerrum pulls another superlative Crime of Fashion out of her vintage cloche." (*Chick Lit Books*)

"As smooth as fine-grade cashmere." (*Publishers Weekly*)

"Totally delightful...a fun and witty read." (*Fresh Fiction*)

Raiders of the Lost Corset

"I love this series. Lacey is such a wonderful character... The plot has many twists and turns to keep you turning the pages to discover the truth. I highly recommend this book and series." (*Spinetingler Magazine*)

"Wow. I loved it! I could not put it down! I loved everything about the book, from the characters to the plot to the fast-paced and witty writing." (*Roundtable Reviews*)

Grave Apparel

"A truly intriguing mystery." (*Armchair Reader*)

"A likeable, sassy, and savvy heroine, and the Washington, D.C., setting is a plus." (*The Romance Readers Connection*)

Armed and Glamorous

"Whether readers are fashion divas or hopelessly fashion-challenged, there's a lot to like about being *Armed and Glamorous*." (*BookPleasures.com*)

Shot Through Velvet

"First-rate...a serious look at the decline of the U.S. textile and newspaper industries provides much food for thought." (*Publishers Weekly*, starred review)

"Great fun, with lots of interesting tidbits about the history of the U.S. fashion industry." (*Suspense Magazine*)

Death on Heels

"Terrific! A fabulous Crime of Fashion Mystery." (*Genre Go Round Reviews*)

"I loved the touch that Lacey was a reporter trying to track down a murderer, but could always be counted on for her fashion-forward thinking as well. If you haven't yet picked up a Lacey Smithsonian novel, I suggest you do!" (*Chick Lit+)*

"Lacey is a character that I instantly fell in love with." (*Turning the Pages*)

Veiled Revenge

"An intriguing plot, fun but never too insane characters, and a likable and admirable heroine all combine to create a charming and well-crafted mystery." (*Kings River Life Magazine*)

"Like fine wine that gets better with age, *Veiled Revenge* is the best book yet in this fabulous series." (*Dru's Book Musings*)

Lethal Black Dress

"Only a fashion reporter with a nose for vintage dresses could sniff out the clues in this brilliantly conceived murder mystery." (Nancy J. Cohen, author of the Bad Hair Day Mysteries)

The Masque of the Red Dress

"It's been too long since the last Crime of Fashion mystery, and fans will delight in seeing their favorite characters return in this eleventh of the series... Author Byerrum makes the scenery come alive not just with descriptions of gorgeous couture of multiple eras, but with the unique personalities populating the struggling-to-survive newsroom. The combination of cynicism and hope is never more apparent than with these jaded reporters, who are accustomed to interns getting blamed by ego-driven politicians... The Fashion Bites articles of tips and the history of D.C. fashion continue to be refreshing and fun, highlighting tips to battle office low-thermostat hypothermia, the need for formal wear rules, and of course, the power of a red dress. This is a welcome return to an enthralling and always entertaining mystery series." (Cynthia Chow, *KRL News & Reviews*)

The Brief Luminous Flight of the Firefly

"Byerrum does a remarkable job of describing what life was like during the 1940s and in presenting an intriguing mystery." (Grace Topping, author of the Laura Bishop home-staging mysteries)

"This is an engrossing mystery set in a meticulously researched and fascinating historical context. The filigree of fashion throughout the book amusingly illuminates character and period. Mimi Smith is a worthy precursor to Lacey Smithsonian and *The Brief Luminous Flight of the Firefly* is a worthy precursor to the Crime of Fashion Mystery series." (Paul Donnelly, award-winning playwright)

"The story is compelling and mysterious and the attention to everyday historical realities brings the era to life." (Martha Horstman-Evans, award-winning director and playwright)

Sherlocktopus Holmes: Eight Arms of the Law

"The rhymes are so happy, some will make you laugh out loud. If you read it aloud to others you can all enjoy the wordplay. And each verse will help you discover clues to your case, to help find where Sally's missing doll may be hiding." (Wendy Kendall, *MLT News, MyEdmondsNews.com*)

"Great rhymes! Wonderful clues! A first detective novel for young readers. The illustrations are marvelous." (Beth Schmelzer, *BestBooksByBeth.wordpress.com*)

"This clever children's book combines rhymes, education and entertainment, in a charming story that's a tale of mystery accompanied by colorful illustrations." (Nancy J. Cohen, author of the Bad Hair Day Mysteries)

The Woman in the Dollhouse

"An ingeniously crafted psychological thriller that bewitches on page one and continues to mesmerize until its shocking conclusion… We can't imagine a better read. Byerrum has deftly structured a compelling narrative that never lets go. You won't either, by the way. This is one book you're practically guaranteed to finish in record time." (*Best Thrillers.com*)

"Reminiscent of the best of gothic suspense fiction, readers will be thoroughly entertained by Tennyson. Her strong will and even sharper wit ensure that readers will be cheering for Tennyson to break free and discover the truth. That the book starts with such a vulnerable beginning only makes the crafty conclusion all the more satisfying." (*Kings River Life Magazine*)

CROOK TALES FOR TWO

ELLEN BYERRUM

Lethal Black Dress Press

Cover art by Kate Lamoure
Book design and cover design by Robert A. Williams

Visit Ellen Byerrum online:
ellenbyerrum.com
facebook.com/EllenByerrum
instagram.com/ellenbyerrumauthor
youtube.com/@ellenbyerrumsfashionbites2378

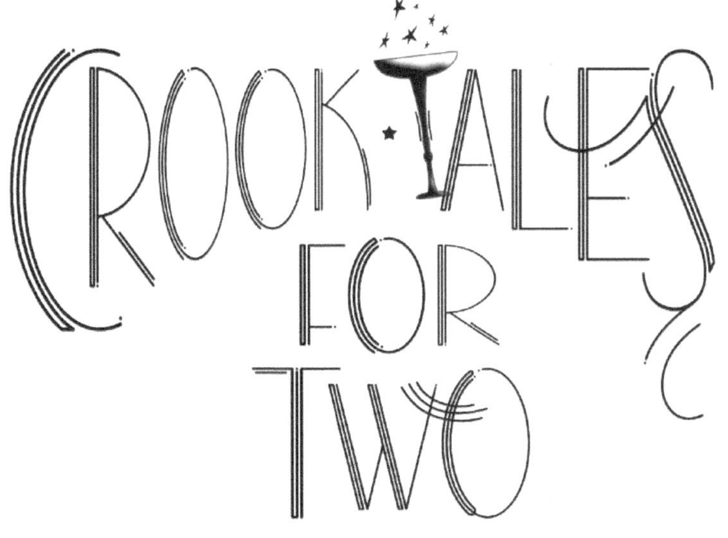

CROOK TALES FOR TWO

ONE

I T OCCURRED TO ME THAT if I hadn't tried to do a good deed and return the gold watch Mr. Scavullo left at the lunch counter, a strange man wouldn't be holding me at gunpoint.

That was the problem with good deeds. Unintended consequences.

I had no idea that following Scavullo would bring me trouble. For heaven's sake, I used to see him and his wife at Sunday Mass at Our Lady of Pompeii. Rumors that he was involved with the Mafia were just that. *Rumors*. I'd paid no attention to them.

And here I was, frozen with fixed gaze on the man with the gun. Was he going to shoot me? People were killed every day in New York City. But it wasn't *my* time to go. Women had power now, and the vote, Prohibition was over, and my play—my first play in this city—was about to open in an almost-respectable Broadway theatre in a matter of days. I was only twenty-five.

There was no way I was going to end up shot dead in an empty elementary school. However, the man with the gun didn't know that.

I stared at him, my powers of speech rendered mute by fear. He stared back but made no sudden moves. He was tall, his brown hair streaked with sunlight. The small space was illuminated by a dim electric bulb that showed the gunman's eyes improbably blue, as if colored by neon tubes. His face was long, and he had a sharp square chin. There were women who might consider him handsome, if they could forget about the gun, but he was some kind of gangster. He had to be. His black pinstripe suit and black shirt were practically a calling card. And his blue tie, matching those electric eyes, was cheekily decorated with martini glasses.

I knew a thug when I saw one. I've been to the movies.

"What are you doing in there?" he asked. I could ask him the same thing. It took me a moment to realize that his accent wasn't from New York or New Jersey. "Well?" He trained his blue gaze on me.

"I'm hiding. I heard shouting. And a gunshot," I managed to say. I was, in fact, in some kind of utility closet in the school building where I'd followed Scavullo. His gold watch weighed heavy in my pocketbook, not to mention on my mind.

I didn't know why school wasn't in session. Then I remembered. It was Columbus Day. President Roosevelt had just declared today, Friday, October 12, 1934, a brand-new holiday, thrilling school children everywhere, and appeasing his Italian-American constituents. That's why the building was empty. Well, almost empty.

"I'm supposed to believe that? Believe you?"

I placed his accent. English. Perhaps high-class English, like that handsome actor, Robert Donat, in that new movie, *The Count of Monte Cristo*. How terribly, terribly improbable.

"You can't command me at the point of a gun."

Brave, silly words. Where were the witty lines I was able to write for my characters?

"I believe I can." He had the nerve to smirk. Still, he lowered the gun, but he didn't slide it into his shoulder holster. "Who are you and why are you here?"

I explained, as efficiently as I was able, under the bizarre circumstances, about Mr. Scavullo and his gold pocket watch and how he had seemed distracted earlier. Scavullo had glanced at the timepiece and left it on the lunch counter at the diner, which was close to the theatre where I worked, the Washington Irving, and where I was having my first play produced. I told the man with the gun I was a playwright. He didn't seem impressed.

On days when I wasn't in the mood for a ten-cent sandwich at the automat and I needed to get away from my job, I sometimes ate at Ray's Diner. That's why I knew Ray was more likely to pocket the watch for himself than to see it returned to its rightful owner. Ray had that kind of reputation. Because I knew Scavullo's family from church, I tried to follow him, to make sure he got it back. He relied on his timepiece.

When Father Rappoli's sermons grew long, I would notice Dante Scavullo surreptitiously lift the watch from his vest pocket and take a peek, no doubt judging how many minutes were left. It was a pretty timepiece. A small window showed the phases of the moon in blue and silver. Sometimes it chimed on the half hour and he hurried to shut it off. Other times he would open the back to check on something.

Why did I know so much about this stupid pocket watch? Perhaps I wasn't listening to the sermon the way I should have either. Scavullo may have winked at me once or twice when he witnessed me watching his watch, as if we shared a secret. His wife Juliette would swat him and glare in that way that wives had, and Scavullo's prized possession would return to his vest pocket until Mass was over.

"I tried to follow him, but Ray made me pay Scavullo's tab first." The Brit looked skeptical. I rushed to explain. "Everyone knows Ray's a skinflint and he takes anything left on the counter. He 'forgets' to bring your change, too. Ray was angry that I grabbed the watch before he could. That's why he delayed me."

"I'm not sure I believe you. How do I know you didn't lure Scavullo here with the watch?"

"Lure him? What are you talking about? I don't even know where he is now! He left the diner before me. I was trying to follow him. To give him back his darn watch."

The gunman leaned against the doorjamb. "Is that what you do? Follow strange men into empty buildings?"

"How dare you! I don't follow men, I'm a playwright. And Mr. Scavullo isn't strange, I know him from Our Lady of Pompeii."

"You're a churchgoer?"

"And you're a Brit with obviously very little knowledge of religion."

"Guilty on both counts. But why should I believe this watch-and-bull story of yours?"

Was he amused at me? "Believe what you want, Brit."

How dare he doubt me. And I had no reason to believe this mug. I was offended by his tone, and his accent. I sneered at him. I realized it could have been my last sneer and I didn't want to waste it on the wrong person.

"And I shall. Continue." The gun wavered but did not take aim.

"Mr. Scavullo was a block ahead of me. I caught sight of him turning into this building." I didn't know why Scavullo did that. I simply wanted to get rid of the watch. Now even more so.

"And you trotted into a closed school?" He sneered right back at me.

"Closed but not locked. As did you," I snapped at him.

We seemed to be in a regular public elementary school with that peculiar smell of pine cleanser that hits you when you stroll through the door, like any school across the land. The red-brown linoleum floors were polished to a high shine. Each classroom door had a clear window through which you could see the green chalkboards sporting the ABCs. Today those windows were free of small smudgy handprints. I'd entered a long hallway, lined with doors on either side. The closet in which I hid was near the far exit.

The stranger stepped closer to me.

"I thought I could dash in and find Mr. Scavullo and hand over the watch. I have to get back to work." I gestured, but he blocked my escape.

"If that's all you wanted, how did you wind up in here with the dustmops?"

"Sounded like a gunfight. One to which I wasn't invited." Even this English buffoon should realize that any sane person would find a place to hide from gunfire. I was too far from the front door to exit the way I came.

"It's hard to hide when you're making such a racket."

"Not my fault," I said.

I had tried a few doors until I found one unlocked, a crowded utility closet where I could lay low. It would have worked too. Everything was fine. I shared the closet with a placid tortoiseshell feline calmly licking her paws, apparently collecting herself after the first shot. I had no idea where the cat came from, although it could have been from a high window, which was open a few inches. Everyone knows cats seem to have no bones. But when more shots rang out, it bolted upwards to a top shelf, upsetting boxes of Christmas ornaments in its wake. It proceeded to create a cacophonous reign of cat terror before disappearing who knows where.

Glass balls of every color fell and shattered around me, setting off a chain reaction of more shiny things cascading downward, clattering and crashing into rainbows of glass shards. The whole ridiculous incident could be in a play. I caught my breath and for a few moments I thought I was fine. I waited to see if anything would happen.

That's when the closet door burst open and this pin-striped gangster appeared, compact blue-steel automatic in hand. We were locked in a staring contest.

More shots were fired on the next floor up. I jumped and caught my breath in a gasp. Thundering feet pounded somewhere above our heads down a similar hallway, or maybe they were on the stairs close by. It was hard to tell exactly where, what with all the blood pounding in my ears. I could feel my eyes watering, my heart beating. Loud voices sounded above our heads, followed by heavy steps running. We both gazed upwards.

Another voice, low and guttural, very New York, shouted down the closest stairway. "Hey Chase, where'd you go? What in hell was that noise?"

The mug reached out with his gun-less hand and grabbed my arm, perhaps in warning. His touch felt shocking, like an electric current that wasn't static electricity. I tried to pull away from him. He seemed to feel something too. His grip was like iron. I struggled to shake him off, but he held fast.

"It was a cat," I whispered. As if on cue, the cat appeared from the back of the closet. The animal meowed loudly and raced through the stranger's legs out to the hall.

"It's only a cat," my captor yelled toward the direction of the other voice.

"Shoot it. I hate cats."

Steps marched away and finished trudging up the stairs to the next floor. The Brit waited a minute before staring at me again. He made no move to follow the voice or the animal. Was he trying to outstare me?

I knew the type. The kind of guy who believes all women swoon at his good looks and slavishly follow his orders. However, I am Irish on one side and French on the other and one hundred percent American, so let's just say there is no love lost between me and the English.

"Give me the watch and I'll see that Scavullo gets it," he said.

I had a very bad feeling that Scavullo would never need his watch again. But I wasn't about to give it away. "I have to do it myself."

Two more painful shots rang above our heads. How many people were up there? How many were shot? How many had died? I put my hand over my mouth to keep from screaming.

"Don't think so." He pointed the gun up.

"Scavullo's up there?"

"He was, but now..." He shook his head slowly.

I could feel tears run down my cheeks. I don't normally cry, but these were extraordinary circumstances.

"Then I'll make sure his wife Juliette gets the watch."

"Look, you," the stranger said. "It's obvious you don't belong here. I'm trying to help Scavullo. Extricate him from this mess he's gotten himself into." *Extricate* was a five-dollar word. Who was this guy? It didn't matter, he obviously was trying to make me give up that valuable pocket watch. "Someone like you shouldn't be involved."

"Someone like me?" What did he mean *someone like you*?

"Chase!" the other voice yelled. I assumed that was this thug's name. First or last, I didn't know.

We continued to stare at each other. I put him at late twenties, maybe thirty, but why I was wondering about that, at that moment, I have no idea. The scent of his cologne danced in the air. It wasn't the cheap stuff that eager boys wear to high school dances or what I thought gangsters might wear. More expensive, and subtle. It made me think of woods and forests. I don't know why. My heart beat like a jackhammer in my chest. I was afraid he could hear it.

"It seems there's a connection between us, Miss Who-ever-You-Are. You feel it."

"I feel nothing," I lied.

"Trying to slay me with those eyes, like green fires."

It sounded like a line he'd used on other women. Must he speak in hyperbole? How dare he be so familiar with me? He pulled me out of the closet, into an alcove behind the up-and-down staircase wide enough to accommodate hordes of children on their way to classes. The stairway led down five steps to the exit door and playground, and up-stairs—to what vile scene of bodies and blood, I could only imagine.

"Chase!" The voice came from upstairs again. "You take care of that cat?"

"Almost there." He yelled in the direction of the voice.

"Yeah, well, get up here. It ain't pretty."

"Stay here," the man called Chase whispered to me. He still gripped my arm, but I squirmed. Then, and I hesitate to admit this, he leaned against me again, pushing me to the wall to the point where I could feel the cold tiles through my sweater and skirt. Now I could feel *his* heart beating.

Why didn't I scream? Because he still had a gun, there were others with guns, and I was not in the mood to die. I was in the mood to run right out of there.

"Shhh." Chase pressed a finger against my mouth. I don't know why that particular touch shocked me, but it did. I pushed him away, but not far enough. Then he kissed me. On the lips. Most familiarly.

Don't get me wrong, people in the theatre kiss all the time. Kiss-kiss, hug-hug. *How are you, darling*? Kiss-kiss. *Lovely, my dear.* Hug-hug. *So good to see you,* kiss-hug. I'm used to that. People you've never met before, hug-hug, kiss-kiss. I like it, It feels rather French. Friendly. I enjoy the glamour of it. Yet this Chase character kissed me as if he knew me rather intimately. Far too intimately. I moved to the side.

"How dare you! Stop," I whispered, because there were other thugs about.

"I couldn't very well let you scream."

"I wasn't about to scream. I wasn't even close to scream-ing." I glared at him.

"My mistake. Stay here. You'll be safe."

"Safe with you? That's an old line," I managed to squeak.

"We'll chat about that later. I apologize, my dear. You simply looked so delicious." I opened my mouth to utter some outraged sentiment and he kissed me again. I beat my fists against him. Slapped him. I clipped his ear pretty hard. Then I lifted my knee. Not hard enough, because there wasn't enough room, but I got my point across. He backed off. We both heard glass breaking on the floor above us.

"Get a move on, Chase." The menacing voice again. Hard, the New York accent. "He's getting away. Fire escape."

Who was on the fire escape? Was Scavullo alive? Who was shot? We heard more rattling, more broken glass.

"Coming." The Englishman wiped his mouth and then mine with a clean white handkerchief. I pushed his hand away. "I will see you again, my sweet," he threatened me.

"Not if I can help it. And I'm not your sweet, you beast."

He had the nerve to grin at me. Obviously, I need to practice my knee kick. "Stay out of sight."

I was relieved he didn't know my name, not that he'd paid any attention when I said I was a playwright. He probably didn't even go to plays.

And wasn't he the optimist to think I'd stay put? His long legs raced up the stairs two steps at a time. The moment he was gone, I bolted down the stairs and out the nearest exit door to the playground, such as it was. There was no one around that I could see, no one looking my way. I was out of breath, but not from exertion—from horror.

I sucked in air, brushed my fingers through my hair, and then I ran.

Two

I COULD HAVE SPRINTED TOWARD the alley, looking suspicious, but I decided it was better to head straight for the crowd milling around the school, waiting for something to happen. Plus, I was curious.

Loud sirens approached. Police cars screeched to a stop. They were followed by reporters in cars and taxis, slim notebooks in their breast pockets and pencils behind their ears, hats worn on the back of their heads. I knew one of the reporters, but his attention was on the action and luckily not on me. I'd catch up with him later.

I sauntered toward the sidewalk where neighbors were gathering. Everyone I saw was focused on the fire escape above my head. No one wanted to miss a thing. After all, a police commotion was entertainment on a beautiful autumn afternoon. They didn't seem to care that gunshots had been flying around over their thick noggins or that someone was now dead, someone who minutes before was alive and breathing. They were an audience, waiting for the main attraction.

"What's going on?" I asked a couple of women standing next to the building. Bystanders were looking up and down, behind them, looking everywhere but at me. Thank goodness.

"Someone got shot inside the school! Can you believe it? Disgraceful. The school, of all places." The harried woman hauling an overstuffed grocery bag sounded outraged. "Thank the Almighty up above, the children weren't there today."

"We can thank Columbus for that." Another woman gestured upwards. I followed her lifted arm and saw the empty fire escape.

"Nah, thank FDR. He gave us the holiday," the first replied. Bystanders around us seemed to agree with that sentiment.

I don't know why we should feel so alive at moments like this. Suddenly I was aware that trees along the street were brightly stained by autumn. So much orange and crimson and yellow set against the blazing blue sky, like a picture out of a calendar. The frosty morning had warmed up during the day. Yet I could still feel its crispness on my cheeks. Had I never noticed the fall so deeply before? I was crazy happy to be alive and living here in New York. Especially alive.

"Did you see anything?" I asked the woman with the groceries.

She juggled the bag on her hip. "Just missed him. Heard some crazy fella was hanging off the iron railing, then jumped into a car waiting for him right under the fire escape. Took off real fast. That's what Gladys said. I always miss the good parts."

"So, Gladys saw him?" I gazed around to see this witness.

"Gladys likes to talk. But not to the coppers. Gladys don't talk to no coppers."

I didn't get to meet this distrustful Gladys; she'd already beat her retreat home.

"What kind of car was it?" I asked.

"Black," the harried woman answered.

Several policemen jumped out of patrol cars that had just screeched to a halt and shouted at us to return to our daily business, which I was more than happy to do. They never said, "Stick around and tell us what you saw."

I had no desire to be interrogated, especially when I wasn't sure what I'd seen. I didn't know what to make of that Chase character, who might exit the building at any second and spot me. Or jump out onto the fire escape. He was surely still at the scene of the crime. I didn't want to see him and I certainly didn't want him to see me. I hadn't actually seen a crime, I'd only heard it. The unknown Gladys had seen more than I did. I told myself I was off the hook.

Now the reporters were crowding the police, running on the adrenaline of a hot scoop. The police barely looked at the crowd of onlookers. It was time for me to get back to the theatre.

Stashed in my pocketbook, Scavullo's prize pocket watch weighed even heavier on me now. Surely he was dead. He wasn't the man who had escaped. I couldn't imagine a man of sixty or so throwing himself out of a window and making like Douglas Fairbanks down the fire escape after shooting up a schoolroom. Dante Scavullo never seemed like the gangster type to me. He was a quiet, soft-spoken man.

Another question occurred: Would the hoodlums know about the watch? Did they care? If they did, would anyone come after me for it? According to the newspapers, these criminals took no prisoners. I could have a target on my back, or wherever they chose to place one.

And what about the blue-eyed mobster who trapped me in the closet? Clearly, he didn't believe a word I said. And why should I believe anything he said? What did he mean about *extricating* Scavullo from the mess he was in? My head was beginning to hurt from all the questions.

The best thing to do was to return Dante's watch to Mrs. Juliette Scavullo as soon as possible. However, I didn't know where she lived. If it was true that there was a mob connection, I didn't care to be seen waltzing up her front steps. If I had her address, I could mail the darn thing and leave it up to Uncle Sam's Postal Service. I hated to think I might have to attend a funeral to turn over the watch.

I wore myself out pondering all that. A bad habit of mine.

Curious about what the afternoon papers would write on the incident at the school, I was betting they'd call it the "Columbus Day School Shootout" or some variation. As a former newspaper reporter, I knew it was too soon for the late afternoon editions to come out. The newsboys were taking a post-lunch snooze.

I'd like to say that I swiftly hot-footed it back to the Washington Irving Theatre, where I worked as a lowly assistant, on my way to fame and fortune. I'd like to say I got back on time and no one noticed I'd been missing, but I don't remember quite how I made it back to my office. Or how long it took. After I talked with the women outside the school and decided I was not going to be shot, it was all rather a blur. With the exception of a few images, those shiny autumn leaves, a woman wearing a bright red coat, a mother gathering her children, a pretzel seller on a corner, my mind's a blank. Those were things I would try to recall later. I didn't know whether I ran or stumbled down the long city blocks to the theatre. I failed to notice the cars or the people or what went on around me. I usually keep my wits about me. It's always been my custom to write down what I see, especially if something caught my eye or was out of the ordinary, as if I were still flinging words at a two-cent newspaper.

Why so unobservant today? My thoughts were full of outrage over this stranger called Chase, though perhaps I should have been relieved he hadn't shot me. I wanted to slap him again.

My other whirling thoughts were of Dante Scavullo. I didn't actually know if he was alive—every instinct said he was not. I didn't know if he'd deliberately met someone in that formerly quiet school, or how many people had guns, or how many people might be dead. I wrote a scenario in my head. And once I'm writing I can ignore all manner of things. I have been known to forget my subway stop when penning a scene or overhearing a particularly juicy bit of conversation with an assortment of accents, only to come out of my haze several stops later, halfway across town.

It was only when I neared the Washington Irving that I paused to look around and wonder how I arrived there. My brain felt numb, my lips were still tingling from that unexpected kiss, and I was starving. I'd never had a chance to eat my lunch at Ray's Diner, even though I paid for it, and for Mr. Scavullo's as well. So far, it had been an expensive, exasperating, frightening, and hungry sort of day.

It was a surprise to see a large hot pretzel wrapped in wax paper in my hands, purchased on my trip back to work. On automatic pilot, I must have gone to a corner cart, pointed to a pretzel, and pulled out my coin purse. The thing was enormous, and it smelled delicious. I was standing on the sidewalk, not far from the theatre where I toiled daily at a variety of tasks, including reading would-be scribes' endless offerings for the stage.

I knew how lucky I was to have a job, any job, in this crazy world, with our endless Depression. But through a quirk of fate and scheduling, and somebody else's fortuitous flop, the Washington Irving Theatre was also the venue that would be producing my first play in New York. And in mere days.

Most of the time, we band of happy little theatrical strivers referred to the Washington Irving as the "W.I." or "the Irv." However, depending on how successful (or not) any given show was, we'd also call it "Sleepy Hollow" or "the Rip Van Winkle." The most dreaded nickname, of course, was "the Headless Horseman," which meant the show of the moment rated a quick and dirty demise, accompanied by a hurled flaming pumpkin.

Its public facade was gorgeous. The lighted marquee, the gilt-edged lobby with its giant crystal chandeliers, the extravagant ornamental metal cage where tickets were sold, it was all designed for teeming theatre crowds. This afternoon it was empty.

I paused next to the side entrance that the theatre staff used. I was reaching for the handle when the door was flung open with a great rusty screech. It sounded like a wounded animal, an angry wounded animal, but all I could think of was gunshots.

I shrieked.

THREE

66 **E**SMÉ! ARE YOU ALL RIGHT?" Andras Szabo, the noted director of my play, grinned at me, looking slightly mad, as usual. "Ah, I know. Finally, my little playwright, you are releasing your feelings to the world." He stabbed his chubby fingers in the air. "Cry. Scream. Laugh. Free your emotions. Your day of judgment is coming."

He meant my play. His Hungarian accent always got thicker when he was excited.

"That isn't it, Andras. I was simply—" Simply what? I couldn't think. I sucked in some air. "I'm merely—"

"A million miles away. Writing a new *pièce de théâtre*?"

"That's it. I might be tweaking the last few lines of *Leaving Alamogordo*."

It had come to me in a flash that I wanted to fine tune the end of my play, even more than I already had.

"What? No! The play is done. It's too late!" Andras's reactions were generally like an exploding, then sputtering, volcano. This was the full Krakatoa. "We have no out-of-town tryouts! No previews, not enough rehearsals! Opening night must be perfect! And now you have new lines? You will drive your leading lady mad!"

"As if you're not steering the asylum bus," I cracked.

"Good point! We shall drive her mad together." He laughed merrily. "Always look for the silver lining."

Szabo was right. Late changes would drive Clarissa crazy. If the dialogue was sharp and the action perfect, she would eventually agree—still, there would be a scene. A dramatic scene. I shrugged my shoulders at my chubby director. Andras Szabo was of medium stature and round shape, attesting to his love of good Hungarian food. He adored sugar and sour cream and anything frosted. He also craved pierogis and goulash. A fringe of brown hair covered his round head, and his face was likewise circular. However, his cherubic countenance was misleading. This director excelled at encouraging, cajoling, or bullying his actors and stagehands. Whatever it took, for the good of the show.

"Don't worry, Andras, it'll only be a few lines."

He sighed deeply. Dramatically. "Playwrights."

"We're not nearly as temperamental as actors," I pointed out.

"Actors. Actresses. Spare me." He put his hand to his heart. "And promise me, Esmé, you have only a very little change. One that Clarissa can handle. Without the fireworks. Those she should save for opening night."

"I promise."

Our goodwill was restored. He patted my shoulder and moved past me out the side door, on the hunt for a late lunch, or an early dinner. Or a legal martini, now that Prohibition was finally over. He was fond of singing that snappy new song celebrating the end of the dry years, "Cocktails for Two." It was on the radio all the time. He was also fond of pointing out all the places that used to hide speakeasies, now shiny new saloons, he said, owned by bootleggers gone legit.

I made my way up the stairs to the offices, past the rehearsal space, where the unseen staff worked. It smelled musty and dusty, a dose of greasepaint, stage paint, and sawdust. I loved it, yet at the moment I found it hard to concentrate. Random thoughts of revenge against the smug mug who had kissed me in a closet crashed into other thoughts of how I was going to rework the ending of my play. It kept me in a fog. I nearly walked into a wall, stopped short, bumped my thigh hard against my desk, and fell into my chair. There would be bruises tomorrow.

I hoped people wouldn't think I was drunk. It wouldn't have bothered anyone, though, so close to opening night. They had their own troubles. In fact, like Szabo, they supplied me plenty of excuses for my absentmindedness.

You know playwrights. Always falling apart approaching opening night.

I was determined not to cry, not to fall apart. My stomach growled. I considered my still-warm pretzel. Only a desperate woman grabbed food on the street like some urchin on the run! But it smelled divine. Tearing it in half to save some for later, I took a bite. It melted in my mouth, hot bread dough, salt, and mustard.

I slipped down into my chair at my overflowing desk in the small corner where I read playscripts for the theatre. Later that afternoon I would be helping at the box office, taking reservations for our very next show, *Leaving Alamogordo,* by *me,* Esmé de LaForet. Esmé *Rafferty* de LaForet. Finally, at seven, I planned to attend rehearsal to make sure *my* words were being spoken, and not off-the-cuff improvisations by actors who had trouble memorizing lines or thought they should rewrite my play.

I stashed my purse with Scavullo's watch in the bottom drawer of my desk, full of stacks of unsolicited offerings and my succinct reports. The floor next to it was piled high with more scripts. There was a rule at the Irv: If anyone touched a play, they had to read it. Most people kept a wide berth of my corner. Today I was even more glad of that. I also knew that even if Scavullo's timepiece chimed, the watch couldn't be heard under all those piles of paper.

"Esmé, what happened to you?" May Scott's voice piped up behind a stack of newly delivered playscripts. She dumped them on my desk. I was the theatre's first line of defense, saving the producers and directors from these unsolicited mountains of dramatic prose.

"I lost track of time."

When I applied for the job there as Jill-of-All-Trades, I earnestly told them I had studied journalism and playwriting (just one course) in college. That didn't impress them as much as my timing. I had walked in at precisely the moment the last office grunt stormed out. I could feel the breeze from his exit. Two years later, I still didn't know what that particular dustup was all about. Could have been anything. Or nothing. It's the theatre.

May's phone rang on the desk next to mine, and she answered. "Manager of hopes and dreams! Don't disappoint me." She quickly dispatched the caller before pushing her dark round horn-rimmed glasses to the top of her head to peer at me. I wondered if my hair had turned white since that morning. "Hey, you! De LaForet. You're not usually late, unlike everyone else around here."

Her eyes were as round as her eyeglasses. She may have been in her thirties, but she looked like an eternal student, in sweaters with white collars and cuffs.

"Long boring story. I'm sorry," I said. "Did anyone notice?"

"Just me." She looked hungry.

"I'll swap you half my pretzel for a cup of coffee," I offered.

May kept a pot of java going on the credenza near her desk. The electric percolator was her personal property and woe to the clueless lad or lass who thought they could lift a cup. May didn't *have* to share with me, this would be a special indulgence.

Her hand was out in the age-old "give-me" gesture. May was as thin as a razor blade, but she could eat anything. She wore her mahogany brown hair in a short and sensible bob. Her clothes were dark and serviceable and seldom featured jewelry or bright colors. May was a brick. You could count on her. She answered the phones and handled a variety of other jobs. She was the queen bee of this little hive, whom no one dared irritate or risk her sting. She changed her job title often, depending on her mood: "box office manager" or "house manager," "supervisor of dramaturgical incompetence," or "ringmaster of wayward boys and girls who couldn't make it in the circus." Her favorite sobriquet was "Queen of the May."

May's actual role was assistant theatre manager and right-hand woman to Sal, Salvatore Rossi, who bounced in and out of the office unpredictably. Sal chose that moment to stride into the room and pour himself a cup of coffee without permission. He raced away before May could yell at him.

Inside, Salvatore Rossi was a handsome young leading man who made the ladies swoon. Outside, he was middle-aged and well fed, hair thinning on top, his buttons straining over his stomach. He loved the theatre but never had what it took to be an actor, or at least more than a spear-carrier. Luckily, Sal's family had money and connections that allowed him to join a small partnership running a theatre and producing shows, for which he had a knack.

His philosophy was like the girl in the nursery rhyme—the one with the curl in the middle of her forehead. When theatre was good, it was very, very good. When it was bad, it was back to the drawing board. Sal was an eternal optimist, but he could indulge in some impressive rages. Nothing seemed to get him down for long—except *Afternoon Tea with Nigel,* the awful play for which I was so grateful. The play that failed, making room for my play, *Leaving Alamogordo.*

While Sal was technically the Washington Irving's artistic director as well as producer, May Scott was the indispensable cog without whom nothing would have worked, the one on whom we called, and to whom we paid homage. We were all in awe of her. Once annoyed beyond all endurance, May would ensure the troublemaker was never cast again or employed on a show there. Still, she could be your greatest cheerleader. I gave her the other half of my pretzel.

"My lips are sealed," she said and indicated her personal percolator. "Help yourself."

I wished May hadn't mentioned lips, because it made me think of the turquoise-eyed stranger who kissed me. My fingertips went there before taking another bite. The memory of him holding me and kissing me was very disturbing. I could still feel the electrical charge of the moment, the scent of his cologne. What was wrong with me? The unwanted thought came to mind that I hadn't been kissed enough in a very long time. Not for lack of men wanting or trying to kiss me, mind you. Aside from all those theatrical kisses, *kiss-kiss, hug-hug*, I was simply very particular who I let kiss me. Extremely particular.

Although I was completely innocent in the incident in the closet, it made me reconsider the ending of my play, which culminated in romantic feelings revealed—and a kiss. *The kiss*. It was expected, it was wanted. Necessary. My heroine had worked hard for it. She deserved that kiss and darn it, *I* deserved that kiss. But now I was thinking that perhaps Annabelle, my character, shouldn't wait for my male character, William, to bestow it on her. She was far too active and impatient for that.

I pulled out my copy of *Leaving Alamogordo* and opened it to the last scene. I grabbed my favorite fountain pen and bit into my pretzel. I was able to push part of the scene at the school out of my mind by mentally rewriting it as well: I put my main character Annabelle in charge of the sudden kiss in the closet. Annabelle wanted that kiss. Me? Not so sure. Not yet.

"Uh, oh. Are those last-minute changes?" May appeared at my desk with yet more packages to drop.

"Just a few lines, I promise. And I already talked to Andras. Besides, no play is ever finished, you know, merely abandoned," I added, quoting a hundred other writers.

"We can always hope." She chewed a bite of the pretzel.

"It will make it better," I said. "It's the very end of the play."

"Endings are important," May agreed.

"Clarissa will love it." I sounded more certain than I was.

"Hmph. You better be sure about that." May dropped the new pile of scripts on my desk. "Or we're all going to suffer."

Clarissa Eldridge, my leading lady. Real name: Sophie Goldblatt. A striking dark-eyed brunette with exaggerated features perfect for the stage, Clarissa was used to men stumbling over their tongues around her. She lapped it up like a Siamese cat. However, she was excessively susceptible to flattery and those of us who worked with her had learned to use it to our advantage.

I didn't begrudge Clarissa her gifts. You want your star to be the center of attention. Still, there were times she seemed to believe that the two of us were in competition. That was not at all the case, I assure you.

With her perfect oval face, Clarissa is clearly more striking than I. My hair is neither blond nor red, but a combination of both, which people call strawberry. It curls easily, and I usually wear it in a chignon or twist, with errant ringlets framing my heart-shaped face. I am slender and of average height, my eyes are green, and my lashes long enough. My features are even and I am proud that I never needed braces to achieve that all-American healthy smile. When men call me beautiful, I am never sure exactly what they want, though I am sure they want something.

Yet, were a handsome man to speak to me in her presence, you can bet Clarissa Eldridge would find a way to slide between us and flash him her charming grin, flutter her false eyelashes, sink her fingers into his arm, and gently pull him away. She could be an excellent actress when the mood struck her. She could also be a pain in the keister.

I knew she would be annoyed by my changes, *any* changes, but I was gambling on her loving the new ending, and the kiss. She loved being the center of attention, and being *notorious* would be even better.

I sipped my coffee. May let me fill my cup a second time. Good thing I'd bought such a large *shareable* pretzel. It was surprisingly filling with that cup of coffee. And without gangsters shooting real guns, my crazy little corner at the Irv felt like peace on earth.

At least I could give my heroine some action. I lifted my pen and let the words flow. Clarissa (as Annabelle) got the last kiss. It would be her desire, her decision. Her action. *Her moment.*

"Make it a hit," May interrupted my thoughts.

"No pressure, May."

She smiled and lifted her coffee cup in salute. I thumped my forehead on my desk and she laughed.

"Do you want to know how I'm changing the ending?" I asked.

"Good heavens, no! I'll find out soon enough. Jeez, preserve me from playwrights' brains, directors' demands, and actors' emotions. Make that actors' tears. Big fat crocodile tears."

The next step was springing the rewrites on the actors at tonight's rehearsal. It was only a few lines. They could write the corrections in their scripts as they worked out the blocking of that final kiss.

If they didn't revolt first.

After I scribbled down my changes, I flipped through one of the playscripts that arrived over the transom: *How to Play Golf*. Labeled a "hilarious comedy of manners," it featured yet another maid and butler performing the task of exposition in the first scene of the play, that centuries-old device. How would an English drawing-room maid and butler, I wondered, describe the surprise mob hit on Dante Scavullo? If that's what it was.

"Oh, I heard it was very bloody, it was."

"Whoever'd suspect the master was a master criminal, being such a wonderful golfer?"

I gazed out the window and kept my eye on the newsstand on the corner, waiting for the newspapers' afternoon editions for word of the killing (or killings) at the school. I wanted to know who was upstairs with Scavullo. The deadly melee had sounded horrible as I crouched in my closet. And while I wasn't an eyewitness, you could say I was an earwitness. Finally, I heard the newsboys starting to sing out the latest headlines:

"MOBSTER MURDERED IN COLUMBUS DAY MASSACRE!"

"REPUTED GANGSTER SCAVULLO SLAIN IN EMPTY SCHOOL!"

"KILLING OF BOOTLEGGER LABELED GANGLAND HIT!"

I dropped the script I was attempting to read, ran down the steps, out the side door, and grabbed a copy of the *New York Post* in its revised broadsheet form. *The New York Daily Mirror* tabloid had also issued an extra edition highlighting the shooting.

The *Post* story was written by Reggie Pendleton, the reporter I'd spotted earlier in that mob of scribes at the schoolhouse. My pal Reggie was smart, and I was especially alert to what he would write. I trusted his stories. He was basically truthful and a less-yellow journalist than the others in his pack of reporters.

Reggie's story was short and succinct. He confirmed that Dante Scavullo was dead, gunned down by person or persons unknown. It was accompanied by a photo of Scavullo's body lying on his back on a classroom floor, blood pooling under his head. He was wearing a three-piece suit and spats over his shoes. Dark stains marked the suit. His pockets were turned inside out, indicating he was robbed, and his own gun was near the body.

His pockets! I wondered: Were they looking for the pocket watch?

Described as a "low-level bootlegger" in a world that had just recently legalized alcohol, this mobster had flown under the radar. No one seemed to know why Scavullo was marked for death. The *Post* reported that Scavullo had fired his gun, but in the gunfight had sustained multiple fatal wounds. For some reason left unexplained, two plain-clothes cops were on the scene. They had fired their guns, and police said Scavullo's shooter may have sustained an injury. The unknown assailant, described as a young Italian man of medium height and build, crashed through a window to the fire escape and fled, aided by a confederate in a waiting car.

From Reggie's story, I gleaned that Scavullo worked as a "distributor" for business owner and gangland figure Frank Romeo. However, with Prohibition over and done with—to much joy across the land—Dante Scavullo's main employment was now in transition. It had been rumored, according to the article, that Scavullo was looking to get out of the mob, trying to broker some kind of exit deal. That echoed what the mysterious Brit in the closet had told me. The guys with the rough New York accents I had heard? They might have been cops.

I worried about how Juliette Scavullo would feel, hearing the news, seeing this terrible photo of her husband's body for all the world to witness.

There was no information in the story about who else had been in the building, who shot Scavullo, and why it all went down in the school. On Columbus Day, of all days. The murder was attributed to "a person or persons unknown." More important to *me*, the papers had no information about a "mystery woman" seen leaving the school right after the shooting. My pal Reggie quoted one of the local police detectives and a couple of witnesses outside. They knew nothing. *Hallelujah.*

The other articles were not quite as long, but conveyed the same information with more adjectives—shocking, heinous, horrible, depraved. It was a relief that Reggie hadn't seen me. Reggie and I had logged many a story together when I was a reporter. He'd be asking why was I there, what was I looking for? Was I writing a play about gangsters? Luckily his focus on his work was so intense, he might not have noticed anyone as unimportant as me, his friend.

When I arrived in New York three years ago, I found a job at a small scandal sheet that went out of business a few months later, forcing me to hit the pavement again. Then I picked up some work for the *New York Post* and met Reggie. I could always tell when he was in trouble by checking his byline. When he annoyed his editors, they used his full name for his byline: Reginald Archibald Pendleton III. I smiled at the thought.

I had jumped between beats, cops, city hall, news of the day. But Reggie had a way with cops that I never could manage, not being a guy. On the other hand, I learned to ignore their jibes and their flirting, and often, their passes. Believe me, I had to dodge many a wayward paw. It was exhausting, something Reggie didn't have to deal with. He could go lift a few brews with the boys in blue, squeeze out some juicy news tidbits, then paint them in heroic colors— or demonize them. Reggie and the cops had a weird quid pro quo going on. I understood.

Back out West where I came from, I toiled at one of those newspapers where women were hazed before being accepted as one of "the boys." Then again, I got more hard news stories there than in New York. My first "hard" assignments were covering boxing matches, both local palookas and famous professional fighters. None were more exciting than the celebrated 'Manassa Mauler,' Jack Dempsey, who ruled the ring in the Twenties.

The boys on the news desk thought sending women out to cover the prizefights was hilarious. All of us reporters, women and men, had to carry twenty-pound typewriters over our heads, fight our way through the crowds to the press seats ringside, and write our stories as fast and as floridly as possible. The boys knew the 'funniest part' of such an assignment was trying to avoid the blood spatter from the fighters in the ring.

Having been warned by another female writer from a rival paper, Nina Oglesby, I wore an old brown smock over my clothes and snatched one of the editors' green eye-shades. I sported a large red handkerchief to wipe the blood from my face and the typewriter keys.

Oh, those golden, bloody memories.

I cycled through the boxing beat and the police beat, where the cops loved to rat out the sheriff's department, and the sheriff's deputies ratted out the cops. I passed all their unspoken tests. I had so much moxie, I may have scared a few men. More than a few. You may not believe that a mere five-foot-four-inches of me could terrify some big dumb galoot in a blue uniform. You'd be surprised.

Ultimately, I fought my way out of the boxing pit and onto the news staff, where I stayed. Until I realized I had enough moxie to leave the Old West for the seductive and dangerous East Coast. I was fortunate, of course. With so many people out of work, any job was considered a coup, humble though it might be. It was as if a leprechaun had tossed a fistful of four-leaf clovers my way.

One of them led to a job backstage at the Washington Irving Theatre. 'The Irv.'

I'd fallen in love with the theatre back home, as rudimentary as it was. I studied playwriting in college with a young professor who didn't even know how to professionally format a playscript. Nevertheless, my characters kept me company. And kept me up at night.

While I had my degree in journalism and found work at a New York newspaper with its regrettably small salary, I also came with my plays, and a few introductions from my theatre professor to random people he knew in the city. If journalism failed me, I was willing to work *any* job in the theatre. When my second newspaper job evaporated, I was hired at the Washington Irving Theatre. I was willing to do nearly anything. Anything not overtly illegal or immoral. Well, not immoral, anyway. Okay, not *very* immoral.

After two years at the W.I., my head was stuffed with lessons learned. I'd read hundreds of (mostly) bad scripts. I'd attended hundreds of rehearsals and witnessed directors and actors screaming at each other. I'd gone to every free seat-filling performance I could, not just at the W.I., but all over the Theatre District. I focused on the people who could assist me on my own plays. And I submitted scripts to agents, to theatres, to directors and producers.

Rejection is never easy and all my plays were rejected. Until I let go of all the rules. I had tried too hard to please everyone and accordingly pleased no one, not even myself. They were too nice—my plays, that is. They were too polite. I know that now.

I had made it to New York full of dreams and cautious apprehension. To land a job in a Real Theatre was beyond amazing. And because nothing paid very well, I might as well work in the theatre, a place I loved, where I could see plays for free, and read other plays. Piles and piles of plays. Sometimes blessings are a double-edged sword.

I had a few qualms about leaving journalism, which had its own crazed energy, but I figured I could always go back. If *Leaving Alamogordo* flopped, I hoped I'd be welcomed back at a newspaper. Some newspaper, somewhere. The pay was roughly as impoverishing as working at the W.I. anyway.

The truth is I was terrified that if *Leaving Alamogordo* failed, the glorious Washington Irving Theatre might let me go. Theatre people are superstitious, and once tainted by a flop, the W.I. would try to bury the very mention of it. And me with it. I prayed my show would not close early, and would find at least a moderate success, which would embarrass neither me nor the Irv. I hadn't grappled with the idea that it could be more than a moderate success, except in my fantasies, but fantasies can take you away from reality.

I pushed those thoughts away, along with Scavullo, the pocket watch, the blue-eyed Brit named Chase, and the whole shooting match. I returned to rewriting my ending and added a second kiss for luck, hoping my stars had the sexual chemistry to make it all work.

It's all up to you now, Clarissa.

Four

"YOU CAN'T DO THIS TO me," Clarissa wailed right on cue, her dark eyes filling with tears. Tears were a talent of hers, almost a parlor trick. The very thought of new lines spun her into a panic. "I can't memorize any more words. My brain is full!"

I stopped myself from making a crack at the expense of her brain's capacity. Before I could say she was simply a pretty parrot and she should just say the lines, Andras stepped in.

"Clarissa, my pet, you will be magnificent. Only a few lines. And you get the last line."

"The last line? Really?" She gazed up at her director with hope in her eyes, even though I was the one who wielded the pen. The last line is the one that can take a play over the top. It's the line that will linger in the mind of the audience. Or at least it *should* linger.

Rehearsal was arduous. The set had finally been erected, with actual furniture instead of tape on the floor, and the actors more interested in navigating new obstacles than listening to new lines. They were forgetting their old lines. They were on edge. I was too.

All the chair and sofa and desk moving kicked up dust on the stage, making me glad I'd changed into my trousers and sweater, my work clothes. My rehearsal togs sent an unspoken message to the cast that I meant business. It was always good to show people who wears the pants. *Me.* Besides, the theatre was chilly. My slacks kept my legs warm as I paced back and forth listening to the lines.

"I'm not saying you don't deserve to be shot by an anarchist," Clarissa declaimed as Annabelle. *"I'm saying I should be the one to plug you! For all the trouble you've given me, you disgusting rat."*

"Hold it, Clarissa," I said, "I'm cutting that whole line."

"I like that line!"

"It's too long. I have a different line for you. The final action of the play is now yours."

"I don't understand. William still kisses me, right?"

William was Annabelle's editor and boss, played by Todd Andrews.

"No, *you* kiss *him*," I broke in. "You take the reins, Clarissa. You have the last line and the last action. You take control of that kiss. Like a tigress."

"That's pretty daring," Todd said. "But if you're game, darling, I'm with you." I knew Todd was dizzy over his leading lady. Todd looked great on stage, but he was a pushover for Clarissa.

"How daring? Like *Jean Harlow* daring?" She flashed her heavy lashes at him. "Do I dare, darling?"

"When don't you dare?" Todd said. They shared a look that left very little to the imagination. Their chemistry could only help the show, I hoped. I let Annabelle keep her old line, in another place. She'd already learned it, and the "daring" new ending clicked. We were in business.

My heroine Annabelle, though daring, was not as polite as I try to be. I am unfailingly polite most of the time. I never lie, and I always try to return lost watches to men who are about to die. That last thought depressed me. Even though Dante Scavullo apparently was a mobster, I felt terrible that he suffered such an ignominious ending, and I felt sorry for Juliette Scavullo.

I watched Clarissa and Todd work out their choreography for the new final kiss. This was more rewarding than facing up to real life. *Leaving Alamogordo* was my what-the-hell play, the one I decided to write for myself using all the stage tricks I'd observed, and I borrowed a few legends of the rough-and-tumble Western frontier and its lady reporters, like Polly Pry. I had finally stopped trying to please everyone else, or anyone else for that matter. I wrote about a smart female reporter with behavior unbecoming a lady. I used a lot of snappy dialogue. And now I was letting *her* seize the moment and kiss the guy. Pretty daring. Still, I knew it was a stroke of luck that *Leaving Alamogordo* was opening at the Irv.

In my comedy, Annabelle struggles for notice and acceptance at her newspaper job. She gets sidelined as the 'society reporter.' When a young bride is suspected of killing her husband, none of the male reporters can get a word out of her, and the cops can't arrest her for lack of evidence. Only society reporter Anabelle can get close to her. She pays a woman-to-woman visit with the delicate suspect and returns with the whole bloody murder scoop.

In exchange, Annabelle demands a hard news beat of her own. Comedy ensues, and at the climax of the play she must defend her editor against the society bride's anarchist lover (and co-conspirator). Annabelle grabs the gun that William, her editor, keeps in his desk drawer, takes down the villain, and saves William's life. Andras and I had come up with the idea of staging the big confrontation using their rolling office chairs, making a comical racket as the actors raced each other around the stage like a demented roller derby.

It was very funny, obviously.

We struggled over the final rewritten lines, and over their staging. The would-be lovers at the end of the play are now faced with a role reversal. Editor William wants to kiss Annabelle, he's falling for her, but he's embarrassed that she's just saved his hide.

The scene took a while to choreograph, amid the actors' whines, their complaints that life (and the theatre) was unfair, the noisy careening office chairs, oh-so-narrowly avoiding tumbling into the orchestra pit—and then the cast's final acceptance that maybe the new ending was a good idea after all.

William/Todd scurries away from her in his chair, while Annabelle/Clarissa rides hers like a chariot, chasing him around the torn-up newsroom. They declare their feelings, shouting at each other, and Annabelle finally corners him, leaps onto his lap, and takes her triumphant kiss.

William: *You were just about to shoot me! Now you want to kiss me?*

Annabelle: *Calm down, lover boy. I can do both!*

She kisses him again, longer. Curtain. Cue wild applause. (Here's hoping.)

Take that, blue-eyed stranger, I thought.

This ending felt right, even though Andras had to interrupt the last long kiss with some notes. There was a feeling in the dusty stage air that, as exhausted and dirty as we all were, we had found the sweet spot in the play. That final feeling of *aha.* The play wasn't run in yet, by opening night, it would work. It had *better*, I thought.

I exhaled and wiped my forehead, smearing the grime.

"All right, it's not as terrible as I thought it would be." Clarissa/Annabelle grinned at me. "It's good, Esmé. You could've come up with it sooner than this close to opening night, you know, but it's good."

"Don't be such a misery, Clarissa," Andras said. "The best shows come together at the last minute. If you're lucky. We just got lucky today." Clarissa laughed and the rest of the cast joined her.

"Better than lucky, we got Esmé," Todd said, to much hilarity.

I could have kissed him, but I didn't. There had been enough kissing today. I agreed that we got lucky, but I wondered, would we have gotten lucky if I hadn't been thinking about that other kiss all day? That kiss in the closet? And the smug Brit in the pinstriped suit?

The relief I felt roll off my shoulders in that moment was marred by my brush with death that morning. Unfortunately, there are no pure moments in life. You never find pure joy or pure excitement or are graced with pure relief. I was acutely aware of how much work it had taken to get to this point, and this moment right here, right now, was so sweet, but the critics could still hammer it into splinters. And sudden death can still find you anywhere, anytime. Even in a school closet.

I wanted a few pure sweet moments of joy, damn it! However, I had no more strength in my shoulders. I could barely lift my fountain pen. We ended the evening in a state of congenial détente. I agreed not to add any more lines, and they promised to learn the words and refrain from changing them. We all left, director, cast, and me, turning off everything but the ghost light.

It was late. I was both exhausted and keyed up. Too keyed up to sleep. I wanted to walk home the many blocks to the Upper West Side where I lived, to walk it off. I debated taking the subway, but I didn't want to slip beneath the surface of the street at this time of night.

I felt safe wearing my trousers and an old cap to hide my hair. I could have been mistaken for a newsboy covered in ink. The October wind picked up and I pulled my jacket close. Still, I kept turning my head at every rustle of leaves and crack of a branch. A car backfired, sounding like gunshots. I jumped and reconsidered my bravado.

I shook out my hair and hailed a cab home.

&

Removing Scavullo's watch from my bag, I took a closer look at this thing that had derailed my day. The gold cover had acquired a patina through age, but it was shinier than I remembered. As shiny as a guilty secret. Ornate initials on the front of the watch had faded, as if they'd been rubbed out. Yet I could make out the impression of Dante Scavullo's initials, D and S.

I opened the front to find an inscription from Juliette to Dante, expressing her eternal love. I felt like an intruder. I turned the thing over and opened the back cover to see a more complicated engraving. This image wasn't faded like the inscription and the initials on the cover. It looked freshly etched. I turned the timepiece in the light and saw that this engraving was like a trick picture. It looked like waves one way, like numbers another way. But not ordinary numbers: Roman numerals. What did they mean? A date? An address? A phone number? I had no idea.

Nevertheless, I wrote everything down in one of my notebooks—an ingrained habit from my reporting days. I jotted down the inscription, the initials, and the general shape of the watch, with its front and back covers. I also sketched out a very poor likeness of the inside image. Art is not my strong suit, so I wrote down the four numbers amid the shaky waves. That being done, I could wipe the watch from my mind and forget about it. I hoped.

I remembered my new camera, the sleek little Leica I recently bought off a drunken *Post* photographer who needed the money. I snapped photos of the watch, front and back, inside and outside, not knowing if they'd turn out until the film was developed.

As I put the camera away, I remembered one more thing. Scavullo *knew* I was in the diner. When he was called to the payphone he gave me a little wink, like he had often done in church. When he returned from his call, he took the watch out of his pocket, glanced at it, and set it down. Then he left as if he hadn't acknowledged me. He was in a hurry.

I found it harder to forget about the man who kissed me in the closet. Perhaps I shouldn't be writing plays about kisses either.

FIVE

SAL'S DECISION TO PRODUCE MY play was weirdly reminiscent of the day I walked into the theatre and filled an empty spot. I had been filling that spot for almost two years when the Washington Irving suffered the infamous flop known as *Afternoon Tea with Nigel*.

Nigel was a real stinker. I know, because I read the script. I told them it was. I told everybody. Nobody believed me. Then I suffered through the rehearsals. And the previews. Dry, arch, turgid, with labored humor, full of pauses waiting for laughs that didn't come. Sal kept waiting and hoping.

As soon as the ink was seared into the scathing notices, it was apparent *Nigel* would have to close, and soon. It was a Headless Horseman of a flop, decapitated by the power of the press. There was one week of performances already half-sold. That final Friday, I was at my desk reading another random offering as fast as I could, counting the clichés. Sal sped by, troubled by closing the show. He could be as volcanic as Szabo after bad news and bad reviews. He stopped and snapped his fingers next to his ear, his go-to motion for trying to remember something.

"Esmé, what was that play of yours?"

"Which one?"

"The new one. The one I liked."

"Leaving Alamogordo," I replied. The theatre had sponsored a table reading of the script as a courtesy to me, and to some out-of-work actors. You have to press your advantages.

"Yeah, that's it. Funny play. Feisty dame reporter, right? Two-three sets max, eight characters? I like it. With the right set, and maybe with Clarissa what's-her-name Eldridge, you know, Sophie?" Sal walked off snapping his fingers. I dared to hope.

Things exploded from there. The theatre was already booked later in the season, but *Nigel* was dying *now*. That left a two-month gap. Enough time to briefly rehearse and mount a new play for a six-week run. Short rehearsal time, no previews, but *my play*. On stage. All of a sudden, I was living the dream. I would have a play on Broadway. I was riding that Broadway roller coaster of highs and lows, with occasional nightmares of failure.

The Washington Irving had had the benefit of my labor for over two years. Now it looked like I would profit from those efforts, as well as a positive reading of *Leaving Alamogordo*. And no matter what happened with my play, I told myself it would be another step on the up-and-down ladder of success.

I had made it—to New York! And Broadway!

My parents were no doubt spinning in their graves at this turn of events. They never wanted me to be a reporter, let alone live a life in the wicked theatre. They had put up with my "little plays," not knowing what they meant to me.

My remaining relatives, aunts, uncles, and cousins, all cautioned me not to think I was "above myself." They had no faith in me. If I dared mention any further ambitions, they scoffed. Reporting was considered a racy enough career. Yet I had treated my father to tickets to several prizefights, even one starring Jack Dempsey, and he hadn't seemed so ashamed of me then.

I lost my parents only weeks apart, felled by a particularly virulent flu that swept through our town. It reminded people of the great influenza of 1918. But they died in 1930. Many people passed away suddenly that winter. My father died first, followed by my mother. After surviving such a difficult hardscrabble life and providing for me, their only child, they hadn't enough fight left in them to survive. The rest of my family had a different interpretation.

"You had to become a reporter? A career unsuitable for a woman," my maiden aunt sniffed. "That alone nearly killed your parents. And now you want to work in the theatre? Glory be to God, they can't see you now! Going down another godforsaken path to Hell!"

Soon after my parents died, my fiancé Roger succumbed to the same virus. Blow after blow after blow. Roger was tall, stalwart, nice looking, caring, and honestly, a little boring. Our conversations often fell silent for lack of interest, or even a mutual subject. If our romance was so lifeless before our marriage, I dreaded what would come next.

We were still in school. Too young to even think of marriage. I was about to call the whole thing off when he came down with the telltale cough. I hoped he would be strong enough to resist. Many people did. But the harder he fought, the faster he failed.

Roger died believing we would be married in the spring. I hope it brought him a little comfort. But not to me. It was time for me to escape.

"What's wrong with being a teacher?" another aunt said to me. "Writing plays? What makes you think you can write a play, Esmé Rafferty de LaForet?"

Rafferty is my middle name. I always thought my whole name would look nice on a theatre poster.

"What makes you think I can't?" I would say, but I never got an answer. Weren't we raised in the U.S.A. to believe we could do anything? Or was that just something that people said?

I couldn't remain in that little Western town where everyone thought Denver was the Big City. My parents had scrimped and saved all their lives. I think they only let me go to college because they thought I was too ornery to find a man. They were both delighted, yet skeptical, when I came home one weekend with a small diamond ring on my finger and Roger in tow. I don't really know why I said yes to marriage, except I felt trapped at home. And yet I didn't see how I could leave my parents, because I was their only child. Roger would be a good, if too quiet, husband. He adored them and they him. We would have stayed in that town. And I would have slowly suffocated. But I was making them all happy. Then they were gone.

To my surprise, there was some money left after the funerals. I discovered they had a savings account and two life insurance policies in my name. They also left me our small house, two bedrooms and one bath, which was paid for in full. It was a miracle that the bank didn't own it, what with the Depression and all. The crash of 1929 spread its long dusty shadow over the land, but my father had always insisted on paying cash. He wasn't a stocks-and-bonds man. He didn't believe in debt. He owned a small general store and kept it running with my mother and *me*, their not-always-willing salesclerk.

I was now the closest thing to an heiress that most people in my town knew. I had a choice—wed some cowpoke who had his eye on my money to grow his herd and his rangeland, where my soul would dry up and blow away? Or I could *escape*. New York City had always been a fairy tale for me, but never a real possibility. Now it was in reach. But I had to leave before it all blew away.

I found buyers for the house and the business. After cashing everything in, I was left with a tidy sum. A very tidy sum for 1931, for the Depression, and for a pinchpenny like me, who grew up in a general store, counting every bean.

The world I always wanted to have might be within my grasp.

Six

M Y BED HELD ME CAPTIVE the next morning, my limbs unable to move, my head stuffed with cotton. Tossing and turning, reciting lines in my head from my rewrites, and alternately trying to re-cast the scene in the school closet with the tall gunman, it all played in a loop in my head for hours. I finally slept, and I slept late.

"Wake up, sleeping beauty. I forgot my key." There was pounding on my front door.

Amelia Applewood cleaned my apartment a couple of days a week, but she offered advice for free whenever the mood struck her, which was often. It was difficult to know what to call Amelia, because she acted as both maid and bossy friend. Recently she had started telling people she was my housekeeper, thus giving herself a promotion, and I had no objection as long as the pay was the same.

Roughly my age, Amelia occasionally occupied the maid's room in my beautiful Edwardian Five apartment. Yes, I bought it with my inheritance. The importance of owning property was drilled into me by my parents, and with times the way they were, the purchase seemed reasonable, if frightening. Dead cheap, according to New Yorkers.

It helped that the seller and the bank assumed I was a widow. When they asked about my husband, I'd just say, "Poor Roger. It was the flu," and fidget with my diamond engagement ring. It would have made things much more difficult, if not impossible, if they thought I was a single woman. Women having the vote seemed to be one thing, but dear God, purchasing power was something else. I kept my mouth shut on the advice of the lady lawyer I hired to help me through some of those obstacles.

I opened the door. Amelia leveled a perky gaze at my rumpled hair and nightgown. Her short blond curls were perfectly in place, her makeup impeccable. Lips the prescribed bow shape, according to the women's magazines. She wore a crisp blue shirt and skirt, topped by a fitted, belted cardigan, making her the most stylish cleaning lady around. When she opened her mouth, her accent was pure New York and not West Virginia, where she was born and from which her family had moved. Every once in a while though, that country twang would seep through.

"Top of the morning, Esmé. You go fifteen rounds with the Sandman? That playwriting biz must be pretty rough."

She had declined my offer of free tickets for opening night. "I'll go if it's a hit," she had informed me, in her own delightful way of ego puncturing.

"Rehearsal went long, and I couldn't get to sleep." I slumped against the wall.

"That's the trouble with your kind of people." She breezed into the room.

"My kind?"

"Writers. Your brain's always full of stuff. You know, thoughts and ideas and stuff."

"And yours isn't?"

"Yeah. But mine don't keep me up at night. They sing me to sleep."

I glared at her. Wouldn't that be nice? It was almost noon on Saturday. I was free as a bird. I didn't have to attend rehearsals today. I tried to rub the sleep from my eyes.

"I'll put on a pot of coffee," she said. "You better clean yourself up."

"I have to get the morning papers."

"Not like that, ya don't." She promised to pick up a couple of newspapers and fix the coffee before she shoved me toward the shower. She grabbed the spare key that I kept on a hook near the front door and exited so efficiently she could give a class on exits and entrances.

I met Amelia casually through friends, not long after I moved into my apartment. But it was the bleak and icy night she banged on my door and I opened it to find her bleeding from the mouth and squinting with swollen black eyes that we really got to know each other. Fleeing from her would-be fiancé, Amelia needed a place where he wouldn't find her. The Upper West Side was far enough away from Hell's Kitchen that she felt safe.

I applied ice to Amelia's eyes and some homemade remedies for her bruises. She had no broken bones, but her spirit was damaged. Soon, however, she started telling me how much I needed her to clean my place and put things in order. Small things like that.

Even with her eyes blacked, Amelia cast them appraisingly on my apartment and despite her troubles, she had plenty to say.

"I never seen a place like this. All this room to yourself. It's gorgeous."

"It's an investment," I said.

"I'll say."

I live on a lovely and quiet tree-lined block. After a year and a half of moving from place to place, living with a variety of roommates, and considering both my options and my inheritance, I decided purchasing a place was the best option. People were losing their homes because of the Depression. I didn't want to feed on their misery, but I needed a place to land.

Prices were way down and many cooperatives were being converted to rentals, but I wanted to own a piece of New York. I found a second-floor 'Edwardian Five' apartment, your not-so-basic living room, dining room, and bedroom, with kitchen and bathroom, plus a maid's room and bath. Imagine that. I don't need all that space, but if times got tough, I could rent out that spare room.

I don't have a mortgage. Because no bank would give me one. They thought that would put me in my place, a lone woman. However, when I offered a cash sale to the owner, who needed the money because his business had failed, being a lone woman, one with dollars in her hand, was suddenly not such a drawback. Money talks. It practically sings and dances.

"This place?" Amelia said. "It's like a fairy tale."

"A good fairy tale or a bad one?" Not the Brothers Grimm, I hoped.

"It's wonderful. How'd you get it to look like this?"

She moved slowly through the apartment, taking in everything. My home is my sanctum sanctorum. My refuge. Decorated in a kind of theatrical excess that most people wouldn't understand. The large bay window in my living room overlooked the trees, the sidewalks, and the pretty brownstones up and down the block. My dining table and chairs fit into the rounded bay where I liked to write and gaze at the people in the street, the seasons, and the changing leaves. My typewriter held pride of place there, unless I had company.

Several pairs of French doors opened to the view and introduced light to most of the apartment, including my bedroom and a petite terrace where I could sit outside with my coffee on those rare mornings when I could spare the time. Connecting doors from my bedroom and the hallway led to a large bathroom featuring a marble vanity and boasting both a large tub and a separate shower.

"Oh my stars, would you look at this?" Amelia stopped at the bedroom, somewhat in awe.

Have you ever wondered what it would be like to sleep in a field of flowers, without the bugs and wild critters? Through the magic of stagecraft, I could do just that.

Hank Turnbridge, a grizzled old set designer at the Irv with a wife and kids and several young grandchildren, took the job for extra cash and the challenge of doing something a little different. His wife Irma kept him company while he painted my 'scenery,' and she and I drank coffee and chatted about actors and directors and the state of the theatre. They took my project as a change of pace because it wouldn't be taken down on closing night.

"I hope you don't think this is too strange," I'd say to Irma.

"Oh honey, you don't know strange." Irma merely laughed and I'd put on another pot of coffee.

Hank was part of the Washington Irving's regular stage crew. With a lot of input from me, he designed a mural of glorious pink and white blooms, which he painted on the wall behind my bed, marching up and across the blue walls and the gold and white cloud-painted ceiling. Roses and hydrangeas on deep green stalks climbed up to the sky and into those fluffy clouds. Together, Irma and I designed a padded, green velvet headboard that resembled a fan-shaped flower vase that the scene shop constructed for me. It was child's play for Hank, she said. And now I sleep beneath it and a matching green velvet coverlet. Alone, I might add.

My girlfriends from the theatre agree that this bower of flowers is spectacular.

"You could really trap a man in here," my battered new guest said.

"And what would you do with him?"

"Depends on his behavior. Not the guy who blacked my eyes," Amelia said. "Some other guy, with manners. It's a pretty big place for one person. You know, you could use some help around here, if you ask me." Always ready with an opinion, even through bruised eyes. Amelia started picking things up after me. She said it was to pay for her room and board for the night, but she had a plan.

I agreed I'd like a bit of help with the cleaning, perhaps once a week. She immediately started organizing my life. Amelia was a polisher. She enjoyed shining the windows, the silver, and me. She dumped the man who beat her and I made it clear that she couldn't work for me if she went back to him.

"What do you take me for? Some kind of sap?"

"Certainly not."

"Then we understand each other," Amelia said, though I doubted if that was true.

We became friends and she became my house cleaner, two or three days a week, depending on her mood and the state of my apartment. She reserved the right to stay at my apartment if the need required.

"And if you have male company, I am the soul of discretion," she assured me. "I will stay in my room and do the maid thing." I assured her that was probably not going to be a concern. "Likewise, I might be with someone and telling my folks I'm with you." Most days she stayed with her family. Other times, I didn't pry.

Amelia was a fresh breeze who brought order to my life, even if she couldn't do it for herself. These days, I don't know what I'd do without her. It's not that I can't be organized, and I am clean, but I tend to be forgetful about household chores when I write—dropping pages in piles, books in stacks, clothes on chairs. Amelia comes along behind me, picking things up, hanging my clothes, and reminding me when the coffee is running out. She is, as they say, a jewel. A very opinionated jewel.

"What would you do without me? You'd never find Scene Two."

"Don't be ridiculous, Amelia. I'll always find Scene Two, and Three and Four. Even if I have to hunt for them."

She could run a corporation. Luckily for me, I am that corporation. Because Amelia Applewood was originally from Appalachia, she viewed housekeeper as high on the list of professions. She also worked in a beauty parlor a day or two a week, which she enjoyed. But as she explained to me, there are some sow's ears that will never make a silk purse.

I now emerged from the shower to the delightful aroma of deep dark coffee. I donned my Saturday clothes, a clean pair of trousers and a thick black turtleneck sweater, on my feet beaded moccasins from back home. I felt completely comfortable and almost human. I stretched my legs on my deep green velvet sofa and kicked off my moccasins.

My hair was damp from the shower, my curls hit below my shoulders. I liked to wear it longer than the prevailing popular short styles because I enjoyed a variety of hairdos. As did Amelia. If I was lucky, perhaps Amelia would fix it later. She was clever that way.

She handed me a cup of delicious eye-opening coffee and tossed the papers in my lap. A random headline read: GANGLAND HIT. BUT WHY? WIDOW ASKS

Scavullo's death was now a rehashed second-day story, a suspected planned mob murder, according to the cops. The paper quoted Juliette Scavullo, who said her husband was working to escape the tentacles of the mob. She was pictured in black from tip to toe and looking ten years older, a sight I never expected to see. There was no mention or information about the man named Chase.

The papers revealed a bit more than they had yesterday. Scavullo was allegedly working for reputed mobster Frank Romeo. I had seen Romeo when he occasionally showed up at Sunday church in his dapper camel hair overcoat, beneath which was usually a sober dark suit. Yet I didn't recall the Scavullos ever chatting with Romeo after Mass.

What did I know about Dante Scavullo? Nothing really, other than he and his family attended Our Lady of Pompeii on Sundays. We occasionally spoke, the way you do when you see people again and again. Dante Scavullo looked like any number of older Italian men. His hair was still thick but gray, and he wore a gold ring with a large amber stone. The newspaper informed me he was fifty-two years old at his death.

His wife Juliette was a striking woman of forty-eight; again, her age courtesy of the morning news. She was soft looking in her middle years and her black hair was shot through with silver. Juliette was stylish, and usually wore the latest fashions in bright jewel colors that flattered her. She was nobody's stereotype of the Italian matron.

Last Sunday, Mrs. Scavullo had assured me she and her husband would come and see my play on opening night. That wasn't going to happen now. Whatever Dante's real profession was, I felt sorry for his wife. She would observe the expected mourning rituals and wear black for the next year and beyond.

As a couple, the Scavullos seemed nice, quiet, and personable. I recalled that people treated them with respect, though usually from a few steps away.

Why was Scavullo killed in a school? The papers and I both asked. They suggested it might be to teach him a lesson—a final lesson? Perhaps the lesson was meant for other small-time operators trying to break free from the Mafia.

My thoughts circled back to another question: Could the man with the gun, the man called Chase, have told me some version of the truth? And what was the truth? Was he some kind of a cop? Luckily, Amelia saved me from brooding over that question.

"You don't expect to catch a man wearing trousers, do you?" She sat down with her own coffee, heavily laced with cream and sugar, on the chair opposite the sofa. She had also split a bagel for us, toasted it, and spread it with a decadent layer of cream cheese.

"Certainly not. I'll catch him with a net." I smiled at the image of me running with a giant butterfly net, or possibly a hook, like the ones they used in vaudeville.

Amelia sniffed. "You're hopeless."

I was never going to leave that sofa, I decided. It was too comfortable. "Why are you here on a Saturday, Amelia?"

"I was bored."

"Bored on a day off?"

"Thought maybe I could get my pay early. There's a Kay Francis picture at the Rialto that I want to take in with a friend. Supposed to be pretty spicy. And you got some silver needs polishing and I could do that for you. Take me about an hour."

Amelia indicated my mother's wedding silver that she had used only on holidays, a coffee service, compotes, and candlesticks. I displayed the items on a tea table. As usual Amelia was right, it needed polishing.

"How much for the silver?" I already had her pay set aside in an envelope.

"Price of the movie, popcorn, soda, and coffee and pie later. Mavis and I always like to go for coffee and pie after the movies."

Amelia always noticed something that needed to be done. I was in a mellow mood and agreed.

"When are you going to break out some of those swell new clothes you got? Ever?" she asked.

"Tonight," I said.

"Really?" Amelia spun around and stared at me. "You're not funning me?" She flew to my mahogany wardrobe and opened the mirrored door. "Which one?

"The lavender."

She brought it forward and we both admired it. The heavy crepe evening gown was a thing of beauty, the lavender hue deep and vibrant enough to make my pale skin glow. The crepe material didn't show wrinkles and was sprinkled with sparkling rhinestones.

The dress was simplicity itself. Cut on the bias, it hugged my body like a waterfall. The bottom of the flared tulip skirt was stiffened, and the hem flared out as I walked or danced. The short sleeves ended above my elbows and fluttered like angel wings. The "extra something" to catch the eye was a large rhinestone broach pinned in the low "V" of the decolletage. Adding to that surprise was a matching jewel sewn-in to the deep V of the back.

"Now this is what I'm talking about." Amelia winked. "Looks like it could be in a play."

We both laughed, because it had been designed for a play, but it never made its debut under the bright stage lights. Amelia also picked up my new silver dancing heels and the sparkly bracelets and earrings I'd planned to wear.

"What's the big occasion?" She leaned forward with interest.

"Going dancing with Wilhelmina and a couple of boys from the theatre. Road test. You know, my pal Willie."

Amelia considered this and approved. "So much better than that old dress you've been wearing."

I was only slightly offended. Up to this point, my social life had consisted of theatre events. Lots of opening nights for shows at the W.I. and other theatres that needed a full house to impress the critics. I had worn my navy "opening night dress" until everybody knew it. Wilhelmina, aka Willie, the resident costume designer at the Irv, had gamely recut the neckline and added sequins, and it looked thoroughly acceptable, but I was thoroughly sick of it. And apparently so was everyone who knew me and had witnessed endless repeats of that gown.

It wasn't as if I ran off to the Ritz every night. However, with my own show opening to a limited run, I was expected to attend the performances, looking oh-so-glamorous. It would also help to impress our show angels, the investors. Even Sal and May were concerned I might show up in my old navy blue warhorse of a dress. They encouraged me to find something new.

"I can't let people think I don't pay you anything," Sal moaned.

"You practically don't," I pointed out. But if I showed up wearing pauper's rags to my own opening, it would send the wrong message, and the theatre is all about image. Some of the more eccentric male playwrights can get away with bizarre haberdashery, but not the women. Once again, the ill-fated *Afternoon Tea with Nigel* came to my aid. First, it flopped spectacularly, thus opening up a limited run so *Leaving Alamogordo* could take the stage. (Thanks, *Nigel.*) And second, it supplied me with a fabulous array of contemporary costumes.

It was the ever-practical May's idea. She convinced Sal to let me purchase some of the show's costumes, at cost. Not from the leading lady's lot, but from the poor understudy, who was about my size, and who never had a chance to go on.

I was able to snag five amazing evening gowns, including the lavender frock, two cocktail ensembles, and several smart day dresses and suits, all courtesy of one failed play. I am the single biggest fan of that fabled theatrical disaster. My new wardrobe came costumed by the amazing Wilhelmina Kim, known as Willie. Those who were dressed by Willie were supplied with the exact outward trappings of the character. She wielded needle and thread like a warrioress. The show might be a flop, but never Willie's designs.

After a show closes, most of the costumes are returned to wardrobe, especially character uniforms for cops, nurses, and the like, which can be used over and over again, and even rented out to other companies or schools. However, the *Afternoon Tea with Nigel* gowns were so very glamorous and so distinctive, Sal and May were afraid the audience could tell where they came from and spread rumors that the theatre couldn't afford new costumes.

Even though these have been lean years, theatre is still about illusion. When men and women attend a play, they buy that illusion, along with their seats. Even more important, May and Sal were superstitious theatre creatures: Costumes worn in a *flop?* Bad luck!

To avert that disaster, they decided the *Nigel* costumes would never appear in any other W.I. show. The staff too; either they couldn't wear them or they decided they had no reason to collect such finery. Practical. The actresses didn't want any of the leads' costumes either. They practically ran away from them at top speed. Superstitious. But the understudy's gowns had never been on stage before an audience. That made them, everyone agreed, *curse-free.* And they were almost a perfect fit for me.

Most of my friends had one or two dresses they saved to wear to the theatre. Why buy more? The indispensable May wore black or silver to all the openings. The gowns all looked the same, but she bought new versions each year. I didn't want to appear greedy, but for a woman from way out West who'd never had the chance to be elegant, those costumes filled a deep need in me. I yearned to be glamorous, one of my many flaws. Maybe it was all the movies and plays I'd seen. Up there on the silver screen or the stage, everyone was prettier and wittier and more fun to be around than the rest of us mere humans. And did I mention their amazing *clothes?*

Because I appreciated Willie's talents, and I always paid her a little extra over what the theatre paid her, she agreed to alter my treasures to a perfect fit. Together we spun dreams of glorious times to come. The costume queen was brilliant at changing a sleeve here, a neckline there, and adding or deleting trim and ornaments to suit me.

Willie and I had been working together after hours in the costume department for weeks. We sparkled up the gowns with rhinestones, faux pearls, and bugle beads, till they looked like something out of Hollywood; only a bit more tasteful, more Broadway, if you know what I mean. However, she wasn't the gentlest seamstress and I wound up feeling like a pin cushion with a thousand pricks.

Under her mop of brown curls Willie Kim was stunning, a lovely blend between her American mother and Chinese father, but people didn't see it at first, under the curls. It slowly dawned on them that she had gorgeous skin and lovely almond-shaped eyes. Then she smiled, and it was dazzling.

Willie reserved for herself two evening gowns and a couple of day dresses from the taller, more buxom leading lady from *Afternoon Tea with Nigel*. Curses don't apply to the woman who made the frocks, she declared. Tonight she was wearing a stunning dancing dress in red satin.

I was almost afraid to wear my new clothes, they were so beautiful. But Willie said we had to try them out in a crowd. The true test of a costume, she says, is an *audience*.

Amelia broke into my reverie. "Now you're going to look like the pearl of Park Avenue. And not so much like the Cowgirl of the Golden West."

"I wasn't that bad."

"No, not you, only your clothes."

SEVEN

WOULD I PASS THE GLAMOUR test? Amelia was determined that I would. Or she would be shamed among her peers. I was always stunned to find out how much my status affected hers, even though I was merely the playwright and not the leading lady.

I barely recognized the woman in the mirror. She practically shimmered in her bracelets and earrings. Her lashes were darker and longer, under more delicately shaped eyebrows than I remembered. Amelia styled my hair with a sugar and water concoction into an arrangement of waves around my face and a braid across the crown, into which she placed some jeweled pins.

The final touch was the lavender evening frock. I had no idea how all these pieces would come together, but Amelia was right. I posed like a magazine illustration.

"I look different." An understatement.

"That's what I was going for." Amelia grinned into the mirror behind me. "Too bad you can't go to work like this."

"But I will be wearing it to the theatre, and that is my work."

"I never thought about it like that. You're going to want me to do your hair and makeup for your opening night." She rearranged a curl.

"If you make me look like this."

"This is just practice, Esmé. I'm gonna be ready for opening night."

"You're sure you don't want tickets?"

"What if it flops? I'd die of embarrassment."

"Thanks for your vote of confidence," I said.

"I'm confident you'll look good. But no way am I going to opening night. I'd be too nervous."

I paid her the extra money for the day and she flounced out to see the latest Kay Francis picture at the Rialto. Said she'd take care of polishing the silver later.

❧

"Esmé, what happened to you?" Willie met me outside Peacocks' supper club, where we planned to try out our new gowns.

"Amelia happened." My dangling earrings brushed my shoulders when I turned my head.

"I may have to borrow her." Willie peered at my makeup, touched my hair, and dusted some imaginary lint from my coat. She didn't need any help. Tonight her perfect cupid bow lips were dark red and matched her satin gown.

"Be my guest, but you'll have to pay. She's quite the little capitalist."

"Worth every penny, if you're any indication of her talents. And that dress is an indication of mine."

There was a delicate balance to the art of dressing, and I was lucky to be tutored by Willie Kim and Captain Amelia. My pal Willie looked fabulous in her claret-colored gown with faux jewels sewn into the bust and the shoulder straps. Her mop of curls was contained by combs and elegantly arranged on the top of her head. Her liquid brown eyes twinkled in the lights.

"Red is really your color," I said.

"Red attracts men." She winked at me. "So I've heard."

Just days away from the opening night of *Leaving Alamogordo*, tonight was a dress rehearsal for our outfits. Willie and I had convinced Sal and May and the other producing members we had to blend into the opening night crowd. Sal agreed to pay for our evening of nightclubbing among the so-called swells. If we fit in, we were golden. And it would be our little joke.

Willie and I were bound not for the famous Roseland Ballroom, which was too large and crowded, or the Stork Club, which was supposed to be the top of the top of nightclubs, or even the brand-new Rainbow Room, but to Peacocks' Supper Club. It was the kind of place you knew, if you were among those in the know.

We moved into the Peacocks' lobby where everything was decorated in blues and greens and golds. Brilliantly colored peacock murals graced the walls, and lights shone above several round velvet sofas. It wasn't a minute before our escorts showed up. Two gents from the scene shop, Tim Johnson and Wyatt Vane, looked like they stepped out of an Arrow shirt ad in their tuxedos and crisp white collars, quite the fashion. There is no way they could afford their haberdashery. I nodded to Willie.

"I see you've opened up the costume shop."

"There have to be some advantages when you make so little money," she replied, always sensible.

We checked our coats. Both Willie's and mine came from the costume shop overflow. I reluctantly let go of the black velvet opera coat with its white fur hood. I had purchased mine, while Willie was only testing this evening's navy brocade coat.

The main room of Peacocks' was located on the second floor of the building, but easily took up an additional floor in height. The dancers and the bandstand were surrounded by two levels of small tables for two and four, each illuminated with a petite lamp in the center. The effect was intimate and romantic.

Peacocks' featured the type of ballroom I'd seen in the movies. Only better, because it was real. This room was gold and white with glittering chandeliers over the dance floor. Newly legal booze was free-flowing, if expensive. The four of us ordered champagne cocktails, because it was a celebration of sorts. The band was playing "Cocktails for Two." That song was everywhere.

I pulled my shoulders back, lifted my chin and felt my face stretch with smiling. I had so often dreamed of being in such a beautiful ballroom. I was taking mental notes. Who knows what could spring from such a setting? Story-wise, that is.

My lavender crepe gown certainly felt marvelous and I caught several men staring at me the way they do, followed by a slow smile if they met my eyes. It was flattering and a little unsettling.

"Esmé, you look like a queen," Wyatt opined. "I compliment Willie on your behalf."

"Why not compliment me?"

"I don't want to give you a swelled head." He smirked.

"Smarty pants." Truly, I don't know why everyone wants to stick a pin in my bubble all the time.

Tim and Wyatt escorted us to the floor. They tripped the light rather fantastically. We'd all been practicing "putting on the Ritz" on the Washington Irving stage at times when it was free. The boys loved to dance, but they couldn't dance with each other, at least not in what was considered polite society. They were so alike in looks, brown hair, brown eyes, and very good teeth, that people often took them for brothers, instead of *very close friends*. They were also witty and fun and good company, and they knew we weren't expecting anything from them in the romance department.

We made a good foursome, and I was happy because I did not have to engage in a wrestling match at the end of the evening. I was practicing hobnobbing with the swells, Willie was on the lookout for an available man, and the boys were happy to be out together at one of the popular hot spots.

Other people stared at the four of us. I chalked it up to our clothes, and the dancing. We all looked as if we belonged in that crowd. But we had the theatrical advantage. Other dancers were obviously rich, but their clothes were wearing them, instead of the other way around.

Wyatt spun me easily from a foxtrot to the Charleston to the Lindy Hop.

I suffered a few pangs for enjoying myself when so many regular Jills and Joes would never see the inside of the beautiful Peacock's Ballroom with an orchestra of such sublime talent. They would never wear such fabulous clothes. I told myself it didn't matter, because everyone danced, even if they only cut a rug at the corner beer joint. Even those sad souls who dropped dead in those horrible marathons, dancing to their doom.

I swatted away my guilt and the champagne kept it away. I was dancing on bubbles, surrounded by bubbles, floating on bubbles. I had pink bubbles in my brain. We danced on, taking breaks and returning to our table, which was on the inner ring overlooking the dancing couples. Much to my amusement and Willie's delight, men kept cutting into our dances.

Most of them could cut a rug, but my toes would testify that there were some gents who were less than graceful on their feet. Some of them asked me out, but the music was so loud, I pretended I couldn't hear.

After a couple of hours, Wyatt and I were circling the room in a jaunty two-step and I was spinning under his arm. I stopped short. Out of the corner of my eye, I caught sight of a tall man with brown hair and blue eyes. Not an uncommon combination, but my first thought was that it couldn't be him. Why would that mug be here?

He was laughing with a few men at the bar before our eyes met. He looked puzzled for a minute. *Where had he seen me?* I was pretty sure he'd figure it out. He wasn't wearing his gangster garb tonight. He was dressed in a sharp looking tuxedo. Almost any man looks good when he's dressed up, and this man appeared to be pressed into his suit. I stopped breathing for a moment.

"Esmé, are you all right?" Wyatt asked. "Too much champagne?"

"Too much something." We moved to our table, where I grabbed my small evening bag, made my excuses, and ran to the ladies' room. I felt reasonably sure that *mobster* wouldn't follow me in there. Then I had to figure out how to exit the building without being seen.

Inside the ladies' sanctum, the fashionable silver-and-pink Art Deco wallpaper, pink sinks, and generous mirrors gave me a pretty hideaway to try to gather my thoughts. I told myself the man I spied was not the man who flashed a gun at me. I almost convinced myself while I touched up my makeup.

I was not alone in the generously proportioned space.

"I thought you were through with him, darling," a blonde in a sky-blue dress was saying to another woman. The blonde had a sweet face and a sharp tongue, at odds with her innocent looks. I deemed her 'Cinderella,' silently of course. My ears perked up. I always love hearing a good story. I waited for the punch lines.

Her companion might have recently escaped from a sanitarium for tuberculosis. Tall, thin, deathly pale under a severe black bob, her glassy amber eyes outlined in black stared back at her in the mirror. She must have loved the effect, because she wore a white satin dress that matched her skin and her face powder. If not for her eyes, the ruby necklace, and deep red lips, she would have been colorless. I dubbed her 'the Snow Queen,' but not Snow White.

"Through with Rupert? I was, but time marches on." She sighed for effect.

"Do you have him hooked?"

"I had and I can again. Why not? I can be fond of him and he looks good on my arm."

"I take it you're sleeping with him?" The blonde applied her lipstick.

"One does these days." The Snow Queen pouted at her reflection. "But since our last breakup he hasn't seemed that interested."

"Imagine that." The blonde had practiced her mocking tone. "If you decide Rupert's not worth it, leave him to me."

I busied myself with my rouge. It didn't really matter. They hardly spared a glance my way. I'm always amused that when women get together, they return to the same subjects, chief among them—sex.

"Don't count on it," the Snow Queen said. "I'll get him back."

"How?" The blonde faced her.

"Turn down my sheets and invite him in." She graced her friend with a predatory smile.

"You don't really like sex, do you, Millie?"

"I don't hate it. What about you?"

"I rather like it," Cinderella said.

The Snow Queen sniffed. "I can live with sex, as long as a ring comes with it. Besides, I have it on good authority that once they're married, men lose interest in that sort of thing."

She certainly was sure of herself, this cold-blooded creature. A human cadaver.

The woman in white glared at me in the mirror. Perhaps I had put on too much rouge. She spoke to Cinderella. "I want to get out of here. I told Rupert I wanted to go to the Stork Club."

"Not the Peacock? At least he knew it was some kind of bird. What are you planning?" Cinderella asked. "To drop a gossip item in the ear of that sleazy columnist? Perhaps an engagement notice? You know he'd hate that."

"I'm aware of that, but whatever it takes. Besides, I want to get out of here, this place caters to the hoi polloi." She tossed her head, indicating me.

"No, sweetie," I said, "just people with blood in their veins." They both stared at me. I don't know why I didn't stifle that comment, but she'd got my goat.

She and Cinderella stormed out, but not before Cinderella threw me an amused nod. I pitied the poor schmo the Snow Queen was targeting to drag down the aisle.

I blotted my red lipstick and stood. I opened the door slowly and peeked out. I didn't see Chase, the mug I was avoiding.

Willie was at our table, delicately dabbing her forehead with a lace-edged handkerchief. She sipped some champagne. Not too far away, Wyatt and Tim leaned against the bar, sipping something more potent than champagne cocktails. And legal, too!

I waved them down, figuring with them on each arm I could simply waltz toward the exit doors, speed down the stairs, collect my coat and go. I didn't have to say much. They knew when, and when not to, make a commotion. I told them I was trying out something for a new play, which was much easier than an explanation. I was simply choreographing my escape from an overeager Don Juan, in some imaginary work in progress.

The band obligingly played a waltz. Wyatt and I twirled toward to the exit door to the stairs, while Willie and Tim spun around us. I nearly reached my objective when a large warm hand grabbed mine, sending a shock through me.

"This dance is mine, love." A British accent.

Startled, I glanced up, and it was *him*. I hadn't been mistaken. The gangster from the school shooting, the closet, the last of Scavullo. I know I gasped, but the swing music covered it. I sent a look of desperation to Wyatt, who merely raised his eyebrow in amused approval and shrugged. He leaned close and whispered.

"Are you kidding? He's gorgeous."

"You're off my Christmas card list, Wyatt Vane."

"I'll try to bear up, my dear Esmé." He saluted me and caught up to Willie, who spread her hands in the age-old "what can I do" gesture.

I turned to the man who held me as he lifted my right arm in the dance pose. The man named Chase. Suddenly I was in his arms. He danced me to the middle of the floor, making it harder for me to escape. Harder, but not impossible.

"I did not say yes." I was furious.

"You did not say no. I assumed you'd try to leave that way. All I had to do was wait." His smooth British accent again grated on my nerves. He was a good dancer. Too good. Neither a toe crusher nor a knee knocker. My feet followed his lead effortlessly. I cursed my ruined escape. I should have gone out through the kitchen. I'd keep that in mind for the future.

"You have all the answers then?"

He ignored that, giving me the once-over and the twice-over. "You look beautiful in that enchanting frock. So very different from the waif in the closet. You're altogether enchanting."

Right sentiment. Wrong man. "You're holding me too tight," I complained.

He gazed into my eyes. "I find it hard not to."

I glared back and wondered where his gun was. If he had it, I would have felt it. He was holding me *that* close. But he didn't look like a gangster tonight. Women were giving him the once-over.

"I read about Mr. Scavullo." I stated the obvious.

"Let's not talk about that now."

"What else do you know about it? You were there."

"As were you. As I recall, we were both occupied at the time."

I felt myself color, but I tried to ignore it. "Do you know who killed him?" I knew Chase couldn't have had time to do the deed before he yanked open the closet door.

"I only wish I did. However, I don't care to talk about that with you in my arms."

"Humor me." I pulled away to show him I was serious. "Who was that guy you were talking to that day?"

"What guy?"

"In the school. The would-be cat killer."

"Him. He's a policeman, off duty at the time."

"Are you saying the cops killed Scavullo?"

"Not at all. Not knowing what to expect, I thought it prudent to have them accompany me. They arrived as the killer began shooting. It would have been much messier to explain Scavullo's death if I hadn't had back-up."

"Did Scavullo know you were bringing them?"

"Yes. He must have alerted someone else." Chase stared at me. "You don't believe me?"

"I don't know." He had no reason to tell me the truth. "Are you going to shoot me?" The reporter in me just wouldn't shut up.

"I would love to do a lot of things to you, my adorable lady in lavender, but shooting is not among them."

"You are very rude."

He had the nerve to smile at me. "Not at all. You misunderstand me. I'm the good guy here. You ran away and I was worried about you. Tell me your name."

"Yours first."

I turned away from him when I noticed the cadaver who had sneered at me in the ladies' room, furiously throwing metaphysical, or was that *metaphorical,* knives at the two of us. But why she should hate *me* was puzzling. Clearly, Chase was the one at fault.

"Darling." Her voice was higher than it was in the ladies' room, but it carried over the dancers. "I believe this is our number."

"The Snow Queen is not happy," I said to him.

"She wouldn't be. She never is." He didn't ask who I meant.

I heard the high-pitched voice whine, "You brought me here. Don't you dare abandon me."

Thankfully, we stopped. He leaned down and spoke into my ear. "Don't go away, please. I must speak with you. I don't even know your name."

Who knew the icy Snow Queen would come to my aid? She placed a death grip on Chase's arm. He looked annoyed. Was he the 'Rupert' she talked about with Cinderella? *'Rupert'?* Seriously?

Her fingernails were blood red, no doubt to match her lipstick and the rubies around her neck. Her eyes looked even more glassy. Fever? Drugs? I didn't know. Even though it was illegal, I was betting on cocaine. People with money could always get what they wanted. Prohibition had taught us all that. I was afraid she might keel over. But even if she was knocking at Death's door, I had no desire to tangle with her.

They began dancing and I picked up the steps with my original partner Wyatt. We quickstepped over to the balcony where we strolled outside for a breath of fresh air. We stood in front of a set of French doors where I could see the Snow Queen and Chase (possibly 'Rupert Chase'?) glide into an easy waltz. Chase scanned the room and didn't find what he wanted. I ducked behind Wyatt.

"Do me a favor, Wyatt."

"Anything, my queen." He reached inside his jacket for a pack of cigarettes and a lighter. He shook the pack and offered me one, which I declined. He withdrew one, lit it, and inhaled deeply. "What do you need?"

"I need my coat and I have to leave right away." The night air was crisp and my skin was covered with goosebumps. "I can take the exit from here if you meet me downstairs in the lobby with my coat."

Wyatt was used to drama. He didn't blink an eye. Willie emerged from the ballroom with Tim. "What's up?" she wanted to know.

"I'm going."

No one knew about the messy incident at the school. I wasn't about to divulge anything now, especially after some champagne cocktails.

"Apparently," Wyatt said, "the wolf dancing with Esmé was a little too friendly and there seems to be a possessive female involved."

"You're off the hook." Willie peered through the glass door. "He's busy with that skin and bones in white. No, I take it back. She's busy with him. In a tango."

"The Snow Queen," I said. "I might be more afraid of her than him."

"Good name for her. She looks scary," Willie said.

"Yeah, banshee scary," Tim added. "Someone get her a sandwich."

"Uh oh, you better scoot, they're coming this way."

"We'll cut him off at the pass," Wyatt added, as if he were a cowboy in a movie.

Luckily, everyone picked up their cues. I opened the exit door and ran down the stairs with Willie, who didn't think it would be wise for me to travel alone. By the time we hit the lobby and grabbed our coats from the waiting Tim and Wyatt had already hailed a cab.

"I'll love you forever," I blew a kiss as he opened the door for Willie and me.

"I know, queenie." He saluted me.

It's good to have friends. And enough change to pay for a cab home. I slammed the door shut and sank back into the cushions, my heart beating too fast.

Willie grinned at me. "That dress is a real success."

Eight

MY HOPES OF RIDDING MYSELF of Scavullo's gold watch early Sunday morning were dashed. It was feeling heavier every day it spent in my purse.

I planned to return it to Juliette, but she didn't attend her usual Mass on Sunday. It wasn't surprising, but still disappointing. I assumed she was too devastated about her husband's death to pull herself together and come to church. Stricken with grief, the burden of making arrangements for his funeral Mass and burial was no doubt overwhelming. Beginning to think I couldn't pull off the simplest of plans, I had to find another time and place to free myself from the gold watch and chain.

I stared at the Italians sitting in the pews around me and the small knot of Irish folk who prayed weekly at Our Lady of Pompeii. We Celts were mostly the pale people with red, blond, and light brown hair. The Italians were dark and dramatic-looking, distinctive. We examined each other with interest.

There was only one Catholic Church where I came from, and everybody of the faith attended. It didn't matter if you were Irish, Italian, French, Polish, or Mexican; if you were Catholic, you all went to the same church. In my small town, you were either Protestant, Catholic, or Jewish. New York was a whole different world.

When I first came to New York, I lived in a small room with a couple of other women. Our Lady of Pompeii was close by and attending had become a habit, one which I was currently rethinking. It was far away from the Upper West Side where I lived now.

Did I know these people? We exchanged pleasantries. We were friendly. Now I hated myself for wondering who they really were. Mere shop owners and small businessmen? Surely, I told myself, they couldn't all be part of the mob. They weren't criminals. Still, the shadow of the Mafia was there, along with mob boss Frank Romeo in his tailored camel hair coat, surveying the crowd with bodyguards at his side.

During his comments, Father Rappoli announced that the visitation and rosary for Dante Scavullo were scheduled for Tuesday evening at a nearby Italian funeral home, and his church and graveside services would follow the next day.

The visitation Tuesday night at the mortuary: my next target.

❧

My plan to hand off the watch and chain at the visitation to Juliette Scavullo, or to one of her sons, and then depart before the prayers began, was thwarted. The widow didn't enter the room until everyone was in place and sitting down. The gold timepiece felt more like a penance than a watch. I had to stay for the full recitation of the rosary before I would have another chance.

A few mourners who recognized me from church nodded silent greetings. I stuck out in this crowd, with my strawberry blond hair and pale skin. I felt as if I were in the stage lights. Nearly everyone else had dark hair, in shades from brown to blackest black, and lovely deep olive skin. My pale flesh practically glowed in the dark. I couldn't hide. All I had was a black tilt hat to wear over my hair, which I wore crimped in waves at the front of my face and pulled back at the nape of my neck.

Because it was going to be a subdued yet formal event, I pulled out another one of my new outfits. I was particularly grateful that *Afternoon Tea with Nigel* had a somber scene and I now owned an appropriate black dress in a heavy crepe, which gave the skirt a dignified swing at the hem. The softly rounded neckline was relieved by a bold pink organdy ruffled collar and matching ruffled cuffs for the sleeves. The collar-and-cuffs could be swapped for several other sets in different colors, including a jaunty tartan red plaid. The fitted matching jacket featured pearl buttons that matched my pearl necklace. It was a warm autumn evening, so I just added a wool shawl and pink gloves. On reflection, it might have been a bit too much.

Dante Scavullo's open casket was in the front of the room, a rosary wound through his fingers. He looked puffy and waxy, in that unnatural way one expects of corpses. A layer of greasepaint makeup and bright rouge tried to cover the pallor of death. They only managed to make him look like a mannequin of himself. I noted the fatal gunshots apparently hadn't touched his face.

As we all took our places and waited to respond to the prayers, several young Italian men hovered around the casket. Juliette shooed her sons away to take their seats in the front row, while other young men remained, offering their condolences. Marco Scavullo was one of them.

The previous year, Scavullo had introduced me to his nephew, Marco, who had emigrated a few years before from Italy. Marco rarely attended church, but I recognized him and some of his friends. He was the pretty boy of the crowd, a year or two older than I.

Marco had conquered a lot of the English language, but he still retained a thick accent. He seemed more comfortable speaking Italian with his pals. He greeted me and held my hand a little too long. Handsome with clean even features, Marco had thick wavy black hair and one of those gleaming white wolf smiles. I was not attracted to him. I left that to a young woman who appeared both fearful and captivated by him. She was a petite beauty with long, black curly hair and unfortunately, a black eye and a swollen cheek.

One of Marco's pals bore an unfortunate resemblance to a rodent, with a pointed nose and quick small eyes. Another had deep olive skin and startling green eyes with long lashes. Though "Green Eyes" was not as classically handsome as Marco, I was pretty sure there were ladies lining up for his attention. He seemed more relaxed and approachable than the others.

I turned my attention to the room. The mortuary chapel was full. I took a seat in the back, aiming to be inconspicuous, but I garnered some stares, making me feel like a terrible outsider. I was happy to sit next to Carina Cimino. Although she was younger than I, about twenty-three, she was married and already had two children. She informed me she was there to get a few minutes away from her kids and score some gossip.

"You gotta know what's going on in this town," she said.

"Do you know her?" I indicated the woman with the bruised cheek.

"Pay no attention to Bianca," Carina whispered, pointing to the young woman glued to Marco's side. "She fancies herself in love with Marco."

"Bianca?"

"Bianca Lombardi."

"I don't recognize her from church. Are they a couple?"

"Depends who you ask. She would say yes. Marco would say no."

"Is he responsible for that black eye?" I looked for signs of violence about him.

"No." Carina shook her head and lowered her voice. "That fat man glowering over there. He's her father. He socked her good when he heard she had her eye on that Mafioso."

"Mr. Lombardi?" There was an air of tension about the man.

"Yeah, Lou Lombardi. Runs a little store, hates the mob. I guess he's tough enough to keep them at bay."

"Why is he here?"

"To show he has no fear."

I was learning a lot. "I didn't know Mr. Scavullo was in the mob."

"You must be the only one. But he wasn't high up. Low level. Bootlegger."

"Who are the others?"

She leaned around me to take a closer look. "The funny looking one? Guido Moretti. Also known as Ratty."

"That's an unfortunate name."

"He's got an unfortunate face. The one with the pretty eyes, those green eyes? Patrick Dentino. 'Lashes,' they call him."

"Patrick?"

"His mother's Irish. Then there's Bones. The skinny one."

"Does Marco have a nickname?"

"Not that I know of. Not yet. Time will tell."

"Is he in the mob?

She shrugged as if she didn't know his exact status. "I hear he wants to be a big man in the mob, but not like his uncle." Not knowing what else to say, I retrieved my rosary. Carina smiled and tweaked her ear. "Always listening."

I hadn't eaten all day and my stomach rumbled. I wanted this portion of the evening to be over so I could leave. I looked up and saw Marco and his buddies staring at me. I assumed it was my strawberry hair. I pulled my black hat lower over my forehead.

Father Rappoli intoned the prayers, and our voices followed along. We all held our rosaries. Mine had been a present from my parents, who acquired it in Rome on a once-in-a-lifetime trip to Europe they had taken while I was a young teen. They visited my genteel French grandparents and left me at home with my mother's rather raucous folks. My grandfather, Marshal Michael Rafferty, taught me how to shoot a gun while they were out of town, and we agreed not to tell them. I got pretty good at hitting paper targets and tin cans.

But the damage a gun could do never occurred to me back then. I didn't think much about guns and death, but I was now. I fingered the mother-of-pearl beads of my rosary, wrapped in their beautiful silver filigree fittings. I counted off the Hail Marys until I could leave.

Juliette Scavullo and her four sons sat in the front row. She was a petite woman with fine bone structure that her severely pulled-back hairstyle did nothing to hide. The circles under her eyes were a testament to the sleepless nights since her husband's murder.

She wore black, as did nearly everyone, but black was not her color. She would have looked better in something bright, a red or a purple. She usually wore ruby and sapphire and amethyst colors to church, but I suspected it would be a long time—perhaps never—before she wore anything but widows' weeds.

On the edge of the crowd near the back was a man in an expensive camel hair coat, which would have seemed out of place, except for the deference he was shown by others in the room. Frank Romeo. I tried to catch a discreet look. I'd never seen him this close before.

Rumor said he had been heavily involved in bootleg booze during Prohibition, among other unsavory activities. Scavullo worked for Romeo, according to some of the newspapers, which also claimed the mob chieftain had ordered Scavullo's murder.

Whether that was true or not, no matter how you looked at it, his appearance here was a shock, even without his famous camel coat. One of his coterie took the garment, revealing a stark black suit underneath. Surrounded by the group of young thugs (at least I assumed they were thugs), Romeo's appearance here was in the worst possible taste.

A morbid thrill rippled through the crowd. I tried to look away, but it was impossible. Frank Romeo was middle-aged and overly groomed, in that movie star fashion that successful mobsters were supposed to favor. The tabloids had dubbed him 'Handsome Frank Romeo' and they weren't wrong.

Objectively speaking, he was fine looking with sad dark eyes, prominent cheekbones and nose. The former newspaperwoman in me might have described his lips as 'sensuous.' Yet I couldn't. He was a thug himself, a Mafioso, and a purported murderer. I was happy to be as far away from him as possible in this crowd.

Although I was staring over my rosary, stifling the occasional yawn, I knew I had to wait until it was all over for a chance to return the anvil on my conscience, the pocket watch.

Finally, I lined up to speak with Juliette Scavullo. Dark-eyed men watched us, but she barely noticed. She seemed slightly surprised but pleased to see me.

"Esmé, so good of you to come and pray for my Dante's soul."

"I— I'm sorry for your loss." Words failed me. I reached into my purse and withdrew the gold pocket watch and I offered it to her. She took a moment before speaking.

"Dante's watch?" She stared at it and then at me. "I thought it was gone. I thought maybe the police stole it, along with all his money."

There were too many people crowding us, so I rushed into my explanation. "Mr. Scavullo was at the diner, near the theatre, where I'd gone to lunch. The day it—it happened, I saw him, and I was going to say hello, but he seemed distracted and left. He forgot his watch on the counter. I picked it up and tried to follow him."

"You picked it up?"

"I remembered how he always looked at it during the sermon." Juliette smiled at the memory. "It seemed very important to him."

"Always such an impatient man." She shook her head slightly and smiled sadly. "But you didn't give it to him?"

"Ray, the owner, was angry that I got the watch before he did, so he made me pay for Dante's lunch before he let me leave."

"Dante didn't pay for his lunch? That doesn't sound like him." Her eyebrows knit together in a scowl. "I don't understand."

"I don't either. Mr. Scavullo must have had something on his mind. He didn't seem to notice me at all." Then I remembered he did see me, before he took that call on the diner's phone. That conspiratorial wink, like he was in church. "I ran after him, but I lost him. I was too late. You see, Ray has a reputation for collecting things people leave and never giving them back. Usually it's just umbrellas, wallets, things like that. But I knew the watch was important to Mr. Scavullo."

"I gave Dante that watch when we were married."

"Ray was mad he couldn't steal it. That's why he made me pay for the lunch," I continued. "I planned to give the watch to you on Sunday at church."

"We never made it to Mass this week."

"I'm sorry. I— I read about what happened." I couldn't manage any more words. I began to worry she wouldn't believe me. Did she think I'd try and shake her down for a reward?

"We thought his watch was lost forever." She stared at the watch, then she turned and called for her eldest son. Juliette gently placed the watch in Anthony's hands. "Your father always wanted you to have it."

"His watch? We thought the cops stole it," he said. "They told the truth?"

"This one time, maybe," she said and turned back to me. "I won't forget this, Esmé."

I wasn't sure I liked the way she said that. "It's not necessary, really." I put up my empty hands and she let it drop.

"You must be very busy these days," she said. "Doesn't your play open up soon?" I didn't know how she could think of me at this time, but maybe it was a relief to think of something other than death.

"Thursday, yes." Final dress rehearsal was tomorrow, then opening night. The producers were hoping the early reviews would bring in the crowds for the weekend and beyond. The very thought made me queasy with nerves. It was part of the process, but still.

"I'm sorry I can't be there. We were looking forward to it."

"I understand. You can't come." The smell of wax candles, incense, and innumerable flower arrangements was beginning to suffocate me. I was dying to get out of there. Not literally, of course. "I will pray for you and the boys."

We leaned in for a quick hug.

"Do you have an escort?" she asked, looking around.

"I'll catch a cab." I had no intention of catching a cab, but it was always a good thing to say. I felt like walking, even though it was after dark. And my stomach told me I had better eat something soon.

Marco stepped forward and offered to accompany me. Juliette shot him a look, then introduced us.

"You remember Dante's nephew, Marco Scavullo." He took my hand and leaned in a little too close. He resembled a would-be leading man who hadn't yet been discovered. He smiled too intimately. I must have stepped back, because Juliette moved in between us. "No, no, you have responsibilities, Marco."

It was his turn to step back, intimidated by his aunt. I was relieved, but I noticed that Marco joined the small knot of men around Frank Romeo. The mobster stepped forward and reached out to Juliette, but she turned from him in scorn.

Romeo and Juliette struck me as particularly ironic. The scribbler inside me would have had a field day with that. I never considered myself a yellow journalist, but what a headline: JULIETTE SPURNS ROMEO!

For God's sake, Esmé, this is a funeral, I told myself.

I am very bad at scolding myself and it only encouraged my scattered thoughts. I was too hungry, I had to eat something before I fell down. I promised myself I'd dismiss Frank Romeo and Juliette Scavullo from my mind. I had completed my mission with the watch.

If 'Handsome Frank Romeo' was responsible for Scavullo's death, I knew it would never be solved officially. It was common knowledge that the police generally didn't interfere in Mafia matters. Unless those matters became too notorious or too dangerous for civilians. Police could be paid off, or they could decide to let "the scum" take care of their own problems.

On the other hand, Hoover's FBI was having a busy year, capturing a spate of bank robbers in the Midwest. Bonnie and Clyde and John Dillinger had been gunned down this past summer. New outlaws took their place in the wanted posters on the walls.

Occupying my mind with trivial facts meant I was counting the seconds before I could leave. I was putting my coat on when I noticed Juliette signaling to someone across the room, someone who wasn't Italian, someone who was taller than the average man in this crowd.

NINE

D AMNATION, IF IT WASN'T *HIM*.
Was the universe laughing at me in some perverse joke? In this huge city the law of averages dictated we would never see each other again, but now Chase materialized at my side. He was back in his gangster suit and dark shirt, but with a different tie, this time an abstract design in purple. He fit right in. I didn't stop breathing, but it felt like I did.

"Graydon, could you do me a favor?" Juliette asked.

Graydon? Graydon Chase? Or Rupert? I threw him a distinct go-away look. She saw it.

"Do you know each other?" she asked.

"We haven't been introduced," I rushed to say.

"I see. Easily fixed," she replied as if that explained everything. "Esmé, this is Graydon Chase. Graydon, this is Esmé de LaForet."

"So pleased to meet you." He took my hand. I was speechless. "Call me Graydon."

Not 'Rupert'? Who was this guy really? Juliette assured me that Graydon would get me home safely. "I don't want you walking alone after dark in this neighborhood."

"It would be my honor," he said, to my horror. In my memory, I heard the gunshots in the empty school that day. The widow turned to the next group of mourners and Graydon Chase and I were dismissed. It was about eight o'clock and the phrase 'starving artist' was completely apt.

"That isn't necessary," I snapped at him. "I can make it on my own."

"You don't say 'no' to Juliette Scavullo."

"She doesn't have to know."

"You don't care for my company?"

"Not really, no."

"Pretty name, that. Esmé. Suits you." His plummy accent grated on my nerves yet again.

"Chase." He was called over by someone else I didn't know.

"Don't move. Please." Chase smiled at me with what I thought was a measure of menace. He turned away and responded to the man who called him. Mrs. Scavullo was occupied with others and I ran for the exit, heading in the opposite direction of the crowd. It seemed I was always dashing down some stairway into the cool night. Outside, I wrapped my shawl around my shoulders and headed toward the subway.

My stomach signaled me as I passed an automat. It was too brightly lit and not appetizing. I didn't feel like dropping a dime in a slot and retrieving a dried-out sandwich. Not tonight. I kept walking and was soon tantalized by the aroma of grilled steak. I turned in the direction of the scent down a side street and followed it to a little restaurant called Bonaparte's. Soft light spilled out of the front windows and I could see hanging lamps and red leather booths with lots of wood paneling.

The place looked welcoming, though expensive. I checked my wallet and decided I could cover it. After all, in light of the Scavullo murder replaying in my head, life was short. My only fear was maybe they wouldn't seat a single woman. God knows what goes on in men's tiny brains.

I was greeted by the maître d', a portly middle-aged Frenchman with thinning brown hair and a thin mustache. He had a certain flair and dignity, wearing a jaunty red vest over his crisp white shirt and tie. He apparently approved of my clothes and demeanor, but he hesitated. This clearly was a respectable establishment, and I was clearly a very respectable woman in an expensive ensemble. He was about to say he was sorry when I jumped ahead.

"Forgive me, Monsieur, I know you probably don't seat single women. I was supposed to have dinner with a—a gentleman, but he stood me up. He is apparently no gentleman." I was prepared to shed tears at the shock and disgrace of it all, if necessary. My lips trembled, and I believe I managed to appear haughty, humbled, and hurt, all at the same time. I have learned a lot from actresses who can cry on cue.

"Oh, Mademoiselle, who would ever stand you up?"

I waved my hands in distress. "And I waited so long! I'm feeling a little insulted, and I'm terribly hungry. I may faint."

"For you, for a respectable young woman, I break the rules. After all, they are my rules."

He smiled and showed me to a red leather-lined semicircular booth, helped me off with my jacket and into my seat. It was nicely secluded. I removed my hat. I fluffed out my ridiculous, and I might add, theatrical, pink ruffled collar and straightened my cuffs. I took the menu he offered, scanned it, and ordered.

I leaned back in the booth and sighed. This dinner was a small indulgence and as the daughter of a Frenchman with discerning tastes, I ordered a glass of cabernet. We had wine with dinner at home all through Prohibition. It wasn't illegal to have it in your house, after all.

Getting it there, however, was another story. It may have shocked the neighbors, but we de LaForets didn't care. My father used to drive down to Mexico with a buddy for cases of cheap wine they called 'Juarez Red.' He would fill up the car with the hooch and hand it out to his friends. The wine wasn't French, he would say, but it wasn't bad, in hard times. So maybe Dad was a bootlegger too, in his own small way, crossing an international border with a load of liquid contraband.

I sipped the wine and waited for my filet mignon, salad, and sautéed mushrooms. I willed my muscles to relax and enjoy this brief moment before being thrown to the wolves—the critics, the Broadway audiences, the world. This quiet moment in a luxurious restaurant in an amazing new dress that conveyed quality—it was a balm for my soul.

My filet arrived, perfectly medium rare. After a few savory bites, the maître d' returned.

"Ah, Mademoiselle, look who I have found. Your date, Monsieur Chase. He is very sorry he is late. Please find it in your heart to forgive him. A very good customer of mine. A gentleman."

I froze in mid bite. *Chase.* They knew each other? Just my luck.

"Yes, you must forgive me, Esmé. Marcel, thank you. I see I still must perform more groveling." Chase had the nerve to smile at me.

"This gentleman would never stand you up, mademoiselle." Marcel was clearly on Team Chase.

"I was merely detained," Chase added.

"A man must do what he must," Marcel answered, as Chase slid into my cozy booth and made himself at home. "Dinner for you, Monsieur Chase?"

He gave a cursory glance at my plate. "The same as Miss de LaForet. And the wine."

"Very good choice. *Parfait.*"

"Pardon, Monsieur Marcel." I gave Chase the evil eye. "Separate checks, please."

Chase shook his head and smiled. "It's already taken care of."

"She is not so easy, this one," Marcel said to Chase. "This one is a lady."

He withdrew with impressive grace. Graydon Chase sat in the booth opposite me while I wondered if I should stage a scene of outrage, or simply run out the door.

"How did you know I'd be here?"

"I presumed you'd take a flier. I asked a friend to follow you at a discreet distance. French restaurant? A mademoiselle with a French name? Voilà!"

"You have friends? How interesting. Are they gangsters too?"

He ignored my comment. "I congratulate you on giving Marcel such a convincing story. He bought it. But when he saw me, he realized I couldn't have stood you up without having a very good reason, and I knew he would do everything in his power to make things right for us."

I glared at him. He gazed at the fabulous meal that I could not finish, now that he was here. My stomach was in an uproar. He had ruined this lovely restaurant for me. And my dinner.

"Aren't you eating?"

"I've lost my appetite."

"Pity. It looks delicious. They do wonderful steaks here."

Marcel bustled over with the wine. Chase lifted his glass to appreciate the color.

"You look like a gangster," I said.

"You look like a beautiful elf." He saluted me with his wine.

Elf. Exactly the kind of compliment I *would* get from this posh thug.

"Elf? I don't have pointed ears, nor am I freakishly small," I said. I am a perfectly normal height, if a bit thin. Most everyone is thin these days, if not downright hungry. It's the times.

"Spoken like a beautiful elf. With such large eyes. What color are they? Not blue? Not quite green? A mix, then."

"They're green. And I'm sure you prefer bony giants like the Snow Queen."

"Snow Queen? If you're referring to Millicent, she is merely a friend. Dear Millie."

"You should tell her that." *Millicent?* Were people really named Millicent? It was a perfectly preposterous and pompous name, like an aged aunt in a play. "She thinks you're practically trotting down the aisle with her. Do you really call her Millie?"

"Only when I want to annoy her." He paused a moment. "You are right though, she is a bit frosty of personality. And by elf, I only mean you seem to have magical qualities, such as disappearing."

I snorted back a laugh. "I wish that was true right now."

"That is not going to happen tonight. No disappearing," Chase said. "I promised Juliette I'd make sure you arrive home safely."

"I can get home by myself. I do it all the time."

He raised an eyebrow. "Listen to me, Esmé de LaForet, there were some very dangerous characters there tonight."

"You think I'm in danger? From the mob?"

His steak arrived and he picked up his knife and fork.

"Juliette Scavullo asked me to take you home, neatly accomplishing two things: making sure you're safe tonight, and by placing you with me, she tells the Italian boys to stay away from you." I didn't like the way Marco and the others stared at me, but I wasn't about to tell Graydon Chase that. "I know now you weren't lying about knowing the Scavullos from church. Still, others might not believe your story about Ray's Diner. I do, by the way."

I stared at Mr. Blue Eyes. "I'm beginning to regret not letting Ray pocket the darn thing."

"That's not in your character though, is it? You seem to be ridiculously honest." He sliced into his steak.

"I'm not ridiculous."

I considered my wine and decided not to drink any more, just to be on the safe side. I pushed it away from me. You never knew who might slip a Mickey in it. He noticed. Observant rascal.

"You had quite an appetite before you saw me."

I truly regretted that I could not finish that wonderful meal. "Sadly, yes."

"I'm not a gangster, by the way."

I could feel one eyebrow lift. It practically touched my hairline. "Do tell. What are you, exactly?"

"Miss de LaForet, I am one of the good guys. I was trying to help Scavullo extract himself from—the Life." He looked momentarily both disgusted and distressed. "He ignored my advice. I told him never to meet with them alone. He promised he wouldn't, and then this."

Was Chase telling the truth? "That's a very nice story. I know all about nice stories. I've heard a lot of them. I used to be a reporter. Tell me, why the schoolhouse?"

"They wanted to lure him to an empty building. No one would look for him at a school."

"Columbus Day. Brand-new national holiday. Why wasn't it locked?"

"Locked doors are nothing to these people." He smiled and leaned back in his seat. "And now that I know your name, I can check out the rest of your tale."

"My tale? Which part do you doubt?" I fingered the edge of my dinner knife.

"At first, all of it. You were hiding in a closet, telling me the wildest nonsense about Scavullo's pocket watch, and then you disappeared. Yet tonight, you produce the timepiece in question and return it to the widow in the middle of a Mafia funeral."

"Hey, it was a *viewing* and rosary! And not everybody there was Italian."

"I checked out your story at that diner."

"You talked to Ray?"

"He balked at first, but after I slipped him a five…"

I shrugged. "He'd sell his grandmother for five dollars. His sandwiches are good, but I won't be going back."

"Ray confirmed your preposterous story. He said you were right there at the counter when Scavullo got some phone call. He claimed he would have returned the watch to the widow. If you hadn't insisted on doing it yourself."

"And you believed him?"

"Obviously not. I spotted him pocketing change that wasn't his. As you said."

I moved on to playing with my fork. "He's all heart, that Ray."

"So yes, I believe that part of your story."

"What don't you believe?"

"That you're a playwright." He stared at me, daring me to spin another tale.

TEN

66“I DON'T GIVE A HOOT in hell whether you believe me or not. *Leaving Alamogordo,* my new play, opens Thursday at the Washington Irving Theatre.”

“Easily checked.” He toasted me, unafraid to sip his wine. “Madam playwright.”

“Still suspicious?”

“On basic principle.”

“I have principles too. And I'm supposed to believe you're some kind of detective?”

“Inquiry agent, or private investigator, if you please. I prefer to think of myself as someone who solves problems for people.”

“For a price.”

“Everybody has a price. Everybody pays a price. Like Dante Scavullo. Unfortunately, it seems Scavullo was holding back, protecting someone, perhaps. Even if people don't lie, they mislead.”

“Who killed Scavullo?” I tried to regain my appetite, but it was no use.

“I don't know who pulled the trigger. Or why he was killed. Our exit plan was working. And then suddenly there was—you.”

“Lucky you. And Handsome Frank Romeo?”

“Romeo is not especially known for killing his enemies, or his employees.” Chase's eyes didn't leave my face. “Bad for business.”

“You don't have to watch me.”

"Oh, I do, you might launch that knife and fork at me. I'm wondering all kinds of things about you, my beautiful elf."

"But you don't believe I write plays?" How dare he.

"It's not a typical profession for a woman."

"I'm not typical! And believe me, there are plenty of us fighting for the chance to have a play produced on Broadway. Too many. And women have written plays for centuries." I was about to launch into a lecture about Aphra Behn and the rise of Restoration comedy when he put up his hands in surrender.

"Thursday?"

"Day after tomorrow."

"At the Washington Irving?" He thought about something, then grinned. "I believe I have plans to attend that opening night. With a friend."

"The Snow Queen?"

"Another friend. She likes to support the theatre, things like that."

"Playboy." So many women, so little time, apparently.

"I've been accused of that. And don't forget, private inquiry agent."

"No doubt you're simply a gigolo."

He seemed amused and cut a piece of his steak.

The scene from the closet replayed itself in my memory. The kiss. It meant nothing to him. I could feel a blush starting on my face, but the lights were dim and I don't think it showed. I needed a way to magically disappear or at least take a powder. But how? Nothing occurred to me. He insisted on taking me home "after our date."

"No." Alarm bells rang in my head.

"I must ensure that your premises are secure and none of Romeo's crew are interested in you, or what you might know, or how that watch found its way into your hands. And back to Juliette. And I promised her you would be safe. It's bad luck to disappoint a new widow."

"To be clear, you are interested in the gangsters and not in me. I was simply an innocent bystander." I placed my napkin on the table.

"So you say. I'm not convinced you're entirely innocent."

We were heading for another impasse. I extracted a promise he would leave promptly after delivering me home. But now Graydon Chase had planted a seed: Could I be in danger from some of the mourners? I picked up my water glass and reflected that I have always had a fatal flaw. Although I wanted to flee, I had to see how this scene would play out.

"I am a gentleman, Esmé." At least he didn't say English gentleman.

"You couldn't prove it by me." I paused for effect. "If I let you escort me home, you have to promise: No more kisses. I realize it meant nothing to you, but I take kisses seriously." I refrained from mentioning the part about the theatre and all the hugging and kissing that went on.

"How refreshing." He indulged in another bite of his steak. "I did enjoy it though."

New York is the stars and the moon for me, and it will be my home forever, yet it is strange to see the ways in which women are held back. Where I came from, women owned property and ran ranches and newspapers. The vote was delivered to us in the last century. We've already had women in the state house.

I have been assured it was only because women were few and far between, so all the Western he-men figured making women happy by marking a line on a ballot was no big deal. It might even keep the women around. But those Western women were tough. They found that a six-shooter makes a man polite.

However, when you are a single woman in a place like New York City in these uncertain times, and you have even the tiniest amount of means, the wolves crawl out of the woodwork. They see a payday. It was one thing to be an impoverished playwright, but another to be a woman of property, even if that property was merely a lovely apartment with a fireplace and a balcony.

My steady job with its small salary also drew the jobless Joes. I realized if I also had a hit play, even a small hit, it would bring more of them. Men who were jealous of my good fortune wouldn't mind using me. It was exhausting figuring out who was who. In truth, I was also terrified of marriage and the unfair laws that allowed husbands access to their wives' money and property. A woman had to be very clever to keep her hands on what belonged to her.

I am reminded of that every day while dodging the whistles and catcalls of men congregating on the streets. Jobless men who have nowhere to go. The stale scent of sweat on unwashed men stings my nostrils as I pass by the soup kitchens. The stench is almost as pungent as the desperation of men on the hunt to find a woman with money. That's one reason I didn't want men to see my place. I was happy to entertain my female friends there, but not the boys who would get the wrong idea.

I didn't want Graydon Chase in my home.

Was he really some kind of private detective? If the pulp magazines were right, that meant he was living on the edge of poverty. He didn't look or sound poor, but he was certainly at home among the Scavullos and Romeos, in his gangster black shirt and pinstripe suit. Or was he just wearing that clan's style as a visual pretext, to smooth his entry into their lives?

Chase was a certain kind of handsome, I admit. Long and lean with a thick head of light-tipped wavy brown hair, he was rather like a magazine cover model. I believe I've mentioned his neon blue eyes. He fit in quite well at the dance club with the Snow Queen in her frost-colored dress and ruby choker. She obviously had money and was in his thrall, planning to hornswoggle him into matrimony, although he didn't seem nearly as entranced with her. Perhaps it would be a financial transaction.

Graydon Chase declared we had a connection. Maybe we did. I could feel it when he touched me, a slight electrical current, like Ben Franklin holding a kite in a lightning storm. I wasn't about to let it knock me down.

Although I didn't want him anywhere near my apartment, I looked over my shoulder for hoodlums while he walked me to his car, a newish navy blue Ford coupé, respectable but nothing fancy. He insisted on opening the passenger side door for me and warning me not to jump out in traffic as he shut the door firmly. He didn't know how tired I was of arguing with him or how desperate I was to be home.

When we arrived, I ran for the building's front door, but Chase hauled me back and insisted on "securing the premises," which meant he wanted to come inside.

We headed to the second floor. My apartment was at the front of the building and faced the street. I pointed out that he had agreed to leave.

"This is your chance to prove you're a man of honor."

He didn't reply, and I calculated how quickly I could retrieve my little blue steel Smith & Wesson .38 from my nightstand, if I needed it. A sentimental present from my Grandfather Rafferty, the one-time town marshal. No need to bother Chase with those details. He was glued to my side. I tread softly up the stairs, Graydon close behind me. No need to wake the neighbors.

"Back off, buster," I said.

He paused, then he put his hand over mine as I opened the lock. He barged into my apartment behind me, ostensibly to make sure no boogeyman was there, slowly closing the door. He took in the layout and my décor.

He failed to compliment my deep green sofa and the gold-and-black chinoiserie screens I found in a shop on the Lower East Side, or the soft emerald green satin-finish paint on the walls. Nor did he mention the marble mantel over the fireplace that held my few family photos, my parents' wedding picture, and the three of us.

My rooms were strikingly handsome, I thought, but I dreaded having this presumptuous Graydon Chase viewing my bedroom, admiring my living room fireplace through my French doors from the vantage point of my bed. Which this man didn't need to see at all.

With one glimpse at my bedroom through the glass doors, Chase casually and slowly moved forward. I put out my arm.

"I did not invite you in."

"And yet here I am. Security check." Graydon's eyes grew wider gazing at the place where I repose. "Oh my God, it's exactly where I would imagine an elf would sleep."

"You're vile, you know that? You're not in any position to judge my taste."

"Once a man sees that bed, Esmé, all he could possibly think of is you, supine on that sumptuous field of green velvet. I like it, it's a lovely work of art."

"That is one reason men are not invited into my home. Now go."

He stared at me with interest. "None? No men?"

That wasn't exactly true. "None who count."

When Hank, the Irv's set designer, had described his work at my apartment as being like a new stage set, I had to give tours to the rest of the stagehands, the stage manager, the actors and actresses, as well as the other staff. May even showed up and approved. So did a few friends of Hank's wife Irma and my friend Reggie, who found it howlingly hilarious.

I shrugged. Elegantly, I hoped. "Some boys from the theatre who generally aren't interested in women have been around, but they do approve of the décor. Time to go, Mr. Chase."

He pushed past me and grabbed my hand, dragging me along, insisting on checking the other rooms, including the maid's soft blue room and bathroom, and all the windows and doors, acting for all the world like the detective he said he was.

"It's a beautiful apartment. Do you own it?"

"Are you a fortune hunter?" My place looked like luxury, I knew. My lovely Edwardian Five.

He grinned. "You still think I'm a gigolo, don't you?"

"Nothing tells me you are not. And don't get the wrong idea," I said. "I can rent out the extra room if things get tight."

"You must be financially independent."

"That is none of your business. Times are tough, have you heard?"

"A dilettante playwright?" He annoyed me. "No. You're a debutante, most likely a Midwestern debutante, I surmise, though admittedly, rather more canny than most debutantes. And is Esmé de LaForet your real name? Or are you a plain Jane Doe from Chicago?"

"That doesn't even merit a reply. I already mentioned my play is called *Leaving Alamogordo*." The W.I. wasn't the largest theatre on Broadway, but neither was it the smallest. He would be lost in the crowd. "I probably won't see you. You'll be occupied with one of your many women."

"Perhaps." He seemed thoughtful.

"All secure?" I asked, indicating the front door. I cracked it open. He stopped before leaving.

"Esmé, you must be careful concerning that crowd tonight."

"At the rosary?"

"They weren't all praying, Elf."

"Don't call me that. It presumes an intimacy we don't have."

"Beautiful Elf, then. Mysterious Elf. Stay away from Frank Romeo and his mob, Elf."

"What about Juliette Scavullo?"

"Her too, to be on the safe side. They will be closing ranks."

"Do you have a business card?"

"You don't trust me?"

"I'd be a fool to do that."

"But we have such fond memories." He pulled out a small private detective license for me to inspect, then withdrew a small crisp card from his inner jacket pocket and handed it to me.

Graydon Chase
Discreet Inquiries
PRAEMONITUS PRAEMUNITOS
Forewarned is forearmed

I turned it over. On the back it read:

VERUM SEQUOR
I chase the truth

It also had a phone number. I thought the Latin was a bit pretentious for a P.I. who worked for mobsters, but I held my tongue. I stared at him and crossed my arms.

"Consider me forewarned."

"Very well, Esmé Elf. I'm leaving, like the good scout I promised to be." I hadn't moved from my post.

"Good. Scoot, scout."

He strode back to where I was holding up the door. Mr. Chase had that wolfish look in his blue eyes. He grabbed hold of me and, damn it, my stomach fluttered.

"You feel it too. Our connection."

Yes, I felt it, but it didn't feel healthy, and his cologne, or whatever it was, smelled way too good.

"You promised not to kiss me," I reminded him.

"Testing to see if I'm made of steel?" He was certainly made of malarkey.

"Perhaps. And are you made of steel?"

"This one time. Lock that door after I leave. Please."

As if I needed to be told.

ELEVEN

THE NEXT DAY I WAS alternately useful and useless. Final dress was always trying. And while there were moments of brilliance, others threw my stomach onto a roller coaster of dread. There were dropped lines, missed cues, costume problems, runaway rolling desk chairs, and a playwright on the edge. It had all the charm of a high school assignment to see a class play.

Yet, although you wouldn't know from dress rehearsal, *Leaving Alamogordo* was really going to happen. The show would go on—if only the leading lady remembered all her lines, and the leading man stopped bumping into the furniture, and the rest of the cast regained their earlier savoir faire and confidence.

Director Szabo was suddenly doubtful about how I had changed the last lines, but Clarissa was on board with her big bossy kiss. It was a stroke of luck that she and the leading man had chemistry. Perhaps too much chemistry. Stop worrying, I told myself, even though there was a collective sense of impending doom. I am not one to believe that 'bad dress means success' (an old saying around the Irv).

Sal strongly suggested that I calm down and get myself a massage before opening night. It was more of an order. He recommended a large Swedish gal, who proceeded to iron my muscles like a shirt through a mangle. And take Thursday off, he commanded.

I am not one to deny myself a gift day off. May made the massage appointment for me at an exclusive ladies' gym, full of women who reminded me of the Snow Queen. Although I was more used to the YWCA and a little intimidated, I acclimated quickly.

"Miss, your knots have knots," Miss Swedish Massage informed me while I was being pummeled on her table. I could hardly stay awake. "Take a nap," she counseled, but I was already half asleep.

I woke up feeling no pain. I also sprang for a pedicure and manicure, and I emerged with ruby red toes and fingernails.

The afternoon papers carried small notices Sal had placed about my play opening at the Washington Irving. Because I wasn't the center of the universe, the scandal sheets also covered the funeral of Dante Scavullo. They particularly noted that mob boss Frank Romeo had put in an appearance.

MURDERED MOBSTER LAID TO REST, read one headline

Blurry photos outside Our Lady of Pompeii Church showed various goons trying to hide their faces behind their fedoras. A heavily veiled Juliette Scavullo was escorted out by her sons. There were no signs of so-called private detective Graydon Chase.

I wasn't surprised, though in my self-absorbed preparation for opening night, I had forgotten today was Dante Scavullo's body's last moment above ground. I took a closer look.

The tabloids set the mobster stories on the front page, which probably owed more to Romeo's presence than Scavullo's death. The *Post* story pointed out in florid prose that widow Juliette Scavullo had once again turned away from the famous mobster.

I wondered about their personal history, and I hoped that snub didn't put her in danger. At the same time, I congratulated myself for finally ridding my life of Scavullo's pocket watch and all its complications, once and for all.

I calculated one more issue in my day: Amelia. I hoped there was enough time for my further transformation, as promised by my housekeeper. I worried way too much about pleasing her.

Back at my apartment, Amelia was waiting to fashion my hair and makeup. She loved bossing me around and proceeded to transform me as she had the night of the lavender frock, only more so. Working at a beauty salon had made her an expert. Or so she said.

She used just the barest hint of foundation on my face under what appeared to be a pound of face powder, darkened my eyebrows, painted on a hint of a smoky green eyeshadow, and lined my eyes with a pencil. I gazed in the mirror.

"Wow." I didn't know what else to say. She'd obviously taken her cues from the movies. A little Kay Francis meets Loretta Young?

"I know, it's subtle, but you don't need too much," Amelia said.

I didn't think it was particularly subtle.

"Now." She reached for the false eyelashes. "For the frosting." Amelia warned me not to talk or move while she applied them. I remembered Jean Harlow in *Dinner at Eight* performing this delicate task, while shouting at Wallace Beery to "never talk to me while I'm putting on my lashes!"

"Can I breathe?" I ventured.

"Very quietly."

I held my breath. She finished and signaled me to behold the glamorous woman in the mirror.

Although the current style for hair was short and worn in a cap shape, I couldn't bear to cut mine. Amelia fashioned my locks in a figure eight at the nape of my neck. Willie had made me a green velvet band covered in pearls to wind through my hair and crown my remaining curls. It looked amazing and completely appropriate.

"It's most fetching, Amelia."

"You're pretty relaxed, for you."

"Massage."

"No kidding? You could use more of those. So, what do you think?"

I pointed to the woman in the mirror. "She looks pretty amazing."

"Yeah, you clean up nice." Amelia oversaw my entire ensemble and helped me into my dress so I wouldn't smear makeup on it. "I wondered when you were going to wear this one. It's my favorite."

"Mine too."

"Good thing that *Teatime with Nigel* thing was such a flop. I just hope your play won't go up in smoke too."

"You're a comfort, Amelia."

"What? I'm honest." She put her hands on her hips and I laughed.

I hoped this lovely remade costume of forest green velvet would provide me with all the armor I required. I had dreamed forever of having such a gown, and Willie swore the color enhanced my eyes and contrasted beautifully with my strawberry blond locks. This evening's frock was a bias-cut masterpiece decorated with rhinestones, faux pearls, and bugle beads on the full sleeves and shoulders. The neckline dipped low in front and much lower in the back. The skirt reached to my ankles, allowing my gold heels to peep out.

I think I looked as pretty as I ever had. It was a little alarming how the right clothes and makeup could give you courage. I knew this when I wrote my characters, and tonight I was playing a new role for myself—successful playwright.

"Hey, you don't want to be late for your own show."

Amelia gave me a gentle shove. She made sure I remembered my purse, and my evening coat, and a couple of bucks. Sending me off like a nervous fairy godmother, she informed me she'd be leaving soon and locking up. She cautioned me to take care and not come home too late.

"You theatre people keep the strangest hours, she said."

"And if it's a flop?"

"Don't throw yourself off the Empire State Building. You'd ruin that amazing creation."

TWELVE

M Y VERY OWN OPENING NIGHT was the kind of evening I'd fantasized about when I was stuck out West, with no hope of a life in the theatre. Tonight would be different. I could feel it.

Before New York, I'd had a few plays badly produced at a little theatre back home. Understand, I was still learning things. Like plot and dialogue and how to keep the action moving. Those experiences were bruising—an old barn of a theatre, with occasionally adequate actors and a part-time director who drank and didn't know stage right from stage left. He yelled a lot and we all hoped for crowds that failed to materialize. Audience members trickled in like a dripping faucet, persuaded to attend by relatives of the cast or ordered there by local high school teachers. I wrote *Leaving Alamogordo* to exorcise myself of all those painful memories. Would it do the trick?

❧

The cabbie and I jolted our way to the theatre, dodging pedestrians and apple carts. All of a sudden the nerves hit me. It must have showed.

"Don't you worry, kid. You've already made it," he said.

"Thanks. I hope so."

I knew I looked ready and the green gown gave me courage, just like the right lines gave my characters life. Tell that to the rampaging butterflies in my stomach, I thought, and I'd be fine.

My driver jerked to a stop. Sal spotted me and ran to open the cab door. He handed a whole dollar to the cabbie, who waited a full ten seconds before a couple waiting on the sidewalk claimed his next ride.

The Washington Irving seated about 1,300, not the biggest theatre on Broadway nor the smallest. It was a gracious and gorgeous space with the right amount of gold leaf, red carpets, crystal chandeliers, and a working light grid. Outside, my name was prominent on the marquee. I retrieved my little Leica camera from my evening bag and snapped a photo, then I was swept along with the opening night crowd.

My expensive Leica came from a staff photographer when I started reporting at the *Post*. Keith was a hopeless, and practically toothless, drunk who regularly bought equipment he couldn't afford. Prohibition did nothing to stop guys like Keith. His benders were legendary around the newsroom, and he was famous for drinking and not working. It was a mystery to all of us why he wasn't fired. Unless he had a lot of blackmail photos.

Whenever Keith found himself in trouble (or out of drinking money), he would sell off some of his trove of camera equipment, and possibly one or two items he'd stolen from the newspaper. I was first in line for the petite camera and I had cash.

Now I snapped a couple of pictures of the swells who were there for my play, dressed up and buzzing with excitement. Inside the ornate front doors, I passed the big board of headshots and paused. My glamorous black-and-white photo was among those of the actors and the director. I felt a hand on my shoulder.

Miracle of miracles, my date for the evening, Reggie Pendleton, was on time and waiting for me. He handed my wrap to the coat check gal and took my arm. He was clad like the gentleman he pretended not to be, in a sharp tailored black tuxedo.

"Pretty snazzy for a humble newshound," I teased.

He was a handsome guy with glossy brown hair, an Ipana toothpaste smile, and normally adverse to evening clothes. I was doubly impressed with his uptown sartorial duds because I knew he would prefer his fifty-cent reporter togs—tan houndstooth jackets, pleated brown slacks, and a colorful array of close-fitting sweater vests.

Reggie claimed we were born companions and swore we'd be married someday. Someday far in the future—after he'd won a Pulitzer or two for excellence in journalism and I'd knocked back a couple of hit plays. First, however, he promised we would have many romances, so we'd earn the privilege of a happy marriage and have no regrets. Reggie loved to talk nonsense, which I always found comforting.

"I don't know, Esmé, I wouldn't wear this monkey suit for just anyone."

"I'm not just anyone," I reminded him, and asked him to take my photo outside the theatre under the marquee, with my play and my name. Who knew if it would ever happen again?

He grabbed my Leica and led me outside to play photojournalist. He insisted we take more pictures in front of the row of headshots, then he handed the Leica to Sal and made him snap shots of us together. Reggie poked me in the side to make me laugh. I'm sure we looked like a couple of hyenas, but I'd have to develop the film to find out. I snatched back my camera.

"You can't order people around like that, Reggie. Not subtle."

He laughed and slapped me on the back. "We're reporters, we're not born to be subtle. And by the way, Esmé, you are definitely not looking subtle tonight."

"Hey," I began, bracing for a backhanded compliment.

"You look fabulous, Esmé. Top drawer. That *Nigel in the Afternoon* or something may have been a dog, but the costumes? Top of the Ritz." I had let Reggie in on the secret of my glamorous new wardrobe, or he might have thought I'd lost my mind and turned to a life of crime. He was aware of what a skinflint I normally was. "It's almost enough to justify these awful *swellegant* clothes."

"Would this gown pass muster with your family?" We didn't often talk about his family.

"My sisters would wonder how many beaucoup bucks you paid for it, where you got it, and how they could find the same. My mother would think you 'very lively' and my father would assume you're too good for me. My brother would make a play for you. They'd like you far too much, so I'm keeping you away from them."

The theatre chimes announced the impending rise of the curtain. Reggie slung his arm around my shoulder and led the way, never one to be late. Our seats were toward the back and on the aisle, so we could make a hasty retreat if necessary. My butterflies hammered out a march inside my guts as the lights dimmed.

"Breathe, Esmé." Reggie gave me an encouraging smile and rubbed my hands to warm them up.

The curtain parted. I held my breath. Possibly until Act One was over. I was lightheaded, my mind racing along with every line. My stomach reminded me I hadn't eaten.

The audience had come not expecting much, because I wasn't a known name. They seemed delighted to find the story moved them, to laughter if nothing else. The actors, even Clarissa Eldridge, remembered all their lines. Well, most of them. I was thrilled that no one stumbled over the props or the sofas or launched a speeding desk chair into the audience. People roared at lines I didn't know were funny. I was cautiously optimistic about the show.

At intermission, Reggie pulled me to the bar, saying we must celebrate.

We beat the crowd up the aisle and to the theatre's watering hole. Being first in line was practically a job requirement for reporters. I often found myself in the front of any crowd, waiting for the news hook and wondering why other people were so slow.

Reggie bought us champagne. I was impressed. "I'll let you buy next time." He gestured with his glass.

"Nope. You still owe me," I said. We clinked our glasses and snickered.

I was feeling giddy—until I spotted Graydon Chase in line for drinks. What were the odds? Reggie noticed me staring.

"Oh no, Esmé. Not that guy. He's a notorious playboy."

"Unlike you?"

"Not at all like me."

"No, you're a sincere playboy. Don't forget, I've seen how many blondes you squire around."

"Flattery will get you nowhere. Listen, I'm still technically on call. They'll kill me if I don't ring in."

"Come back for Act Two or I'll kill you."

"Be right back." Reggie went in search of a phone booth to call his editor. I waved him off and turned for another glance at this notorious playboy, Graydon Chase.

He wasn't with the Snow Queen tonight as he had said. This time he squired a tall thin woman with palomino-colored hair and an unfortunately long face. She had large brown eyes and prominent white teeth. I dubbed her Miss Palomino. Kinder than calling her 'horse faced,' as so many upper-crust blondes were dubbed. I pondered why she would pick such an expensive-but-dull beige dress, with nary a sequin or trim to be seen. Miss Palomino did not reach the height of Chase, but she towered over most women. She smiled at him with her predatory teeth.

Graydon, on the other hand, looked splendid in his tuxedo. It's annoying that men can usually rely on a tuxedo to make them look dressed up. His eyes widened when he saw me. I had the feeling he still didn't believe I'd written the show, but there I was, my photo shining among the headshots. My name in lights.

Take that, Mister Private Detective. If you really ARE a detective.

Chase waved me over, but I stood rooted to the floor. Grabbing their drinks, Chase brought his pal over to me and introduced us. I didn't catch her name, but she wore impressive topaz jewels. To make up for the bland dress, I assumed.

"You look lovely, Esmé." He lifted his drink in salute. "And your play is going great guns."

"Thanks. It seems so." I sipped my champagne.

"You're the writer? I always wanted to be a writer." The Palomino had a voice like a Bryn Mawr debutante, dripping with money and disdain. Yet she seemed friendly. "Writer" must have been the magic word.

"You should try it."

"I might at that. I was quite good at writing notes in school."

Reggie materialized next to me and gulped the last of his champagne. I took a sip while he and Graydon stared at each other.

"Pendleton," Graydon said at last.

"Chase," Reggie acknowledged. So they really knew each other. And were not the best of friends. The familiar chimes summoned us into the theatre again.

I squared my shoulders, finished my drink, and smiled at Chase and his date before proceeding regally stage right.

"Excuse me," I said to a portly gent who held a cocktail in each hand. The crowd parted for me. Sal and May signaled to me with thumbs-up gestures. They wore big smiles with their evening duds. So far so good, but I was all too aware the second act could kill a play. Sal clapped his pudgy hands and reached for his wife Della, who was dolled up in pink satin and furs. Her freshly dyed blond locks glistened in the light. They ushered their friends back into the theatre.

Reggie sat down next to me, but I could tell he was ready to jump on a story. He tweaked my arm.

"We're on our way, kiddo."

"What do you mean? Exactly?"

"You got your play, and I may have a major story. Unfortunately, I gotta blow this glitzy joint."

"Oh, Reggie, you promised."

"After the curtain call," he reassured me and lowered his voice as he whispered in my ear. "Mobster gunned down. I got a tip."

"Another one? Who's the goon?"

"Not sure, but I'll let you know."

"Connected to the Scavullo hit?" I asked.

"There's a possibility."

Was I not going to be able to enjoy my own opening night? Chase shows up like a bad penny? Another gangster bites the dust? And now Reggie has to sprint away like a racehorse in approximately fifty minutes, leaving me dateless on my own opening night.

Poor, dead, soft-spoken Dante Scavullo had caused more ripples in this pond than anyone had a right to expect. I felt a rush of relief that I was rid of his fancy pocket watch, and I wished Juliette Scavullo peace with it.

And I wished eternal peace to whoever had killed her husband.

Thirteen

EVERYONE EXPECTED A KISS AT the end of the play. After all, it was a comedy, as well as a mystery, and a romance, but my new ending evoked gasps and laughs when Clarissa/Annabelle chased down the leading man, argued with him, shoved him down in his rolling chair and planted her victory kiss, which went on longer than strictly necessary.

"So that's how it's going to be?" William/Todd said from downstage center, after coming up for air.

"Yes, that's how it's going to be," Clarissa/Annabelle answered, with another lengthy kiss. *"I'm in charge of this romance."*

"You were just about to shoot me! Now you want to kiss me?"

And then her final line. *"Calm down, lover boy. I can do both!"* And the final kiss, one that went on and on.

The lights dimmed. There was a beat before the applause started and grew, sounding like the accolades of angels, feeling like sunshine, like warm honey pouring over me. I basked in it before making my way to the lobby in a daze.

"You knocked it out of the park, kid." Sal smacked me on the back. "I knew you could do it." I guessed I still had my job. At least until the reviews were published.

There was much hugging and kissing after the show, and I reveled in it. Most of the crowd who lingered in the lobby were waiting for a glimpse of the actors, particularly Clarissa Eldridge, the daring dark-haired vixen of the piece. They crowded in on her with programs to be signed and flattery to be gushed.

A few well-wishers waited for me and I heard whispers from the crowd. "That's the playwright," I heard. "Really, she looks so young," and "Are you sure? She doesn't look like a writer." And "I know, where are the owl-framed glasses?" Best of all: "She looks like an actress."

Before he sprinted out of the theatre like his pants were on fire, Reggie nudged me. "It's a great ending, Esmé. I think you and I should rehearse. We could refine it even more, with plenty of rehearsals."

"You're a scoundrel, Reggie." He always made me laugh.

"How does it go again? You push me around in the chair and then shower me with kisses? Let's try it."

"Incorrigible cad."

He leaned over and pecked me on the cheek, then whispered, "Forget the chair, but I'm not kidding about the kissing." He looked very handsome in that crowd of theatre swells. And though he was flirting, I could read the clarion call of the free press in his face. "I barely have time to make the early edition. Don't be mad, it's a juicy murder."

"And a scoop. What can you tell me?"

"Some guy sitting in his car, and then boom! He takes a couple shots to the head."

"How horrible. I hope he didn't feel anything."

"I guess it was quick. I can't write it the way you penned your play, but I'll try to get a kissing angle in there." We maneuvered our way through the crowd.

"Get out of here." I understood about deadlines. "Or you'll be bylined Reginald the Third again."

"Sweet-talker. I'll catch up with you this weekend."

I paused at the lobby door. "Don't you have plans with Janice?"

"Janice was last week. You have to keep up. New kid at the paper, Ingrid, invited me to a picnic this weekend."

"You really are too attractive for your own good, you know that?"

"As are you, my sweet."

I was not impressed. Reggie was too taken with himself, I knew, and he used those good looks to get what he wanted.

"Pencil in a walk in the park, Reginald Three. It's your turn to buy me coffee." I reminded him.

"It's a date, doll." Another peck on my cheek and Reggie was gone.

"Go get 'em, newsboy," I said to his departing back. I wondered about this 'juicy murder' and told myself any number of mobsters could get themselves killed any day of the week, not just Frank Romeo's gang.

Reggie and I had been on several casual dates, meaning they didn't cost any money, but between my life in the theatre and his on the city beat, chasing crime scoops and corruption, finding time was tricky. Also, he could never pass up a cute blonde, while I was a mere *strawberry* blonde.

Our potential future relationship hadn't progressed beyond a few stolen kisses, hence his desire to rehearse them. The truth was, though I adored Reggie, he was a little too much the boy next door for me. Still, as I once more caught sight of Graydon Chase and the Palomino, something made me hope Chase had seen Reggie flirting with me.

Yes, I *am* that petty and this was my night! Was I jealous or merely annoyed? I didn't stop to analyze. Reggie had promised to come with me to my opening night party. Now I was minus a date on the biggest night of my life.

The evening was rushing past and I tried to catch hold of it, the crowd, the applause, the beautiful gowns. The audience lingered, laughing, quoting lines from the play, instead of fleeing into the night like accomplices to a crime, to avoid having to say something nice.

I was moving with a group of other theatre folk when I spotted Marco Scavullo with Bianca Lombardi, the young woman who had looked at him with big doe eyes. The woman whose father slapped her around to keep her away from the Mafia. So far, her father was losing. She must have had it bad for Marco.

I wasn't shocked at that. But it was in the worst possible taste for them to show up at a play tonight. His uncle's funeral was just the day before. His family and friends should be at private mourning rituals. Neither he nor Bianca should be out on the town, he in a dark suit and she in a shiny blue dress that accentuated her dark beauty and her curves. They did not look like mourners. Besides that, Marco didn't strike me as much of a theatregoer.

He stepped in front of me, Bianca trailing behind. He seemed to be waiting for me. He graced me with his bright smile.

"How is your Aunt Juliette doing?" I asked.

"She's a little sad," Marco said with a shrug.

A little sad? My God, if I had lost a man I had been married to for twenty years, especially in such a brutal way, I'd be fractured.

"You didn't have to come tonight. But thank you." I tried to keep the shock out of my face.

"My aunt gave me her tickets," Marco said. "She said to pay her respects to you."

"Really."

"It was very nice of her," Bianca spoke for the first time. "The tickets. I think she wanted to be alone with her sons. The house has been so crowded with neighbors and friends since—since everything happened."

That I could understand. Juliette was no doubt overwhelmed by everything, and with having company descend on her. Well then, let her have some peace. But certainly, this couple could have chosen a less conspicuous place to step out. Bianca touched my arm.

"We enjoyed the play."

I turned toward her and smiled. Her black eye looked better, I noticed. The bruising had faded and her Helena Rubenstein powder covered most of it.

"Mr. and Mrs. Scavullo had said they'd come to see my show. I'm so sorry they couldn't be here tonight." Life and death had funny ways of interfering with our best laid plans.

"Who knew. Right?" she said.

"Lots of words in that play of yours." Marco seemed puzzled. He was clearly not sure about those words. His accent was thick Italian. "How you think of so many words? So many thoughts?"

There's one in every crowd and tonight it was Marco.

"Yes, there are," I agreed. I may have raised my eyebrow at Bianca, who looked perplexed. "I like words."

"You look so beautiful." He leered at me and I stepped back as Bianca scowled at him. "Why talk of words?"

Anyone with a brain would know that on the opening night of a playwright's work, the event is about those words. Feel free to flatter my words at length, even if you are lying. And Marco had to make a comment about my looks. It was also disrespectful to Bianca, who clearly saw depths in this mug that I did not.

Dante Scavullo's nephew was too handsome, one of those men who thinks every female will swoon at the sight of him. I, on the other hand, need the stimulation of some intellect. Some challenge. Some words.

Behind the happy couple came another man I recognized from the Scavullo visitation, the man with the pretty grass-green eyes, Patrick Dentino, known, I'd been told, as "Lashes." He waited for them to notice him, bouncing on his feet impatiently. His mission was with Marco, yet he had time to give me the once-over. I must have looked puzzled. Marco turned to see who it was. He favored the man with a small toss of his head as if to say *wait*.

Lashes rolled his eyes and kept bouncing. Their compatriot known as "Bones" stood outside the glass doors. Lashes barked something in Italian and Marco replied, sotto voce. Bianca understood the conversation, but I did not.

"We won't keep you." Bianca tried to pull Marco away, but not before he wondered aloud, "How much money you make for this play?" I was used to people wondering about my royalties, but not in such a bald manner. "Three dollars a ticket? Lotta moolah. How many seats?"

He was adding it up in his head. He may not have liked words, but numbers clearly were different.

"Enough," I said, a little sharply. Thirteen hundred seats was a good house and all those seats were filled tonight, but many were comps from the theatre or cast and crew. "Thank you for coming."

As they left I heard him say to Bianca, "What? What I say?"

I watched them leave. He and Lashes caught up with Bones, still outside. I could see them speaking animatedly with lots of hand gestures. I wondered what the excitement was all about. But they turned around and left, walking briskly. I may have caught a glimpse of a camel hair coat, but I couldn't be sure. I wondered about the dead mobster Reggie had mentioned and I felt skeleton fingers on my spine.

The lobby was emptying out. I knew there was a big letdown waiting for me, when my energy and elation would deflate. First, however, there was the party at Sardi's. Sal was leaning against the ticket booth. He mimed that we all were expected there.

"I'll be along in a moment," I said.

Remembering my wrap, I bumped into Graydon Chase on the way to the coat check. He caught me by the elbow.

"Have you been abandoned by that rogue Pendleton? When the night is still young?"

"He has a story to cover. And he did make time for my show."

"Miss de LaForet, it was lovely to see you. Priscilla and I must be off."

Priscilla? Millicent? What was it with these people and their names? At any rate, she was at his elbow, so I disengaged mine.

"I hope you enjoyed the show," I said.

"I adored it!" Miss Priscilla the Palomino was beginning to grow on me. "So lovely to meet you, I'm Priscilla Summerdine." She seemed nice and, unlike Marco Scavullo, she said all the right things ("Such a delightful play!") before signaling "Rupert" she was ready to go. She slipped her hand into his pocket, making sure I noticed.

And he was "Rupert" again? Clearly this man used too many names. Did he really prefer Graydon, or was it easier to compartmentalize his life by whichever name people used for him?

He gave me a long steady look and I smiled brightly. Had he seen Marco?

Rupert/Graydon grasped my hand, and I felt the charge of his touch race through my body. Maybe I had some kind of physical oddity, some kind of disease. I hoped it wasn't fatal.

"I'll see you later." He had the nerve to wink. Priscilla didn't see it.

"Goodnight—Rupert." I smiled as brightly as I could. "And Priscilla."

"Call me Priss. We must meet again," she said. "We'll talk about *writing*."

As they made their way through the crowd, Willie swooped in, draped in a dramatic gown she had fashioned out of purple satin and silver lamé. With Seth, one of the designers, on her arm, she proclaimed, "You knocked it out of the park tonight, Esmé!"

"I had help. Lots of help." I twirled my velvet gown.

"A home run!" Seth added. "Now, let's make tracks to Sardi's before they run out of food."

The three of us linked arms and strolled over to Sardi's and marched up the stairs. We gaped at the caricatures on the red walls as we settled into a table. Bubbly and hors d'oeuvres were passed around on trays and I would have eaten every last the appetizer, but I was too nervous to eat. We waited anxiously for the reviews.

Aside from that, all I saw was caviar and I am not a fan of that particular salty delicacy. I couldn't remember the last time I'd eaten actual food. Sal and May made sure there was an elegant spread and a surfeit of champagne. Guaranteed to give you a headache. And it would not do to choke on a cracker in my lovely dress.

As for the reviews, I'm not sure if we were waiting for the late-late editions or the early-early ones. It seemed an eternity before they showed up.

There was a change in the atmosphere as newspapers suddenly appeared in the hands of a street urchin who traded them for nickels. I couldn't breathe until I turned to the right page and saw the first one was—decent. The next was better, even good. And then they were *great*. Beyond my expectations. I'm not sure I took in all the words. Willie reached for the papers and read them aloud.

She swiveled in her seat and hugged me. "See, they even mention you, the playwright! 'A winning team at the Washington Irving Theatre...'"

My glass of champagne sat half-drunk in front of me. I felt half-drunk even without the champagne. *The Times* pronounced *Leaving Alamogordo* well written and 'a fine comic play with a fresh new voice.' They mentioned the director and actors by name and finally me, the playwright. Miss Esmé de LaForet.

At first I only remembered a few key phrases. I knew I would read the rest of them later, much later, and more than once. Even though I'd been pummeled thoroughly with that Swedish massage, the invisible rubber band that had held me together all day was about to snap. The tension released its grip and dropped me in an imaginary puddle. My arms felt as if I were letting go of a heavy load.

For some of us, the party grew louder and funnier until partygoers started to drift away. Leading man Todd and leading lady Clarissa exchanged a passionate stare and left, hand in hand, no doubt wanting to rehearse their love scenes.

Wilhelmina and Seth cuddled at our table, leaving me odd woman out. I could have had some male company if I wanted it, but drunken advances weren't my style tonight. A couple of guys, friends of the actors, called after me, wanting to paint the town red with them. But I'd had enough thrills for today.

FOURTEEN

SNUGGLING INTO MY LUSCIOUS EVENING coat, I escaped, though I doubt many of the pie-eyed celebrants noticed. I ran down the steps of Sardi's and into the night air. It wasn't exactly fresh, but it was bracing. I picked up my feet in their gold-strapped high heels and headed for some real food.

It was too late for dinner and too early for breakfast, but I didn't care. I slipped away intent on finding sustenance. I promised myself I'd catch a cab afterward, grateful that New York City didn't roll up the sidewalks after dark, the way they did in other places.

"Esmé, Esmé, don't go." The boys from the Irv who were stoked up on liquid courage called after me. "Author, author!" They stumbled down the steps laughing, but I was already halfway down the block.

I ducked into a narrow diner, the kind with a counter on one side and small booths on the other, decorated with bright green Formica tabletops and dark blue vinyl seats. It was nearly empty, save for an elderly couple who'd been out on the town, but not too out on the town. This wasn't the Ritz, or Sardi's, but it was affordable, and quiet.

I sidled into a booth toward the back where I could see everyone inside and anyone who walked through the door. The night cook took one look at me and decided I wouldn't cause any trouble. He eyed my evening coat and dress.

"Night at the theatre?"

"Quite a night at the theatre." I couldn't help sighing, filled with satisfaction.

"So what's a nice kid like you doing without a date, all dolled up like that?" He wore a name tag: MICK. He sported an anchor tattooed over one bulging bicep, U.S. NAVY inked underneath. A veteran.

"I had a date. He had a deadline."

"Newshound, huh?"

"Yes, and I'm a playwright. Tonight was opening night of my play." Except it was way more than that. It was my first opening on Broadway and I wanted to remember every moment and not drown it in alcohol. I wanted to let it roll through my mind. I handed Mick an extra program.

"Look at that! Congrats, lady playwright. And you're not crying. That's a good sign. Hey, can I keep this?" I noticed a few other playbills tacked to the wall.

"Sure. I'll even sign it for you." I laughed. Mick was clearly familiar with theatre types and he looked like someone I would rather befriend than offend.

"Thanks." I scrawled my name on it and he put mine up with the others. "Now you're official."

Eat your heart out, Sardi's. "I'm starved."

"You came to the right place. What'll it be, sweetheart?"

"Grilled ham and cheese on rye and a side of fries." I added a glass of milk. I knew it was prosaic, but that's what I wanted.

"You got it. My specialty."

With that I retreated to the ladies' room, patted my hair, and smoothed a cool damp towel over my face. Dabbing on a bit of powder, I decided I looked presentable, though why I cared, I had no idea. I returned to find someone occupying my table, someone tall with blue eyes that I'd know anywhere. Was he following me? Again? And where had he parked Priscilla the Palomino?

Chase stood and indicated I should join him, as if it weren't my table to begin with. I sat down, eyeing him as suspiciously as I could.

"Congratulations on your play, Esmé. Looks like a hit."

"You want I should throw him out?" my buddy the cook asked.

"He can stay. For now." Quite frankly, I didn't know what I wanted. I was tired and hungry. And curious.

"Just let me know. I don't let anyone upset my favorite customers." Mick grinned. "Especially my playwrights."

"Much appreciated," I said.

Graydon leaned in close. "It's uncanny. People come out of the woodwork to protect you."

"Not everyone, but I'm grateful when they do."

"No doubt it's your elfin powers."

"You annoy me." He smiled broadly in reply. "You shouldn't annoy people with special powers. And what are you doing here?"

"I wanted to offer my congratulations on the success of your *Leaving Alamogordo*."

"Have you seen the reviews?" I reached for the papers I'd collected.

"I don't need to see them to tell me it's going to be a success. Your elfin ways are powerful." He shrugged as if there was nothing he could do.

"You're a critic then?"

"Merely an avid theatregoer."

"Where is your lady friend? The Palomino?"

"Who?"

"Long face, beige dress, good strong teeth."

"That's very mean," he said, laughing. "Priscilla. I dropped her at her place."

"That's right. I remember now. She seems nicer than the Snow Queen."

He raised an eyebrow at me. "You mean Millicent?"

"The Snow Queen and I weren't introduced." I remembered her insult in the ladies' room. "If you call me an elf, I can call your friends anything I please. And I'm working on a name for you."

"Really? What is it?"

"I'm working on it." In fact, I had no idea. "It might well be Gigolo Gangster."

He seemed ridiculously pleased with this. "Snow Queen does rather suit Millicent."

"But you escorted Priscilla to the show."

"We're old pals. Then I took her straight home."

So old she felt free to put her hand in his pocket. "Why didn't you go home too?"

"I was thinking about you."

Sure he was. "You saw who showed up?" I prodded him.

"Marco Scavullo and Bianca Lombardi don't strike me as your average playgoers."

"No, Italians seem to prefer the opera. Mostly Puccini. Anyway, they didn't seem that keen on my play."

"How do you figure that?"

"Too many words, according to Marco Scavullo."

Chase snorted. "He probably didn't care for your heroine failing to bow down to the man."

Mick arrived with my milk and grilled cheese. "What about you, buddy?" I guess he had decided Chase was okay, as I hadn't asked Mick to throw him out.

"Coffee."

Outside the front door, I heard the randy boys I'd evaded before. I picked up the menu and hid my face. They opened the door and hollered my name. "Esmé, where are you?" Graydon moved slightly to thwart their entry, but Mick was already on it.

"No one by that name in here. And you bums are too drunk and disorderly to enter this establishment." He flexed his impressive muscles.

I heard them grumble and close the door. They had no desire to tangle with a large cook who carried a large cleaver. I lowered the menu.

"Thanks, Mick," I said.

He grunted in response. "Theatre people." It was that kind of neighborhood. "One coffee coming up."

Speaking of theatre people, I wondered whether Graydon, or Rupert, or whatever his name was, was interested in Clarissa Eldridge, the actress. I saw him gazing at her and her crowd of admirers after the show.

"You have so many lady friends. If you need another, Clarissa is single."

"Who?"

"The leading lady. Played Annabelle."

"Oh, her. She was fine. My interest is you."

"Because of Scavullo."

"It's more than that and you know it, my dear Esmé. You have special powers. Our connection is strong, it's alluring, it's worth exploring."

"You're horrible."

"And you enjoy kissing as much as your heroine. Are you even aware of how passionate you can be, hiding in a dark closet in a closed school on Columbus Day?" I was aware all right. However, I had no intention of exploring my passions with some damn Brit. "I love that look, he said. "You're even more elfin and beautiful when you're plotting something."

"I only plot my plays."

For some reason, Graydon thought that was hilarious. He reached over and relieved me of some of my fries. They were delicious, hot and crispy. He waved to the cook.

"On the other hand, Mick, I think I'll have the same as she."

Chase's English accent seemed to work wonders with everyone, including the cook. But not me. He reached for part of my sandwich, and I slapped his hand away.

"Yours is coming and we are splitting the bill."

"Are you by chance afraid I'm hard up for cash?"

"I don't care whether you are or not. I pay my own way."

He rolled his eyes. "Where I come from a gentleman pays."

"Oh, so you're a gentleman now? And not a gangster?"

In my opinion, splitting a bill was nothing compared to what a woman was expected to pay. Afterwards.

"I see I must work on convincing you. By the way, you are lovely in green."

I touched the beautiful velvet and smiled. "Thank you. My favorite color."

"Even lovelier than you were in the violet gown you wore the other night."

"You remember it?" I was surprised.

"I am paid to remember details. Such lovely and extravagant clothes in these hard times? Something to behold."

He wasn't exactly wearing rags himself. I bit into my sandwich, a slice of melted ham and cheese heaven. But I needed to set him straight about my clothes so he wouldn't think I had money to fleece.

"You don't need to have a million dollars to *look* like you do."

"Well said. And your quite astonishing apartment?"

"Are these detective questions? Do you think I acquire things though shady money? Like your clients?"

"Was I prying? Sorry." He wasn't sorry at all. His meal arrived and I snatched a couple of his hot fries as payback.

"Yes, you were prying. Here is the truth, which I'm happy to tell you because you never believe the truth. I'd appreciate it if you didn't share what I tell you with your uptown girlfriends."

"Never. On my honor."

"That word again." I took a moment before speaking. "I came into a small amount of money after my parents died. They were older and not healthy. They died within weeks of each other. The flu wielded its scythe over a lot of people in our town. I couldn't bear to stay, so I sold the house and escaped to New York, where the Depression has made it smarter for me to buy than rent. I try to be careful with my money and my reputation. In addition to writing plays, I have my job at the theatre."

"Enough for such exquisite clothes? Priscilla remarked on them. She said your gown must have come from Paris."

"Must it?" I picked up my sandwich again. "Paris. Well. I must tell Willie." I snickered at the thought.

"What's so amusing?"

"The theatre, darling. This delightful frock started life in a failed flop of a show. Sal Rossi, our producer, let me buy the clothes at a rock-bottom price, because he's convinced it would be bad luck to use them in another production. Willie, my friend and costumer extraordinaire, remade them and tweaked them for me. She made them fit and flatter."

"And fabulous. All from your theatre's own costume shop? Brilliant."

"This gown was made for the understudy, who never had a chance to wear it. Lucky her. And it's different from the leading lady's costume, which was a lot bigger, in another color. My gown is unique. Sal's superstitions are my gain."

"Your secret is safe with me. I liked it very much, you know, your play," Graydon said after a pause. I had to give him credit. He was smarter than Marco Scavullo. Graydon Chase knew to flatter me by talking about my work. Not the ticket prices.

"Tell me more."

"She's very lively, your heroine. I daresay those kisses she insists on will keep the audience talking. Bit daring, that."

Daring indeed. That had already been mentioned in some of the reviews.

"She's a modern woman, and it was just a few kisses."

"Which she took on her own terms. A statement of her independence."

"How clever you are. You said you liked it."

"I enjoy spirited women." Again the neon-blue stare. "I suppose you simply draw on all the drama in your own life."

"I keep all my drama on the stage, thank you very much."

Most improbably, he started to laugh again. It was a strange sight. Graydon Chase had exceptionally good teeth for a Brit. He looked younger and more approachable, and that compelling cologne wafted through the air. I had to beware. He shook his head, still laughing.

"What drama?" I demanded.

"First, you pop up in a closet like an elf out of nowhere in the midst of absolutely murderous mayhem, then you follow that up by causing a stir at a mobster's funeral, with a missing pocket watch in hand."

"I was merely returning it."

"So you say. Then you again appear out of nowhere at a dance club, a vision in violet, and disappear as quickly as Cinderella. A lovely Cinderella."

"I hailed a cab, not a pumpkin."

"And just now you had to hide behind a menu to evade Tweedledee and Tweedledum."

"Those are mere circumstances," I sniffed. "Let's return to Mr. Scavullo. What went wrong, if you were there to protect him? Did you fall down on the job?"

The supercilious expression on his face morphed into one of puzzlement. "Not sure. Everything was worked out. The deal was done. Then at the last minute, without any reason, Scavullo changed the meeting location and the shooting started. The killer was waiting for him in that school."

"Scavullo never explained why the meeting place had changed?" I really had known nothing about the man, except his church habits.

"He hung up on me."

"Where were you supposed to meet?"

"A restaurant two blocks from the school."

I bit into my last fry while wondering how many phone calls Scavullo had made from that phone booth at Ray's

Diner, how many nickels he dropped after he was initially called to the phone. I focused on remembering the last time I saw the man: A waitress came over to him and asked if he was Dante Scavullo. She said he had a call in the booth. He was gone maybe ten minutes while his food congealed. When he returned, I was going to say "Hello," but he seemed too distracted. Ten minutes left plenty of time for more than one call. Did he call Graydon Chase and change the location after the first call?

"What is it?" he asked.

"I had forgotten how distracted he was after taking a phone call. There's a phone booth in the back of the diner, near the restrooms. He put on his overcoat, and he seemed to forget about his meal." It wasn't unusual, people who had no phones arranged for calls at handy locations, neighborhood drugstores, bars, diners.

"Anything else?" Chase asked. "Do you know who he was talking with?"

"Was it you? Or someone else, or multiple someones? He was gone long enough for his blue plate special spaghetti to cool." Now I remembered it was spaghetti and meatballs that day. Though strictly speaking it was also a Friday and he should have ordered the clam chowder or the spaghetti without the meatballs. Being Catholic and all. In hindsight, not a terribly faithful Catholic.

"Is that all? Please, Esmé, it could be important. Anything."

I was surprised I remembered that much. "Nothing else. Scavullo said nothing to me. And now I probably won't be able to sleep." I yawned and remembered his quick wink at me. "What does the phone call tell you?"

"Something someone said caused him to change the plan on which we agreed. Something urgent. He called me, but we spoke for only a minute. I was at my office, not far from here."

"You were trying to help Scavullo leave the mob? How?"

"Negotiating a sort of settlement. He used to be part of a conduit for illegal liquor. With Prohibition over, he wanted out. The time seemed right. There wasn't a big part for him in the organization now. Scavullo wanted to go legit, as legit as possible, with his own legal liquor store. Frank Romeo was on board with this. He'd supply the booze and take a cut. He was happy to have Scavullo out. Too much history there."

"With Juliette?" Apparently the rumors were true. "Romeo could have ordered a hit. He's some kind of mob boss, right?"

"But why now?" Chase asked. "He could have had Scavullo eliminated at any time. And Romeo was always thinking about Juliette. He would never want her to think he was responsible."

"What went wrong?" I was turning it over in my mind. I hadn't known the Scavullos at all, it seemed.

"Other than somebody objected? I don't know."

"How did you get involved, Rupert, or should I say Graydon?"

"It's Graydon. He called me. Dante made it clear he wanted someone far outside the mob. He believed my being English was far enough. He'd heard my name in financial circles. I mostly chase after missing funds, people who embezzle, things like that. He had a referral."

"And why did you take the case?"

"It was outside of the norm. A bit scandalous, intriguing. Possibly a bit dangerous."

Dangerous? "Why was Marco Scavullo at the theatre there so soon after his uncle's funeral?" I drained the rest of my milk.

"Can't imagine. Marco enjoying the theatre is quite a stretch."

"I suspected he wanted to be an actor. He's got the looks. They often do, those pretty boys, but—"

"This boy doesn't want it?"

"If he finds it hard to sit through a play, it would be even harder for him to learn all his lines," I said. "Too many words, remember?" I waved a French fry.

Graydon nodded. "What's your impression then? Did he mention the timepiece?"

"No." I glanced at my wristwatch. It was late, or early, depending on how you looked at it. Long after midnight. "Maybe Bianca was right. Perhaps Juliette wanted him out of the house so she could mourn in peace. He was curious about one thing."

Chase finished his fries. "About what, besides you?"

"He wanted to know how much money I'm going to make. The ticket price, how many seats in the theatre. He was ballparking the gross. He doesn't like words, but he seems to enjoy figures, if they relate to cash."

Chase didn't say anything but he looked annoyed. "Bounder."

"Not so sure about the other characters he buddied up with at Scavullo's funeral. Lashes Dentino was there, along with the skinny one, Bones, in the lobby tonight waiting for him."

"You should have just kept the watch," he said.

"And I wouldn't have been in that closet and we would never have met," I said as sweetly as I could. "If I hadn't gone to the visitation, you wouldn't have been foisted on me as an escort home. Too bad."

"We would have met somehow, someway, Elf Queen."

"You ought to write for Hollywood."

I reached for my purse to pay my half. Chase tossed enough money on the table to pay for both meals and plenty extra to make Mick happy. I threw Mr. Moneybags a poisonous stare.

"Don't worry, I'm not keeping track," he said.

"I am. If I had known the trouble it would cause, I would have mailed the watch back anonymously. However, I didn't know the address."

"You didn't know Scavullo was in the mob?" He searched my face for a lie.

"Remember, I'm not from around here. There were the rumors, but I don't suspect everybody of heinous crimes. Except maybe you." I stood and picked up my coat. In a flash, Graydon was there to help me into it. Mustn't let Mick think he was impolite. "Really, are you Graydon or Rupert?" I asked.

"Graydon is my middle name. I prefer it."

"Your lady friends call you Rupert." Name of the dead poet. Dead poets are less trouble than live detectives.

"Some of them."

"Let me get this straight, you're some kind of detective, but not with the police department. And you have two names. Or three. Maybe more."

"Do you have a point, Esmé Elf?"

"It's Esmé de LaForet."

"Yes, I've seen it up in lights."

"You can see how I might be skeptical." I put up my finger to indicate another point. "You're leading on Millicent, aka the Snow Queen, *and* Priscilla the Palomino. Then there's this business with having too many names. And my friend Reggie says you're a notorious playboy." I headed to the door. Chase kept pace with me.

"Pendleton? Yes, of course, that's to be expected. Kettle, meet pot."

"I know Reggie's a playboy, but at least he's honest about it. And we're just pals."

"Says the elf who hides in closets."

Graydon, or Rupert, Chase insisted on driving me home. We could have argued over it, but cabs were not as plentiful this time of night. It was late, and my spring was unsprung. I set the ground rules: He could drive me home, escort me to my door, but he could not come in.

He countered that he must ensure the premises were safe because we couldn't know about the characters who populated New York City. He was also uneasy, he claimed, about Marco and his friends.

He grabbed my hand and waved goodbye to Mick. Outside he indicated a different car than the Ford from the other night. He opened the passenger side, then ran around to the driver's side as if afraid I'd jump right out. I might have, but by then I could barely keep my eyes open.

Besides, I'd never before been in a brand-new Pierce-Arrow sedan in dark green and gold. Or in any old Pierce-Arrow, for that matter. This car was a thing of beauty, luxurious, and much more elegant than the Ford he had driven, which I should point out, was perfectly acceptable. My father drove a Ford.

"How many cars do you have?" I asked.

"It belongs to a friend. It seemed more appropriate for a night on the town."

"Does it belong to Priscilla?" She looked like she had the kind of money that would buy a Pierce-Arrow.

"Aren't you nosy."

"I was a reporter. Nothing is adding up, Mr. Rupert Graydon Whatever-Your-Name-Is."

"It's too late for arithmetic." Chase remembered my address and found a place to park across the street.

"You can drop me here."

"Must we always have this argument, Esmé?"

I glared at him, too tired to fight. Chase parked and escorted me to my apartment, because, he said, that's what gentlemen do.

"My place is just as secure as it was last time," I informed him. I had my hand on the doorknob. He placed his hand on top of mine. It was very warm and despite my best intentions, I felt that familiar thrill and ordered it to go away.

We opened the door together. He moved inside while I stationed myself at my front door. He ignored me and checked all the windows and doors, apparently trying to impress me with his thoroughness. Finally, he returned and pulled me into an embrace.

"You cannot kiss me when you're having affairs with two other women. Or possibly more."

"I am not currently having affairs with any other women."

I didn't believe him. He kissed me anyway. I can't deny I was interested in comparing it to the first two kisses and I wanted to be held. Held on my opening night. Held by a man with strong arms, who smelled delicious, and seemed to release electric currents all the way through my bloodstream.

When we came up for air, I asked, "Did you kiss her goodnight too?"

"On the forehead. I told you. We're old friends." Graydon seemed annoyed.

"Mere friends?"

"Yes."

"Let me tell you something, Graydon or Rupert, she believes you're more than friends." I remembered the way the Palomino beheld him with awe. "As does the Snow Queen. And I'm not part of a harem, so you'd best leave."

"I'd never keep a harem, it's far too complicated, Your Elfin Ladyship."

"My name is Esmé."

"Yes, it's here on the program." He pulled one out of his pocket, then bestowed on me one more soul-searing kiss. "Good night, Esmé de LaForet. Lock up behind me. Please."

FIFTEEN

I STUMBLED OUT OF BED at noon the next day. No sooner had I put the coffee on the stove than there was a knock at the door. Amelia, all bustling and efficient, glided past me into the apartment like a queen.

"I didn't know you were coming over," I mumbled.

She handed me a paper bag. "Bagels. And I brought you the newspapers, including *The Times*. I figure you can use extra copies. It looks like I may actually have to go see it."

"Careful, Amelia. You'll turn my head." I tried to rub the sleep out of my eyes. My arms felt unusually heavy.

"Late night, huh?"

"Got home about two, or maybe three."

She seemed slightly impressed. Another knock was followed by a delivery of flowers. An exquisite bouquet of white orchids, pink roses, and ivy in a crystal vase. The accompanying note read, "A simple pleasure for a dangerous beauty." No name—but it was from Chase. It had to be. Reggie Pendleton was not known for extravagant or expensive gestures.

I gasped. Amelia squealed and grabbed the note. "Dangerous beauty? You carrying a gat? Is that you? Got a roscoe in your pocketbook? Should I be afraid?"

"Give it time."

She considered for a moment. "Wait a minute, what did you do to get these?" Then in a whisper. "He's not still here, is he?"

"No! He walked me to my door and then he went home, or somewhere. You thought I slept with him?!"

Amelia shrugged. "Crossed my mind. Though you're pretty particular."

I sent her a scathing glare that bounced right off. I examined the flowers. The previous night, Sal had kindly arranged for a bouquet for me, but they were nothing compared to the leading lady's. These flowers from Graydon Chase were something else completely. Still, I didn't want anyone getting the wrong impression.

"They must've cost the moon." Amelia opined, grabbing the vase and running to the kitchen to add water. "Who is this guy? A Rockefeller?"

"No." At least I didn't think so.

She peered at me. "What does he want from you?"

"I don't know, but he's not getting it."

Amelia smirked. "He may have a different opinion. I hope to meet Mr. Orchids-in-a-Crystal-Vase."

Could Graydon afford these pretty posies? What kind of friends did he have? The kind who would lend him a gorgeous Pierce-Arrow to drive?

Money is always close to the top of my mind. It's an unattractive quality, but it's a habit. So was eating regularly. Bread lines were everywhere. Banks had closed, though they were slowly reopening. In my family, we had always worried that the wolf was at the door and panting on our necks.

Not everyone grows up feeling so impoverished, saving every penny, every shred of paper, wax paper, tin foil, coffee tins, and glass jars. Twice mending every tear or hole in a pair of socks and wondering whether the bills would be paid this month. It was only after my parents died that I found they had squirreled away a good sum of money. And they'd never had a chance to enjoy it.

The winter they left me, following the terrible flu that took so many lives, I started finding envelopes full of dollars hidden here and there. Under the mattresses, between the pages of old books, in my mother's old purses. Bills and coins in rusted coffee cans hidden in my father's shed. That was all in addition to the bank book. It was money they could have used to live a more comfortable life and I questioned why they wouldn't have spent it on a few basic necessities. What in God's name were they waiting for?

I resented them for that. Life never had to be so hard. Irony was staring me in the face.

In the midst of the Depression, I, Esmé Rafferty de LaForet, was facing the prospect of better days ahead. If *Leaving Alamogordo* was indeed a hit, or merely had a respectable run, I could expect a decent sum of money for it. If today's newspapers were any indication, I could stop worrying about the wolf howling at the door. I rejoiced in my luxuries, my apartment, and my tailored-to-order theatre finery. The ones that Chase's girlfriend believed came from Paris.

But like a play on a stage, the illusion of my life felt like a fairy tale and belied the hard work it took to get there. Fear of poverty had always been my constant companion. It was hard to shake.

Amelia set the vase of freshly watered flowers in the middle of the newspapers on the hall table. I set the flowers on the coffee table so I could see them from the sofa. I selected the *Post* and reassured myself that the review was positive.

Then I searched for Reggie's story from last night. It was inside, on page three, with a typically lurid headline.

YOUNG MOBSTER MEETS HIS END IN HUDSON TERRAPLANE
by Reginald Archibald Pendleton III

As I predicted, Reggie's editor had retaliated for his late story by using his full name. That's what he got for staying till the end of my play. Still, he had also finished his article. Another dead gangster seemed to indicate that the various tribes were at war, Reggie wrote.

The accompanying picture showed a couple of cops inspecting the death car, a dark brown-and-tan Hudson Terraplane, a favorite of mobsters like the late John Dillinger. A bullet hole was visible in the shattered front windshield, which was splattered with what I assumed was blood. Reggie reported that the killer apparently hid in the back seat of the car while Guido Moretti went to get a coffee, waiting for him to come back. Moretti was shot in the back of the head. Another bullet had gone through the window. Police theorized the killer was familiar with Moretti's habits.

The car belonged to Frank Romeo, but it was not known whether he was the target, or where he was while his driver was murdered. The victim's body was laid out on the street, but only the feet showed in the photo. I'd had quite enough of mobsters lately. But not enough information. I read on.

The story jumped to the next page, accompanied by another picture, possibly from a high school yearbook, identifying the victim as Guido Moretti, known among his friends as "Ratty." I recognized him as one of the men at the visitation of Dante Scavullo. My pal Reggie didn't know I had attended the rosary, nor did he need to know that I had previously met his 'notorious playboy' acquaintance, Graydon Chase.

Yet I was pretty sure Reggie and I could exchange some information. I didn't know what I was looking for, except to satisfy my curiosity. Old habits die hard, I guess.

"What are you doing?" I asked Amelia who was bustling around with scissors and a jar of rubber cement.

"Making you a scrapbook of your notices, obviously."

Obviously? I would never have the patience for that. "Carry on then. And thank you."

"I have no idea what you'd do without me, Esmé."

"Neither do I. I assume I can pay you for your time?"

"Yes. And my effort." She lifted her work to show it off and she handed me a receipt for the scrapbook. The cover was black leather with gold script that said "Memories." "I'm thinking, you should get to work on writing another play."

"I need some time."

"Don't take too long. Strike while the iron is hot."

I sent her a warning look. She shrugged.

Several cups of coffee helped wake me up. I eventually showered and donned some casual Saturday trousers (of which Amelia despaired), then I caught a cab downtown to catch up with Reginald Archibald Pendleton III. Even though it was his turn to buy coffee, I wound up paying for a couple of hot chocolates in paper cups.

"You owe me, Reggie."

"Next time I'll buy you dinner. At a real restaurant. Promise." He turned his charmer's smile on me. I snorted. Reggie came from a monied family, but he rejected their financial help, most of the time. He was determined to stand on his own two (gold-plated) legs.

"I'm keeping tabs."

"It's part of your charm." He flashed his grin again.

We took our hot chocolate to Washington Square and sat near the arch. "I see you're in the doghouse again."

"No big deal," Reggie said. "Where else are they going to find a good police reporter?"

"Have you counted how many times your byline has been changed?"

"Not this month."

I scoffed. We both knew there were dozens of would-be reporters on every corner. "Tell me about Guido Moretti. 'Ratty.' What else did you find out?"

"Not much to tell. Typical mob hit. Far as I can figure, Moretti was small potatoes. Just a grunt, a foot soldier. Involved in running liquor during Prohibition. Allegedly."

"Any connection with Scavullo?"

"Why, you know something?" He trained his eyes on me.

"Me? How would I know?"

"Something you're not telling me, Esmé. Did you know Scavullo?"

I merely smiled. "I used to see him at church. You know, that place you never go on Sunday mornings."

"Heard of it. Every time I see my folks."

"Scavullo was a regular, always there with his wife. We'd say hello. So yeah, I knew who he was." I tossed that off casually and Reggie nodded. "Obviously I'm interested. And about Ratty Moretti?"

"His mama can't stop crying. Swears he was the sweetest boy who ever lived. Oddly, everyone I talked to agreed. Even the cops. Ratty wasn't the sharpest knife in the drawer, but whenever he was arrested, and it was a fair number of times, they said he was polite and soft-spoken, friendly, a nice guy."

"What kind of offenses?"

"Minor stuff. Joyriding, petty theft, nickel-and-dime crime. Mostly when he was a juvenile. He spent some time in reform school. Learned not to get caught so often after that."

It was another beautiful day. Golden light sifted through blazing crimson leaves, and an azure sky dotted with clouds seemed to highlight the old men in their plaid coats, content to sit and play checkers. There would be no more beautiful days for Guido 'Ratty' Moretti, a poor fool who was apparently not a rat, just a mouse caught in a trap.

"What do you think about the poor sap?" I asked.

"Ratty was the designated fall guy for some minor stuff. Not bright enough to think of the crimes himself, but smart enough to know Frank Romeo would go his bail and take care of his family. Family was important to him. One more thing," Reggie continued. "His ma lives in a crummy tenement, but she has a brand-new radio, and a few other things, like a new sofa, table, and chairs. Everything else is threadbare."

"Did she mention where those things came from? Or did you ask?"

"Did I ask? Everything came from the dead kid. He worked for that nice Mr. Romeo."

"That nice Mr. Romeo." The breeze was chilly on my skin. I sipped my now-lukewarm chocolate.

"Mama Ratty assured me Frankie Romeo is a gentleman and a fine businessman, always good to his family and friends, not a gangster like everyone says. And if he was, she says, these are difficult times and he only did what he had to do, surviving in a cold cruel world. He feeds people. Romeo is a saint."

"And you wrote that bit down, what with all that pathos," I deadpanned.

Regie pulled out his best-boy grin. "Never waste a heart-wrenching quote."

"Anything else?"

"Too many tears, Esmé. Four younger kids, husband long gone, and Guido the rat-faced boy who supported the family now dead."

"That's horribly sad." I felt the crush of the times press against me, against Mrs. Moretti. "Maybe if he hadn't looked like a little criminal, he would have had a better life."

"Maybe. I knew a guy looked just like him. Studied at Princeton. Now a doctor. Life is weird."

"Are you writing a follow up?" I'd bet on it.

"Can't waste all those tears. Obviously."

"I'll look for it. If Ratty was Romeo's driver, where was Frank?"

Reggie sported a sly grin. "Frank's got a lady friend he visits twice a week. Maybe he pays for her company, maybe not. No one's touching that angle. Yet. Too dangerous."

"He was supposed to be in love with Juliette Scavullo. He's never married."

"What of it? A guy's got needs."

"And you would know," I said.

"I'm like any guy who plans to trip the righteous path, stay faithful, when he marries." He winked at me. "You don't have to worry, Esmé, when we marry it will all be out of my system."

"You won't have any energy left in your system. Not even for me." I saluted him with my cup.

"O, ye of little faith."

"Just being realistic." I snorted a laugh.

"At any rate, no one's gonna call out Handsome Frank Romeo for having a female love interest. Not me and not the cops."

"If it was a regular thing, how long was Ratty waiting for him?'

"Hour, maybe two. So why the sudden interest? Why this story?" Reggie was suddenly on alert, eyeing me with interest. Well, a little more interest than before.

"I'm always interested in your career, Reggie. I'm waiting for the day you can buy me dinner."

"That's cold." He sipped and made a face. "So is this drink."

"I'm a cold-hearted woman. I never know what my next play will be about. There are lots of gangster pictures, so maybe the world needs another gangster play."

Reggie was a pal. He believed me. "Maybe you're the one to write it. Hey, maybe we could write it together."

"Trying to ride my coattails?" He laughed, and I added, "Guess you better go, before your editor messes with your byline again."

He gazed at his watch and groaned. He kissed me on the cheek and sprinted away. It was late. Sal had told me I could take the day off, but I headed to the theatre anyway, to see if I'd missed anything.

There was a small pile of congratulations telegrams on my desk, from friends, and even from my old editor back home.

CONGRATULATIONS, ESMÉ. YOU SAID YOU'D
DO IT AND YOU DID.
LEAVING ALAMOGORDO A HIT. I KNEW YOU
COULD DO IT.
POP THE BUBBLY, KID, YOU MADE IT.

None were from my remaining relatives back home. It was only to be expected.

Sixteen

"ESMÉ? GRAYDON CHASE." THE PHONE was ringing when I unlocked my door.

"I see you have a telephone directory."

"And you were the only de LaForet in the book, initial E. I called the theatre and they said you'd left."

"Short day, arrived late, left early. C'est la vie." Amelia was gone, but my brand-new scrapbook was waiting on the table next to the flowers. They made a pretty picture. The pages were cream colored. I flipped through the book with one hand while holding the receiver in the other. Amelia had pasted up my newspaper notices meticulously. "Thank you for the flowers, Graydon. They are lovely."

"As are you. That's not the reason I called. We need to talk in person."

"About?"

"Guido Moretti. Also known as Ratty. Your friend Pendleton and the other yellow scribes splashed the story all over the papers."

"The story wasn't untrue, merely sensational." I felt like I should stand up for Reggie. "Too bad about Ratty Moretti though. He didn't sound that smart, but a nice guy, everyone said."

"The papers squeezed out all the emotion they could. Yet he was a dangerous character. Let's talk tonight."

"I'm going to the theatre tonight. Opening weekend, you understand. If it never happens again, I want to be there for this moment in time."

"Every night?"

"I might skip Sunday night, if I'm tired. When do you want to see me?" And what was his real reason? "Why can't we just talk on the phone?" The telephone was a wonderful invention and I was lucky to have one.

"I can't see your face over the phone."

"To tell whether I'm lying or not?"

"Because you're prettier than most people I deal with. Sadly, I have an engagement later tonight. I'd rather see your show again," Graydon said. "A lot of the lines were lost in the laughter."

"Who are you seeing?"

"No one exciting. This is business."

"Blonde business or brunette business?"

"So many questions, Esmé. I can tell you were a journalist."

"We keep asking only until we have credible answers."

"Cocktails before the show, then. I'll pick you up at six. And Esmé, there will be other opening weekends for you."

I hoped he was right.

Amelia had set out my gold lamé gown for tonight's show. My opening-night velvet number was a success and this was a lovely follow-up to my first dress. Not to mention that gold and silver lamé were the absolute rage. I had thought about wearing the lavender, but I could wear that tomorrow and Graydon hadn't seen this one.

I don't know why it mattered to me that he hadn't seen this one. Most women had one good evening dress. I now had a handful, each one a showstopper. The lamé was darker and richer gold than many and complemented my coloring. I decided to wear the dress's matching bolero to cover up my bare arms and back, more suitable for this time of day.

I wondered if I could replicate the makeup magic that Amelia had wrought. She'd thoughtfully laid out all the necessities on my dressing table, including the eyelashes. Those were particularly intimidating. And then, like a miracle, Amelia stopped by, after this week's movie and before she and her friend Mavis were meeting for pie. Another Saturday, another movie and pie.

"I couldn't leave you alone in your hour of need," Amelia said.

I suspected she was waiting around to see if the man who sent me the gorgeous flower arrangement would show up.

"Thank you. Do you suppose you could you teach me?" I indicated the pile of cosmetics.

"Thought you'd never ask."

Like a drill sergeant, Amelia instructed me and then quizzed me and gave me a passing grade. There was a knock at the door as she helped me into the gold gown. Amelia wore a triumphant smile as she closed the curtains over my bedroom doors and strode to the foyer.

"Miss de LaForet will be a few minutes," I heard her say. She told him to wait in the living room.

He introduced himself and then said, "I haven't had the pleasure."

"I'm Amelia Applewood, Miss de LaForet's personal assistant. And housekeeper. And girl Friday. Part-time."

Thanks to my girl Friday, the apartment was presentable and shined to a high gloss. I was also glad to know what Amelia's job titles were these days. I supposed I could use whichever I chose. I emerged from my bedroom to cut short any more revelations.

Graydon wore a sharply pressed tuxedo and looked quite distinguished, though he stared at me for a long time. Amelia was impressed. She raised her chin to me and indicated the flowers.

"Mr. Chase," I said.

"You look stunning in gold lamé. Same little shop?"

"Exactly so."

He took my coat from Amelia and helped me into it. I waved goodbye to her.

The navy Ford was parked outside. Not the green Pierce-Arrow. He opened my door and helped me in.

"You're lucky to have Amelia," he said.

"She thinks so. She was checking you out, you know."

"I hope I passed muster. She seems quite formidable."

"Not to mention judgmental. She is under the impression I did something shockingly immoral to merit your flowers."

He flashed a predatory smirk at me. "We'll have to start working on that. I'd hate to disappoint Amelia."

"Cad." I glared at him.

Soon we were settled in at a hotel bar near the theatre, all wood and glass and sparkling chandeliers. We sat on a gold velvet sofa with a small marble-topped coffee table in front of us. The setting matched my ensemble. It was all so genteel, belying the subject at hand—murder. Graydon looked severe when I said the word.

"This is no game, Esmé. This mob business."

"I assume our subject is Guido Moretti?"

"I don't know that his demise has anything to do with Dante Scavullo's death, or that it doesn't, and I don't want to. I'm stepping away from that carnival and I want you to do likewise."

"I'm not in that carnival."

"Innocent bystanders get hurt too."

It was the first time Graydon referred to me as innocent and meant it.

"Oh, so you've finally decided I'm innocent?"

A waiter came by and stopped for our orders. I requested an iced tea with orange slices and Graydon ordered a brandy and soda. It was too early to start drinking when I knew I would be expected to have champagne later. At least one glass, for toasting.

"Why was Moretti killed?" I asked.

"I only have guesses."

"I'm sure you have more than that."

"He was Frank Romeo's driver."

"What about Romeo? Was he a target?"

"He's fine. I don't know if anyone was after him. Any more than usual, that is."

"Why shoot the chauffeur?"

"Good question. When they start going after the smaller blokes, the rest of us should move out of the way." He lifted his glass. I sipped my tea. I realized I was famished and afraid of being lightheaded. Graydon noticed. "Hungry?"

"I didn't have a chance to eat today. Wait, half a bagel."

"Dear Lord, Esmé, do you ever eat?"

"I've been busy. I'll eat when the show closes."

He ordered a couple of sandwiches and mentioned something about talking to Amelia to make sure I had 'daily sustenance.' I ignored him, but I was grateful for the egg salad when it arrived. I changed the subject.

"Do you have other clients?"

"I do. But they are not in the mob. Standard bread and butter."

"And they are?"

"Not for public dissemination, Elf. My business requires discretion."

"You say you want to know about me, but you won't tell me anything about yourself."

"That's not true." He merely watched me and sipped his drink. Let him have his business. I had mine and I checked my watch. "We have plenty of time," he said. He made me uncomfortable. "You are so desirable. You must know I want you, Esmé."

Mr. Smooth! He said it, just like that. Like it was nothing special. Like "let's have hors d' oeuvres." Well, I wasn't on the menu.

"People in Hell want ice water."

"Like you're throwing at me now. You want me too."

That may have been true, but I hold myself with more value. "I've never been one to follow the crowd, and I'm not following the crowd to your bed." I refused to admit how much I was tempted by him. "That's what men want, isn't it? Most men," I said.

"I'm not most men." He wasn't, he was more devious. "But I do desire you. What a picture you would make."

"Where?"

"Anywhere."

I know I might not be as sophisticated as I look. I wasn't used to all this free love, as the rest of the world was, or at least New York City. It was different for me. I wasn't interested in a failed fling of a relationship.

"I'm a keeper, Graydon. Not your type."

He took my hand and kissed it. "How do you know I'm not a keeper?"

He gazed at me with those blue eyes that now seemed quite guileless. *Bastard*.

"Let me talk to the Snow Queen and Priscilla the Palomino and I'll get back to you."

He snorted, not unamused. "Ye of little faith."

I stood up. It was time he escorted me to the theatre. As promised.

There was no reason to think Chase would show up at the theatre later that night. He'd been so attentive, and I was becoming used to him. The flattery and the flirting were fun, yet I knew I was enjoying his kisses and his embraces a little too much. Particularly after he made it clear that his intentions were nothing but carnal.

He was no doubt being chased by the likes of the Snow Queen and the Palomino, otherwise known as Millicent and Priscilla. The Snow Queen was determined to marry him, at least so I gathered from observing her stick figure in the ladies' room at Peacocks'. It appeared unlikely to me now. Graydon Chase enjoyed playing the field. Everybody seemed to know he was a playboy, even my Reggie.

Darn it, why did he have to look so handsome and smell so divine?

Leaving Alamogordo that night played even tighter and funnier, especially when William/Todd accidentally pitched himself out of his rolling chair and slid across the stage like Babe Ruth stealing home. Szabo, our director, ordered him to do it that way from now on. The cast was happy, Sal "The Hitmaker" Rossi was tasting a hit, and so was I.

But I skipped all the after-parties, save for a single glass of champagne, and hailed my own taxi home.

SEVENTEEN

I SHOULD HAVE BEEN RIDING high, reveling in the show's good reviews, Miss Full-of-Herself and loving it. Yet in my head I could hear my far-flung relatives tell me it was only a play, and I was simply a speck in the universe, and not to think too highly of myself.

If I hadn't run after Scavullo, all that followed, including the boy shot to death in a car, would only be a story for a day. I wouldn't know that people called that dead boy Ratty. Guido Moretti would be only a name in the newspapers, and I'd be wallowing in the success of my play. Thinking about nothing but me. It sounded pretty great, that pure moment of enjoyment, and I was missing it. But that might be the Irish side of me speaking.

No more good deeds, I told myself. *That's it.*

Amelia was not coming over later, everything was ship-shape and polished, except me. I was rumpled and sleepy. Yet despite her doubts, I was capable of looking after myself. I fixed some coffee and scrambled eggs and tried to chase grim thoughts away.

Every paper, even *The New York Times*, had reported the murders. Not as splashily as the *Daily News* or the *New York Post*. Yet everyone, not just the Italians, knew that Scavullo had been a bootlegger for the mob. Or at least the bootleggers' bookkeeper, according to Reggie's story. Someone who knew where the bodies were buried. And now Juliette Scavullo would have to raise her boys alone and try to avoid the snares set by the likes of Handsome Frank Romeo.

I recalled Columbus Day, when I grabbed the pocket watch off the counter. Was there something I'd missed? I retrieved my notes and studied them. The ambiguous image on the inside back cover—waves that turned into Roman numerals—was very distinct, and it looked recent.

What did the watch's image mean? Some kind of a hidden message, or not-so-hidden message? I let my thoughts run, which got me nowhere. Except the possibility that it was a new image, etched by a master watchmaker. An image dictated by Scavullo for a purpose known only to him.

Life was full of symbols and mystery. As far as I understood, the Mafia had many complicated and curious rituals. Did the waves represent something like that?

My first serving of java was beginning to work its mischief on my brain, so I poured a fresh cup. I had the afternoon free to come up with more crazy ideas. They might be nothing, or they might suggest scenarios for a new play.

Where would Scavullo have gone to have the watch serviced? New York was full of jewelers, Italians and Jewish men and many others. Suppose Scavullo didn't want everyone to know about the image. If he planned to exit the mob and chose Graydon Chase because he had no ties to the organization, perhaps Dante felt the same way about his future, and placed his secret in the watch?

The gold watch had looked clean and shiny to me. My father had had a pocket watch he called his "railroad watch," and he had it cleaned and oiled every year. What if Scavullo's watch had just been serviced? Maybe he'd picked it up on Columbus Day morning. Then his jeweler might be near Ray's Diner, where he ate lunch, and a stone's throw from the Theatre District and the elementary school. Was I thinking, or plotting?

This was ridiculous, I told myself, merely a device for a play. It was nothing but sheer fancy—and caffeine jitters— on my part. However, that afternoon I strolled the neighborhood of the diner, looking for likely candidates. There were a few watchmakers and jewelers, where I stopped and asked about a pocket watch that had been recently serviced, describing it the best I could. I kept striking out. I was about to give up this improbable quest, when I spied a tiny storefront marked with formal gold-and-black lettering.

Gwyllyms' Clocks, Fine Watchmaker and Jeweler. No one would notice this little shop unless they'd walked past it a dozen times. I had, and it had never registered with me before.

I opened the door and an old-fashioned bell jingled. There was a single glass counter displaying rings, necklaces, and earrings, as well as silver baby cups and other items ready for engraving. Sitting at a workbench near the window with a view of the door and the limited floor space, a man lifted his head from his work and peered at me. His jeweler's loupe was attached to his glasses, his face etched with wrinkles, his longish hair salt and pepper. He was not quite medium height with a thin frame.

"May I help you? I'm Mr. Williams."

He was joined by an equally petite woman with graying hair worn in a bun. She smiled as sweetly as anyone's granny. With a cleaning rag in one hand, she was polishing the sparkling glass of the jewelry counter. I must have looked confused.

"Isn't this Gwyllyms'?" I asked.

"Oh, that. That's the Welsh version." He smiled. "Here in the States, we go by Williams. Might you have a clock or a watch in need of service, Miss?"

A Welsh watchmaker? An odd choice, perhaps strange enough to suit Scavullo. After all, he'd already hired an English detective.

I introduced myself and rushed into questions about the late Dante Scavullo. In lieu of any reasonable explanation of why I wanted to know, I simply said I had admired Scavullo's watch when he gazed at it in church.

"He seemed very fond of it," I added lamely.

"Ah, Mr. Scavullo. Terrible thing that. We read about it in the papers," the woman said.

"We don't usually see many Italian gents in this shop, but turning down customers is bad business," the watchmaker added.

"Then Scavullo was here?"

He lifted his glasses and stared at me. "You're nothing to do with the police then?"

"Oh no. I'm a playwright." They smiled and seemed to relax. The whole neighborhood was lousy with theatre people.

"Evan and I are quite fond of the theatre." Mrs. Williams indicated her husband. "What with being so close to the playhouses and all."

"Poor Mr. Scavullo picked up his timepiece the very day he died," the watchmaker said. "A very fine specimen. Gold, silver, blue enamel, a double hunter."

"Double hunter?"

"Double means both the front and back covers open." He took a watch from his work desk to show me. "A hunter has one cover that opens. The covers are to protect the watch when you're riding to the hounds. You understand."

The hounds? I nodded. "Why did he come here to your shop?"

Mr. Williams leaned forward and scratched his head. "As I recall, Mr. Scavullo didn't want to go to any place where he was known."

"So he had the watch serviced here?"

He nodded. "Always. Serviced, oiled, and polished. We adjusted the mainspring this time, and a little something special. It wasn't a complication, but..."

"A complication?" I asked.

His wife smiled at my question. "A complication means any additional function in the watch that doesn't simply tell the time." I must have still looked stumped. "Mr.

Scavullo's watch had several complications, like this one. The day and date, the star chart, the phase of the moon, the chimes. Very pretty chimes, they were."

"We call that a grand complication," Evan Williams added. "Don't we, Nell?"

"What was the 'something special'?" I was trying to keep all this straight.

"Now that the poor man's left this world never to return, I suppose I'm not breaking any confidentiality. He never asked me for my silence." He scratched his head again. "It was that ambiguous image we engraved on the inside back cover. Nell did most of the work on that." He winked at his wife. "She's a fine engraver."

"The Roman numerals and waves?" I asked.

"You have an eye," she said. "Not everyone can see those numbers."

"Yes, the numbers. Did he tell you what they mean?"

"Oh, no. And we would never ask. A gentleman's pocket watch can be a very personal thing."

"Did he mention why he wanted the engraving?"

"It's not our job to be curious," the husband said, yet I sensed they were curious. No doubt they were used to keeping secrets, like engravings for birthdays and engagement surprises.

"Fair enough. Do you remember if he was anxious or fearful that day? He visited your shop not long before—the incident."

The watchmaker stared at me for a long moment. "No. In view of the fact that he died that day, I have thought about it. No, I can't say he seemed to anticipate the outcome."

"Was he distracted?"

"Not at all. He was very interested in the pocket watch."

Nell Williams stepped forward. "Mr. Scavullo was quite pleased with our work. He laughed to himself, and he paid with cash, paid in full."

Then Scavullo didn't know he was going to die, and he hadn't become distracted until after the phone call at the diner when I saw him. I thanked Mr. and Mrs. Williams for their information. I didn't offer them money for it. That would make it seem like something out of a cheap detective play.

"Do you enjoy the theatre?" I pulled out a pair of comp tickets to *Leaving Alamogordo* for the run of the show, writing my name on them. One of the perks. "Just call the box office and work out the dates you're free. If you would like to go."

Mrs. Williams thanked me, beaming.

As I was leaving, a pretty pair of amethyst earrings caught my eye. They dangled delicately and captured the light. They were not inexpensive. Yet a fair purchase for some interesting information. I wore them that evening with my lavender gown.

Eighteen

66 "THANK YOU FOR COMING TO the show," I said at intermission to the vaguely familiar figure standing in the theatre foyer. Greeting well-wishers was part of the job.

The man was a walking Ichabod Crane, very tall and very thin, with prominent facial features, very appropriate to the Washington Irving Theatre. It took me a moment to remember him. Then I did. *Oh dear.*

The fellow with a sneer on his face was none other than the author of *Afternoon Tea with Nigel,* Julian Davis-Montclair. "I simply had to come and cheer on a fellow playwright," he said, as falsely as he could.

"Thank you." I waited for the anticipated insult or back-handed compliment. I was relieved to see that he didn't recognize my stunning dress. In fact, he may not have inspected the understudy's costumes. He seemed to be with a male friend, whom he failed to introduce.

"Your reviews were kind, very kind for a freshman effort, Esmé," he said. "Don't take it to heart, they're just waiting to stick a pin in you when you least expect it. The way they did to me."

His wit was dipped in poison, as was his pen. I took a wary step backward.

"Don't think I don't appreciate your keen insights, Julian." We'd only met in passing, and yet here we were on a first-name basis, like familiar old enemies.

"Well, I had comps. When your next play fails, call me. We'll commiserate."

"And I'll return the favor." I didn't try to keep the sarcasm from my voice.

Davis-Montclair clearly seemed to think he had an exclusive on sarcasm. He peered at me disapprovingly over his horn-rimmed glasses, the style that all the intellectuals seemed to wear at the moment, along with his black beret and his borrowed tuxedo.

Navigating the crowd of well-wishers, Sal spotted the playwright who had cost him so much money. He spun on his heel and sprinted away in the opposite direction. Taking umbrage at this snub with a loud sniff, Davis-Montclair exited the lobby with his friend, a short, chubby, sweating fellow. They stood outside the glass doors gesturing wildly, no doubt savaging my play, or Sal, or possibly all of Broadway. I stared at them and decided their tuxedos must have come from some costume shop, either borrowed or simply taken. They were worn at the sleeves and badly fitted. I didn't know if these guys would return for the second act, but I didn't care.

Before I could sigh dramatically, some friends hustled over to congratulate me. Among them was Nina Oglesby, freckled ex-cowgirl, a sister refugee from my old newspapering days out West. I remembered her chestnut curls flying and fringed skirts flapping as she ran down her sources like a roughrider. Nina had traded her Western wear for a sleek New York style since arriving in Manhattan this year and landing a high-society beat. She was a quick learner—but she could never quite hide those freckles.

"Great play, Esmé, reminds me of those good old fights we had in the newsroom." She winked. "Can't wait to see how it ends. Tell me, does Annabelle move to NYC too?"

I laughed and we admired each other's smashing outfits. She was in a pale pink satin number with rhinestone clips. She admitted her new high-society beat was rubbing off on her.

"Wait and see," I said.

"Even though this is Saturday, this really beats covering the Friday night fights. Not that I'd mind, every now and then. On the other hand, I don't usually have to dodge flying fists, excited fans, or all that blood."

Neither one of us had to wear smocks covering our dresses to visit the theatre.

"We never would have missed it. Or gone back," I said.

"You always had your eye on bigger things. It's a fun play, Esmé. Reminds me why I left the Old West for the land of the Knickerbocker."

"They're keeping you busy at the *Post*?"

"Penning society gossip? It's like getting paid to party. I could claim I'd love to go back to covering 'real' news, but this is delightfully different. It's a nice break."

"You know what they say, Nina, every reporter you meet is a would-be playwright."

"Not me, I'm working on the great American novel."

"Good for you." One less playwright to compete with. The chimes interrupted our chatter and we returned to our seats, after agreeing to get together for lunch. Sometime soon.

The audience was even more enthusiastic than the previous night. They'd had time to read the reviews. Now they had permission to laugh from the opening curtain.

Sal provided free champagne in the lobby on opening weekend. I sipped my obligatory toast and met a couple of news scribes who wanted a quote from me about my play. I was cautious and modest in my reply. I knew how easily words could be turned around, especially if you weren't as scrupulous as I had been back in my ink-and-newsprint days. Not to brag.

I debated whether to go out after the show, but I was as limp as a rag doll from the tension and the excitement, and content to simply observe the crowd. Dressed in their finery, shop girls and their dates, society matrons and their distinguished escorts, all off to parties and bars. I loved them. Most of them. I stood on the side until the crowd thinned. Sal invited me to his private after-party. I waved him off and started to flag a cab.

"That's some dress," a man's voice sounded behind me. I turned and found myself staring at long-lashed green eyes, a pleasant face, and dark hair. He seemed Italian and yet not Italian. If I wasn't mistaken, those were Irish eyes.

"Patrick Dentino, isn't it?" He nodded and shook my hand.

"Pat to my friends. Thanks for not calling me 'Lashes.' I hate that name. I remember you from the Scavullo visitation."

Neither of us mentioned that we hadn't been properly introduced. Lashes Dentino (I didn't call him that) wasn't in evening clothes or mobster attire. He wore slacks and a tweed jacket, topped by a hand-knitted scarf, and a hat. He wasn't accompanied by any of his compatriots I could recognize. I gazed into the crowd to make sure. After my drink with Graydon, I was wary of anyone who hung around Marco Scavullo.

"Where'd you come from?" I looked around.

"Just walking. I was feeling kind of bad about Ratty. Didn't know I'd wind up here."

"Guido Moretti? I read about him in the papers."

Without his pals, Patrick seemed to have less bravado. He was more down-to-earth than I expected. "Ratty was just a kid. He didn't deserve this. His family relied on him."

"The papers said he worked for Frank Romeo."

"Scandal sheets say a lot of things. Guido was Frank's driver. That's all."

"Why would someone shoot him?"

Patrick exhaled loudly. "Driving is a sweet job, most of the time. Drive around in a nice car, hang with the boss, pay's good, no heavy lifting. Yet you never know when you turn the key if it's going to blow. But Mr. Romeo, he's straight with all the big boys and never had a problem."

"So you think someone was after Guido himself, and not Romeo?"

"But that don't make sense either. Ratty didn't have no enemies." He shook his head and measured the crowd around us. "What are you doing out here alone anyway, don't you have a date? Woman like you?"

"The audience was my date. I'm catching a taxi home, it's been a busy week." A cold wind lifted my hair and I snuggled into my fur collar.

"I'll stay and make sure you get that taxi. You should be safe."

I glanced up at him, wary. "You think so?"

"It's a big unsafe world, Esmé de LaForet. But don't worry," he said with a big Irish grin. "I'm safe. I don't bite." I wasn't so sure about that. I shrugged. We were probably about the same age. Both half Irish-American. "You wrote this play?" He gestured to my name on the marquee. "Marco mentioned it. I'm impressed. Truly."

"He thought there were too many words."

Patrick laughed at that. "Sounds like Marco. But you should hear him swear in Italian. He's got a big vocabulary. He likes you."

"He was with Bianca Lombardi."

"He has a lot of admirers. Bianca's more persistent than most."

"Good," I said. "I hope those admirers keep him busy."

"What, you don't think he's the most handsome thing that's ever lived?" Smirking now.

"Not my type." I could have said more, but I let it go.

Patrick thought of something else. "I saw you at church once or twice, over in the middle with the Irish, where my ma sits. You're rare, Esmé de LaForet. Irish with a French name."

"My middle name is Rafferty. Family name."

"I like that. Rafferty. You showing up at the viewing was a surprise, let me tell you."

I tucked my coat closer in the breeze. "I don't know why it should have been. We went to the same church. The Scavullos were going to come to my play."

"No kiddin'?" He seemed impressed. "First, you ain't Italian. I'm only half and I get the business about it all the time. Second, you returned Scavullo's gold watch and that really got tongues wagging, like there wasn't enough to talk about, what with how Scavullo was taken down and all. And it wasn't Mr. Romeo who done him in, I can tell you that. I know what people are saying."

I didn't want to hear any more about reputed mob boss Frank Romeo and what a great guy he was.

"Pat, this is the deal. I saw Mr. Scavullo at Ray's Diner where I was eating lunch. He left his watch on the counter. I tried to give it to him then, but he was out the door so quick, I lost him." I took a breath. "That's all. Anybody would do that."

"Nah, only an honest person would do that, and there aren't a lot of them, at least in this town. And to tell the truth, not too many at that viewing either. Good thing Father Rappoli wasn't hearing confessions or we would have been there all night." He joked like an Irishman. He tapped me on the arm. "Don't worry, Mr. Romeo sent a couple of us over to Ray's to check out your story."

"You did what?" I could feel my mouth open wide. I may have gasped. "Are you some kind of truth squad? And how dare anyone think I'd lie?" Graydon Chase had already muscled Ray to check out my story. And now the mob too?

"Ray confirmed it. No problem. He's a big sissy, you know. Big squealer."

I could just imagine how they "confirmed" it. Chase paid for his information. Somehow I don't think Frank's boys were so polite with Ray, the 'big squealer.'

"I don't go to Ray's anymore." Certainly not *now*.

"Yeah, his meatloaf ain't that great. Hey, I'm just giving you a hard time."

It wasn't the first time I regretted not leaving the stupid watch at the restaurant.

"I'm sorry now I tried to do the right thing."

"No, no, you did do the right thing. From what I hear that watch is important to Mrs. Scavullo. Sentimental and all. Meant a lot to her, you getting it back to the family."

I was going to ask him more, when out of the night, beret-wearing playwright Julian Davis-Montclair showed up in my side vision. He was speaking just loud enough for us to overhear.

"I suppose that's what happens when you let women have pens and paper. Or God forbid, a typewriter. It goes to their heads."

I growled beneath my breath, wondering what I should say. Turns out I didn't have to say anything.

"You there, in the beret. That didn't sound so polite," Patrick Dentino said to the beret wearer. He glanced at me before grabbing the disagreeable playwright by his worn-out lapels. Pat wasn't a huge man, but he was quick and well-muscled. He reminded me of some of the lithe young boxers I'd seen in the ring when I covered the prizefights. "You want I should teach him some manners, Rafferty? Maybe break his pen?"

"No, Pat, please. He's not worth it," I said, even though I wouldn't have minded punching this particular playwright myself. The thought of mob interference on my behalf was a little alarming.

Patrick tossed him backwards with a shrug. Davis-Montclair staggered back and retreated a few steps, before quickly striding away in the opposite direction. We watched him go.

"I kind of always wanted to write, you know," Pat said. "I was always that kid with my nose in a book. My ma says I should go to college and make something of myself."

"You should try it. She might be right. There's still time."

He seemed amused by the thought, and he smiled at me. It wasn't the leer of a wolf on the prowl, but a pleasant companionable smile. From a guy who was willing to beat up another playwright for me. Kind of endearing. He jumped into the street and hailed the next taxi. He opened the door for me and warned me not to talk to strangers before shutting it firmly.

Pat Dentino waved goodnight.

Nineteen

I T WAS TIME TO SEPARATE myself from all the Scavullo mess, so for a change, I attended Sunday Mass at St. Patrick's Cathedral. I skipped Our Lady of Pompeii, my usual place of worship. The cathedral, the crowds, and the music of the choir soothed me.

When I was growing up in a dirty windswept town, hot and dry in the summer and unforgivingly cold in the winter, among the many shabby paint-peeled buildings, St. Bridget's Church was the only place of grandeur I saw. It was small but made of stone and carried a sense of permanence. Its stained-glass windows, gold chalices, candles, and incense promised me there was beauty and music and another world outside the sagebrush and tumbleweeds that fenced me in. I wasn't thinking about Heaven. I was thinking of that green and promised land, the mythical East Coast, and its crown jewel, New York City.

Far grander than little St. Bridget's, New York City's St. Patrick's Cathedral dazzled me. The soaring columns and arches offered both awe and anonymity. I drifted along with the music and tried to forget all about Dante Scavullo and Ratty Moretti and the rest. There was nothing I could do about their deaths. I sailed along, kneeling, standing, praying, and lighting candles. All was well. Still, I couldn't help watching over my shoulder as I left.

One of the true joys of a Sunday morning was picking up a newspaper after services and heading to a nearby diner to enjoy it. I found a likely restaurant a couple of blocks away and settled in with *The New York Times*. The

Sunday edition was worth more than the dime it cost. It was as if the whole wide world was right there at my fingertips.

Turning the 168 pages of this behemoth Sunday edition, I indulged in news about the upcoming trial of Bruno Hauptmann, the man who allegedly killed the Lindbergh baby, and the abduction of Mrs. Alice Stoll, and pondered why there were so many kidnappings these days. On the other hand, I puzzled over why so many old and ragged people stashed fortunes in their basements and beneath the floorboards. Fortunes found only after their owners had shuffled off their shabby mortal coils.

The Depression affected everyone in strange ways. I reflected that my parents had hidden cash away in unlikely places as well, but they also had bank accounts, and they never wore rags. My mother often shared with some of the railroad tramps near our house a bowl of her Irish potato soup, that was usually simmering on the stove.

I returned to the shocking front page news that the Episcopal bishops were in favor of birth control information. Risking centuries in Purgatory, I too was in favor of getting the word out about contraceptives. Too many women were beaten down and physically broken with their ever-expanding flocks of youngsters. I pictured them all living in a shoe, like the nursery rhyme, old before their time, with too many children to know what to do. Without money and support, they had no visible funds or husbands to help. I kept to myself my many radical ideas, such as that birth control was not the worst thing in the world.

I strolled home, *The Times* under my arm, enjoying the clouds that drifted over Central Park. Another one of those perfect fall days, cool and crisp, but enjoyable with a warm jacket, a colorful shawl, and a saucy hat. The park was full of families and tourists and seemed a place of wonder.

The sheep meadow was lushly green and serene, while the sheep themselves had been trucked over to Brooklyn's

Prospect Park. More exciting for me was that after so much back and forth on when and if it would be ready for commerce, the Tavern on the Green's doors had swung open to the public just the day before. I paused and admired its handsome exterior.

How difficult would it be to convince Reggie to take me to lunch at the Tavern in payment for all those coffees for which I had picked up the tab? It wasn't cheap and people were no doubt fighting for reservations, but Reginald Archibald Pendleton III would surely have some pull, either for his name or for his position at the *Post*.

And I would surely be able to pull something from my closet of wondrous costumes to wear. Dressing up and going to the Tavern on the Green? That would be positively *theatrical*.

Twenty

THE RINGING WAS INSISTENT AS I opened my door, reminding me how lucky I was to even have a telephone when so many people had to run to a friend's or the drugstore to use the phone booth.

"Esmé, it's May. Not to scare you, but Clarissa is sick, as well as our leading man, Todd."

"Sick?" Just today I'd decided not to attend this evening's performance. The first three nights had gone beautifully, and I was tired and wanted to be at home, catching up on my reading, playscripts, books, magazines. No one would miss me. But now, a potential disaster loomed. "How sick? That sounds suspicious."

"It's too early in the run for them to be pulling stunts." May sounded very matter-of-fact. "And despite the obvious romance between those two, I doubt it's an excuse for them to run out of town to make whoopee. There's a virus cutting a swath through the Theatre District. The understudies will have to go on."

"Oh May, that's awful."

"Don't worry, no one's as eager to please as an understudy looking at their big chance."

"I mean it's awful for Clarissa and Todd."

"Yes, but this bug is supposed to be quick and vicious, over in twenty-four hours. Some of these flu things are like that, one minute you feel fine, then twenty minutes later, you're down for the count. Clarissa and Todd have two days to recover and return to the show. Three, if they convince Sal they're dying."

"Do you think the rest of the cast will catch it?"

"Not all at the same time. I hope."

"How did Clarissa sound?" I knew there was a phone in the rooming house where she resided with other hopeful actresses.

"Dramatic. Very dramatic."

That cheered me. If Clarissa could still present her excuses with dramatic excess, she probably wasn't at death's door.

I sank into the sofa and tried to just breathe. "Are they off book? The understudies, I mean." As far as I remembered they were fine, but they didn't have the drawing power of Clarissa Eldridge and Todd Andrews.

"Theoretically. Are you coming?"

"Yes. I'll come to the show." I felt sick to my stomach, and it wasn't the flu.

"Take a sedative," May counseled.

"I don't have a sedative." I'd never taken anything to calm down, though I knew plenty of people who had.

"Necessities are in my bottom drawer. See me before the show."

"I'll be fine," I said, feeling numb.

"Listen, Esmé. It could be a train wreck or a triumph. You never know. Either way, you don't want to miss it."

"When you put it like that, how could I stay away?"

The only thing keeping my mind off the potential disaster ahead was my wardrobe choice, what to wear to the theatre on a Sunday night. Full evening attire seemed ill-advised. I opted for one of the two cocktail dresses from *Afternoon Tea with Nigel.* Wearing another costume from that show was like scoring a point against its ill-bred beret-clad author.

I chose the deep cranberry dress in velvet. The low-cut back ended with a large satin bow that settled into a V just above the hips. There were tiny matching ribbons on the wrists, and a small crimson velvet cap with an attached veil. It featured a matching satin flourish that dipped low over the forehead. Willie had included a large costume jewel in the middle of the back bow and another for the hat. The ensemble was fetching and yet nothing quite like I'd seen before. It made me feel vaguely mysterious, especially with the dark red veil.

Unfortunately, everyone recognized me the moment I ventured backstage to spread luck to the cast, wishing them all to *break a leg*. Clarissa's understudy instantly clutched her guts and sprinted for the lavatory. I hurried to my seat, ignoring May's drawer of sedatives. She waved me on. Nobody wanted to miss a good train wreck.

Though I held my breath a few times over shaky lines, I was relieved to find our understudies had their own fresh takes on the material. Plus, their terror enlivened everyone's performance. Although there were missed lines and some bits of dialogue looped in the wrong places, the actors—in a state of sheer panic—ran their lines at breakneck speed and got the laughs they needed. Tonight, *Leaving Alamogordo* played like it was shot out of a cannon. Happily, the audience left the theatre cheering and speaking of attending the show again to compare the two versions.

A jovial Andras Szabo slapped me on the back. "You see, Esmé, that's what I was going for. We cut eight minutes off the play. I'm going to give notes, you want to come?"

"No thanks, Andras. Just happy to be alive."

I was very aware of the inevitable adrenaline crash to come. I collected my coat and he helped me on with it. Making it home in one piece was my only remaining goal for the rest of the night.

Twenty-One

66 "EY PRETTY LADY, WHY YOU not go out with me?" An Italian accent. "Tonight."

The words came from behind me and promised an invitation, not a complaint. I spun around and collided with Marco Scavullo. I disentangled myself and backed away from him, Possibly I shrieked a little. I was feeling a bit delicate these days. He was first in line for the last person I wanted to see. After him and Lashes Dentino, who was next? Handsome Frank Romeo himself? I wished Reggie was there with me, with his brash bravado.

"I'm so sorry, did I frighten you?" Marco was suddenly all concern and conceit.

"You startled me. You should be careful."

Full of swagger and wearing a bright lavender shirt with his suit, he apparently took female screaming in stride.

"You remember me, Miss Playwright?" He flashed a mouthful of bright, even teeth. "Ladies never forget me."

I took another step back. "What are you doing here?"

We stood outside the theatre, under the marquee flaunting my name and the title of my play.

"I been thinking about you." He rubbed his chin thoughtfully. He'd seen that gesture at the movies, or maybe he was just showing off his pretty face. "I'm thinking you should write a play for me. I'm a good-looking guy. I could be a star."

He didn't see me rolling my eyes. There was no lack of ego about Marco, and he was handsome. A guy who hated words but wanted to be an actor? It figured.

"You didn't care for my play," I said.

"I wouldn't say that. I liked it." Dramatic gesture. "I don't have to have all the words. I can change your mind when I take you out for spaghetti dinner."

I put up my hands to fend him off. "Marco, stop right there. I'm too busy with my play and sick actors and I won't go out with you."

"Why not? Is it because of my—friends? You liked my uncle."

"I didn't know your uncle. I only saw him at church." I took a deep breath. "And what about Guido Moretti?"

"That was a sad thing. Sure." He was momentarily downhearted. "Ratty was a good kid."

"I'm not getting involved with anyone in your line of work."

"You hear too many rumors." Now he employed the fingers-to-his-ear gesture, but smiled to indicate he was not offended. "Maybe you can make me a better man." He moved in front of me to stop my progress. I dodged around him and raised my arm for a taxi. "Many men flatter you, I know, but Marco Scavullo is sincere."

"Not that many," I responded.

He reached out for me but did not touch me. "You are very beautiful. We look good together."

"People need more than that." At that moment, Marco reminded me of Chase's Snow Queen and her friend in the ladies' room at the dance hall. She had spoken of Chase as an accessory on her arm. "*I* need more than that. I need someone who likes the theatre and plays. I think you should be happy with Bianca."

"Bianca is a nice lady, but she is not Esmé de LaForet. I am single guy. I won't give up. You will come out with me one day?"

A black-and-yellow taxi dropped off a couple of passengers. I lunged for it, and this time Marco grabbed for my arm.

"No." I shook off his hand and another couple jumped into the recently vacated cab. "Don't follow me."

A shiny Ford screeched to a halt in front of the theatre. I recognized it. The driver's door opened and Graydon Chase jumped out, leaving the engine running. I peered inside to see who this evening's lady might be. It was empty.

"Chase," Marco said, taking a step back.

"I'm taking the lady home." Chase practically puffed out his chest and pounded his fists. Metaphorically speaking.

"I didn't know you were together tonight. Excuse." Marco bowed slightly to Chase and then nodded toward me. "Another time, Miss Esmé. It's a promise."

I was in no mood to argue about Chase's chivalry. While he and Marco were facing off, I ran for the passenger door and jumped in, leaving the door open in case I had to leave suddenly. Marco strutted away, but not before I noticed him flirting with a couple of shopgirls who were closing up their store. Graydon shut my door firmly, then ran to his side and slammed it. He pulled away from the curb.

"Are you all right, Esmé?"

"I'm fine. May I hitch a ride home?" I don't know why I trusted him. Maybe I only trusted him more than I did Marco Scavullo. It was a surprise to see him here. I had given up on the idea of Chase appearing out of nowhere.

"I thought you weren't attending the show tonight and yet here you are. Were you lying to me?"

"Oh please. I hadn't planned on it. The leads are out, allegedly felled by some flu. The understudies had to go on and May said something about a potential train wreck. Couldn't miss that."

"How was the performance?"

"An under-rehearsed show running on adrenaline and fear? Very exciting. They pulled it off." I let my breath go, not realizing how apprehensive I'd been all day. "The audience was enthusiastic, and I also learned that Clarissa Eldridge and Todd Andrews are not irreplaceable."

"The leads? Are you sure they weren't making the two-backed beast?"

"Oh, you Shakespeareans. May says it's too early in the run for shenanigans like that. Besides, they won't be happy when they hear how well Understudy Night went." I gazed at him while he kept his eyes on the road. He was more casually dressed than I'd seen him, wearing trousers and a brown tweed jacket over a sweater and shirt and matching knit tie, loosened at the neck. It was something Reggie might wear. "What are you doing here anyway?"

"Working late."

I gave him the old side-eye. "Really?"

"It's true. It's not always parties and nightlife, though some of my clients expect that. I do actually work. Boring work. Tying up loose ends."

"Financial clients?"

"All that Scavullo business kept me from my regular tasks."

"Right. Were you on a late date? Or spying on me?"

"Merely on my way home, when I see you tangling with Scavullo's pretty-boy nephew."

"I wasn't with him. I was just trying to hail a taxi. And I appreciate the ride, Graydon. Thank you."

We drove through the lights of Times Square and finally into quieter streets.

"I'm guessing you're hungry," he said.

"I ate brunch." I wish he hadn't mentioned food.

"That was hours ago. I'm hungry too."

Graydon guided us to a small restaurant on the Upper East Side, a place I'd never been, but you could have drawn a straight line from it across the park to where I lived on the Upper West Side. It looked pricey and that made me nervous. I was still unsure about my future as a theatre scribe. Nothing was promised.

On the other hand, I was tired of fighting with this guy about paying my way.

Chase ushered me into a small intimate restaurant, where the staff was polite but not intrusive. He helped me off with my coat and checked it.

"You look lovely in red. The hat and dress are particularly fetching. Let me guess, another costume courtesy of the amazing Willie Kim?"

"From a cocktail party scene. I am grateful that Julian Davis-Montclair was so self-indulgent with his settings. Too bad about the plot." I straightened out one of the bows on a cuff. I would have to report to Willie that once again her togs were unsurpassed.

The waiter ushered us to a small round table near the fireplace where a candle flickered in the center. The light glowed the way it always does in romance novels. Graydon put his finger on my face and let it linger. It didn't seem a very English thing to do. "Beautiful," he said.

"Ha. I just clean up well. Just ask Amelia."

"It's not only me. Marco Scavullo, for example. It's charming that you're unaware of your power over men."

Not completely, I thought. I seemed to have an amazing effect on gigolos.

It was late and the restaurant was not full. We ordered French onion soup paired with Chardonnay. I inhaled the aroma before indulging. Just like my father used to make. He usually let my mother cook, but *soupe à l'oignon* was his specialty, a simple homey dish.

"Esmé, I fear I may have been a bit too direct the other evening."

"When you said you wanted me?" I silently ordered him to squirm, but he didn't.

"Yes."

"And you remember what I said about Hell?"

He laughed. "Good line that. Perhaps we could start again."

"I don't like standing in line."

"What line?"

"The Snow Queen, the Palomino, and your other assorted ladies-in-waiting."

"There's no line, if there ever was one."

"Maybe not here, not now. Maybe I should check the ladies' room."

"And what about Marco Scavullo? Grabbing at you on the street. What does he want? What was he doing there?"

"Other than my incredible allure? He wasn't there to see the show, but he told me he would be a great actor in a play, but not one with a lot of words. Maybe I could write one for him." I dug into my soup. "I'm sure he has lots of ideas. With guns and a limited vocabulary."

Graydon focused on his own bowl of soup, and we lapsed into a companionable silence. I wished I didn't suspect him of ulterior motives. I wanted us to simply be two people. Maybe he still distrusted me because of how we met. I distrusted him for the same reason. But if we hadn't met then, the day Dante Scavullo was murdered, we wouldn't have met at all.

"It's not that I don't adore your intriguing company, but I can hardly keep my eyes open," I said, after the soup. "Would you mind? Or I could walk." I was kidding, of course. I'd never choose to walk across Central Park that late at night.

Back at my apartment, where he again insisted on inspecting the premises for suspected bad guys, I prompted him to leave. He was not the best at picking up an exit cue. He was, however, excellent at extended goodnight kisses.

Twenty-Two

LEAVING ALAMOGORDO HAD BEEN BOOKED for a six-week run, barring a first-night disaster, bad reviews, or lagging audiences, which could shut down the show in a heartbeat. No one wanted to struggle with a half-empty theatre. We were all interested in putting bottoms in those seats, and after this weekend, I was cautiously optimistic.

The Irv was usually dark on Mondays and I slept late, but I decided to pick up a stack of scripts at the theatre. I was behind in my reading. Assuming no one would see me, I wore khaki slacks, a soft warm sweater, jacket, and a trim fedora.

I arrived to find that Sal had called an all-staff meeting on the stage for a postmortem on the play. I'd left my apartment just before his call came. This felt like the same kind of meeting that was called after Sal decided to pull the plug on *Afternoon Tea with Nigel*. I held my breath. All kinds of horrible scenarios rampaged through my brain, including me cleaning out my desk.

After a dramatic pause, Sal sailed onto the stage, where all the healthy cast and crew were in attendance. He carried all the reviews he could find, an armload. He tossed the papers up into the air with pure glee. Some poor stagehand would have to clean them all up.

"Ladies and gentlemen, it looks like we have a hit on our hands!" Sal was generally a pleasant person, but I'd never seen all his pearly white teeth before. The man was actually grinning. This was a moment to remember. "The phones have been ringing off the hook and we are booked solid, except for your comps, so use them wisely," he said.

Not only that, Sal added that he was looking for another stage where he could continue and extend the run.

There were shouts of joy from the actors amid wild gestures and impromptu dancing. It took me a while to catch my breath. As the creator of the work, I held a different kind of responsibility. After all, if a play is a success, the director gets all the credit. If it fails, it's the playwright's fault. At least according to the newspapers.

Relief flooded my body, a hot wave breaking across my shoulders, undulating down to my toes, a furious fever of happiness. If I hadn't been sitting, I would have fallen down.

Our temporary leads took bows. Director Andras Szabo, with whom I had butted heads on numerous occasions, graciously shared the stage. But it was Sal, the producer, who pointed toward me and acknowledged my contribution.

"We wouldn't be here without Esmé de LaForet, the woman wielding the words." Calculating in my head, I would make a tidy little sum from my royalties. By banking most of it and not losing my mind, it would allow me the freedom to write and create more plays for some time to come. "But you still have scripts to read," Sal said. I lifted my pile of plays to show him. It got a laugh.

I planned to keep my day job. It got me out of my apartment and gave me something to do while giving those days shape. I also loved the outsized personalities of the people who frequented the theatre. They were mostly fun-loving lunatics who provided drama (and comedy) and they almost never murdered anyone. They preferred to stun their enemies with good (or bad) performances. And gossip.

The meeting ended and we all dispersed. No mobsters that I knew of were hanging around the theatre that day, nor playboy private eyes, about one of whom I had mixed feelings. However, *The New York Times* featured a front-page story on another mobster: RACKETEER SLAIN IN MIDTOWN STREET.

The victim was found missing a thousand dollars, so the papers said, and his pockets had been turned inside out. I had no idea if it was related to the hit on Scavullo, but I assumed I'd hear something sooner or later.

❧

"This looks like the real thing." I carefully handled the Perrier-Jouët champagne bottle with its delicate flowers on green glass.

"For you, Esmé, only the best." Reggie looked smug, but he grinned. "My folks' wine cellar is full of the good stuff, the real stuff. They'll never miss a couple of bottles."

"Thief. You learned this in school, didn't you?"

"I was merely an amateur then."

"Are you going to keep us here at the entry?" Nina Oglesby lifted another bottle of the precious bubbly. I opened the door wide and they pushed past me into my apartment. "Crazy place you got here. Like in the movies," Nina said. "Sure beats my place, my roommates' and mine."

"Esmé's got an eye for décor," Reggie said. "Just pretend you're on stage."

I looked from one to the other. "So that's how it is? You two are an item now?"

They looked at each other in consternation. "We're just work buddies, just two thirsty scribes," Reggie said. "And that's a fine thing for my future wife to say."

"What's this?" Nina was suddenly all ears like the society writer she was. "Future wife?"

"It's a joke," I said. "For when we're old and gray and unloved."

"When I've got my Pulitzer and Esmé has a string of hit plays."

"And after he's squired every available leggy blonde in Manhattan."

"You're lucky I have so much regard for you." Reggie took my hand and kissed it.

"Are you going to open that hooch," Nina demanded, "or just crack wise all night?"

Reggie expertly peeled the foil and popped the cork. I retrieved champagne glasses, still puzzled. I wasn't used to having this much company, especially outside the theatre world.

"Why are you here, Reggie?"

"You think we wouldn't find out that your run is sold out? It's a hit. Success is fleeting and we must capture the moment. Carpe diem!" He poured. Reginald Pendleton's champagne handling was as proper as his name. "To the mistress of the moment, the wielder of witty words, and playwright of note, Esmé Rafferty de LaForet."

"You heard." I was touched that they cared enough to come and bring champagne, even though I wasn't dressed for a celebration. They likewise were in work togs, a navy suit for Nina and the inevitable sweater vest and corduroy jacket for Reggie.

"My desk is right next to the theatre department," Nina shrugged. Sal must have sent them a press release. Listening to bits and pieces of everyone else's stories was just part of the newsroom brew, I knew. Being able to concentrate on your own work in that mix of chaos and deadline was a time-honored skill.

I sipped the bubbling nectar and kissed Reggie's cheek. "Thank your parents for me."

"Hmph. When *I* take all the risk."

Nina lifted her glass. "May your successes multiply! And take us all along for the ride."

The champagne bubbled, it tickled, it soothed. I slept soundly for the first time in weeks.

Twenty-Three

THE NEXT EVENING, THE AIR was full of promise and the forecast predicted rain. It also was loud with the singsong cries of the newsboys waving the latest edition. I planned to look for the notice about my play, but that news took a backseat to the sensation of the day. Some headlines were plainly stated, others were declaimed loudly in rhyme, the song of the newsboys.

"PRETTY BOY FLOYD SHOT DEAD IN OHIO!"

"O-MY-O-MY-O, PUBLIC ENEMY NUMBER ONE DIES IN OHIO."

"PRETTY BOY FLOYD DEAD! PUMPED FULL OF FEDERAL LEAD!"

Now George "Baby Face" Nelson would take over as Public Enemy Number One. The news raised an uneasy sense of anticipation in the air. It was October 23rd. Who would be next? Women looked over their shoulders and walked swiftly. Men snugged their jackets closed, narrowing their eyes. Nickels and pennies flew into the hands of the newsboys as people crowded around, demanding the latest editions that described the demise of this famous outlaw. I picked up my own papers, though by now I should have been sick of mobsters, even out-of-town ones.

Minus the sensational news, on most nights like this, I loved sitting at my front window overlooking the street to absorb the scent of rain and indulge myself with a bowl of semi-homemade soup. I had roasted chicken in the refrigerator, and I picked up last minute ingredients to throw it all together.

After growing up in the dry heart of the drier West, where rain was a mere prayer on the wind, I was enchanted by rainstorms, soft ones and furious ones. I loved the lush green of the East and I could feel my heart swell every time I strolled through Central Park. I never missed the sagebrush and tumbleweeds, not at all. I could smell the rain coming.

I stopped into the neighborhood deli and purchased chicken stock, lemons, fresh baked bread, and rich farm butter. I was taught the secret of the soup by the wife of a Greek sheep rancher back home. One of the few useful things I'd ever learned there.

As I left the deli, I caught a glimpse of Graydon Chase, and then he was at my side. Had he been following me? Did the news of another dead gangster remind him of me? How romantic. I turned and faced him. I couldn't tell if I was annoyed or pleased.

"Esmé, it's going to be a wet dog of a night. I'd love to take you to dinner. Intimate restaurant. Cozy fireplace."

"Sounds romantic, but not tonight, Chase. A rainstorm is on its way and I'm going to make some lemon chicken soup. And I have a fireplace."

He looked comically dejected. "You're making a meal? All alone?"

"Do you doubt me?" I stopped. Perhaps I could even up the dinner tally, as Chase had always insisted on paying. "Would you care to share some soup and hot bread and gaze at the storm?" It was neither here nor there for me. I was intent on gathering my goods and fleeing home before the torrents arrived.

"You're inviting me to your private abode? Yes, rather. It sounds lovely, Esmé."

"There's a catch. You must leave by eight o'clock. Friends are coming over and we'll be discussing clothes and costumes. You'd be bored. I hope."

"Glass half full, I suppose. I'll take it."

There was a heavy mist in the street. We were only a block from my apartment, but by the time we rushed through the downstairs door, the skies had opened up and poured forth. We pounded upstairs, laughing, shaking off raindrops. I handed him my coat to hang in the front hall closet, while I unpacked my grocery bag in the kitchen and began on the soup.

I wore a heather-colored sweater and knit skirt with a smart belted jacket and matching scarf. Being friends with a costume designer was having a positive impact on my life, and my wardrobe. Willie had tutored me through my choices for opening night, and now we needed to discuss what we should wear to see Duke Ellington and his band at the Cotton Club in November.

The chicken was prepared and shredded, and a big bowl of rice was ready to go. It was now mostly a matter of assembly and simmering, carefully blending the lemon and egg mix, before adding that mixture to the hot soup.

Graydon wasn't as big a nuisance as I had feared. However, he felt compelled to comment on all the contents in my refrigerator. "I say, you have champagne in there."

"I know."

"Decent stuff, though not the best."

"I have a philosophy about champagne," I responded without turning around or hitting him. "Always have champagne on hand in case there is something to celebrate. It shouldn't be the most expensive stuff, or else you'll never drink it, always waiting for something more important to toast. It should be just good enough to enjoy without guilt."

"Very practical."

To be honest I kept a store of bubbly because I feared the government might repeal the Repeal of Prohibition, and then how would I celebrate those little moments? Besides, life felt more sophisticated with bubbles. I also thought Willie and May might like something to drink, although it seemed rather soon after last night's impromptu party with Reggie and Nina.

"I also have a couple of bottles of beer on hand for company, if you prefer," I said.

"By all means then, let's have champagne. This is a moment to remember, you entertaining me in your sanctum sanctorum."

"I was going to have water." I lit the oven and turned it on low for the bread to heat.

"Don't trust yourself around me?"

"I don't trust you." I concentrated on stirring the savory mixture in the large pot.

It smelled divine. Graydon found wine glasses in the cupboard. I heard the pop of the champagne cork. He made himself useful, finding soup bowls, plates, and silverware. He folded the napkins with an expert's hand.

"Never let it be said a lady couldn't trust me. But I see I'm still on probation."

The soup was ready. The bread came out of the oven. I dished up the lemon chicken over rice and carried bowls to a small table near the front windows, and Graydon managed to carry over the rest. I tasted it, noting how the lemons gave me a delightful pucker and made my mouth water.

He handed me a glass of champagne and lifted his. "A celebration of soup and adventures with an elf. An elfin queen."

"An elf again?" I sipped the champagne. It wasn't the Perrier-Jouët, but it was tasty and not overly dry. Perfect with the soup.

"The best I could do on short notice. You fog my brain, Esmé."

"Sounds like a useful talent to me. Like the Shadow, who clouds men's minds."

Graydon snorted in response. He had set the table rather formally for soup and bread. It was as if he had practiced this sort of thing. Was it with the Snow Queen or the Palomino? Or both? Or many others?

"You look pensive." Graydon interrupted my thoughts. "Anything I should know?"

"No. Shall we eat?" I turned on the gas fire and cracked open the door to the balcony so I could smell the rain. "How did you happen to be passing by the deli when I was there?"

"I was waiting to see if you'd show up."

"At the deli?"

"In the neighborhood."

"Part of your detective work?"

"Timing is one of my skills. It gets dark early and I like to know you're safe. It seems particularly dangerous these days."

"Still worried about Scavullo's goons?"

"A bit."

"Do you think the same person killed Dante Scavullo and Guido Moretti? And what about that third mobster?" I retrieved a newspaper to show him.

"It crossed my mind. It has also crossed Frank Romeo's. He is not happy, even though the third man was not part of his gang."

"You could stay away from him."

"He contacted me."

"You aren't going to work for *him*, are you?" I felt the shock on my face.

He shrugged. "I told him that if there was anything I could do, within the parameters of the law..."

I picked up today's news stories. "It's been a tough year for gangsters."

"And their victims," Graydon took one of the papers and scanned it.

"Scavullo was robbed. From the picture in the papers his pockets were turned inside out. Was it like this other bootlegger?"

"Matter of fact, yes. But there's no proof they're connected. Most killers will go through their victims' pockets, if they have a chance." We ate in silence for a few minutes, tearing off pieces of the bread and buttering it, enjoying it with our soup. The blue-eyed stare was on me. "Delicious soup, Esmé. It really makes a meal."

"Are you surprised?"

"I shouldn't be. A little, yes. Most of the debutantes I know don't cook."

"Very funny."

He gazed around the room. It was a pretty picture. Amelia had been by, and everything seemed to shine in the firelight. Graydon paused, staring at the mantel where I'd placed the empty bottle of Perrier-Jouët. It was too pretty to toss.

"I see you do indulge in the higher-grade champagnes. That bottle wasn't here before."

He was more observant than I thought. "It was a gift from Reggie. He and Nina, Nina Oglesby, society writer for the *Post,* brought it over last night, after they found out about my show."

"Your show?"

"Successful opening. The run is sold out." I turned my paper inside out and looked for the notice. I showed it to him. "Sal is even thinking of extending, if he can find another stage."

"Pendleton? He gave you the champagne?"

"Pinched from the family manse in Boston, no doubt months ago. You remember Reginald Pendleton the Third. He's always saying he and I will marry one day. It's a joke."

"My dear Esmé, perhaps to you, and I hope to you. But not to him. When men say things like that, they are testing the waters. If you brush it off, they can say it's simply a little joke."

"Don't be absurd. Reggie is all about blondes and the occasional brunette. He's just a pal. An old reporting pal."

"An old pal of mine, too. For now, he wants to sow his wild oats. Pendleton can be a cad with every other woman but you. He doesn't want to show his true colors. And that's a damn expensive bottle of champagne."

"That he stole from his parents' wine cellar. I only had a couple of glasses. I think he's sweet on Nina, although she's not a blonde. She had at least three glasses. Anyway, we had to toast my success, because you never know when it will come again."

Graydon returned to his bowl of soup. "Congratulations on your play's success. Enjoy it. By the way, what did Pendleton say about the murder of Romeo's driver?"

"You're pumping *me* for information now?"

"I wouldn't say pumping, Elf."

"Everything Reggie mentioned was in his stories." It was time for me to do some info seeking of my own. "Where are you from in England? And how did you wind up here?"

"London. I was rather an impossible youth and my parents decided I would be less embarrassing across the Atlantic, in a military school."

I laughed. He seemed the impeccable gentleman. On the other hand, he wore gangster pinstripes rather well. "You were the bad boy?"

"I wouldn't say that. I simply possessed more, ah, *energy* than was seemly in my family."

"Are you the younger brother?"

"Yes, thankfully. I have a younger sister as well, back home." He stared at his empty bowl. "Do you mind if I help myself to another? This is absolutely delicious."

"Of course." I waved him on to the kitchen. "And then? You didn't go back?"

"I rather liked it here. So I decided to stay, went to Harvard, did a two-year stint in the Army." He returned with a brimming soup bowl. I hoped I had enough left for my friends.

"The American Army?"

"That's what one does, and where I learned to make a mean cup of coffee."

"I'm bowled over by these accomplishments, Graydon. I want to know more and I have many questions." I glanced at the clock on my mantel, right next to the Perrier-Jouët champagne bottle. "However, Willie and May will be here soon."

"You're not kicking me out?"

"Not until you've helped me clean up."

"I must sing for my supper?"

"Do you sing?"

"Occasionally."

"That would be pleasant, however, tonight you must scrub." I started to sing "My Melancholy Baby," and he joined in as we cleaned up. Graydon Chase had a melodious voice. Why wasn't I surprised?

"See how nicely we harmonize, my beautiful Elf." He looked longingly at my bed. "You could take me to Elysian fields."

"Dream on." I could hear steps outside my door. I reached for the doorknob. "Time to go, Graydon."

"Not quite." He pulled me close to him and brushed my lips with his. I hated how excited my body became when I was that near him. I hated it and I loved it. I leaned into him and melted into him. I wanted his kiss to go on forever, and in different places. It was hard to come up for air.

His mentioning my bed was so unfair! It painted too many pictures in my head, which unleashed a slew of impure thoughts. I tried to push them aside when one came unbidden: that being with Graydon might be far more enjoyable than it was with my late fiancé Roger.

I had tried to mourn Roger, but it didn't work. He faded further and further away in my memory. Our lovemaking had been awkward, and I was more enthusiastic than he was. He believed it was wrong before the wedding. I argued it was merely a bit advanced, and surely we should know if we were compatible in every way, rather than to marry and regret it. However, by that time I was already regretting my planned future with Roger.

Graydon went further with his hands. I was melting.

There was a loud knock at the door, which startled both of us. I managed to break away from him and brush my fingers through my hair. I opened the door. Willie and May bustled in, shaking rain from their coats, hats, and umbrellas, staring at Graydon Chase.

"Another time, Elf. Lock the door behind me." He gave me a slight bow to me and my guests and flashed his mocking blue eyes before heading down the stairs.

As he disappeared from view, Willie smirked. "Elf?"

I could have kicked him for calling me that.

"Was that an English accent?" May inquired. "He looks aces to me. Is he a duke or something?"

"Wasn't that the guy you ran away from at Peacocks'?" Willie again. "I knew I'd seen him somewhere before."

"Probably on a Ten Most Wanted poster," I said. "No more questions!" I reached for the garment bag Willie offered.

"Something smells delicious." May was always hungry. "We just left work and the cupboard was bare."

"I'm guessing you're starved."

Their eyes lit up, and I offered up soup and bread. I was glad it was a very large batch of soup. In the meantime, I unzipped the garment bag.

"You made out like a bandit on that Headless Horseman of a show," May said.

"I'm lucky Sal is so superstitious. But it wasn't the clothes that killed *Nigel*. Did you see the script? I told Sal it was a dog. Just like that particular playwright."

"Clarissa turned green on opening night when she saw you," May said, slurping her soup. "She's too big-boned to wear anything of yours."

Clarissa Eldridge, jealous of me? I'll take it. "But why didn't Sal think it would be bad luck to sell the costumes to *me?*"

"The exchange of money always erases the lesser evil when Sal's involved. This soup is really delicious. It's Greek, isn't it?"

"According to the Greek sheep rancher's wife who taught it to me."

I grabbed the bag and ran to my bedroom to try on the treasure. It was a light emerald-green chiffon gown with a tight-fitting bodice made of interwoven strips of material that met at the hip line. Layers of skirt fluttered below my calves. Reaching my elbows, the sleeves were anchored to darker green straps studded with faux jewels, and they danced like an angel's wings around my shoulders. The metal zipper was on the side, expertly hidden by Willie.

I twirled into the living room and modeled this bewitching frock for my appreciative buddies. "What do you think? This one for Duke Ellington?"

I had never seen the Cotton Club, nor had the others. It was a long way Uptown. It wouldn't be hard to talk some of the stage crew into escorting us to the show.

"That dress was made for breaking hearts," May said.

"I certainly hope so."

Yet I wasn't quite sure whose heart I wanted to break.

Twenty-Four

A DEPARTMENT STORE TEAROOM: ONE of the safest places for a woman alone or women in pairs to relax at lunch without unwanted male attention. I stood and waited for a table.

This was another test for my theatrical wardrobe. I sojourned to Lord & Taylor on Wednesday to take lunch in the tearoom and see whether I felt comfortable in that elegant establishment, and whether it was comfortable with *me*.

This was the other suit from *Afternoon Tea with Nigel* and it was a pip, slightly conservative but with surprising details. It was an ocean-blue wool crepe, featuring a long tight skirt with kick pleats to the side. The hip-length belted jacket sported bright lilac lapels and trim, and the matching chapeau carried a wide lilac velvet band and bow on the right side. In the pocket, I wore a pale blue hankie trimmed in lilac lace. I secured it with a sparkling broach.

I spied several well-to-do shoppers appreciating my ensemble, and I smiled back at them. It's funny how people don't appreciate the magic of clothes, which can turn a shop girl into a debutante. Women want the clothes they see in the movies, but they don't know why.

"Miss de LaForet? Esmé de LaForet?"

I turned toward the voice and spotted the Palomino blonde who had been with Graydon at the theatre. She waved. I struggled to pull up her name. "Priscilla?"

"Yes! Call me Priss. Would you care to share a table?"

"That would be lovely." I'm always up for a little gossip.

Besides, Priscilla/the Palomino had complimented my play, even as she hugged Graydon's pocket that night. Today, she wore a brown-but-uninspired day suit of good quality. I joined her at her table, and a waiter appeared as if by magic with another table setting.

"Fancy running into you here," she said.

"I enjoy walking during my lunch hour, and I need to pick up a few things." I took off my lilac gloves and put them in my bag.

"You get a lunch hour as a playwright? Oh, I don't know what I thought, maybe that you're sitting up all night in a garret, a room full of books, communing with the writing gods. What a wonderful life."

"While that sounds delightful, I also work at the theatre during the day, reading scripts. I do need to make a living." Unlike the Priscillas of the world. I must have made a face.

"That must be difficult, when all you want to do is write." Priscilla really had that debutante drawl down.

"I love the theatre, actually. After all, you have to meet characters to write about them. And now is such an exciting time for me." I didn't mention the murders that seemed to be circling around everything.

"It must be, being the toast-ess of Broadway." She was working so hard on being clever. *Toast-ess?*

"I think my actors prefer the accolades. I'm merely the scribe."

Priscilla leaned in close over her menu. "Rupert said you're a debutante from the Midwest, but you're keen on making it here on your own."

"He's playing with you. I'm not. A debutante, that is. Nor am I from the Midwest."

"I so admire that." She winked at me. "I understand about the deb thing. You don't want people to know. People are so nosy. I admire your independence. We debs must stick together."

"I do want to make it on my own."

"Your secret is safe with me."

"Thank you." I didn't know what to make of Priscilla. I was through correcting her, it was too much work. She struck me as the kind of person who just wanted the next tidbit of gossip. "You mentioned you wanted to write?" I asked. "And what would you write?"

The waitress appeared tableside to take our orders. Mine was the Virginia ham sandwich and Priscilla chose the chicken salad. Two coffees.

"I do, I do, but who has the time? And I don't know that I have a good story, not yet. Maybe something set in Paris, but everyone's doing Paris, don't you know?"

"Not everyone," I managed to say, trying not to be jealous of her obviously moneyed background.

"Perhaps someday it will all come to me, and I shall be sure to ask for your advice." She leaned forward again. "I must say that suit is marvelous. Is it from Paris? I haven't seen anything quite like it."

'Not Paris. No. I have a wonderful tailor and we work on my wardrobe together." I smiled and she knew better than to ask more. "Your suit is quite elegant." Even though it was boring, it must have cost buckets of money.

"Last year's, I'm afraid. I'm here for a refresh." She sighed with the sheer anguish of that task. I changed the subject.

"You're friends with Graydon?" She looked blank. "Rupert?"

"Oh, yes. We adore each other. Rupert is such a delightful and naughty boy."

"Naughty?"

"Oh, you know."

My stomach sank. "You're a couple, then?"

"Not anymore, alas. Rupert will love you and leave you. I've always known that. But it's fun while it lasts. And we're terribly good friends." My sandwich arrived.

"Do you know the Snow Queen? I mean, Millicent?"

"Millie the Witch? Hmph. You really call her the Snow Queen? How droll. I shall take that up immediately."

"Oh, please don't, I didn't mean to say it."

She merely laughed. "Yes, we all know each other. Self-defense, you know. Millie's a vamp. She's wanted Rupert forever, under the misguided fantasy he'll walk her down the aisle someday. The funny thing is, I don't think she really even likes men."

"Just Rupert?"

"Just Rupert. He's more of a trophy for her, but being the Snow Queen, you know, perhaps she'll freeze him to death." Priscilla laughed at her own wit.

I'd lost my appetite.

How was I supposed to feel about Graydon now? Or Rupert? Or whatever his name was? Mr. Love 'Em and Leave 'Em. And why was he *Graydon* with me and *Rupert* with everyone else? Was it a detective thing? A mob thing? A playboy thing?

Lunch with Priscilla Summerdine was probably the cold shower I needed, but it wasn't as bracing as it should have been. My mind was jumbled with how being close to Chase made me feel, compared with Priscilla's cold-blooded analysis. Or she could be lying. I didn't know whether she wanted to throw me off my game, or stake her claim to him, as she had, with her hand in his pocket. At least I left her wondering where I got my great suit.

I retreated to the accessories department on the first floor. I needed a fresh pair of elbow-length evening gloves, but I had trouble making up my mind. Silver or white?

When I held them up to compare, I spotted Bianca Lombardi in one of the mirrors. As if my stomach wasn't upset enough. What was she doing here? She didn't strike me as a Lord & Taylor kind of shopper.

She seemed startled to see me too. It's always strange when you see someone out of context and it takes a few seconds to place them. I strolled over to where she was selecting hosiery. I didn't want her to see me ignoring her.

"What do you think? White or silver? The gloves." I lifted them for her opinion. "I'm Esmé de LaForet."

"I know you. From the funeral, from church. From the play." She turned her attention to the gloves. "Both look nice. I really don't know from gloves." Bianca's eye was healed, but now her lip was swollen and red. Someone was beating up on this woman.

"Are you all right? Does that hurt?"

"I'm fine." She touched the lip and grimaced. The wound was fresh.

"Was it Marco?"

"No!" She turned to face me. "No, Marco wouldn't do this. It's my pa. He doesn't like Marco, but it's my life, you know? I'm going to live my life, not his."

"I know."

This was only the third time I'd seen Bianca. Although she possessed a dark beauty, there was no sparkle about her. Instead, she had a disquieting intensity about her, something simmering beneath the surface. Maybe it was just the desire to get away from her home. I knew that feeling.

"Papa thinks he's going to stop me from being with the man I love."

Oh dear. There's a bad drama in the making. "Do you work around here?"

"Not really, I get away at lunchtime. I work as a secretary for my father. If I'm late, he can't say nothing. He runs a small business. Just family, and I can only take so much, you know? This place here? Lord & Taylor? It's like taking a trip somewhere, to a magical pretty world." She lifted her head and glanced at the stunning displays. "All the pretty clothes, all the pretty people."

I nodded in sympathy. I wondered if Marco Scavullo, the object of her desire, was nearby. I had no time for him or his false flattery. I silently wished her well and remembered he said Bianca was a nice girl—even as he was flirting with me.

"Don't you think it's dangerous to be around Marco?"

"Why should I? Marco and me, we got an understanding." I had a bad feeling about that understanding. I feared they understood different things.

"Did you know Guido Moretti?"

Bianca opened her eyes wide. "Yeah, everybody knew Ratty. That was real tragic. Funeral's tomorrow. Even my pa is going, for Mrs. Moretti. I'm buying new stockings. Show some respect, you know?"

A saleslady in a crisp brown dress with white linen collar and cuffs interrupted us. Bianca bought two pairs of stockings and a bright blue handkerchief.

I bade her goodbye and decided the evening gloves could wait for another day. In the noon-hour crowds I caught a glimpse of Marco sliding up behind Bianca, putting his hand around her waist. She covered it with her hand. They definitely had some kind of understanding.

"I heard a rumor you're writing a play about the syndicate." I lifted my head. Patrick Dentino was casually leaning against the granite wall outside the department store's front doors. He had a lazy smile, green eyes half-closed under his famous lashes.

"What? Of course not. Where did you hear something that insane?" He shrugged. "From Marco Scavullo, right?"

"And you're writing a part in it for him." Patrick laughed out loud.

I could feel the color rise in my face. "That's outrageous. First of all, it's a stupid idea. Second, I don't know anything about—that world. Third, I write my own plays and I don't write them simply because someone wants a part. Especially not Marco Scavullo."

Lashes Dentino found this amusing. His eyes crinkled and he tried to stop snickering.

"Your face is worth it all. I figured he was lying. Nobody believes him. He can hardly read a menu in Italian, let alone read a play in English."

"Could you set people straight about this, as a favor to me?"

"No need. No one takes him serious. And right now he's working too hard on being Mr. Romeo's little pet. Marco's his new *driver*."

Chills ran up and down my spine. "Isn't that dangerous? After what happened to his uncle? And Guido?"

"You want the job, you take the risks. Since booze turned legal, things are getting tight. Lots of fellas are looking for other ways to make a dollar."

"You really should think about that college thing, Patrick. New York is lousy with colleges."

I could see him thinking. "You ganging up on me with my ma?"

"If I knew your mother, I probably would. College is safer than what you're doing and you could do it part-time. Why are you here anyway?"

"Romeo's inside buying ties."

"Frank Romeo? Here in Lord & Taylor? Ties?"

"Blue ties for the funeral. Ratty's favorite color. Frank wants us all to be there in solidarity and he's buying all the ties. A nice blue. Subtle-like, he says." Patrick shifted position. "Hey, I might want to go see your play, but I hear it's sold out. All those seats—pretty good paycheck, right?"

"Maybe a once-in-a-lifetime thing. I still have to work for a living."

"Rafferty, I could tell you're Irish just from that." He remembered my middle name. "Us Micks are always afraid everything will be taken away at any moment. Hide your good fortune in the cookie jar or under the mattress."

"We had to hide it. From the English, you know." I was thinking of one English gent in particular, who clearly wanted something from me or my cookie jar. "Maybe I can get you a couple of comp tickets. Free. You could take your mother. You might want to write a play."

"Yeah? I like those Irish poets and playwrights, Synge, O'Casey, Yeats, all those guys."

Lashes? A reader? Who knew? I reached into my bag and pulled out a couple of comps I had in reserve. "Call and name the date."

"Really? I'm impressed, Rafferty. My ma would love it. And me, too." He looked around to make sure no one caught him talking about the theatre out here on the street.

I filled in my name on the tickets. I didn't have that many left, I needed to be careful with them.

"Contact the box office, they'll find seats for you. They may not be the best, but they'll be seats."

"Long as they're inside out of the rain. Hey, I got to get dressed up in a monkey suit for this? I seen lots of swells wearing that kind of getup."

He waved the tickets in his hand excitedly, and I wondered if he'd ever been inside a Broadway theatre before. The funny thing about Patrick Dentino was that he could speak properly, or he could speak gangster. He was bilingual.

"A suit will be fine."

"Good, I had to buy a nice one for the funeral. Hey, Rafferty, you ever need a bodyguard, you let me know. On the house."

I stood still, shocked at the suggestion. "You think I need a bodyguard?"

"You never know. All I'm saying is we got lots of desperadoes out there these days. Like stealing cars and holding them for ransom? Talk about lowbrow. Robbing people on the street in broad daylight? Women with money, looking like you do, that's another kind of target. You say the word, I'll make sure you're safe, that's all I'm sayin'."

"That's a favor I may call in someday. Thank you, Mr. Dentino."

Patrick spotted Handsome Frank Romeo, tipped his hat to me, and left.

Twenty-Five

66 YOU LOOK LIKE A THUNDERCLOUD, Elf."

That's the problem with having a face that constantly expresses all my feelings. Or at least most of them.

"I feel like one. A thundercloud, not an elf. And my name is Esmé."

Graydon had asked if I was free to meet him for a late afternoon coffee. I informed May I'd be reading scripts at home for the rest of the day, then detoured to the café where Graydon—or Rupert—waited, looking damnably handsome and cocky, blue eyes lighting up his face. Yet Priscilla's words replayed in my head. *Naughty Rupert.*

"Why, what's up? Should I be afraid?" He signaled for another cup of java.

"I ran into your beige friend Priscilla Summerdine at Lord & Taylor's tearoom, and she spilled a lot of tales about what a naughty boy you are, Rupert."

"Oh, dear. You ran into Priss-Pot." His face gave away nothing, though he sat straighter in his seat.

"Priss-Pot?" It suited her in a funny way.

"Pet name from the crowd. Priss is a delightful woman, but she adores idle gossip, indulges in it, trades in it. Hates the name Priss-Pot. Was it educational?"

"If it's true that with women, you love 'em and leave 'em, then I suppose it was educational. I heard you are fun while it lasts, but it never lasts. Such a freewheeling set of friends you have. They sound oh-so-modern, Graydon, but I'm afraid I could never be that modern."

"I thought you were more skeptical than to believe everything people say."

"I also heard that I'm a debutante from the Midwest and my clothes come from Paris."

"Did you disabuse her of these notions?"

"Miss Summerdine was going so fast, I couldn't keep up. I assumed she got that misguided information from you. Who am I to call you a liar? You liar."

Outside our window on the street, the usual crowds were rushing about. Women with shopping bags, men with briefcases, all wearing hats. In between lunch and dinner, the café was not full, but would be soon. The red checked tablecloths were unpretentious and the wooden counter scarred and old. It had a comfortable feel about it that I should have enjoyed. Yet I didn't.

"Misinformation from me?" He half smiled. "Perhaps I was going on first impressions. Debutante. Smashing wardrobe. Banking family, I suppose."

"Why the Midwest?"

"Strength of character."

"But not the West?" I was grateful for that. I'd been shaking off the dust and tumbleweeds ever since I arrived in New York.

"I didn't see you as a cowgirl."

"I never was one."

"Not with that fabulous theatrical wardrobe. By the way, another smashing suit. Give Willie my compliments. You fill it out wonderfully."

"Flattery cannot get you out of this one. I know nothing about you. Do your women call you Rupert? Or just the rich, silly ones? And what would Priss-Pot say if she knew the truth about me?" He looked blank.

"Something silly, no doubt. Esmé, someday I'll tell you a tale." He leaned back and considered me.

"Why not now?"

"Today is not the day."

"Why do you want me? Just to put another notch on your bedpost?"

"My, my. Is that how Midwest debutantes talk?" He lifted his coffee cup to me.

"No. It's how we talk out West. The Snow Queen is obsessed with you as well."

"Wounded pride. What about you and Pendleton?"

"Pals."

"He's more than just your friend. Esmé Elf, what can I do to prove I'm honorable? At least where you are concerned."

I didn't know. My coffee sat untouched. I could barely swallow. However, I was curious about other things. Although I was irritated, I told Graydon the rest of what I learned at the elegant department store. I wouldn't be accused of hiding anything.

"By the way, Frank Romeo and his cronies were buying ties today, for him and his underlings to wear to Guido 'Ratty' Moretti's funeral tomorrow. Lord & Taylor was very crowded."

Now I had his attention. "You saw him?"

"Got a glimpse of him later. Camel hair coat and all. Bianca Lombardi was there, with a bruised lip. Also Marco Scavullo, who apparently is now Romeo's driver, and Lashes, aka Patrick Dentino. And possibly Bones, but he's so thin, I may have missed him."

"You've been busy." Graydon did not look happy.

"Merely shopping. As were they. I've never before thought about where gangsters shop for their ties. I would have imagined a store that specializes in pinstripes, gaudy ties, snappy fedoras, shoulder holsters."

He thumped his fingers on his cup. "The whole crowd at Lord & Taylor? That would be something to see. Thank you for telling me. Anything else?"

"I don't know if this will amuse you or not. I am not amused. Patrick—Lashes—said there were rumors that I am writing a play about the mob. It's garbage, of course." I shuddered as if to rid myself of the very thought.

Graydon sat up straighter. "Who started the rumor?"

"The man who thinks I should write a part for him. Lots of people say they want parts in plays, but Marco Scavullo could hardly sit through a show. He couldn't even deliver a line, plus he'd show the audience how bored he was."

"You shouldn't be associated with any of them in any way." I could see Chase thinking, in that overprotective manner he had.

"If I had it to do all over again. I would have left the darn watch on the counter. And we would never have met."

"Don't be so sure about that, Elf. I would have noticed the Chicago debutante in the Parisian wardrobe. That night at Peacocks', for instance."

I was supposed to be flattered, but I'm not sure I was. "I don't want to associate with Frank Romeo's crowd. Especially after Patrick—"

"After Patrick what?"

"After he said if I needed a bodyguard, I could call on him. I gave him comp tickets for him and his mother to see the show. For the information, and for trying to squash Marco's rumor. Pat's half Irish and not really a full member of that crowd. He's been thinking of going to—wait for it—*college*."

"I'm always surprised when any of those goons can read and write. Why does Lashes think you need a bodyguard?"

"Not sure. Wait a minute, you didn't hire him, did you? To watch me?"

"No, and I never would. Just stay away from him, Esmé. From all of them. Please."

"Are you going to Ratty's funeral?"

"As I said, I'm staying out of this."

I wondered if Scavullo's planned exit from the mob, and his subsequent murder, was part of some bigger plan of Frank Romeo's.

"Any closer to catching Scavullo's killer?"

"I didn't sign up for catching killers, and when it comes to the Mafia, they tend to clean up their own. Even the cops don't want to get in the middle of that, and Juliette is afraid of anyone else getting hurt."

"She feels guilty, doesn't she?" That was always the woman's part, taking on blame where none existed. He lifted his cup and signaled for more.

"Juliette wanted Dante out of the bootlegging business, since well before the end of Prohibition. She especially wants to keep her boys out of the Life."

"And her nephew? Marco?"

"I don't have a read on him. Far as I can tell, he thinks it's a glamorous life."

I shivered, remembering the day Scavullo was killed, the sound of the gunshots still ringing in my memory.

"Are you off the case, then?"

"Almost. Mrs. Scavullo's worried that Dante left some money for her, but she doesn't know where. She claims he'd never leave her unprotected."

"And he didn't tell you?"

"He was reluctant to tell me more until he was safely out of the organization."

"Did he hate Frank Romeo? He would, wouldn't he?"

"I'm sure he did, but he never mentioned it. He was looking to the future, retiring with his family."

"Did he say where?" I asked.

"No, but I assumed New York somewhere. Maybe Long Island. Maybe New Jersey. No place very far away."

"Has Juliette said anything else about the pocket watch?"

"No."

Even after I ferreted out Mr. Williams, the watchmaker, I still didn't know what those numbers etched into the pocket watch might mean. The numbers and the waves had obviously meant *something* to the dead man. After all,

Scavullo ordered the etching, and he picked it up right before he was murdered. However, I wasn't about to bring this up to Graydon. Because— Well, he's the hotshot detective, let him figure it out on his own. And my clue might be just a red herring.

Besides, he might accuse me of being too *dramatic*.

I don't know where people get the idea I'm always being dramatic. Much more often, I am merely a writer. A playwright, or a reporter. I can't help it if the situations around me are dramatic.

TWENTY-SIX

H E LOOKED PARTICULARLY CHEEKY IN his tweeds, not like a movie private detective in a trench coat, skulking behind doors and down shadowy hallways. More like a roguish English gentleman out and about. I was finding him way too attractive. Priss-Pot's words came back to me again: *Naughty Rupert.*

"Graydon, do you have an office, or someone who works for you, schedules your days, and files your paperwork? Or do you dwell in a dark alley somewhere? With the trolls?"

"You still don't believe I am who I say I am, Elf?"

"The jury is out. You pop up at the oddest moments."

"While you disappear at a moment's notice."

"I am always where I say I'm going to be," I said.

"I doubt that very much. Well, come along then."

He took my hand, we left the café, and he hailed a cab.

"Where are we going?"

"To my office."

"An actual office?" Not a dark alley?

"An actual office."

How could I turn that offer down? Curiosity and the cat. And all that.

The taxi took us to a building in Midtown. It was tall yet anonymous-looking, new and shiny, the kind of place where you might find an accountant or a dentist. Chase's office was on the second floor.

"You must understand, Esmé, you're the first—lady friend to whom I've ever shown this place."

"I'm probably the only one who asked about it."

He tipped his hat at me. "That may be. I prefer to keep business and pleasure separate."

"And I'm pleasure?"

"I hope you will be."

"You never stop, do you?" I grinned back at him. "Keep hoping."

We walked up two stories to his office, though we could also have taken the elevator.

"The second floor?" I asked. "Why not the penthouse?"

"I don't like to give people too much time to change their minds. It takes some courage for people to see an investigator, no matter what the subject. If they have to wait for the thirtieth floor, it's much easier for them to flee."

"What kind of jobs do you take, other than the occasional mob extraction?"

"Something where there's a business or financial aspect. Embezzling is one of my specialties, also fraud, malfeasance. And I take care of a bit of my family's business, quietly."

"Follow the money. Why go to you and not the police?"

"Businesses come to me because they don't want word to get out. If everyone knows a bank has been embezzled, their customers lose faith, they go somewhere else. By finding the money leak, I prevent further loss of funds and they retain their customers."

"Then how did you get tangled up with the mob?"

"Long story. Scavullo heard about my services. He wanted a legal way out. We were going to talk personal finances later."

We turned down the hall to our destination. The sign on the office door said CHASE INQUIRIES. It sounded very English to me.

Graydon opened the door and we ambled into a small reception room. I don't know what I expected, perhaps something threadbare and down at the heels, but it was immaculate. Though not expensive, the furnishings were neat and modern. There was a small washroom and a door leading to an office. A pot of coffee was brewing behind a black-and-gold Chinese screen.

A woman who sat behind the desk stood up. "Mr. Chase, I wasn't expecting you." I noted that her wooden desk was tidy, with a phone and appointment book and all the usual tools. A typewriter stood on a small table where she could wheel it close to her when needed. She had a padded chair in good repair. "Coffee or tea, Miss?"

"Coffee, please," I said. "Black is fine, cream if you have it." All that caffeine would probably make me jumpy. At the moment, I was in a state of amazement.

"Make it two, Mrs. Carter." he added.

This didn't look a thing like our ramshackle offices at the theatre, which on any given day could be knee-deep in playscripts or heaped with props and costumes. And our scarred wooden desks with initials carved into them said no one was afraid to put their feet up on the furniture. We had posters of previous shows tacked to the walls, while this space featured a tasteful English landscape in oil.

"Mrs. Carter, this is Esmé de LaForet, the renowned playwright." To me, he said, "Mrs. Carter is indispensable. She knows where all the bodies are buried, so to speak."

"How do you do, Miss de LaForet?" She spoke like she was from somewhere outside the city. Well-schooled. Perhaps Connecticut.

I shook her hand. "Nice to meet you, Mrs. Carter."

"Esmé is not a client," Graydon said, implying we were friends.

Mrs. Carter glanced at him and smiled slightly. "I didn't think so."

We studied each other. Mrs. Carter was middle-aged, neither a raving beauty nor unattractive. Her brown hair was cut into a trim bob. Her dark purple dress was subtle yet flattering. She seemed friendly under her air of starchiness.

"Esmé thinks I'm a gigolo. I had to prove her wrong," he offered. Mrs. Carter seemed slightly startled.

"That's true. I used to be a reporter. I'm fond of facts. Not gigolos."

Apparently not knowing what to say, she turned to Graydon. "I've put some folders on your desk, Mr. Chase." She cranked a fresh sheet of paper into her typewriter.

"Thank you. Mrs. Carter also keeps track of all the receipts and payments." Graydon reached for his office door and gestured me inside.

Her no-nonsense approach was soothing. I don't know why I was so relieved to find his office was not fictitious and he had a real secretary. While Mrs. Carter deserved praise for her work, it wasn't for her physically decorative properties. Graydon Chase was able to keep his mind on his business around her.

"In addition to Mrs. Carter, I hire other—associates from time to time." Graydon broke into my thoughts.

"Like the cops at the schoolhouse, when Scavullo was dispatched?"

"Exactly so. They are from a wide variety of backgrounds." I gathered he liked people from different places in society. One point in his favor.

His polished mahogany desk was neat, with pad and calendar and a leather case for pens. All placed just so. As Mrs. Carter had said, there were folders on his desk. Four oil paintings graced his walls, soothing hunt country landscapes. Two for Graydon's view and two more for clients. His comfy-looking swivel armchair was padded in dark brown leather, and his window offered a view of the street below. Two smaller green leather chairs were for visitors, and the walls were a pale green.

"Tell me about Mrs. Carter," I said.

"Lydia Carter is extremely competent. She has two nearly grown children, and a husband who disappeared one day."

"What happened to him?"

"A blond showgirl happened."

"Did you find him?"

"Mrs. Carter wasn't interested in finding him when she came to me. She wanted a job."

"Very sensible," I said.

"That's what I thought. She also types seventy-five words a minute with zero errors."

"I like her."

"Good. She likes you too."

"How can you tell?"

"I simply can," he said.

In retrospect, this impromptu visit felt more intimate than it should, but I am an optimistic sort. "You're a very organized worker," I observed.

"Aren't you?"

"I wouldn't say so and neither would Amelia." She would laugh at the very thought. "When I'm writing, I have notes scattered everywhere. I keep a notebook and pen in my purse, but I've been known to jot down ideas on cocktail napkins, play programs, envelopes, and the back of my hand."

He stared at me, perfectly organized folders with impeccably typed papers frozen in his hands.

"How do you keep it all straight?"

"Who knows? I generally know where I put my notes. And Amelia follows behind me and organizes things, my closet, my cupboards, and my writing. I often write in the middle of the night, so there are multiple papers on my nightstand. Or the floor. Or the fire escape. I'd like to have a more sensible system, but it might make me nervous. Does that scare you off?"

"I'd have to check your nightstand. In the nighttime, of course." He lifted an eyebrow.

"Fantasies, Mr. Chase."

"Look around, Esmé. Do you believe me now?"

"That you're a private detective? This place would be a very expensive ruse just to convince me."

"It would be worth it. Though I fear I may have shocked Mrs. Carter. You're the only female friend I've brought here." He reached for my hand and the familiar electric shock ran through me. I pulled back, but he held on. "Esmé. Elf. You affect me in ways that no other woman has."

I may have lifted my own eyebrow in doubt. He kissed me, deeply, intimately. During office hours. It was a long moment before we broke apart. I had to catch my breath.

"I never do this sort of thing in the office," he said. He reached for a handkerchief to wipe lipstick stains from his face.

I checked my face in my compact, wiped away a smudge and carefully reapplied the color on my lips, taking care to blot them several times. I could hear Mrs. Carter's fingers clacking away on the typewriter. Graydon shuffled through his folders while I picked up a magazine. He signed a few pages. We took a beat, as we say in the theatre.

"Alas, my dear Elf, I have an appointment," he said at last. I caught my breath again.

"I'll leave you to it then. I've got scripts to read, notes to write. Thank you for the tour."

He escorted me out, dropping his papers with Mrs. Carter. It was reassuring to know he really was some kind of private investigator. That didn't mean he couldn't also be a playboy. I pictured Dante Scavullo in that office, explaining to Chase his desire to find a way to exit the mob. It was an unusual request that required finesse. Professional finesse. And luck.

Graydon seemed to make up his mind about something and took my hand again, and damned if I didn't feel that same lurch in my stomach.

"Elf, Esmé, I'd like to ask you out on a date. Are you free tomorrow?"

"Thursday? Are you talking about a real date, not simply running into you at various unexpected times and places?"

"Exactly so. Is there any place in particular you'd like to go?"

Many days I'd passed a particular place while wandering through Central Park. That brand-new restaurant, Tavern on the Green. What a pretty picture it made and how I longed to see it from the inside out. I suggested lunch there.

"Lunch? Why not dinner?"

"Lunch is always safer with a known rake. Like you. And I should probably pop into the theatre tomorrow night to see how the show is holding up."

"Very well. Lunch, and we'll see what develops after."

He looked smug, as if he believed he could change my mind.

❧

That evening when I called crime reporter Reggie Pendleton he assured me he would be watching Guido Moretti's funeral from a safe distance. And taking notes.

"Thanks for tipping me to the tie color, Esmé. Wouldn't do for me to accidentally wear the same color as Romeo's boys."

"You'll be writing something about the funeral?"

"Won't amount to a lot of column inches, unless a fight breaks out or someone throws herself on the casket, but it'll bookend Ratty's short life."

If there was a connection between Ratty Moretti's death and Scavullo's, I was pretty sure that Reggie would discover it and bring it up. However, it seemed Scavullo's death had disappeared from the press. Just another Mafia murder. And the thousand-dollar bootlegger gunned down in the street hadn't been favored with any more press coverage either. The level of death and violence in the mob was becoming ho-hum.

Guido's unfortunate face, nickname, and youth made him a more interesting subject to Reggie than middle-aged Dante Scavullo. Then again, Reggie hadn't been hiding in a school supply room when the shooting broke out and Scavullo died. It was hard to beat that first-person connection.

"Be nice to Guido's family," I said.

"Always. And my editor also mentioned that. He liked the last story. Say, aren't we due for coffee?"

"Depends on who's paying," I said.

"You're such a stickler for details, Miss de LaForet. I'll check my calendar."

We made a tentative coffee date for the weekend. In the interim, I had a pile of scripts to read and rate.

The theatre was still adjusting to actors ill with the flu. I took advantage of the peace and quiet and knocked out a pile of scripts the next morning. One of them made the "maybe" pile. Others went in the growing reject pile. I informed May I planned to knock off early and work at home. I neglected to mention I had a hot date.

May was not fazed by my assertion that I would be working at home later, though she sniffed that I was awfully well-dressed for just a half-day of work.

"I might have lunch plans," I admitted.

"I hope so. I'd assume you were an idiot if you hadn't. The outfit is splendid. Does the lunch plan have an English accent?"

I groaned loudly for her benefit and flounced out as if I were a leading lady. I heard her laughing as I left.

TWENTY-SEVEN

T HE SUN WAS HIGH IN the sky. It was about the time of Ratty Moretti's final funeral rites at Calvary Cemetery, and the final clumps of dirt thrown over his coffin. I wouldn't be there. I wouldn't see anyone from the Frank Romeo mob today.

I pushed those thoughts away and left for my lunch date at Tavern on the Green. The leaves were in their full kaleidoscope glory, creating a colorful mosaic against the blazing blue sky. The peppery aroma of autumn and woodsmoke in the air was intoxicating and I wanted to remember everything the way it was in those moments.

Artists with their easels were busy with brushstrokes, capturing the trees and passersby. I wandered over sidewalks flanked by rows of painters, some wearing smocks and berets to entertain the tourists or simply to add local color. Perhaps they were inspired by the proximity of the grand and glorious Metropolitan Museum of Art. As I glanced at their work, they seemed to have varying degrees of talent, but all appeared to be deep in the clutches of creativity.

How Graydon had managed to wrangle a reservation at the new restaurant, I didn't know, but he was resourceful. I was probably as interested in what I was wearing as the event itself, and in seeing who lunched with whom. This would be our first official date.

Romance generally has not worked out for me, whether I listen to my brain, my heart, or my body. All three are rebellious, and none listen to reason. I had fantasies in my head about Graydon Chase, but also trepidation. Priss-Pot Summerdine had warned me against him and at least some of what she said had to be true.

For my lunch date with Chase, I chose a moss-green knit sweater and skirt. The contrasting navy blue belt matched the trim on the sleeves, which coordinated with my hat and gloves. I also wore a frothy light green lace collar with ruffles that floated down the neckline. I felt very smart, and because the day was bright and temperate but could turn colder, I carried a warm navy wool jacket over my arm.

I was glad to be out of the office today.

More of the staff were being felled by that strange flu, one by one, as if they were dominoes. A few were returning to work, pale but brave. Our leading lady was ready to take the reins back from her understudy and tread the boards once more.

Luckily, no one had died from their illness, but as mine was a dramatic workplace, everyone had escaped the grim reaper by *the merest thread.* No one had ever been so sick and so afraid of leaving this earthly plane.

The virus affecting the players at the Irv was quick and vicious, lasting for up to two days. Newspapers reported that a significant number of people had died, though whether the deaths were from the virus or some other flu hadn't been determined. I wondered if it would strike me too, and I brushed the thought aside. I had no time for illness.

I waited for Graydon outside the restaurant. I spotted his long legs across a green swath of grass, moving slower than usual. Dressed quite nattily in a dark suit with a subdued tie in shades of green, he smiled when he saw me and my heart lurched, if such a thing was possible. Or maybe there were butterflies dancing a tango inside my stomach. I told myself to be sensible and I suspected I wouldn't be able to eat all my meal.

It turns out my personal warning was unnecessary. There was to be no lunch that day.

I took hold of Graydon's outstretched hands—and had to remove my gloves, because they were so hot. He was flushed and we moved into the shade. I reached up and touched his forehead.

"My God, Graydon, you're burning up."

"I'm fine." His stiff British upper lip was firmly in place. "Just a touch of sun."

"I have to get you home."

"Not necessary, I merely need to sit down." He was breathing hard.

"Give me your address. We'll catch a cab."

"It's nothing. Just a slight bug, Esmé." He was the opposite of all those overdramatic actors. Both were equally annoying.

"A slight bug could kill you."

The memory of people dying from the flu, including my one-time fiancé, and my parents, would haunt me for life. I was not going to see one more person succumb to it. Perhaps I was turning into a hypochondriac by proxy, but I was suddenly afraid for Graydon. He seemed reluctant to tell me where he lived.

But I didn't care if he lived in a hovel. In fact, I might have preferred it.

It suddenly occurred to me that he might be married and had never bothered to mention it. Why else would he refuse to tell me? Had I read too many bad plays? Still, I could hardly leave him in this shape. Sweat beaded on his forehead. I pulled his immaculate handkerchief out of his pocket and wiped his face.

He finally murmured an address on the Upper East Side. Breathing hard, hot as a stove, he leaned upon my shoulder. I insisted that he loosen his tie and take the jacket off, no matter how unseemly. He did so reluctantly. His matching vest looked equally formal, over a white

Arrow shirt. Still formal, still impeccable, still burning up with fever.

The address wasn't far, yet it felt like an epic journey simply to reach the street to hail a taxi. Luckily, the cabbie just thought Graydon was drunk and not contagious. I assured him I would pay the tab.

Even though I had seen his office, I still thought Graydon Chase must be one step away from being a gigolo or living on a stoop somewhere. Was I supposed to be prepared for a many-stories-high luxury building? With a doorman?

"This is it, lady," the cabbie announced.

"This?" It couldn't be.

"Yes," Graydon managed to utter. "Home sweet home."

"You will pay me back, Graydon."

I handed money to the cabbie. The building doorman recognized Graydon and helped pull him from the car.

"He's not inebriated," I said to the man. "He's ill, he has a fever."

"Don't you worry, Miss, we'll take care of him." The doorman, who gave his name as Thompson, supported Graydon with his shoulder. "Mr. Chaseborn, come inside. I'll call Robbins."

Chaseborn? Robbins? I had no idea what was going on. But I have learned that when you can't improvise, stay silent and let others do the talking. Graydon 's face was slick with sweat. I wiped it off again.

"Thompson, meet Miss de LaForet," he managed to say, remembering his manners. "The eminent playwright." That was stretching it a bit. Or maybe it was sarcasm.

"Pleased to meet you, Miss."

"And you."

Thompson never batted an eye. I assumed it was because I was exceedingly well dressed for lunch. Thank goodness, this costume was meant to convey an upper-class socialite with money. Dramatically.

     Ellen Byerrum

We were helped through the marble lobby to the handsome black-and-gold Art Deco elevator. When the doors opened, a tall distinguished-looking man in a dark suit met us. He introduced himself in another set of dulcet British tones.

"I'm Robbins, Mr. Chaseborn's valet. Allow me to assist you, Miss."

TWENTY–EIGHT

WHY WAS I STILL STANDING? I felt like falling through the floor. *Valet?* All the facts, all my assumptions, all the rules had just changed.

"Esmé de LaForet," I said. "I'm—" At a loss for words, apparently. What was I? His date? His friend? I didn't know any *Chaseborn.*

"The noted playwright, Miss de LaForet?" Robbins filled in as he helped Graydon into the elevator.

"Yes, the playwright." Noted? Not a terribly bright one at the moment, as I had just found out the man I had been seeing was someone else. "I only know a Graydon Chase. I don't know a Rupert Chaseborn."

"Ah, yes. I see." Robbins was a wonder of understatement.

I didn't see. The elevator whirred and delivered us to the highest floor. To the penthouse.

"Afraid I haven't yet been completely forthcoming with Esmé," Graydon or whoever-he-was uttered.

Yet? Was he planning to tell me? And who was this Chaseborn? I had nothing but questions, but it wasn't the time to utter them.

Robbins handled him expertly, leading us to a penthouse apartment with a large foyer with yet another marble floor of polished Art Deco black-and-white diamonds. There were silver mirrors, white and pale blue furniture, and deep colorful rugs. From the windows you could see tall buildings and a long swath of emerald grass in the park, and I was only in the living room.

I turned on the man I knew as Graydon. "Are you married?" I practically fell down anticipating the worst. "If you are, I will leave immediately."

"God, no. It's the truth, Elf." He was still sweating and shaky and he needed to get out of his heavy wool suit.

I glared at Robbins, demanding the truth with my expression. "No, Miss de LaForet, Mr. Rupert is not married, nor has he ever been, to my certain knowledge." The valet was taller than his employer, dark haired, as distinguished as a marble monument, and just as straight. Yet he knew I was a playwright. A playwright of note. I gave him points for that.

"We have to get him to bed," I said.

"Yes, Miss de LaForet. Immediately. Is it the virus?" Robbins's face expressed some polite distress, while at the same time, remaining very starched.

"I think so. Please call me Esmé."

I followed them to the bedroom. I didn't care how it looked, I wasn't going to let anyone else die on me, even if it was this lying fool. I would deal with him later, after he lived. Then I would make his life miserable.

"Do you have a thermometer and ice?" I asked.

Robbins nodded. "I'll bring them directly, Miss. After I tend to Mr. Chaseborn's needs."

"And a bourbon," Rupert Chaseborn uttered weakly.

"Can the comedy, *Rupert*," I said, then I turned toward the tall valet. "Ginger ale, if you have it. No alcohol. And a basin of water and towels, please."

I couldn't believe I was barking orders to this complete stranger. Who nominated me the director of this little farce?

"Better do as she says, Robbins." He collapsed on the bed, laboring to breathe. "She sounds serious."

The valet nodded to me and addressed Graydon. "You look to be in a bad way, if I may say so, sir."

"This damn virus, apparently."

Good God, were they always this formal with each other? I wanted to scream.

"Apparently, sir. You seemed fine this morning."

"It's a swift and vicious virus," I said. "It's sweeping through the theatre community. I haven't had it." I wanted to make sure no one was blaming me.

Robbins didn't seem to think it was odd when I followed them into the master bedroom. His impeccable training, no doubt. I suppose I shouldn't have noticed, but I could feel the money that went into this room's fine furnishings. It oozed from the very woodwork.

I recognized the Aubusson rug, the large bed and luxurious silver-blue headboard with matching cover and linens. The walls were an exquisite pale blue. A pair of black chinoiserie dressers were topped with mirrors and similar side tables sat on either side of the bed. *Ka-ching.* Hear that cash register ring.

I turned my back while Robbins helped Graydon out of his clothes and into a pair of silk pajamas. Graydon was looking rather green, and it wasn't long before he sprinted to the bathroom and vomited. Eventually, he stumbled back and fell half across the bed. He was dizzy and I couldn't lift him. The reliable Robbins helped him back onto the mattress and straightened him out.

"Robbins, do you have an apron or something I could wear over my dress?"

I was wary of having "the patient" get sick all over my clothes and yet didn't feel quite right about asking the valet to do my bidding.

Chaseborn lifted a hand and waved. "Please accommodate Miss de LaForet with whatever she wants, Robbins." He breathed huskily and the valet retreated.

I removed my lace scarf to protect it and rolled up my sleeves, happy that this quality knit resisted wrinkles. Robbins efficiently provided ice, tepid water, and towels, and a white apron that practically swallowed me up.

Graydon lay against a mound of pillows as his breathing settled down. He was as hot as a brick left out in the sun. I filled an ice bag and settled it at the back of his neck. He sighed with relief.

I decreed that he must drink cool liquids, and Robbins returned promptly with a tall glass of iced ginger ale. Robbins also informed me he had telephoned the restaurant and canceled our reservation.

I lifted the glass of ginger ale to Graydon's lips and he drank. I wet a towel and unbuttoned his pajama top.

"My dear, are you making advances?"

"Shut up, you two-faced, double-named, prevaricating sidewinder."

His eyes opened wider for a moment. "That's hardly the thing to say to a sick man. You might kill me."

"Shall I finish the job now, or come back later?"

He grabbed for my hand. "No, please, Elf. Don't go."

I slipped the thermometer into his mouth so he couldn't talk, took the wet towel, and started wiping down his chest to cool him. I helped Robbins remove his pajama top to continue with his arms. I tried not to get too personal or gaze too long at his muscled chest, with its mat of brown curls.

The heat from his fevered limbs transferred to the wet towels, which I re-dampened and applied again and again. His temperature was well over a hundred degrees and rising. I encouraged him to drink more liquids and stay hydrated. Before long, the oversized apron was drenched and my arms were tired.

He said he felt better for a moment, then the chills started and his teeth chattered.

"I feel bloody awful, Elf. I'm cold. Hold me."

I covered him up with his blankets, and when he didn't stop shaking, I held on to him, half on the bed, half off, willing his shakes to stop. That peculiar pull between us was still there, damn it.

Robbins entered the room with more supplies and caught me in this terribly compromising position. I held on to the sick man until the chills passed.

"Robbins—" I began.

"Not to worry, Miss Esmé. The chills, no doubt."

Still, I needed to explain. "I'm here only because Mr. Chaseborn was suddenly taken ill. That's how it is with this virus. I'll be gone as soon as he's out of the woods."

"Then I plan to be sick for a long time," he said weakly. "And the Elf Queen knows I prefer being called Graydon."

Robbins lifted an imperious eyebrow at him. "Indeed, sir."

"My name is not Elf, you understand."

"Robbins knows everything," Graydon murmured.

If this man died, I felt as if I would never find anyone to love me, not that he was necessarily the one. Definitely *not* the one. This was too hard. Even though my feelings were in an uproar, and I despised him for lying to me, Graydon Chase needed to live, for my soul's sake. It was very selfish of me.

Although I had been under the impression he had feelings for me, I had no illusions that he loved me. He had proved it by his enormous lie. He proved he had no respect for me. It was as if I could hear my dead mother leaning over my shoulder whispering in my ear. *The lad is a Brit then, is he not? Well, then he's not our kind, dear.* I knew all about the Brits, and my French father wasn't fond of them either.

I dipped the cloth in the water and cooled down Chase's forehead again, perhaps a little roughly. Graydon was delusional, spouting nonsense about elves and magic and elves popping out of closets. No one would believe him. Hours passed. Graydon was better after he slept, and then he was worse. He was sick often. I held the basin for him and lifted glass after glass of water to his lips, and then ginger ale.

This was not quite the Tavern on the Green dream date I had envisioned.

Finally, I asked Robbins if he had a phone number for a doctor. It was obvious the man in the bed could afford one.

"It's just a precaution. I don't think he belongs in the hospital, because that's where they keep sick people who infect everyone else. But I want to rule out anything worse," I said.

"I'll call Mr. Rupert's regular physician." The valet collected empty glasses and soiled towels and left the room.

Mr. Rupert. I tumbled his name over and over in my head, *Rupert Graydon Chaseborn*, and I wondered where I'd heard or read it. It finally clicked.

Oh hell. Though I didn't know any Chaseborns, I realized I was aware of *this* man's reputation, the way a reporter stuffs random clippings in a mental filing cabinet. One 'Rupert Chaseborn' was a notorious and wealthy playboy whose name was bantered about in the society pages, which I seldom read. Nina must have mentioned him, fragments that sailed in one ear and out the other, but now I was putting the pieces together.

His name had been linked with a new and lovely upperclass lass every month or so, appearing at this opening or that, a gallery, the opera, my play that he attended with Priss-Pot Summerdine. Another one of those gossip column names. He proved a slippery target at best for the women who chased Chaseborn.

The Cinderella tale has never appealed to me, the idea of chasing after some rich Prince Charming who would rescue me from my sad, impoverished life. I wanted an equal, not some man who thought he was better than anyone else. Or who could buy half the real estate in Manhattan. Many of the women who chased him, including the Snow Queen and Priss-Pot Summerdine, probably had fortunes of their own, but they ran after the Chaseborn money and prestige for the thrill of it.

At the same time, people on street corners were eating beans out of tin cans.

And worse, in my opinion, Chaseborn must be a millionaire! He was obviously filthy rich. In charge of some family money or some corporation or other, which apparently left him scads of time to pursue his hobbies, such as womanizing and "detecting."

I couldn't very well hold the Great Depression against Chaseborn, but I could blame him for not revealing who he was. Was pursuing me some kind of game? Slumming with someone from the hoi polloi? A mere struggling writer? How he must have sneered at me. And what was this private investigation scam he was pulling? How dare he lie to me! How dare he play with me! Had he told people how we met? I could die of humiliation.

So where did that leave my friend Reggie, other than, at the moment, writing his article about today's mob funeral for Guido Moretti? I knew Reginald Pendleton III was from a wealthy and privileged background, but he worked hard to separate himself from it. Except for filching the occasional pricey bottle of booze from his parents, he seemed to live within his means on his newspaper pay. I respected Reggie for that.

To my friends, I was an heiress by the slimmest definition, simply because my parents had died and I inherited a small amount of money and property. We laughed about it. To Chaseborn, I must have looked like a ragamuffin, a would-be socialite. Or had he really thought I was a debutante? He seemed to be impressed by my wardrobe, yet now I wish I hadn't told him how I came to have it, as brilliant a feat as that was. My silent rage was interrupted by the doctor.

"Ah, yes, Miss. We'll take care of him now."

The sawbones was called Dr. Zydeco, who seemed to have a practice in a building down the street. He arrived promptly. An affable man with a prosperous-looking tummy and a pocketful of cigars, Dr. Zydeco had apparently attended Chaseborn in the past for minor ailments. This physician seemed friendlier and kinder than I thought Graydon merited, but he was efficient. He pronounced the patient extremely ill, but agreed it was better for him to stay in his apartment, where he could receive the best care that money could buy.

To my great relief, Dr. Zydeco also came up with the name of a nurse who could come over that very evening and stay all night. Cost obviously being no object.

As the day wore on and the patient showed no improvement, I was more and more determined he wouldn't die on me. I wanted Rupert Chaseborn to live long enough for me to read him the riot act, and then storm out of his life and out his front door forever.

Dramatically, with a lot of fire and passion. And the most devastatingly perfect curtain line. Which I was still working on.

TWENTY–NINE

NURSE JESSE O'BANYON ARRIVED A few minutes short of 8 p.m. She was crisp of manner and starched of uniform and her white cap featured two slim horizonal black ribbons. She was professional and reassuring. The starch in her spine relaxed over the course of the evening, and we became acquainted and then comfortable with each other.

Jesse had an open friendly face. Not one that could be termed pretty, but she was vibrant and attractive in her own way. I liked her immediately, though I was predisposed to liking whoever came through the door to relieve me of my burden. She complimented me on how I'd taken care of her patient so far.

"You got gumption and stamina. You've been tending him all day?"

"Since noon." I was beginning to feel it.

"Well, take a load off, get yourself some coffee if it's available. You've done good. But you need a rest, unless you want to come down with this menace yourself."

"Have you treated a lot of these cases?" I asked.

"Enough. Don't worry, kid." She nodded toward Rupert Graydon. "He'll be here when you catch a second wind."

Granted her official permission, I realized I must have looked as exhausted as I felt. I remembered I hadn't had my promised lunch at the bright new Tavern on the Green. I'd spent all my energy getting liquid down Chaseborn's throat. I staggered into the hall outside his bedroom to stretch my legs. Rubbing the back of my neck, I proceeded to the dining room where a silver service with coffee and cream and sugar was set up on a massive buffet. Robbins poured me a cup, although clearly, I could have done it myself. His brew was rich and I drank it quickly.

"Will you be leaving, Miss— Miss—" He clearly wanted to call me "Miss de LaForet," which was far too formal for me.

"Miss Esmé," I said. It seemed like a good compromise. The patient was asleep for the moment, but he still looked ghastly. "And not until he's out of danger. With Nurse O'Banyon here, my reputation should survive."

I was fortunate that theatre people, like reporters, were known for working all kinds of crazy hours. My neighbors were used to it. There were times I'd worked at the Irv all night and staggered home in the early hours of dawn. They never accused me of illicit behavior. Probably they didn't care.

"Don't leave, Elf," Graydon spoke up from the bedroom. I peeked in.

"I thought you were asleep."

"Off and on." He closed his eyes, and Nurse Jesse slipped the thermometer in his mouth yet again. She urged him to sip "a fortifying drink," which was mostly chicken broth. He turned his head away, weary of this little game. I'd been anxiously looking for that ashy, almost-blue color I'd seen on people who were ready to die. So far, Graydon remained eerily pale, with a somewhat-greenish cast.

"He appreciates your care, Miss, and your being here." Robbins sounded less imperious than before.

"You see, Robbins, I've lost people to the flu— My mother, my father, and my late fiancé. I'm starting to feel cursed."

"Do you believe in curses, Miss?"

"Not generally." I comforted myself with the thought that Chaseborn's kind rarely succumbed to life's inconveniences and problems. "I didn't know who he was."

"Does that matter? He holds you in high esteem, Miss. And now that you know he is Rupert Chaseborn? Is he still your friend?"

"My friend was a phantom. Chaseborn is definitely not my friend. And neither is Graydon Chase."

I may have detected the slightest hint of amusement in his expression.

"Miss Esmé, you must be hungry. May I bring you something?"

"I would be eternally grateful."

"I can serve you here in the dining room, Miss, or if you prefer, in the study."

"I feel dwarfed in here, all alone." The room was grand, decorated in great swaths of silver panels and twin chandeliers. I could imagine it as a dance floor as easily as I could a dining room. "How about the study?"

Robbins served me a simple ham and Swiss cheese sandwich in the study in front of a fireplace, complete with roaring fire. It was remarkable how tasty it was. I relaxed on the Chesterfield sofa and gazed around the room. The shelves were full of leather-bound books and *objets d'art,* including delicate bronze nudes.

Next to the fireplace stood a shiny Art Deco Philco Radiobar. They had been all the rage during, and now after, Prohibition. The wooden cabinet featured waterfall oak lines and a radio with fabric over the speakers on the bottom. The top opened to reveal a hidden mirrored bar, complete with shiny glasses in various styles to suit different cocktails, from shot glasses to highballs to brandy snifters. There was room for at least four large liquor bottles filled with Scotch, gin, bourbon, and brandy. The good stuff, presumably, not bootleggers' rotgut hooch.

Rupert Chaseborn could play the radio on his Radiobar and fix himself (or his company) a drink at the same time, and then hide the entire bar away when the vicar came for tea. Very swanky.

I turned on the radio in time to hear Fred Astaire singing "Putting on the Ritz." I was not in a Ritzy mood. I turned it off and noticed a smaller room with a door half open. Attached to the study, it seemed to be some kind of studio. I peeked inside and gasped loudly.

Robbins passed by with my empty plate and noticed me staring into the room. "Everything all right, Miss?" He paused for a moment. "Ah, this is Mr. Rupert's studio. He occasionally—paints."

There were two portraits, not quite life size, well executed. Two female nudes looked familiar, and I found myself staring at Rupert's girlfriends. I was surprised I could still be shocked by Rupert Graydon Chase, yet I was.

The first painting featured the Snow Queen gazing saucily over her shoulder. She was completely starkers, except for her telltale ruby necklace. Every hair of her strident black bob was in place. She was thin with flat flanks. The same woman I had encountered in the ladies' room at Peacocks', with the glassy eyes and an imperious stare. In the bottom right-hand corner were the initials R.G.C., presumably for Rupert Graydon Chaseborn. Did the Snow Queen pay him for it? Did he pay her? I wondered. Why didn't she take the dratted thing to her own home? Unless of course she considered this majestic apartment her future home. Or he simply wanted to keep it. A souvenir of a conquest?

This must have been the "naughty Rupert" that Priss-Pot Summerdine had mentioned, and this painting contained more information than I had expected.

The second nude was the honey-haired Palomino, Priss-Pot herself, stretched languidly on a chaise lounge and fingering her breasts. She was merrily sans culotte and sans everything else and sporting an inviting smile, appearing much ruddier and healthier than the Snow Queen. Again, Naughty Rupert's initials were in the lower right-hand corner of the painting. Clearly, I had underestimated these East Coast debutantes. They had unsuspected hobbies. I felt sick to my stomach, and I backed into the study.

I became aware of Robbins, still holding the plate. "Are you quite all right, Miss Esmé?" I retreated to the sofa, needing the warmth of the fireplace. "Shall I pour you another cup of coffee?"

"Please. Listen, don't worry about me, Robbins. I'm far too provincial to take up any more space in Mr. Chaseborn's life. After he recovers, he won't see me again."

"I would count that as a shame, Miss. And a great loss." He gestured to the portraits. "These paintings, as *technically* accomplished as they are, seemed to have been a mere phase for Mr. Rupert. The landscape over the mantel is also one of his."

The small brass plaque read, "Hudson River in Autumn." It was a glorious sight, with trees of every color rendered with accomplished brushstrokes.

"Does he like landscapes?"

"He says they don't talk back, Miss. And generally, they don't move."

I was laying up a trove of grievances against Chaseborn. My face was hot—not with embarrassment—but with rage. Who did he think I was? What kind of woman? I sipped the coffee, slower this time, as I simmered.

Graydon lied with such ease. Many of his lies were of omission, but still. I was half interested in hearing his stories of these paintings. I could just imagine how smooth and fatuous they would be. He had told me his hobbies included painting and drawing. I presumed that meant bowls of fruit or something similarly unthreatening. How he must have laughed at me.

I was not against nudes per se. Nudes could be beautiful, even gorgeous. I was simply not used to seeing people I barely knew smirk at me in their birthday suits. And what must Robbins think? For he had surely met them all. In various states of dress and undress.

Had Chaseborn expected to seduce me into a similarly compromising position? I quailed at the thought. And here I was, flirting with the ruin of my reputation by merely being in his apartment—a man's apartment—*a notorious playboy's apartment!*—even though Robbins was there, as well as Dr. Zydeco, and now Nurse Jesse. I was never alone with the patient. But who'd believe that?

Robbins left me staring into the flames of the fireplace. I don't know how long I sat there, listening to the distant moans of the sick man in the bed. Was Graydon living a double life, or even a triple life? I sat, my shoulders drooping, thoughts swirling in my head. Oddly, I reflected on how I would miss the special scent of him, the one that made my head spin.

"Why don't you catch some shut-eye?" Nurse Jesse interrupted my thoughts. "Robbins says there's a guest room. Or three."

I didn't have the strength to move from the sofa, but I was determined to stay awake. "I'd rather stay here, where I can hear what's going on. I'll just rest my eyes. Robbins needs some rest too."

"He's going to retire soon, don't worry. I'm on the job." She exuded confidence and competence, for which I was grateful.

"How's the patient?"

"Still feverish, but his temperature has dropped. I expect it to spike again. Just the way this thing goes."

Before long, Robbins came in with a pillow and a soft blanket. I apologized for being there. He assured me my presence was a pleasure. Indeed, he said, Mr. Chaseborn would express his gratitude to me when he recovered. Unfortunately, both he and Nurse Jesse somehow had the impression that I was in love with the sick man.

I tried to stay awake, but I closed my eyes, and that was that.

THIRTY

HERE WAS A COMMOTION IN the front hallway. It was about seven a.m. I pried my eyes open as I jumped up from the couch, disoriented and unsure of my surroundings. Where was I? Was the apartment on fire? I didn't smell smoke. I heard feet pounding on the floor in high heels.

A woman confronted Robbins. She spotted me next to the blanket and demanded to know who I was and what I was doing in Rupert Chaseborn's apartment, and had I spent the night? The mad gleam in her eye told me she was enjoying this scene greatly. Was she an actress? I didn't recognize her.

"Who are you?" she demanded.

"I could ask the same of you," I said.

"How dare you question me!"

"How dare I?" I couldn't help it, I stared to laugh. I was still sleepy.

She was thin and pretty in a brittle sort of way, as if she would break in a stiff wind. I assessed her age as several years older than I, close to thirty. Her hair, the color of mahogany, was worn in a stylish short bob, so popular these days. Her eyes were small, or maybe she was merely squinting, making the lines around them stand out. Her face was long and thin, appealing now, but as she grew older, she might well resemble a witch. Her voice was high pitched with a faint-but-distinct New York accent.

"I am Rupert's fiancée," she declared. "I am Tricia Dunlop."

Was I supposed to know who she was? I immediately christened her "Trixie," because I had no idea what she was up to, although she did carry the air of an aging debutante.

Wait, his *fiancée?* No! I don't know why my stomach lurched at that moment. I shouldn't be surprised. Not after the nudes. What else could be left? Tricia/Trixie was the cherry on top of this particular mess. I wondered if a nude of her, one I hadn't seen, lingered in another room. I stared. Was she the kind of woman Chaseborn wanted?

Graydon on his sick bed uttered, "Do I hear the screech of the she-dragon?"

"Who are you?" she demanded of me, quite ignoring Graydon. If she was his fiancée, shouldn't she be running to his side? "I asked you a question!" She aimed one talon at me.

"No she-dragons allowed," Graydon yelled, before his coughing interrupted him.

I assessed her, she who was clad in pink from head to toe, including her hat. Her clothes were respectable, but several years old and her shoes a bit scuffed. However, I couldn't see her gracing Chaseborn's arm, like the Snow Queen or Priss-Pot Summerdine.

Robbins turned his head my way and spoke *sotto voce.*

"They are not engaged, Miss. Though Miss Dunlop has attempted that feat repeatedly."

She shouted over him, "I must see Rupert!" Still, she did not move. Instead, she thrust out her left hand so I could admire her diamond engagement ring, a thin gold band with a modest diamond. A ring any woman in love would adore. Yet surely, the wealthy Rupert Chaseborn would have given her something much larger, more distinctive, perhaps an heirloom, something handed down for generations in his proper British family.

Nurse Jesse arrived to the fray next, carrying a basin of clean water and fresh towels. I took them from her and shoved them at Tricia.

"Fiancée? I'm so glad you're here," I said, as Jesse and Robbins watched me. "Rupert is quite ill and terribly contagious. People have died from this, you know. Listen to me, his fever is still very high. You must continuously wipe down his skin—his head and neck, back, arms and legs. He'll fight you, so watch out, because you must know how strong he is. However, since you're here, you must help get his temperature down."

Jesse, bless her, backed me up. "Keep that basin close, sweetie, he may need to upchuck, and you'll want an apron to cover those pretty clothes. This virus is unpredictable and deadly, so don't forget the fluids. Force them down his throat, if necessary."

Trixie/Tricia stood frozen in place, horrified. Robbins, for once, seemed bemused and at a loss for words. Tricia Dunlop refused the basin and towels. She turned on her heel and fled the premises without speaking to Chaseborn, and without another word to me. I realized I had never introduced myself. A serious breach of etiquette.

"How did she know I was here?" I asked.

"Miss de LaForet?" Robbins asked.

"She knew a woman was in his apartment at this unseemly hour. Has she caused a scene like this before?"

"Not like this, no, Miss. Scenes, rather often."

"She's a piece of frail material, that one," Jesse said. "But you're in the clear, Esmé. You had two chaperones all night."

Robbins cleared his throat. "Miss Dunlop's family lived in this building for some years, until her father lost most everything in the Crash. They were forced to find other lodgings. She has been making a play, as they say, for Mr. Rupert for some time now."

"If she's familiar with the building staff, someone could have tipped her off," Jesse offered with a shrug.

"That was very neatly done, Miss," Robbins put in. "My compliments. It usually takes some time to 'encourage' her to leave."

"Esmé, Elf, come talk to me," I heard the patient say. "I can explain!"

"You do not want me to come in there, Rupert Graydon Chaseborn." I raised my voice. "You really don't."

Brave words, but my arms and legs were wobbling like rubber bands. I staggered back to the study and sank into the cushions.

I smelled coffee. I must have fallen asleep again. Sitting in a chair next to me, Nurse Jesse was drinking a cup of the rich aromatic brew. Anticipating my needs, Robbins was there with a cup for me. I was silent, but I sent him a question with my expression.

"Mr. Rupert is out of danger, Miss Esmé."

"He's weak, but the fever's broken," Jesse said. "He'll live."

I nodded and took the cup. Robbins had added a hint of cream and sugar. I inhaled the comforting steam.

"Thank you, Robbins. You must be exhausted."

"I have had some rest, Miss. Nurse Jesse made me retire to my quarters for a time. She can be quite convincing."

"Bullying, more like. No sense in all of us staying awake just to wipe Pretty Boy's fevered brow," Jesse said, with a soupçon of sarcasm and starch.

The clock on the mantel informed me it was now tenthirty. I had stayed the night in a man's apartment, and to my extreme horror, had no fun. Except for exorcising the so-called 'she-dragon' in pink.

I excused myself to use the guest bathroom to freshen up and repair my makeup. The spacious room was stocked with fresh towels and soaps and creams. I also noticed a bottle of scent, "Hickory Wind." Now I knew why Rupert Chaseborn smelled so alluring. I splashed some on my wrists and my hankie.

My face was flushed. I vaguely wondered how long it would be before I'd come down with this particular virus. I washed my face and combed and pinned back my hair. I reached into my pocketbook for my face powder and lipstick. I smoothed my eyebrows, touched them up with a bit of pencil, and darkened my lashes. It was the best I could do on short notice. I emerged to find Nurse Jesse assessing the patient.

"He's resting more comfortably now," she said. "Without your quick action, he'd be a lot worse off, if not dead."

"He's too young and healthy to die," I protested.

"Funny thing about this virus. It takes the young and healthy first. The ones you never think would die. But their bodies fight so hard, they burn out and succumb. Some of the old folks just let it wash over them, and live."

I figured he'd beaten the odds. "Do you know where I could find my jacket?"

No sooner had I said it than Robbins was there with my wrap, and a silver coffeepot to top up my cup.

"Must you leave, Miss? When he awakens, I'm sure Mr. Rupert will want to express his thanks for all you've done."

"Let him rest," I cut him off. "I'll just finish this."

"That man makes a mean cup of coffee," Jesse said. "I could get used to this kind of treatment." She headed for the bedroom to pour some more liquids down her patient's throat.

I didn't want to cast my eyes on Graydon again. I didn't trust myself not to slap him, or kiss him, one last time. I stood up again but before I could shrug on my jacket, Robbins was there to help me. Jesse came out of Chaseborn's room to say goodbye.

"You were terrific, Jesse."

"Between you and me, I don't often get these swanky assignments."

We shared a conspiratorial smile. "Do you enjoy the theatre, Jesse?"

"Don't get much of a chance to see it."

I pulled a theatre voucher from my purse and wrote, Good for Two Comps, Run of Show, for *Leaving Alamogordo*. "Here. It's my show and I get to sprinkle around a few complimentary tickets as I choose. It's sold out, but just call, they'll fit you in somewhere."

"Thanks," Jesse said. "Don't I feel like a swell!"

I turned to the tall valet. "Robbins, would you be interested in seeing my play?" I handed him another pair of comps. The noted playwright plays Lady Bountiful. "Your coffee and hospitality revived me. I'm very grateful."

I headed for the door. Robbins got there before me. "Is there a message for Mr. Rupert, Miss?"

"Unnecessary, Robbins. Kindly tell that man never to call me, follow me, or contact me ever again. I am not a rich man's plaything. Jesse, would you please walk me downstairs? Might help protect my reputation if people see I was with an Angel of Mercy all night long."

"I'll put my cap straight and get my cape, so people will step out of my way."

She dropped me at the front door, where the doorman inquired after Mr. Chaseborn's health.

Word travels fast.

Thirty-One

IF MY NUMBER WAS UP for this virus, I figured it would be a day or two or three before it hit me. I would prepare for it. Not just with some aspirin and ginger ale, but with facts about Rupert Graydon Chaseborn. I felt sure that revenge would give me the strength to live.

I showered and changed into a more casual skirt and sweater, still proper and comfortable. I would have preferred slacks for working, but I'd already caused enough potential scandal. Collecting a fresh notebook and pens, I headed to the New York Public Library.

Libraries are marvelous, and this one was the best. All you had to do was throw yourself on the mercy of the librarians and before you knew it, you had a stack of bound books of newspapers with society pages from the last two years. I settled down to work.

Rupert Chaseborn showed up with regularity in those pages. I jotted down the dates, the events, the names of the women he escorted, and I copied all the florid prose describing the high and mighty at the top of society's pecking order, as it related to him. There were many allusions to his wealth and position, as well as dances and auctions attended, and balls and charity events to which he had squired many a lovely lady. However, he rarely escorted these damsels more than once or twice.

I didn't know if he was playing the field or was simply reluctant to settle down. There was no mention of Tricia Dunlop, "Trixie." She was clearly lying about being his fiancée. The Snow Queen and Priss-Pot Summerdine were both pictured with him at various times. In most of the photographs, Rupert/Graydon looked preoccupied or bored. At least I thought so. He may simply have been fed up with being photographed.

By closing time, my hands were covered with ink, and my notebook had at least thirty entries about that sought-after catch, Chaseborn, and his companions. If I was ever tempted to backslide in my feelings about him, I had his history at my fingertips. Part of his history, anyway.

I felt better for my research mission. Gathering facts was second nature to me, something I'd forgotten about in the excitement of my play's production and the foolishness of picking up Scavullo's watch that day in the diner. I liked having more facts, but after sitting and staring at newspapers all day, turning page after page, I was lightheaded and filthy with newsprint. My notebook was full of Rupert Chaseborn's fabulous social life, a mad whirl of parties and opening nights and the cream of society.

On the way home, I stopped at the market for supplies, some ginger ale, aspirin, and menthol chest rub. And just in case, honey and a bottle of whiskey, the all-purpose Irish cure for any illness. I placed them near my bed, adding towels, a basin for warm water, and my thermometer. I also set out my two extra nightgowns. Judging from Chaseborn, if I contracted his virus, I'd be sweating through them and risking chills.

I decided against attending tonight's performance and I didn't want to spread any germs. Instead, I lifted the phone receiver.

"Why didn't you tell me about him?" I complained to Reggie.

"I thought you knew. It's an open secret that Rupert Chaseborn is Graydon Chase. Apparently, in addition to escorting the latest lovelies, he's the guy to call to look into upper-class financial crimes. He may have personal experience. And of course he's managing the family fortune."

"But *I* didn't know."

"Really? That doesn't sound like the reporter I've worked with."

I pouted. "No, it doesn't."

"Oh, Esmé, don't tell me you fell for him," Reggie lamented. "That soulless moneybags?"

"Not completely." I sighed loudly. "I'm such a chump, but I didn't fall all the way."

I could have, it would have been easy. His bed looked so inviting, if there hadn't been a desperately ill man in it. I didn't want to think about men in beds right now.

"Don't beat yourself up. Heels like him happen. And from what I've seen, Chase is a complete cad. No lovely lass left un-lusted-after."

"Says the man who can't resist a blonde." I cuddled up on the sofa and rested my head on a pillow. He laughed.

"I can resist the women with a hungry look in their eyes, the ones who check out my family's entry in the social register. They think I'm the guy they'll nab."

"The ones after your money."

"I'm a lowly scribe, Esmé. I don't have access to that money. Can't help it if women out there think I do."

"Another reason they chase Chaseborn." I could see that if everything was true, Graydon was walking around with a price on his head, a price of at least several million dollars.

"That high-tone Brit accent gets them every time." Reggie shifted from his native Bostonian tones into New York Cabbie. "Not a regular Joe like me." I giggled, but it didn't help. "So Chase chased after you? He has fine taste, in spite of his other flaws."

"In my defense, I thought he was a gigolo. Possibly a gangster."

"How did you two meet?"

Reggie was my dear friend, but I couldn't possibly explain that. What would I say? Pocket watch, school supply closet, cat, Mafia, guns, shooting? Or if I said we were introduced at a funeral, Reggie would want to know *whose* funeral, why was I there, and why hadn't I mentioned it before?

"I have to go, Reggie. We'll talk soon."

"Hey—"

"Bye."

I took the precaution of unplugging my phone before tumbling into bed.

~

On Saturday, I slow-roasted a chicken, which made everything smell homey and gave me the illusion I had a few domestic skills. Amelia said she'd show up the following day for her pay. Apparently she had enough left over for pie and a movie with her friend.

The rest of the afternoon, I spent reading my notes and typing them up in a clear and concise format. It turned out to be ten pages long, double-spaced, all about Rupert Graydon Chaseborn, aka Graydon Chase.

I started to label a file folder—but I didn't know which name to put on it.

Thirty-Two

I MADE MY WAY TO St. Patrick's Cathedral Sunday morning, still sore at Rupert Graydon Chaseborn. Having no expectation of seeing him all day Sunday felt just fine. He would, no doubt, be taking it easy. I would be too.

It was yet another glorious fall day. The trees were in full flame, and the air was warm with a cool breeze. I wore my black suit, the one I had worn to Scavullo's visitation, but I switched out the pink collar and cuffs for a different look, the seasonal red plaid, a little costume magic.

I took a pew toward the back and was surprised to see Juliette Scavullo with her son, Anthony. Why wasn't she at Our Lady of Pompeii? Perhaps the familiar was all too much. Too many people offering their condolences, or worse, ignoring her because of the scandal. Her nephew Marco wasn't there, but he didn't strike me as much of a churchgoer. She wore black as I had expected, though she was still attractive in her widow's weeds. I was sorry that she would have to stay in somber clothes for years to come.

I inhaled the incense and listened to the choir and tried to pray, but I didn't know where to start. Following the service, Juliette lingered at the front of the church while people said hello or offered their condolences. When there was a break, I approached.

"Esmé, hello." She reached out her hands to me and I grasped them.

"I've been thinking about you, Juliette. How are you doing?"

"Better some days, not so good others. But I have my children and we are out of that gangster life, finally."

I hoped it was true. "What do the police say?"

"Police! They know nothing, even if they know who did it. They don't care. But that nice Mr. Chase is still trying to find out something. He feels bad about—everything. Everything was settled. There was no reason for anyone to kill Dante." She seemed to notice me again. "Sorry, my thoughts run in circles."

So did mine. "It must be the hardest thing to go through. I can't imagine."

"What does Graydon say?"

"I'm not really seeing him anymore."

Juliette seemed surprised. "I'm sorry, I thought you would make a good couple."

"I flirted with that idea for a while, but—" I lifted my shoulders and let them go. "I hope you find some peace."

"For my sons' sake, I am trying. I'm trying to figure out how we go on from here." Her voice dropped. "Dante promised we would be set for life. I would never have to worry, he said, if anything happened to him." She shook her head. "The things a widow thinks, but I cannot find where he left that money. We need it for the boys, for college, for Anthony."

"You might ask Chase. They were working together—"

"He's been trying to find it. He didn't tell you?"

"He told me nothing. He certainly can keep a secret."

Anthony came forward. He lifted Dante's pocket watch from his vest and checked the time, the way I had seen his father do. "We should go, Mama."

Juliette turned the full force of her smile on him. "The spaghetti will wait."

He smiled back, handling the timepiece carefully. He retreated a few steps.

"See how he treasures it. Thank you. I believed you, about Dante and the watch, but Graydon, he checked out the details. At the diner." She sighed and changed the subject. "I was sorry to miss your play. Such an important night for you."

"Don't give it a thought." I waved my hand.

"It wouldn't look right, "she said. "A new widow at the theatre."

"I was surprised that Marco showed up. To represent you."

"Marco?" She looked puzzled.

"He said you gave him the tickets."

She put her hand to her head. "I was in such a fog, who knows? Maybe. I don't remember."

Anthony was waiting impatiently. She reached for her son. He put a protective arm around her and steered her away.

♫

I either forget about food or else I'm starving. I hadn't eaten since last night, in order to take communion. My stomach growled and I remembered a different breakfast place a few blocks away that wouldn't have an overflow church crowd. I love being in a city where restaurants are open on Sunday. Imagine.

Inside this small diner, a waitress showed me to a petite aqua two-seater booth toward the back. She brought me coffee before I ordered eggs and an English muffin. It was my kind of place.

I lifted the hot cup to my lips and in a moment the atmosphere in the restaurant changed.

The couple in the booth next to me stood up, threw money on their table, and rushed out. I heard chairs squeaking and rustling. More people left. The waitress let out a big sigh. She seemed to be the only one unimpressed by whatever was happening. I caught her rolling her eyes as she turned her back to retrieve her coffeepot.

I set my cup down and glanced up. An expensive camel hair coat came into view, and I found myself staring into the face of Handsome Frank Romeo, notorious mobster.

The only way to deal with a bully is to stand up to him. A lesson I learned back home with a pasty-faced fat boy in the eighth grade, Mitchell Malone. *Never show fear.* Mitchell tried to take my lunch money, but I pasted him in the face with a snowball packed with rocks. I made sure everyone saw it and I called him terrible names, like "scurvy lout" and "lily-livered boy" and "bull's pizzle." All courtesy of Shakespeare. Everyone knew the Malone boy was a thief and a big baby, but few stood up to him. Mitchell was so flustered by my resistance, and his snow-covered face, that he burst into tears. He was marched away by Sister Mary John for some special punishment, while Sister Angelina Rose took me in hand.

"Bull's pizzle, Miss de LaForet?" she inquired.

"It's from Shakespeare," I explained.

"So it is. Shakespeare is not always polite."

"But Sister, I was afraid for my life! And my lunch money."

She tried to hide a smile as she discussed the expected etiquette of ladies and Catholic school girls. I was not punished, and we agreed that you need not always be polite to bullies. But in *other* cases... One reason I loved Sister Angelina is that she believed the girls and she had a gift for divining the truth. She believed me. Mitchell Malone, after many infractions—mine being the final straw—was expelled.

Now I stared at the man who stood next to my table.

"You really know how to clear a room, Mr. Romeo." Remind me not to invite him to the theatre.

"But not you. You're not afraid of me?" He allowed himself a half-smile.

"Should I be?" I told my inner coward to stop quaking. After all, I had seen him at church.

"No. May I?" He indicated the other side of the booth.

"Of course." I appreciated his asking.

Everyone knew the man who ran the operation over Scavullo was Frank Romeo. But he was almost a myth. A local legend. Finally, I was seeing him up close. I also saw the waitress carrying a full coffee for him, unasked, setting it down very carefully.

As I had noted before, he was an attractive middle-aged man in a camel-colored cashmere coat. Way too old for me, of course. None of the stereotypical words seemed to apply. If rumors were correct, he was either a cold-blooded killer or a strictly hands-off-the-violence type. His long black hair was tinged with silver and combed straight back, shiny with Murray's hair pomade. Brown eyes under prominent brows and high cheekbones gave him a regal look, but he was going a bit soft around the jowls.

At a respectful distance behind him I saw Marco Scavullo, Patrick "Lashes" Dentino, and "Bones," just Bones, a tall, thin man whom I had never heard speak. The Cisco Kids, I dubbed them. Only they weren't heroes. They stayed close to the front door, out of earshot, but where they could monitor everyone who entered.

"I'm not the one responsible for Dante Scavullo's death," Romeo said without preamble. "I never ordered a hit. I'm a lot of things, but I am not a killer."

"You *are* Frank Romeo?" I just wanted confirmation. This guy looked like the kind of person who preferred to keep his hands clean. He made a sound halfway between a growl and a chuckle. I think he was amused.

"Yeah, but I'm not the guy in the papers. The notorious 'Frankie the Cat'."

"I wasn't aware they called you Frankie the Cat." I'd only heard him called 'Handsome Frank.'

"You gotta read more of the tabloids, kid. They're very colorful. I haven't seen you at Our Lady of Pompeii recently."

He drank half a cup of steaming coffee in one swallow. He was keeping track of my churchgoing habits? That was disturbing.

"I've been going to St. Patrick's," I answered like a schoolgirl.

"Good. You shouldn't just stop going. Not on my account. Why did you change churches?"

I glanced quickly at Marco. Was I supposed to say he made me nervous? "It's closer to where I live."

Romeo nodded. "I had nothing to do with Scavullo's death," he said again. "Dante was a smart guy. As a measure of goodwill, I'm even employing his nephew." He cocked his head toward Marco Scavullo. "And the kid's no brain trust, believe me.

I could believe that. "Is it true Dante was leaving the business?"

"He was making an exit, yes. Retiring. It was time." He swallowed the rest of the coffee in one more gulp, then held out his cup for the waitress. She threw me an exasperated look as she stalked over with the pot. They'd done this dance before. She heated mine up too.

"You weren't stopping Scavullo from leaving?"

"No. To tell the truth, he was an okay guy in the bootleg booze biz. He was a numbers kind of guy, he kept track of shipments, payments, debts. The guy was honest. Imagine that. No skimming, ever. But he lacked vision. It's a whole new world now, after Prohibition. Dante didn't want to explore other—opportunities." He sipped his fresh cup. "Take this place." He gestured toward the back of the diner. "Behind that door over there? Looks like a broom closet? Used to be a speakeasy. Lots of room back there. Now we're expanding. Couple months from now? Big fancy restaurant, big bar, top-shelf liquor, dance floor, swing bands."

"All legal and everything?" Did I really just ask that?

The mob boss made a sour face. "I know, I know. But you do what you gotta do."

I nodded. "Do you have any idea who killed Scavullo?"

Why on earth was I asking him these questions? The guy was a mobster, but the reporter in me, well, she just couldn't stop.

"No. I'm not feeling sad about Dante being gone. Good at his job, but to me, always kind of a nobody, you know? But my boy Guido, that's different." Romeo's face clouded.

"Guido Moretti? You think there's a connection?"

"I assume so. Guido—" Frank stared at his coffee. "He was a good kid. Not the brightest, but the most willing. To please, to take the fall if he had to, the most loyal. He was good to his mother. Everybody liked Guido. His killing makes no sense. And if it was to get to me? Still makes no sense. Kind of people who want to get to me? They come after *me*. Not my boys."

Sounded like a case of hero worship on Ratty's part. Frank's eyes darkened and the muscles in his face hardened when he spoke of the boy's killer. Whoever had dared cross Frank Romeo had better be long gone, I thought.

"Do you know anything about the man who was gunned down near Broadway? The papers called him a 'racketeer'."

"Heard of him. Not one of my boys. Met him once or twice. We don't have a lot of sales conventions in this business. I heard he was quite the highflier. I read the papers too, but they're trying to draw a connection where there ain't one. Trust me."

We were silent a moment. The waitress sauntered over again with the coffee pot. He brushed her away.

"I heard Ratty liked blue."

"Yeah, he liked blue. Sky blue. We all wore blue ties to his funeral. Respect. You understand?"

I wasn't going to say I didn't. "Why would you let Scavullo quit?"

"For her. For Juliette. And I got tired of looking at him."

Mr. Romeo seemed mentally to go somewhere else for a moment. So the rumors were right.

"You love Juliette Scavullo." It sounded like a stupid thing to say. But I had to say it.

"Always have." He closed his eyes. "She wouldn't take me, so she married that big lug instead. She didn't want to be associated with my—business affairs."

"But Dante Scavullo was in the mob too."

He shrugged as if that were old news. "I prefer to call it 'the organization,' but yeah, I hired him long ago, right after they were married. He had a hard time getting a good job. The Italian thing, it stops some people from hiring us. But I, Frank Romeo, I gave him a job. Revenge, see?" I wasn't sure. "See, it took his manhood away to have to work for me. I knew that and he knew that. And I always knew where Juliette was, what she was doing."

"Why would he agree to that, when he knew how much she hated the bootlegging business?"

"Money. Makes it hard to say no. Especially when you got a kid on the way." Frankie the Cat thrummed his fingers on the table. "Should have been my kid, should have been my wedding. Should have been my wife. *Capisce?*"

I had to give him credit. It was a devious sort of payback. "All for revenge?" Might make a good title for a play.

"Revenge is a funny thing, Esmé de LaForet. Sometimes it fills a need and it's sweet. Other times it just fills your mouth with the taste of blood and ashes. Dante wanted out and I was ready to let him go. He reminded me of her. Every single day. I thought maybe if I didn't have to look at him every day, I could stop thinking about her."

"Do you know who killed him?"

"No, and believe you me, I want to find the guy."

"And if you find him?"

"Maybe I won't be so nice that day. Whoever killed Guido and Dante has got to pay. And I gotta find out, to prove to everyone I wasn't the one. Juliette has enough of my sins to hold against me. I figure her forgiveness is not an option. So revenge it is."

Graydon had told me the truth, or at least a version of it. From her station by the door, the waitress flashed me a look that seemed to ask if I was doing okay. I gave her a nod. Romeo tilted his head at her.

"Hey, Mona, what you think I'm gonna do? Make a scene? We're having a friendly cup of coffee here. Everything is copacetic." She shrugged.

"Why are you telling me this?" I held my heavy green mug for its warmth. He lowered his voice.

"For Juliette. She's gotta know I had nothing to do with his demise. Frankly, I can't imagine who'd want him dead. Dante? A nice nobody. It was hell to know she preferred that guy to me. I saw her talking to you after Mass. You're friends. I want you to tell her."

"I'm not Italian. Why should she listen to me?"

"That's why. If you were Italian, she'd think maybe I paid you off. Or I scared you, or leaned on you. But she knows you from church. You're Catholic and a Mick, even with that Frenchy name. That counts. I seen your name in the papers, I know you write plays. You're no pushover, or you wouldn't have gotten this far." He suddenly grinned. "And I know you're going to remember this conversation." Frankie the Cat was certainly right about that. I was furiously memorizing every word. "You got a look on your face, Esmé de LaForet. What does that look mean?"

"I was wondering if there was a moral to this tale."

He shrugged. "The moral is don't marry the wrong person. Don't waste your time on the wrong person. Don't live your life with regrets. And if you think about writing a play about this, about me—"

"Oh no! I am not writing a play about any of this." I must have looked horrified.

"So Marco's just blowing smoke? I figured. I tell you one thing, Marco thinks you're swell. For that matter, so does Lashes. Bones? He don't have no opinions. But Marco ain't smart enough for you. Or classy enough."

"I have no interest in Marco. None. He wanted me to write a play with a part for him, but I am *not*—"

"No, not for Marco, he's a nobody, but maybe someday you might. Write the play, I mean. Just don't make me the bad guy. I got feelings."

"I would never knowingly hurt your feelings, Mr. Romeo." Those big terrible vengeful feelings.

"Thank you. You put me on stage, I'll deny it's me. But this guy, this guy you might write about someday, this guy who's not me? He's in love with the woman."

"Really, there's no play."

"Who knows? It could be a gangster play." He gave me a sly smile. "But make it a romance, too. There should be music. And dancing. And make the guy handsome."

He smiled, for real this time, and I could see the young handsome Romeo pining for his Juliette as she married the less flashy, a little dull, stolid but safe, Dante Scavullo.

"If I ever write it, which I won't, I promise he'll be handsome." Everyone's a critic. And a director. And an editor.

"And listen, Chase is a good guy, I'm telling you. He regards you greatly."

"How can you tell?" I felt myself bristle at Chase's very name.

"He won't let anyone talk about you. He won't talk about you. He won't let anyone go near you."

"He and I are no longer meeting."

"Right. Like the way we just met? Fate, Miss de LaForet. Fate plays the last card."

It was Romeo's turn to laugh. Notorious gangster, mob boss, booze runner, maybe killer, but he was surprisingly easy to talk to. And Romeo's Achilles heel was a woman named Juliette.

❦

Esmé, you're going to make yourself sick!

That's what my mother would have said to me, and I was pretty sure she was right. That's why after my encounter with Frank Romeo, aka 'Frankie the Cat,' I decided to make myself the lemon chicken soup that had disappeared so quickly the last time. I shredded the chicken and assembled the ingredients while I simmered the broth. It was reaching a delightful fragrance when the phone rang.

"Miss de LaForet, I am so sorry to trouble you." It was Robbins, Chase's valet.

"No trouble." I had no grudge against Robbins.

"Would you be able to give me your recipe for a soup? Something with lemons and chicken? Mr. Rupert is— Well, he is much improved, but he swears he must have that soup, Miss. He says he enjoyed it so at your flat."

I seethed. Was Chaseborn psychic? Did he know I was making lemon chicken soup at this very moment? He seemed to want to keep bothering me, even after I had given him the air. On the other hand, Robbins had been kind and considerate of me. Twenty minutes later he was in my kitchen writing notes and helping me put the dish together. It would make a big batch. I told him he could take half of it with him to keep Graydon quiet. I may have made a reference to poisoning it as well.

"I do apologize, Miss. I know that Mr. Rupert can be irritating when he is not feeling his best."

"Irritating is a pale word, Robbins," I said. "A very pale word."

He smiled. We were interrupted by a familiar knock at the door. Amelia had dropped by to pick up her pay, but she stayed when she caught a good look at the distinguished valet in the kitchen. Robbins had a way of looking formal, even with his jacket off and wearing an apron.

Amelia stood open-mouthed for a few seconds before straightening her shoulders and fluffing her hair. She tilted her head as a sign for me to introduce her. I did and they held eye contact for several moments past necessary.

"Miss Applewood, a delight. I am Mr. Chaseborn's valet," Robbins informed her.

"I'm Esmé's housekeeper, part-time. I never met a valet before." She put her hand out and he took it.

He seemed to be as fascinated by her as she was by him. She looked delicate, but she immediately started directing him and handing him the right kitchen tools. She peppered him with questions, kept the conversation moving along, and she managed to invite him and herself to sit down for a bowl of soup. We three sat at my dining table after Amelia lit candles and laid a fire in the fireplace. I learned that although Graydon was recuperating he was not happy, and he believed I had "abandoned" him.

"Hardly! I cooled his fevered brow all night! At the risk of my reputation, I might add, and I left as soon as I knew he wasn't going to die."

"Do not worry, Miss Esmé, he's simply not used to women walking out on him."

Amelia turned her attention to me. "You walked out on him? The man who sent those gorgeous flowers? I don't believe it."

"That may be his story. He's welcome to it." I concentrated on my soup.

"This is quite a savory dish, Miss. I can see why he enjoyed it so much," Robbins said.

"It's a bowlful of comfort, it is." Amelia batted her baby blues at Robbins. I wondered if she would be able to find out his first name, so I didn't mind when she offered to accompany him back home to keep the big bowl of soup steady. You would think she was a queen walking out the door. I suspected she wanted to see Chaseborn's lair.

I helped myself to another bowl of soup. It was delicious, but it made me sad. I would never see Rupert Graydon Chaseborn again.

Thirty-Three

O N MONDAY MORNING, I BOOTED up and strode through the first snow of the season to the theatre, catching fluffy flakes on my tongue, enjoying the frosted look of the city. I wondered how many dirty secrets were covered by the snow and whether some unseen gangster was watching me. The snow would not linger, it was merely a preview of coming attractions.

When I arrived at the Irv, it was half staffed and May was out with the virus. I assumed she would be more stoic than our actors, yet after seeing how ill Graydon Chase had been, I was inclined to give grace to anyone who caught it.

Willie was sketching costumes at May's desk for an upcoming show while answering the phones, feet up and wearing slacks. She claimed she loved the theatre best when it was empty, and on Mondays when the stage was dark. As long as the ghost light was lit.

I tried to catch up on reading my pile of playscripts. But the pile never magically disappeared.

"What is the deal, Esmé? You keep sighing."

"Bad plays. Sorry." I was lying, but I cut down on the sound effects.

My brain circled around from reading scripts to thinking about Chase, and then about Frank Romeo, and back again. One of the things I loved about New York City was the ability to get lost in the crowd. But I'd lost that. Why were so many people aware of my every movement?

That damned watch! I wished I'd never touched it! Apparently, no one on God's green earth had ever returned some lost item to some mobster without having some nefarious angle. It was *that* suspicious.

Frank Romeo suspected I knew more than I did. And from Juliette, I heard there was a stash of money that Dante Scavullo had hidden somewhere for his widow's future. A stash that hadn't been found. Romeo had said Scavullo was an honest man, but doesn't every man want to provide for his family? I reflected once again on the numerals in Scavullo's watch. And wondered what they meant. But it grew chilly in the offices and I'd had enough.

By the time I walked home, the frosty snow had melted and left a cold dark night behind. Pumpkins were beginning to dot the landscape, decorating stoops of homes and shop display windows. Homes with children featured windows with cutouts of witches and owls and slivers of moons, reminding me the Halloween holiday was close at hand.

❧

Tuesday was much the same. Filled with small, quiet tasks. The show would go on. Leading lady Clarissa Eldridge and her swain Todd Andrews were back on the boards at full strength, feeling relieved to be alive, jubilantly taking the reins back from their replacements. So far, I'd dodged the virus and was enjoying my mysterious resistance. I was relieved that I had kicked Graydon Chase to the curb, while I exited stage left. Pursued by mobsters, but not by a bear.

Even so, I missed his kisses, that peculiar electric current that ran between us, and the self-assured way he held me. He wasn't afraid I'd break. It was probably the same way he must have held all the others. I threw the thought away.

Graydon—somehow I found it hard to think of him as Rupert—also had that wonderful aroma. I couldn't forget it. Luckily, that spicy-citrusy-woodsy scent came out of a bottle. The bottle that had been on his dressing table, as well as in his guest bath. I was merely missing the *scent* of him, I decided. I didn't need Graydon Chase, I needed his cologne, Hickory Wind.

I marched over to Fifth Avenue. A scent that alluring had to come from Lord & Taylor's men's counter, where I found myself during my very flexible lunch hour. To be sure Hickory Wind was the one I wanted, I made myself dizzy sniffing all the colognes available, and I wasn't even halfway through. It seemed that men everywhere had discovered the power of scent in all its overpowering variety.

And then I spotted Hickory Wind. I signaled to the salesclerk, who assured me of my superior choice.

"Why, Elf, what are you doing here?" Oh no, not that plummy British accent! It had sneaked up behind me, all smooth and low, jarring me out of my fog of colognes. Graydon had appeared as if I'd conjured him up from his very scent. But it was only his scent I wanted, not his superior attitude. I peered at him. He looked remarkably healthy.

"You're alive," I said.

"Thanks to you, Elf. I still can't believe how fast that virus hit me and then sped away. Like a hit-and-run driver. Unfortunately, you hit and ran too. How can I thank you?"

"I'm not even talking to you, Graydon. Please leave me alone or I'll call for security."

"Please do. I know all the store detectives. Charming fellows."

Bastard. I refused to look at him. "I'm looking for a cologne for a friend."

"Really, a friend?"

"I have friends!"

"Many, I've no doubt, but which friend?"

"None of your business, especially if it's detective business. What do you wear?" I asked, as if I didn't know.

"This one." He reached across the counter to a small brown bottle, very understated. The one I'd selected. I picked it up. "Hickory Wind." I closed my eyes and sniffed. I gasped a little when I saw the price. "It's quite new. How good a friend is he?" Graydon asked.

"This good." I lifted it up. Graydon was also making some purchases, but I paid no attention. I decided my purchase would be my first-successful-play present to myself. A moment to remember.

I would also remember that my arms and legs felt suddenly very heavy and hot and my head began to ache. Unmistakable signs that I had perhaps half an hour or so to race home and climb into bed before I was violently ill.

"Esmé, what is it?" he asked.

"Too much cologne," I lied. The clerk handed me my package and change and turned to Chaseborn to handle his purchases. I seized the moment. "I have to go."

Without looking back, I scurried away through the crowd of shoppers. Outside, the sunlight hurt my eyes, and I hailed the nearest taxi. The driver was fast and reckless, but under the circumstances, I was grateful. My fever rose as he screeched to a stop in front of my building.

I met my neighbor, Mrs. Jenkins, outside the front door and asked if her son Freddy could pick up a bag of ice at the store down the street for me. I handed her more than enough coins. Freddy, a budding entrepreneur at twelve, was always willing to put down his baseball and glove and run errands for nickels and dimes.

My stomach was somersaulting violently and I made it through my front door just in time to reach the bathroom and be sick. Afterward, shaking, I tossed my clothes on the divan near my bed and struggled into a nightgown. I felt so hot, I wanted only to lie down.

A knock on the door interrupted me. It was too soon for the ice to arrive. "Who is it?"

"Esmé, open the door. It's Graydon."

"Why don't you leave me alone?" I didn't want the neighbors to hear me fight with him. I cracked the door open. "I mean it, Rupert Chaseborn. I'm sick." I tried shutting the door.

I felt faint and I'd never felt faint before. He stepped inside and caught me before I slipped to the ground. He carried me to bed. In a minute I had to stumble back to the bathroom, slam the door, and be sick again.

I had anticipated feeling bad, but not this bad—outside I was on fire and my insides were twisted up in knots. When I could stand, I washed my face. My head was banging. I opened the bedroom door quietly, holding a wet cloth to my forehead, and I flung myself on my bed. He was there with his jacket off, rolling up his shirtsleeves.

"Making yourself at home?" My voice sounded quavery to me. "I told you to go away."

"Clearly, I did not listen." His Brit accent sounded extra smug.

"Please go." I laid down without taking the covers off the bed. I had to lower my temperature. Where was the ice? I had ice hats ready at my bedside.

"You obviously need assistance. Let me help."

"In that case—" I gave him orders. I needed ginger ale, water in the basin, and ice. Some semi-conscious part of me wanted to see if the rich boy could follow instructions.

A rat-a-tat-tat at the door announced Freddy Jenkins with the precious ice and supplies. Chase dealt with him, and I suspected slipped him some extra tip money. I heard something about "fever" and "highly contagious" and "stay away unless I call."

Graydon helped me drink some ginger ale, lifting me up and holding the glass. He prepared the ice hat for my head. He carefully wet and wrung out the towel and wiped down my face and neck and arms.

"Where did you learn all this?" I asked.

"From you. Don't you remember?"

I growled. "I want to forget that."

"It's a pity you're under the weather, you look quite fetching in that gown."

I have a weakness for pretty lingerie. It was silk, pink, and edged with lace. It skimmed my body. And it was rather sheer. Curse it. "Stop looking."

"Not an option, Elf."

Chills hit me next. I was shaking. The bed covers felt impossibly heavy, but Chaseborn lifted them with ease. He helped me under them. I couldn't stop trembling. He crawled on top of the bed and held me until I warmed up again.

"You can't do that," I whimpered. "Who told you to do that?"

"Robbins told me you kept me warm until the chills stopped."

"He swore he wouldn't tell." My teeth were chattering. I could barely get the words out.

"I vaguely remembered you being there with me. A lovely image. Robbins merely confirmed the details."

"You beast."

"*I, Beast!* Thank you, I'll use that title for my memoirs."

This isn't funny, I thought. Why is he so amused, I wondered through my fog.

Soon the quivering stopped, he released me, and the fever began again. I threw off the covers. It went like that—fever and chills—until I slept. I was out for hours before I awoke, hot again, and dying of thirst. It was dark outside, and just one lamp was lit in my room. My head was pounding.

"You're awake." Graydon was sitting in my easy chair near the bed under my reading lamp, sipping my medicinal whiskey. "The theatre called. I said you were ill. The flu virus. Whoever it was said they'd see you in a few days."

"What time is it?"

"About seven."

"You've been here the entire time?"

"Yes."

"Can't you leave me in peace? Don't you have some detecting to do? Or money counting? Or mob coddling?"

He had some papers in his hand. My dossier on his social life.

"Seems to me you've been doing a little detecting on your own. Such fascinating reading, and it's all about me."

"I had no idea who you were. I wanted to know."

"And you had to run off and find all this? I would have told you anything you wanted to know."

"Liar," I said, and then I was out again.

Thirty-Four

"**I**'M NOT GOING TO APOLOGIZE," I said, "if that's what you want. Your social life is public information."

I reached for the ginger ale and lifted the cool glass to my forehead. Someone was driving a locomotive through my cranium. Where was the aspirin? I reached for the side table.

"You must be very annoyed with me." He opened the tin and handed me two tablets.

"You're the detective. What was your first clue?"

He sighed and set the papers aside. "We were having such a nice time. Just the two of us, Graydon Chase and Esmé de LaForet. I loved that you didn't know any silly, stupid, scandalous Rupert Chaseborn."

"I haven't got as many names as you do." Or as many adjectives.

"Though sometimes with your close friends, you go by Rafferty."

"My Irish friends. I like Rafferty." I slumped down to a horizontal position. "Were you ever going to tell me you lead a double life, or, I don't know, maybe a triple life? Are there more?"

He felt my forehead. "You're heating up again."

"I'll survive. You did."

"I'm not sure I would have lived without you, Elf."

I reached for the ice cap. Water sloshed inside it. The ice was all melted. He noticed.

"Let me refill that," he said.

Graydon left and returned with the cap full of ice and a cold glass of water.

"Thank you."

He took the damp towel and started wiping me down again. I tried to protest, but my limbs lacked strength. He put the thermometer in my mouth. "Listen to me, Esmé. I am chagrined and flattered that you decided to research my social history, and a little annoyed."

"Ha. I am furious with you," I said, though I think it wasn't terribly clear, what with the thermometer stuck under my tongue. He took it out and pronounced it one hundred and two degrees. Down from my peak, he noted.

"A favor. I'd like to borrow your information and have Mrs. Carter type it up." I must have looked surprised. "Tricia Dunlop is suing me for breach of contract."

"Trixie? That's what I call her. You said you weren't engaged."

"We are not and never were. I knew 'Trixie'—good name for her, by the way—because her family lived in my building before her father lost his shirt. I escorted her to a party once at her request. One time. Never again. Poor woman is quite deranged."

"She needs the money, doesn't she?"

"Yes, but why do you say that?"

"I only saw her once, but her clothes were years out of date, yet clean, and fashionable when they were new. Her shoes were worn. Polish couldn't hide that. She wasn't dressed like the Snow Queen or Priss-Pot."

"You noticed a lot. For not being a detective."

"I woke up and there she was. All I could do was stare."

"This lawsuit of hers is a form of blackmail. Figured she'd sue me and settle for a nuisance payout. She'd take that, I'm sure, though she'd rather be married, both for the money and the Chaseborn name."

"If she grew up rich and it was all taken away, it couldn't be easy for her."

I struggled to sit up. He helped me adjust my pillows.

"Trixie alleges a good many things that aren't true. Dates and times we were together. Your dossier proves I was at very different places. Apparently, I was with a number of other ladies, contradicting her suit."

"With photographs." I held my aching head with both hands. "I didn't think that engagement ring was something you would give her. Too small, too plain, and not an heirloom. But what do I know? Just a Midwestern debutante, right?"

He ignored that and fanned the file. "With all of this that you put together, I think we can get the case tossed out before it gets nasty."

"Before it spreads in all the newspapers?"

"She would view that as a bonus."

"Is she in love with you?"

"Don't think she's capable. I simply represent dollar bills. And pounds sterling."

"That's terrible, Graydon. Has Trixie considered working for a living?"

"That doesn't happen in her social class. She'd rather live on past glories." He reached for my hand and kissed it, which sent another hot chill through me. "You come from a different place than the Tricias and Trixies of this world, Esmé."

I rubbed my head and fell back. The thundering was beginning to subside and I was feeling sleepy again.

"May I borrow this document?" he said. "I will return it. You know all about me now, you don't really need it."

"Yes, I do. I haven't committed it all to memory yet."

"Please, Elf."

"It seems you have me over a barrel."

"Don't tease me with that visual, Elf Queen." He smiled, wickedly. "I'll have a copy and carbons typed up for you. Interesting, isn't it? Even when you annoy me, you help me out."

"Annoy you? What do you think you do to me? I walked out of your life. Curtain call."

Graydon pulled the chair closer to my bed. His voice was low.

"For the record, Robbins is quite taken with you. He's very impressed that you never wanted to see me again. And your parting speech, that you're not a rich man's plaything. Those were the words?"

"Yes. And I am not seeing you again. I can't. I will never be your plaything. You're just making this messy."

I punched my pillows trying to get a more comfortable position. I was so hot, it was hard to think.

"I told him it sounded like a curtain speech. A nice touch, with a bit of drama."

"I'd throw this pillow at you, but I'm too sick."

"Esmé, Elf—" He hovered over me.

"We can't see each other anymore."

"Don't say that."

"Have Mrs. Carter return the file in the mail." I squinted at him. "Are you wearing a different jacket?" This one looked like a more relaxed tweed, but it made me hot just to look at it.

"Robbins came over with a change of clothes for me."

"When did all this happen?"

"You were sleeping."

"You've been busy." I looked at the clock. "You have to leave, Graydon. My reputation—"

"I would never harm your reputation. But you stayed with me all night. You can't expect me to desert you now. And don't worry, Robbins has contacted Nurse O'Banyon. She will be over soon, I expect, and we will have a very starched official chaperone."

"We really can't see each other," I protested.

He kissed my forehead and left the room.

A couple of hours later, I woke to find Nurse Jesse taking my pulse. "It's slightly elevated, doll, but you'll live."

I smiled at that. I adored her dry competence.

"I daresay I will."

"This is a swell place you got here. Not as grand and glorious as his, but it's got heart and soul. Comfort."

"That's what you get when you have a Broadway set designer paint your place."

"Ha. You must be feeling better."

"A very tiny bit." Once again the thermometer was in my mouth and I clenched it while I spoke. "Where is Chaseborn?"

"Out there. Taking a break, doing some kind of work. He's using your telephone." She indicated the living room with a turn of her head. "I told him he could leave, but he's stubborn. Almost as stubborn as you. He wanted to make sure your neighbors saw me come in, white cap and navy cape. He called me a veritable angel of mercy."

"A chaperone with a thermometer. I can't believe how exhausted I am."

"Best thing for you. Go to sleep."

Before I did, she helped me into my blue silk nightgown. The pink one was soaked through and she didn't want me to catch another chill.

I was aware of him in my dreams. When I awoke late the next morning, feeling weak but much cooler, Graydon was gone. Jesse was there, along with Amelia, fussing over me with a cup of tea.

"You shouldn't be here," I said to my unpredictable housekeeper. "I don't want you to catch this."

"I had this stinking flu weeks ago," she said, as if it were some kind of contest. "On my days off."

Her days off and on were unpredictable, to say the least.

"Sorry, you didn't mention it."

"My ma played Florence Nightingale. Made her happy."

She and Jesse got along famously, chattering away like birds at the end of the day. When Jesse said she wasn't sure she could make it to my play because she didn't have anything to wear, Amelia helped me convince the nurse to take my old navy-and-gold-trimmed evening gown that I had replaced with the costumes from *Afternoon Tea with Nigel.*

After some fussing, Jesse finally tried it on. She agreed it shouldn't go to waste. She looked like a different person in the dark gown.

Me, I didn't feel like a person at all. I felt like the watery contents of my ice hat. Melted.

Thirty-Five

Halloween came and went. In my little corner of the theatre world, everyone was either too busy or too sick to pay much attention. Besides, in the theatre, every day is Halloween. Or something like that.

By Friday, I was well enough to return to work for a few hours, capable of reading scripts and the newspaper, full of a shocking Halloween tale of jealousy, rivalry, and revenge: Apparently eight thousand copies of the Harvard Lampoon had been stolen. The editors were blaming Yale.

By Saturday, I was in danger of relapsing. I hadn't seen Graydon since he walked out of my apartment, nor had I seen my file on him, which he promised to return. Perhaps it made him angrier than I thought. Fine. He took up too much room in my brain anyway. I could retype those notes. I was still in the process of letting him go and thinking about him and how much better off I was without him, when there was a forthright knock on my front door.

I popped open the brass peephole to see a middle-aged woman. I'd never seen her before and she looked harmless at first glance. Rather severe, but harmless.

"May I help you?"

"I must see Miss Esmé de LaForet in private."

"I am Esmé." I swung the door open and she marched right into my entryway.

Her stride was imperious, shoulders back, chin up. Perhaps mid-fifties. She wore her hair in a short-cropped bob over bright blue eyes. A touch of lipstick and powder. Her clothes were expensive, a robin's-egg blue silk dress, matching knee-length jacket, a fur wrap draped over one shoulder. Her blue hat was neat and tidy, her navy shoes matched her bag and her gloves. She'd added three strands of pearls. For midday, it was an impressive ensemble.

"I had to meet the creature who broke up my son's engagement and ruined my last chance for grandchildren." Her accent was very English and very crisp. "I had to see what this monster might look like."

With a declaration like that and the high-toned English accent thrown in for nothing, how could I resist the dramatic possibilities?

"I may be that creature. Would you by any chance be Rupert Chaseborn's mother?"

I smiled at her. Surely I should win points for being quick on the uptake. I never imagined him even having a mother, let alone one residing in America.

Although I usually wore slacks on Saturdays, but after being sick and wearing nightclothes for so long, I felt like a bit more formality was due. I'd selected a comfortable crocheted dress in purple over a blue slip. I knew the colors and the fit flattered me, even though this outfit had started life in a department store, not a costume department.

"I am Mrs. Cyril Rupert Montague Cedric Chaseborn. My given name is Jane." These people and their names. She gave me the once-over. I sensed she was disappointed that I didn't have scales and fangs. Trixie must have given me quite the buildup, trying to ruin my reputation. "I am Rupert's mother."

"Pleased to meet you. Now, you were accusing me of ruining your life. Let me guess: Trixie?" She looked blank. "Tricia Dunlop?"

"Poor Tricia. She informed me in confidence— Well, this is very—indelicate."

"I can imagine. Come in. I'll put the kettle on and we can discuss it over a pot of tea."

"Tea?" She hesitated, but she was just as curious as I was. There might be as many gaps in her knowledge about her son as there were in mine. "Very well. I mustn't be long, my chauffeur is waiting outside."

Tea was a necessity when dealing with the English, I'd heard. And my Irish mother set great store by a good cup of tea, and even though her family had been in this country for well over fifty years, she observed four o'clock tea every day. As for me, I would be happy to toss tea in any harbor, but I indulged now and then. It reminded me of my family.

"Earl Grey or breakfast tea?" I asked.

She seemed surprised, then she asked for the Earl Grey with cream and sugar. "If you have it."

"I do." For some reason after meeting with Robbins, the tall valet, Amelia had taken to making tea. She made sure I had all the ingredients on hand.

"You're more civilized than I was led to believe."

"I can imagine."

I ushered Mrs. Chaseborn into the living room. She may have expected tears or protestations of something, or even questions, but she didn't get them.

"Is it Lady Jane?" I asked.

"If you like. People do call me that here. The title is more formally Lady Chaseborn."

'Her Ladyship'? Color me surprised. This bit could be funny, smartly used in a play, somewhere, sometime.

"Would you care for scones?" My mother always insisted on serving scones for company. Indeed, I had been planning to bake some this afternoon. Scones were the first thing my mother always made me after an illness.

"I do rather care for scones," she said. "But I haven't found any decent scones *here*."

Oh yes, she threw down *that* gauntlet. I can make scones. I went to the kitchen and she followed, though she was welcome to wait in the living room and be captivated by my décor.

"Tricia said she visited Rupert rather—*early* one morning and found you there. Asleep."

I separated the scones, sprinkled them with sugar, put them in the oven, and set the timer.

"Did she tell you that I was asleep on the sofa and Graydon was in his room, deathly ill with the flu?"

"What? My Rupert was ill?"

"Burning up with fever. It was dangerously high. For the record, he and I were supposed to have a lunch date. His illness struck so fast, our lunch never happened. I insisted on taking him home and making sure he was tended to. Yes, I was there, but so was the doctor, and a private nurse that the doctor called, and of course Robbins."

The kettle whistled and I heard the front door open. Amelia entered, as if I had written her into the scene.

"Miss Esmé, you should be conserving your strength," Amelia lectured me, turning off the burner. We both turned to look at her. *Miss Esmé?* Apparently, Amelia was still under the spell of the very formal Robbins.

I introduced the two of them. Amelia glowed with pleasure. She loves British accents.

"Something smells good. Must be your special scones." Amelia donned an apron and shooed us out of the kitchen. "I'll bring in your tea."

I cast an inquiring glance her way. She beamed her all-knowing smile in response and pulled me aside.

"Robbins warned me she was on her way," she whispered.

This was an interesting development. It appeared that Robbins had Amelia's number, in more ways than one.

"Rupert was ill? You escorted him home? And then you stayed by his side all day and night?" Lady Chaseborn was really trying to understand. "Putting yourself at risk?"

"My mother, my father, and my fiancé all died from a flu very much like this one. I couldn't bear seeing anyone else succumb to it. Anyway, there were the three of us tending him, four if you count the doctor, and your precious Rupert is now hale and hearty."

She seemed to soften a bit, but I had no doubt that this could be an act.

"That may be commendable, but ill-advised. Who else was there again?"

"Robbins, obviously. Doctor Zydeco—you may know him—and Nurse Jesse O'Banyon. I have her number if you like. In the early morning hours, I sat down on the sofa in the study, and closed my eyes. I didn't mean to, and I woke up when Trixie arrived, making quite a racket. Graydon wasn't happy to hear her."

"Robbins was telling the truth?" Lady Jane had already checked with Graydon's valet.

"Robbins doesn't strike me as a liar," I said.

Amelia diverted us with a tray, complete with a pot of tea, cups and saucers, napkins, and hot scones with jam and butter. She arranged everything attractively on the coffee table and served us. There was more than enough. Did Amelia think I was the Ritz?

After Amelia retreated to the kitchen, Lady Jane sipped her tea. Her eyes widened at the first mouthful of fluffy, buttery scone.

"What are your intentions toward my son?" she asked.

"None, Lady Jane. Graydon didn't tell me he was engaged. Nor did he tell me his name was Rupert or Chaseborn. You may rest assured I am not running after him. He has lied to me. Constantly."

That didn't seem to faze her.

"I do so want grandchildren before I die." She poured more tea into her cup without offering to pour for me. That's all right, I am able-bodied. I had the feeling she didn't really care who gave her grandchildren. She simply wanted the dynasty secured.

"You have another son," I said. Lady Jane sighed. "And you're still young, and Rupert has more ladies-in-waiting than you could shake a stick at. But don't bet on Trixie. She's not for him." I refrained from saying she was for the loony bin.

"I know the girl and her family. She was acceptable, if not preferable. She informed me they were engaged, although telling me should have been Rupert's responsibility. However, I was prepared to overlook certain personal feelings." What could I say? This was all fascinating. Lady Chaseborn nibbled at her scone. "This is quite delicious."

"Family recipe." I smiled. "Passed down through generations on my mother's side."

"And your maid—"

"Amelia acts as my housekeeper a few days a week."

Lady Jane nodded as if this were all fine and proper. "She seems quite capable."

"She has great timing." I was grateful for that, and at that moment, Amelia came back with a fresh pot of hot tea. Did I really have *two* teapots? I didn't recall that.

"This is a lovely flat. From your family?" Lady Jane was nosy.

"No. I came into a little money after they died, and I came East. I bought it myself. I am a working woman."

She stared at me intently. "Not a nurse?" She didn't have to say nurses had a racy reputation. "Or some kind of teacher?" Dull but safe.

"Sorry, much worse." I laughed at her discomfort. "First I was a newspaper reporter, now I am a playwright, but always a writer."

"A playwright? Wait, you're not *the* Esmé de LaForet? You must be the one on Broadway. I believe I saw a review of your play. *Fleeing the Alamo,* or something like that?"

Thirty-Six

66 _L EAVING ALAMOGORDO._" I CONFIRMED the awful truth.

"Esmé de LaForet. Of course. I don't know why I didn't put that together. I was told it's sold out. Tricia didn't tell me you were a playwright."

"I doubt if she knew." It would be amusing to be the one with the power for a change. "I could see what I could do about a couple of comps, but seats are very tight."

"My goodness! You could arrange tickets to a sold-out show?" _Now_ she was impressed.

"Perhaps." I merely smiled, calculating how it might irritate Graydon. "But not if you're planning to take Trixie Dunlop."

"Good heavens! That conniving little weasel? Never. And if she thinks she'll damage your reputation with her loose tongue, well, I will nip that in the bud."

The power of the theatre! "I'll see about those comps, Lady Chaseborn."

"Please call me Lady Jane." Lady Jane lifted the pot and poured, and this time she included me. "Do you know, I've always wanted to be a writer."

"What's stopping you?" Good Lord, this woman had servants, time, money, no doubt a weird family life for material, and possibly some haunted manor house she could draw upon for inspiration.

She hesitated before answering. "My husband doesn't think I can do it. He's back in England. Politics and all that, you know."

"Wouldn't it be rewarding to prove him wrong?"

The dignified Lady Jane suddenly giggled like a little girl. "What a delicious thought that is. He is the perfect man, don't you know? Never wrong, always right." She rolled her eyes and I stopped myself from making a crack about her son. She sat up straight and stared at me. "You don't think I'm too old to be a writer?"

"Don't be ridiculous. Writing is the one profession you can practice till the day you die." And she was as well preserved as money could buy.

"Never thought of it that way. I'm not yet sixty." She was thinking of it now. There was a gleam in her eyes.

"It could be quite a smash in your circles," I said, "whether you write a novel or a play or even some poems. Some racy sonnets, perhaps." She would have the kind of social credit that would get her attention. Amelia bustled in to clean up the mess from the scones and tea. Graydon's mother made no move to leave. "Tell me, Lady Jane, what would you write, if you could write anything you wanted?"

"A novel." A faraway look came into her eyes. "I suppose a big gothic romance, with danger and adventure and a beautiful heroine, the kind that is so popular now. Not that I've spent any time thinking about the question."

I'd bet she'd spent a lot of time thinking about it. "That sounds very promising. Have you written any of it? You could start on it at home this afternoon. I'm sure your driver must wonder where you are."

"Andrew? No, he's used to my little quirks. Would you happen to have a pen and paper?"

Was that a trick question? I'm a writer. I handed her a fresh notebook and a pen.

She simply wanted to jot down a few ideas, she said. But instead of leaving, she peppered me with questions about the craft of writing, the theatre, and my early days as a reporter. We spent the rest of the afternoon discussing her 'theoretical' book. She took to the task like a major general commanding her troops. It crossed my mind that perhaps I should have left her to the machinations of Trixie Dunlop.

In the meantime, Amelia took charge of the chauffeur, offering him tea and sandwiches, which they took out to the terrace to enjoy in the sunshine. Lady Jane seemed oblivious to him. She was lost in the foggy terrain of her imagination.

An hour or two passed, but she didn't tell me much about Graydon, except that she was appalled no one had told her that he was deathly ill. She knew he had some sort of investigative business, but assumed it was a phase, or a hobby. He never told her about any of his women, so when Tricia came forward, Lady Jane Chaseborn was optimistic there actually was an engagement at hand.

"Good Lord, look at the time." She checked her watch against my clock on the mantel. It was almost five o'clock. "I generally have a spot of sherry this time of day. I don't suppose—"

I gazed around the room in confusion, wondering if she would rather accept a brandy, when the amazing Amelia materialized with two glasses of sherry on a silver tray.

"I didn't think I had any sherry," I whispered to my housekeeper. She grinned. Later she told me that Lady Jane's driver Andrew let it be known that Her Ladyship could be fractious without her daily nip of sherry. Amelia gave Andrew a dollar from the housekeeping fund, and he slipped down the backstairs to the new liquor store on the next block. Amelia, the original fix-it gal.

Even more peculiar, after spoiling for a fight with me, the notorious engagement wrecker, Lady Jane seemed to be enjoying herself. And though I pointedly mentioned I was an independent working woman, of French and Irish descent, and a Roman Catholic, she was in no hurry to tear herself away. Surely, she should be out hunting for an appropriate mate for her son, and not someone so eminently unsuitable for her family.

Down deep, I supposed Lady Jane was a lonely woman who was taken for granted by her husband and sons. Clearly, she had to be, in order to consider a faker like Trixie for a daughter-in-law. She needed something to do. But I was becoming very weary. I yawned meaningfully, for the tenth time, and she finally noticed.

"My dear, I am sorry for taking up so much of your time. I am in your debt for your assistance with my Rupert in his hour of need. I am the last person to know he was at death's door. Very few women would do what you've done. And to risk your reputation doing it. A spot of sherry and I'll be gone."

She downed her sherry and took the liberty of filling half a glass more. I realized I was in need of sherry myself. I'd spent the last three hours with Graydon's mother, and while it had been amusing—or something like it—I simply couldn't keep it up much longer. Lady Jane's fingers were covered in dark blue ink. She gazed in wonder at them.

"I had no idea how lovely it would feel to finally put pen to paper."

I felt like I'd been run over by a milk wagon, and the horses too. A loud knock startled both of us.

"Esmé, it's me, Graydon."

Amelia opened the door for him. I downed the rest of my sherry. He came straight to me and took my hands in his. We stared at each other for what seemed like a long time. I could feel Lady Jane's interest.

"Esmé, are you all right?"

"Don't I look all right?"

"Are you perhaps afraid I've done something to her?" Lady Jane inquired. He spun around.

"Mother. Good God. What on earth are you doing here?"

"I was chasing down a scurrilous rumor. And visiting my new friend, Miss de LaForet. My only mistake was in believing that horrible creature, Trixie. Tricia Dunlop. Spreading her vile lies."

He raised an imperious eyebrow at me. "Trixie?" To her, he said, "You are unbelievable."

"If I had not come here, I would not have met Esmé Rafferty." She was unrepentant, and I liked her for that.

"You had best leave before you wear out your welcome, Mother." Graydon called for Andrew and I remained silent. "Esmé has been quite ill. She didn't tell you?"

"With the same malady?" She looked from me to him. "You were at death's door, I understand, and yet no one called me."

"It ran its course in a couple days. Andrew!"

Her driver emerged from the kitchen with Amelia, who would certainly want extra wages for today. Graydon grabbed Lady Chaseborn's wrap and put it around her shoulders.

"I must remember my notes." Lady Jane grabbed the notebook and lifted it in victory. "For my novel."

"We'll discuss this later," he said.

"Will we? I look forward to that." Much to his annoyance, she kissed him on his cheek. It seemed to me she was really quite happy with the chaos she had caused.

Graydon escorted her down to her car. I wasn't going anywhere. Not yet. Amelia took the armchair nearest me and sat with a sigh of contentment. She poured herself a sherry, making herself at home.

"You are a wonder, Amelia. I didn't expect you here today."

"Robbins called me. He said you might be needing me because her ladyship was in 'high dudgeon.' Whatever that is. What is a dudgeon? Anyway, it sounded important."

"It's going to cost me, isn't it?"

"That's capitalism." She grinned. "I do for you and you do for me."

Amelia still hadn't seen my play. She didn't want it to disappoint her. She could, however, quote from the reviews.

"Indeed. Don't know what I would have done without you."

"And you don't have to worry about this going any further. You're my meal ticket, Esmé."

She helpfully explained that she took her fee today out of the housekeeping fund and left an accounting of her pay, as well as the cash for the sherry. She patted her pocket, then retrieved her coat. After all, the evening was young and she had plans.

"Thank Robbins for me," I said.

"Already done."

Amelia opened the door and Graydon marched in as she marched out. She winked at me.

"Why on earth did you let my mother in?" he asked me.

"Playwright. The dramatic potential was simply too compelling."

"She's a stranger to you."

"Not anymore, she's not. Apparently, Lady Jane had some interesting little chat with your Trixie, who is hell-bent on ruining my reputation. Your mother said Trixie's been after you for years."

"I honestly never even noticed until this last fiasco."

"What a terrible insult to her, not being noticed." I had to get up and move, or I'd fall into a post-sherry nap.

"I suppose so. What are you doing?"

"Putting on my walking shoes. I'm going to get some fresh air. I haven't eaten, except my scones, of which your mother enjoyed several. I need real food." With him there, I was feeling decidedly lightheaded.

"You make scones too?"

"Don't get excited, I have a limited repertoire."

"I'm going with you."

"No society dates tonight?"

He pulled me to my feet. "Esmé, I was called out of town on a job. When I arrived home, Robbins alerted me to the situation."

"Your mother is a situation?"

He laughed. "She certainly is."

I reached for my coat and he took it and held it for me.

"We weren't going to see each other again. Remember?"

"I never agreed not to see you." He followed me out the door. "I see you now, Elf."

THIRTY–SEVEN

EVER SINCE LADY CHASEBORN LANDED at my door, I'd been thinking about Lafferty's Pub, quiet and protective, full of neon green shamrocks and dark wood. Lafferty's stained-glass windows featured the Irish harp, and the bar featured Guinness stout and Jameson's whiskey. Though there was nothing like it in my old hometown—there were no antlers in the décor—I felt at home the first time I walked through the front door.

As a plus, I wouldn't run into any of Frankie the Cat's Italian boys there. And if Devlin Sullivan was present, actor and bartender extraordinaire, I'd be well taken care of and protected from randy Englishmen.

I had known Devlin since I saw him in a production of *The Cherry Orchard*. He played the passionate land-buying peasant Lopakhin and I complimented his acting. He remembered me and allowed me to claim a small table by the fireplace. He always kept the wolves away.

Strolling through the crisp autumn evening had cleared my head and got Graydon out of my apartment. At least for the time being. I thought perhaps all the Irishness at Lafferty's would send him running home. Nevertheless, he kept his upper lip stiff as we arrived.

He observed the Gaelic décor of Lafferty's suspiciously but opened the door for me. We sat, we ordered, and we stared at each other in silence. This is going well, I thought.

"She was spouting some nonsense about writing a book," he suddenly complained.

"She is. You should encourage Lady Jane."

"Nonsense. And don't call her that, it just gives her airs."

"Listen, smart guy, a book takes a long time to write. Time when she's thinking about imaginary people with imaginary problems and not involving herself in your *real* life. Capisce?"

He rubbed his face and he seemed weary, though still handsome. Darn it. "You have this weird power, Esmé. All kinds of horrible scenes filled my mind, and then I arrive and find the two of you nipping at the sherry like old chums. How do you do it? Mother likes you—and she likes no one. No one I've ever liked, anyway. What did you think of her?"

"She amused me. She exhausted me. The sherry was a complete surprise, because Amelia, with Andrew's wise counsel, decided to make herself essential to the scene."

"Aha. Mother is fond of the sherry."

"Trixie apparently informed Lady Jane that I was a fallen woman, and I had stolen you away from her. Miss Up-to-Her-Tricks is angry that she is not your fiancée and she'll do whatever she can to destroy my reputation."

"Trixie's always been a childish chit. She'll never grow up."

"Is she still suing you?"

The waiter arrived with our meals. Chicken pot pie for me and fish and chips for Chaseborn. We were apparently both starved, and we dug into a bit of comfort.

"I presented Tricia's attorney with your rather extensive and not-all-that-flattering file on me. He promised they would drop the matter. Your document proves I couldn't have been with Tricia Dunlop on the dates alleged."

"Well, there's an irony. You always seem to be everywhere all at once."

He ignored that. "He said he would have a chat with Miss Dunlop about bringing false lawsuits." But Graydon still wore an air of annoyance.

I was beginning to think that I could be an investigator too. After all, I had supplied all the vital information. Reporter at heart.

"You haven't returned my papers yet. Just remember, as a mere scribe I retain my original notes by law," I taunted him. "I spent hours in the library. Oh, the drudgery. All those silly women linked to one Rupert Chaseborn, notorious playboy. When I typed it up, I didn't realize I'd need so many carbon copies."

"Could you possibly change the subject?"

"After you left my apartment. I believed we had concluded our business."

"You underestimated me."

Devlin Sullivan left the bar and sauntered over to our table. While I was at Lafferty's he considered himself my protector.

"Rafferty, what are you doing with this Brit?" Since learning my middle name, Sullivan always called me Rafferty. He glared at Graydon.

"I'm an American, mate," Graydon said softly. He leaned back in his chair. "Naturalized citizen."

"Are you now? Left the old empire behind for the shores of Ameri-kay?"

"That's right."

"He's picking up the bill, Sullivan," I said. "He's good for it."

"Oh, well, that's different then. Drink up. If you're needing any help, Rafferty..."

I smiled to let him know I was not in any trouble. "I know who to call." Graydon stared after Devlin and shook his head.

"Are you really a citizen?" I demanded.

"Indeed, I have papers to prove it. Before you ask, I seem to belong here, for some reason. My brother belongs in Britain."

"And your mother?"

"She belongs in a castle somewhere. With a moat full of alligators. She had a falling out with my father some years ago. He bought a townhouse in New York and uses it when he visits, which is seldom. She lives there, when she's not flitting about. They are, I believe, in a state of détente."

"How long has she been here?" I assumed that being supplied with a car and driver, Lady Chaseborn must have established herself firmly in New York.

"Several years, long enough to meet people like Trixie. I assume she's here due to her never-ending disappointment with my father and my brother. Without grandchildren to anchor her somewhere more civilized, she decided to claim New York for her personal empire."

"And you?"

"We stay out of each other's way. Mostly."

"You didn't tell me you had a mother here."

"Why would I? She's a steamroller."

"Encourage her to write her book. She may discover things about herself."

"You promise she'll leave me alone?"

"No promises. Can't she bother your brother?"

"He's a terrible prig. Even Lady Chaseborn thinks so. Yet I'm terribly glad to have Sir Cedric."

"Cedric? Sir Cedric Chaseborn?" It sounded like a very priggish character out of a bad English drawing room comedy, and I snickered.

"It is rather comical. So is he. However, he has to deal with all the familial duties, keep up the family name and all that. Never got along though. We prefer to be on opposite sides of the Atlantic."

Although my meal was creamy and delicious, I found it difficult to eat much when I was with Graydon. He had a terrible effect on my appetite. I wished he wouldn't look at me the way he did, as if he could see right through me. Then I remembered my mother saying that men generally had the insight of gnats, and I felt better. I took another bite.

We fell silent for a while and a three-piece Irish band set up. They started out playing soft mournful songs, but I knew they would get louder later, with rebel songs that could really rile up the Jameson-and-Guinness-fueled crowd, still celebrating the end of Prohibition.

I had to change the subject matter before it would be too noisy to talk.

"Graydon, you mentioned you were out of town on business and that's why I haven't seen you. Were you looking for Scavullo's missing money?"

He tore himself away from his food. "Who said anything about Scavullo's money?"

I shrugged as if it were unimportant. "Juliette Scavullo was at St. Patrick's Cathedral last Sunday. We both thought changing churches was a good idea. I didn't bring up the subject, believe me." I lifted my fork for another bite. "Juliette said Dante intended to leave her well off, but she couldn't find anything, no trace of any money, and she doesn't know how they are going to live. I thought she would ask you."

His voice dropped and he looked almost dangerous. "What else do you know?"

I played it light and airy. "Other than Marco Scavullo is the new driver for Frank Romeo? Not much."

"Describe the 'not much'."

I sipped my drink. "Frankie the Cat followed me to a diner after church. Can that man clear a room!"

"Frankie the Cat?" Graydon's eyes blazed, but he held his temper.

"I didn't know that was one of his tabloid nicknames. Has a certain ring. He mentioned Dante's money as well. He says he wants Juliette to be well taken care of, but he is a gangster, so maybe he just wants to get his hands on the dough."

"I warned you not to get involved with Scavullo's people."

"Nor would I. Frankie the Cat wanted to speak to *me*. People scrambled out the door the moment he showed up. The waitress wasn't impressed. It was all I could do to keep from spitting out my coffee. But he was a perfect gentleman. Unlike some gentlemen I could name."

Graydon sighed. "What did he want? Specifically."

"For me to tell Juliette he didn't kill Dante. He said she'd listen to me, even though I'm not Italian. *Because* I'm not Italian. Because I'm not part of the Italian, um, social scene."

"What else, Esmé?"

I hesitated. "He heard from Marco that I was writing a play about the mob."

"What? You are not!" If I didn't have Graydon's attention before, I had it now.

"In a world with a million ideas, why on earth would I write about those sleazy criminals? And they're not funny enough. Marco made it all up, and he wants a part in this fictitious play that I will never write."

"Did he believe you? Romeo, that is."

"Yes. But Frankie the Cat requested that if I ever did write such a play about someone like him, I'm to make his character *handsome*. And to make it a love story, with mob stuff. And music. And dancing."

Graydon stabbed his fish. "Good Lord. It seems Romeo still loves Juliette. But it doesn't mean he's not a dangerous thug. Protestations aside, he could still be a murderer."

"That's an unsettling thought. I had coffee with a murderer?"

"Good. I hope it keeps you awake at night."

ے

The music was deafening and the crowd rowdy. I stood to leave. Graydon settled the bill with Devlin Sullivan and we exited. Outside, the temperature had dropped. Blue and green and gold light spilled from the colored windows of the tavern, marking patterns on the sidewalk. The night mist was settling on the grass and the car windows.

"I'll call us a cab," Graydon said.

"Go ahead. I prefer to walk."

He treated me to his best exasperated expression and took my arm. "I would hardly abandon you to the inhabitants of the night."

"I'm sorry you thought you had to rescue me. From your *mother*."

"I'm sorry I underestimated your ability to deal with my mother."

"Nothing can come of this, Graydon, the two of us. You must see that."

At that moment, it felt like the darkening sky allowed us to speak more freely than in the restaurant facing each other. It was quiet on this side of town. If someone was following us, they weren't close enough to hear.

"Elf, let me get this straight. You don't like me because I have a little money?"

"It's not a *little* money. You're a bloody millionaire! People on the streets are killing themselves trying to make a couple of bucks a week just to survive."

"I can't help that, and you have your own money."

"A tiny inheritance that allowed me to buy an apartment. And being a woman, that wasn't easy."

"In addition, you have a hit play on your hands. You must be hauling in royalties from *Leaving Alamogordo*."

"Not yet. Royalties are evanescent things. It could all be ashes tomorrow." I lifted my head, but the sky was obscured by clouds. Sort of like my future.

"If it matters, I was charmed that you took me for a gigolo."

"Instead of merely a heartless playboy?" I felt duped, embarrassed. He laughed.

"Elf, you wound me."

"When one person has more than the other, it creates an unequal relationship. I want an equal."

"I could never be your equal, Esmé."

"Smooth talker. I'm not a notch on your bedpost. I'm not an easy mark."

"Where do you get these ideas?"

Where, indeed. I'd overheard the Snow Queen discussing 'bedding the man,' even though at the time, I didn't know the man under the microscope was one Rupert Chaseborn. And although Priss-Pott Summerdine gossiped about 'Naughty Rupert,' she neglected to tell me about the charming portrait for which she had posed. Nude.

"I saw your paintings! Your nudes. The night you were sick, the same night I was risking my reputation. To my surprise, I recognized them. How many more are there? So many talents."

Though I didn't look at him, I could feel his surprise.

"Robbins didn't tell me that. At any rate, those paintings were just a phase. And there are no more."

"I assume this was the famous Naughty Rupert Phase?"

"Priss-Pot, I suppose." Clearly, he didn't want to discuss it. "Too many complications. We all thought it was fun, a little wild. A bit of a diversion. They aren't lewd, you know."

"Very tasteful, I'm sure, but I wonder what Lady Jane would think. Your mother wants you married, Graydon. Rupert. I assume to someone *acceptable*. But if she writes that book she's planning, you'll have time to sow more wild oats. And paint. Paint them all."

He changed the subject. "You were engaged before. That fellow who died. I understand I owe my excellent care to his demise."

"I decided to release Roger from that promise right before he got sick, but I never had the chance. We were too different to make a happy marriage."

Poor Roger. Good looking, kind, and so very dull at the bottom of it all. I wanted only good memories of him.

"Tell me about him."

"Roger wasn't my equal, either. He had no interest in things like plays and novels and going out to a fine restaurant every once in a while. And his lovemaking wasn't all that enthusiastic. In fact, he really wanted to wait until we were married. I suspect he would have happily waited much longer than that. I insisted we needed to find out if we were compatible."

"And were you?" He seemed irritated by this. *Men.*

"Not really. He seemed to consider sex a duty. Sort of like washing his socks."

Graydon perked up. "And here I was sure you intended walking down the aisle as a model of purity." It seemed to be a question.

"Two people should know each other before they commit to fifty-plus years of marriage." I couldn't imagine anything worse than being with a man who had no interest in me, other than cooking and cleaning and drudge work, without even the saving grace of a happy relationship in bed.

"In the biblical sense?" He was calculating something.

"Obviously. I've seen too many women get married because they've been told all their lives that's what they should do. And I know women in the theatre world who didn't find out until the wedding night that her knight in shining armor was more interested in other men, and her job was to be a respectable smokescreen."

"What about your fiancé, was he interested in men? Because frankly, Esmé, I cannot imagine a man not wanting to bed you."

"He didn't prefer men. Roger simply wanted a godforsaken ranch in the middle of nowhere, surrounded by sagebrush. He was more interested in the price of cattle than in me."

"I take it you're not opposed to sex? In principle?"

He hadn't asked me this before. Being half French, I thought that question was idiotic.

"I'd say it was my right. Get one thing straight, Rupert Graydon Chaseborn, I indulged because I was engaged to be married. I'm no flighty roundheel."

"Never in a million years would I have thought that of you."

"Although marriage is nothing I plan on, I take it seriously."

"You plan to be a sex-starved single woman?"

"I hope not forever. But when you look at it, marriage is a bad deal for women. For most women. My mother seemed quite in love with my father. They had a hard life, but one they shared as equally as possible, running the general store. They giggled a lot behind closed doors. For me, on the other hand, being engaged is a possibility. That could go on forever, without being trapped."

"You think marriage is a trap? Funny, I've always felt that it's the females who were on the hunt and wanted to trap me."

"Or your bank account. Men have chased me for the same reason. Not at your scale, of course."

"Not very flattering, is it?"

"I might be engaged someday, but I'd never give up my career or my apartment that I've worked so hard for."

"Some people say the only real power women have is marriage," he countered. "Not that either of us is interested in that, of course. But I am interested in you, Elf." He leaned in closer.

A loud noise exploded near us, smothering Graydon's sweet nothings. It sounded like gunfire and all I could imagine was Frank Romeo gunning for me. I jumped and Graydon pushed me into a doorway where we were protected by granite walls. We waited for more shots—when an old car lurched to a stop in front of us.

I succeeded in not screaming, nevertheless I found it hard to breathe. Graydon caught his breath too and brushed it off with a cough. He released me from his hold.

"Just backfire," he said. "Damnable old Model T. It's nothing."

The driver of the car got out, kicked his tires, and swore at his machine. My sense of relief was enormous. "Frankie the Cat is never there when you expect him," I said.

"He could be there when you don't. They weren't following us. Not this time."

"You were afraid they were? What do you know that I don't?"

"Just being cautious. Now, where were we?"

The man with the car managed to hand-crank the engine and start it again. He threw a passing glance toward us, returned to the driver's seat, and drove off.

"It's too hard on me to be near you, when this relationship can go nowhere." I picked up my pace.

He stopped me, stared into my eyes. "Esmé, you saved my life."

"And you saved mine. I hope we're even."

I considered all the windows that were lit above our heads. Who lived there? Were they arguing the way we were? Were their romances sliding into oblivion? Were they making love? I obviously didn't know how love should go. I was no expert.

He uttered something that came out like a growl. "Anything else?"

"It's embarrassing that you showed up this evening. I had just made a dramatic pronouncement to your valet that I never wanted to see you again. It was a great curtain line."

"Yes, the one about how you're not a rich man's plaything."

I'm glad he couldn't see me blush in the night. "That's the one. But he told you your mother was gunning for me."

"We keep the family guns away from her. I'm sure he's sorry for stepping on your dramatic moment. However, even Robbins was afraid for you and felt he needed to alert me to the situation."

"I meant it, you know."

"I'm afraid I do."

The dying leaves on the trees called to each other and clattered as the wind made itself known. Somehow, several pumpkins had remained on a front stoop. They made a lovely tableau. A sense of grief landed on me.

"We can't go on this way." I neglected to say it was killing me.

"You can always count on me."

"And your money?"

"It's not that terrible a burden, you know. Better than having none."

"Except when women like Trixie show up to bleed you dry and then sue you."

"Not so terrible when I have you to protect me." I wasn't amused. "You have a fear of poverty that breaks my heart, Esmé."

"It's not poverty so much as loss of control of my life."

I certainly didn't want to wind up like those old women in the newspapers, who held on to their money in coffee cans buried beneath the floorboards. I believed in and used banks. I didn't want to be alone, but I knew a lot of women who were lonelier in their marriages than they were before.

I stopped at the front door of my building. I knew he'd follow me upstairs.

"Securing the premises, you know. Then I will follow your wishes."

He went through his familiar routine and returned to where I was stationed at the front door. I didn't want it to end like this. One of the saddest things in the world is not knowing that your last kiss will be the last. I wanted this last kiss to be on my terms.

"Graydon, this is goodbye." I reached for him and kissed him for a long while. He responded with passion, but I denied him any further pleasantries. My body was screaming for more and didn't know why I was so intent on denying it. It would have been so easy to give in. Eventually we came up for air.

"You are confusing me, Esmé. My darling."

"Good. I shouldn't be the only one. I want to remember this moment. It's a lesson."

"This is ridiculous." He pulled his coat up near his ears and stormed away and down the stairs. "It's damn cold out there. Damn cold world."

I shut the door and watched him from my front window. He hailed a cab and disappeared into the night.

THIRTY–EIGHT

ON SUNDAY, I WAS TEMPTED to try Eglise St. Jean Baptiste, the Upper East Side church that began life catering to French Catholics in the city. But that was the coward's way out. I decided I would try at least to rid myself of Frank Romeo's one request, his urgent message to Juliette Scavullo.

She and I bumped into each other as we exited St. Patrick's. She still wore black and a veiled hat. I wore the blue and lilac suit I'd worn to Lord & Taylor. Wearing my outfits from the theatre was a relief. I never had to worry that they looked perfect.

She seemed more at ease hiding in her widow's weeds in a place where she wouldn't be gawked at by everyone, people she knew. People might look and wonder, but they wouldn't know she'd been the wife of a dead bootlegger. In addition, there were several other women in black mourning clothes. Strangers stayed away for fear that death was catching.

"May I speak to you, Juliette?" I motioned to her and she followed, leaving her sons to wait closer to the church's entrance.

"What is it?"

"Last week after church, Frank Romeo approached me at the diner where I was eating breakfast."

"Francis?" She closed her eyes for a moment, but she didn't seem surprised. "What did he want?"

"He wanted me to tell you he didn't have anything to do with Dante's death. Mr. Romeo wanted your husband to leave the business because of— Well, you know. Because of his feelings for you.”

She laughed in derision. “His feelings. Always his feelings.”

“He wanted me to tell you. I didn’t want to, because, well, he’s a little scary.”

“Once, he used to be a completely different Francis Romeo.” She touched my shoulder. “He knew you would tell me the truth, or at least tell me what he said.”

“He knew Mr. Scavullo saved some money for you, but he swore he didn’t know where it was. Or really what Dante had collected.”

“You mean something else, like gold or diamonds? That would be pretty fancy for that man.” She touched her plain gold band. She lifted her hands, signaling her boys to stay away. I turned around to make sure no one was nearby. It was a typical busy Sunday morning in New York. I saw that Marco and “Lashes” Dentino were positioned across the street from us. To make sure I relayed Romeo’s message? I couldn’t be sure.

“Dante never said anything specific to me about what he had arranged. He said we had all the time in the world.” She sobbed on the last words.

“What about his bank?’

“He wasn’t so big on banks. They fail, he said. But he was reconsidering.”

“Yes, but the new law—”

“He said when the time came, I would know.”

“Weren’t you curious? He was in a dangerous kind of job.”

“There is nothing in his will. Dante took so much pride in taking care of us, even though it killed him to have to work for Francis. To ask Dante about money? It would make it seem like I didn’t trust him.”

I reflected that not asking questions was not in my blood. I thought about the watch. The pocket watch and its fresh etching wouldn't leave me alone, but because I didn't know what it meant, I didn't want to bring it up. It may have been intensely personal. If Juliette could only give me a clue, maybe I could figure it out.

On the other hand, the watch might have nothing to do with Dante's plans for her future. The message might have been for the son who inherited it. Some code only the family would understand. And yet they hadn't recognized it.

"Could he have left a message for you? Something hidden?"

"Like in the movies, in the mystery stories?" She shook her head and her black veil danced in the wind. "Dante kept his business to himself. He wasn't a mysterious man, except for the way he died. I thought he was safe. I didn't love him when we married, but I grew to love him."

"And Frank Romeo?"

"He ruined all of us. I gotta go. My boys look hungry."

Thirty-Nine

REGGIE LOOKED SPLENDID IN HIS tuxedo and a top hat, an unexpected sight in the crowd leaving the theatre Sunday night. He swept off his hat and bowed to me.

"I wish I had my camera." I loved the thought of capturing Reginald Archibald Pendleton III on film and I mimed clicking the shutter. He grinned back.

"I'm glad you don't, that would be blackmail-worthy."

The show had gone well and I didn't expect to see anyone I knew. Nevertheless, I dressed up, hoping it would improve my gloomy mood. My lavender gown and amethyst earrings did the trick, but they also reminded me of the Welsh watchmaker and that still-cryptic timepiece. My coat was in my hand and Reggie rushed to help me into it.

"You're no slouch yourself. Stunning dress. Another secret from the costume shop?"

"You know me too well," I said. "Why are you here, Reggie? Not to see the show again?"

"Sadly, no. That would have been far more entertaining. Tonight was a command performance for my family. A great uncle's birthday. He's supposed to be fabulously fixed and no one dares insult him."

"Oh, so you do dress up."

"An order from my mother. I left as soon as I could. I was already in this get up, and Sardi's is nearby, and I owe you a coffee or two. So how about it?"

A night all about me? That sounded pretty great. I hugged him. And then a shadow hovered over us.

Marco Scavullo appeared to be strolling casually past the theatre, as if by accident. He moved through the crowd towards me. He was not formally dressed, but he swaggered my way and puffed out his chest. He threw a look toward Reggie that I didn't like.

"Evening, Miss de LaForet." He nodded but did not remove the black fedora from his head. "You working on that play for me, like we talked?"

My last nerve was frayed and I snapped back. "Just because you want it, doesn't mean we discussed it. I am not writing a play for you, Marco Scavullo. Get that through your thick head. And it will be a while before I'm ready to take on a new play. I'm still babying this one."

He narrowed his eyes. "You will. Write it for me."

"I don't take orders from you."

"Esmé doesn't take orders from anyone," Reggie said. "I know this. She's got a serious case of independence."

Marco moved closer until he and Reggie were nearly nose to nose. But if punches were going to be thrown, they should at least know each other. I introduced them.

"You're one of Frank Romeo's boys," Reggie said.

"I drive for him, high hat," Marco sneered back.

"Thanks for your interest, Marco." I moved between them. "Reggie and I have plans. Do give my regards to Bianca."

He shook his head. "You'll come around to Marco."

Reggie took my arm. I merely waved back as we made our way to Sardi's.

"How do you know that goon?" Reggie asked, flustered.

"Scavullo's visitation. I know I shouldn't have gone, but I knew Dante and his wife Juliette from church."

I could see Reggie mentally putting things together.

"And Chaseborn, how do you know him?"

"We were introduced there, at Scavullo's visitation."

I would go to my grave before telling anyone about our encounter in the school closet.

"Seems like I should have gone to his visitation, and I'm not even sure what that entails."

"You are so Protestant," I said.

"In name only. I'm really just a heathen. Ask my mother. You've been holding out on me, Esmé. Must have been quite a funeral."

"Not a funeral. That happens the next day. First the mourners gather and visit and view the corpse, and then everyone says the rosary and their prayers. Takes a while."

"How many mourners?"

"I didn't take a poll. Enough to fill the mortuary."

I ordered an old-fashioned. Reggie made it two. We were tucked into a table against the wall, sitting against a tall, upholstered bench at the famed restaurant. Above and all around us were caricatures of celebrities. Glamorous gowns and tuxedos were *de rigeur*. I tried not to gawk.

"You still having Chase problems? Or is it Chaseborn?"

"I'm such a fool, Reggie. I didn't know he was *that* Chaseborn, the one in the papers. I knew him as Chase. I'm usually rather discerning in my taste in men, except of course for you. And tell me, how in a city of too many millions, do I keep running into the man?"

"Maybe he's following you."

I pondered that. "He couldn't possibly think I have any information he wants."

"There's always attraction."

"You think? But Chaseborn's being followed by every debutante on the loose."

"That's it, they're too loose. And he's some big game trophy to bag. And before you say it, my dear Esmé, I don't have his kind of money or prospects. Not yet. The women who chase after me are in it for my charm and savoir faire."

He lifted his glass to me.

I rolled my eyes. "My dear Reginald, you are full of it."

"And that's why I love you, future wife."

FORTY

THREATS ARE NEVER THE BEST way to start the day. A letter addressed to me was on my desk at the theatre. Though I mostly received scripts from struggling playwrights, along with heartrending typewritten pleas to produce their plays, I occasionally received personal correspondence. But seldom like this.

This missive came in a pink envelope and matching pink notepaper and a dose of sour-yet-flowery perfume I didn't recognize. Or like. It wasn't signed, but it was brief.

> *Esmé de LaForet,*
> *You will never have my man. I will ruin you and destroy your reputation. I was there before you and I will be there after you. Stay away from him. This is a warning.*
> *A friend*

"A friend?" I seriously doubted this was from "a friend." I was relieved it didn't go to my apartment. At least whoever wrote it didn't know my home address. Yet who would threaten me? I had one guess, or maybe three.

I grabbed some Washington Irving stationery and jotted a brief note. I stuffed it, along with the offending pink missive, into a larger envelope, addressed it to Rupert Chaseborn at his office, and summoned a stagehand to deliver it. Let Chaseborn and Mrs. Carter sort it out. I tried to put it out of my mind, but it kept coming back. Neither could I get the stench of cheap perfume out of my nose.

You will never have my man. I didn't want her man. Did I have to put up a sign? But which *her* was it? Was Graydon such a prize, and was I really some kind of a threat?

≈

"You have a visitor." May was way too interested in the handsome blue-eyed man striding my way.

"I didn't expect you to come right over," I said.

"You didn't?" Graydon answered.

"It's simply that I don't like threats, even if they come wrapped in pink paper and dipped in a poison perfume bottle."

"May I steal her away from you?" Graydon asked May, who gazed at me for a sign that I was willing to go.

"I'm sure we could talk him into buying two subscriptions, for the next season," I said to May.

"You're pretty free with my money." He was amused.

"I'm still scheduled for another hour here."

"Two season subscriptions, it is." Graydon withdrew his wallet.

May had the paperwork ready to go. Prime orchestra seats too. He lifted me up by my elbow. "Shall we go, Miss de LaForet? You shameless hustler, you."

≈

"I am sorry for disturbing you, Graydon. I know we're trying not to see each other. And you didn't have to come in person. I merely thought you'd be interested."

We were sitting at a polished wood table in a too-bright automat, but it wasn't crowded at this time of day.

"You disturb me whether we see each other or not, Esmé. I don't like threats either. This one seemed pretty obvious."

He withdrew the letter from his pocket, grimacing at the scent that hadn't faded.

"You're saying Trixie is too obvious a suspect?"

He had picked up a cup of coffee and I bought coffee and an egg salad sandwich.

"Let me guess, you didn't eat lunch." He just cocked an eyebrow at me and refused to let me pay with my coins.

"I was distracted."

"I suppose death threats can derail the appetite."

As can infatuation, I thought. It was infatuation that I had, not love, I decided. I would just have to get over it.

"You seem to be the subject of someone's intense ardor, Graydon."

"And unfortunately, you find yourself in someone's crosshairs. But not Tricia Dunlop's. Even if she was foolish enough to write this, and her attorney strenuously warned her against any contact, the handwriting is off."

"It is? You've checked? And against what?"

"An old invitation. A cocktail party from when the Dunlops lived in the building. Tricia appended a personal note to me. Robbins files all my correspondence."

"Interesting. For your memoirs? *I, Beast!*" He sighed in exasperation. "But what if it was the Snow Queen or Priss-Pot? Possibly working together."

He lifted his cup. "Robbins compared them as well and discounted both. They didn't pen this either. Robbins was quite smug, I might add. He's always told me his files would be of use someday." I was flabbergasted.

"But you've only had the note a couple of hours."

"You don't think I'd wait on this? Toss it in the inbox and get to it sometime next week? When a potential lunatic could be after you?" Graydon seemed so outraged I couldn't help but giggle. "Besides, Robbins is ruthlessly organized and he likes getting out in the afternoon. I phoned him and he was at my office in thirty minutes with all the necessary documentation."

My own correspondence, and no, I didn't keep every-thing, resided in a couple of messy shoe boxes in my closet. The congratulatory notes I received at the theatre were packed into my bottom desk drawer. I simply must have Amelia "archive" them all sometime.

"Do you think they found someone else to write this for them? As a diversionary tactic?"

"Why bother? Priss-Pot did her worst when the two of you had lunch. She's gone on to other pursuits." He had a point.

"And the Snow Queen? She could have had a friend do this as a lark." I remembered her friend, the blond, blue-gowned lady I'd named 'Cinderella.'

"Preposterous. Millie and I bid adieu a while ago."

"A few weeks anyway. Yet, one naked portrait and her declaration in the ladies' room tells me otherwise."

"What are you talking about?"

"At Peacocks' that night. She told a friend she was going to marry you, though I didn't know at the time she meant you."

"Millie? Good Lord. That's a fate to be avoided."

We stared at each other. "May I see that?" He handed the letter over and I studied it. The words were simple. But the penmanship was beautiful, as if the writer had learned longhand in parochial school. Or an exclusive girls' board-ing school.

"The theatre's dark tonight," he said. "Will you be stay-ing at home?"

"Safe and sound." I had plans for a cozy fire and my in-evitable pile of reading.

It was twilight when we left and I would have preferred to walk home, but he escorted me to a taxi, for which of course he paid. He apologized for leaving me. He said he had a pressing appointment. I did too. With my fireplace, my muse, and a spot of sherry.

FORTY-ONE

THE DAY AFTER THE SCENTED pink threat arrived, the sky was a lovely silvery shade that seemed lit from within. It accompanied a drizzly day that alternated between mist and light rain. It was a perfect afternoon to take a photo stroll in the Ramble with my Leica, one of my most prized possessions. You never know what you'll catch on film.

I'd arranged to slip away from work that afternoon while it was still light. Central Park was quiet, and unlike the days of full sun, the crowds were scarce. I assumed most people were tucked inside or at a cozy restaurant with a pot of hot comfort, or sipping cocktails for two.

I was well prepared in my black turtleneck sweater, khaki slacks, and a warm wool jacket. I headed to the park, my camera on a strap around my neck, out of sight beneath my jacket.

The falling leaves were bright against the somber day, creating a multicolored carpet over the emerald grass, bright yellow, pumpkin orange, russet, bright crimson. The Ramble's bushes were thick and poetic in their march toward winter. It was misting heavily. I breathed deeply. Like Greta Garbo, I wanted to be alone.

A figure in a black pinstriped suit appeared on the path, appearing oddly formal.

"Esmé de LaForet, why you not go out with me?" It was Marco Scavullo. These 'unexpected' meetings were clearly deliberate and I didn't like it. He must be following me. "Tell me when."

"No, Marco. I'm not going out with you. I've told you before." I avoided saying mobsters were off my list of preferred dates, especially ones who showed up bizarrely out of the nearby trees of a secluded walkway in the Ramble. I tried to move on. He reached out and stopped me.

"We make a pretty couple."

"There's more to romance than that." I tossed the line off as if I were in a frothy play and not trying to flee from him as fast as possible.

The memory of three murders, of his uncle and Ratty Moretti and the unlucky racketeer gunned down in the street, hovered around my head. I picked up my pace.

"Stop." He commanded as if that was going to work.

"Leave me alone." He stayed one step behind me. I heard rustling in the bushes. Perhaps a rabbit or a fox. I turned around, looking for his constant companion. "Where's Bianca?"

"I left her at the zoo. She likes the animals."

"That's terrible. She's crazy about you. Appreciate what you have."

"I catch up with her later. I buy her some popcorn." He had the nerve to smile like he was granting a favor. She certainly deserved better than Marco. "Esmé, I just want to take you out to dinner sometime. Nice Italian place. We make a date. You're pretty, but too skinny."

"I said no. I have a career, I'm a writer, I'm busy, I have no time for you." That's always a good fallback, but I doubted that he understood writers' deadlines. Or women's lives.

"A career." He shrugged. "You need a nice man to take care of you. Your play is done. You're making lots of money. You can stop writing, until you write a part for me."

"I don't know where you get that idea. It's infuriating. I will write what I like and you have no part in my work."

He looked at me as if that were the most incomprehensible thing in the world.

"More plays? Without me?"

"That's right. Forget about me, Marco. You have Bianca Lombardi and she's too good for you."

The rustling grew stronger. Now I guessed it was a dog or a squirrel. I turned around to see what kind of animal it was. At the same time, someone fired a gun. Two rounds. Two huge booms. The sound was deafening, which meant it was close. Without thought, I hit the ground and rolled under a bush, happy the Ramble was so thick with foliage, if quite muddy. I heard Marco yelling in Italian, very loud. I lay there for a few moments, then I propped myself up on my elbows to see. Marco was clutching his perfectly sculpted cheek. Blood poured down his face.

"Marco!" a woman screamed. Suddenly Bianca was there with a handkerchief, pressing it to his face. Outrage and blood marred his matinee idol features. She was crying hysterically, like a terrified child, almost swallowed up in her baggy brown coat. He was shouting in Italian, turning this way and that, looking for the shooter. But the bullet had only grazed him, or he wouldn't still be standing.

Was it just a warning? If so, someone was a very good shot. The kind of trick shot you'd see at the rodeo. I was used to shooting guns with my grandfather, the former town marshal, but with wax plugs in my ears to soften the noise. Now my ears were ringing, my heart was thumping, and my hands were cold.

Still, I remembered my Leica. I pulled it from its case and snapped photos of Marco and Bianca yelling and gesturing at each other. And the torrent of blood from Marco's face wound. The Leica's shutter was so soft, no one heard.

The blood would absorb into the trail soon enough, I knew, it would be covered with leaves and vanish without a trace. In a few more seconds, Patrick Dentino was there. He put one arm around Bianca's shoulders to reassure her, then he spun around, gun in hand, looking far more lethal than the "Lashes" I knew. I took more pictures, one frame after another, until I was almost out of film.

Something suddenly felt hot against my wrist. I had squirmed deeper under the bush until I was lying on a small brass shell casing, nestled in scarlet leaves. The assailant had fired an automatic. I had no idea where the shooter was, but he must have been near for the casing to have reached where I lay. The small brass object seemed to glow in the grayish light. It was still hot to the touch. I rolled back far enough to focus and snapped a photo of the casing before popping it in my trouser pocket. It smelled of gunpowder.

Fearing that someone might see my camera and object to my photographing this scene, I slipped it off my neck and tucked it into my jacket pocket. I didn't plan all my actions, they were simply what any reporter—or ex-reporter—would do.

Marco was someone's target. But whatever mob business it was, I was not interested in finding out.

I rose to my muddy knees and stood. Marco was still bleeding, still screaming, Bianca was yelling. All in Italian. They paid no attention to me. I noticed he had pulled his own gun from what I guessed was a shoulder holster, but he was calming down and submitting to Bianca's ministrations. She still held the blood-soaked handkerchief to his face. I made my way to them.

"We should call the police." It wasn't the smoothest thing I could say, considering Marco's line of work.

"You out of your mind?" Marco said. He scanned the area and said something in Italian, but his voice was getting weaker.

"Did you see who it was?" I asked.

"No." He looked sullen. "But I will find him. I will kill him."

Bianca was sobbing. She had it bad for Marco and he clearly didn't return the feeling, at least not to the same degree. I wanted to tell her she needed another boyfriend in a less dangerous business. She sent me a look of utter loathing. I returned one, along with a gesture that I hoped said, *He's all yours.*

Marco was no longer focused on me, which I counted as a blessing. He'd run out of rage-fueled energy and he leaned on Bianca.

"We gotta get out of here," Patrick Dentino said. He ran a few steps ahead to make sure the shooter was long gone. "Follow me." Pat gave me a look that I should leave too, in the opposite direction. "Stay safe, Esmé Rafferty."

I nodded and backed up into the woods, where I had a view of them leaving, and the pond and the trail behind me. I repeated the details of the afternoon in my mind, so I could write them down as soon as possible. In the meantime, I seemed to be covered in leaves. I rubbed my sleeves, but the leaves hung on to the wet wool.

I had grown up in a town where the local lunatics shot up the street signs and the signs on the highway. Every sign was riddled with bullet holes. Oddly, since moving to New York City, I hadn't heard that much gunfire, except from blanks in prop guns in stage plays.

The shots I had heard today were neither the high sharp crack of a .22, nor the low heavy boom of a big-bore gun. I guessed the gun the shooter used was a .32 auto, a pocket gun. I pulled the casing out again and peered at it: Sure enough, a .32. What can I say? My grandfather, the former marshal, had a lot of guns.

My knees were scraped and my pants were covered in mud. My cheek stung. I was still shaking and in desperate need of comfort.

No, not Rupert Graydon Chaseborn.

FORTY-TWO

"RAFFERTY, YOU BEEN ROLLING AROUND in the bog with the Little People?"

I limped down the stairs into Lafferty's. My khakis were streaked with mud and my coat was now a coat of many-colored leaves. I must have smacked my knee when I hit the ground, because it hurt like the devil. I suspected there was dirt on my face too. Just another day in show biz.

"Looks like it. I'm sorry, Devlin, I'm probably too filthy to come in." I would regret leaving, because the tavern felt warm and welcoming.

"Nonsense. You look all in. Take a seat by the fire. Leave a trail of bright leaves and I'll find ye. Now, there's a marvelous potato soup on the stove. I recommend it with warm bread and butter." He had a knack for recommending just the thing I wanted. I could have hugged him. I didn't.

"Sounds like heaven."

"And you'll be drinking?"

"Hot buttered rum and a glass of water."

He nodded. "So what happened to you, lass?" Devlin Sullivan looked concerned and ready to fight off any enemy I might have.

I looked down at my filthy clothing. I made sure my camera was safe in its leather case, in my pocket. "Long story."

"Good thing you're a playwright. Weave us a tale, Rafferty. It wasn't the Englishman you were here with, was it?"

I shook my head. "No, wrong place, wrong time. Italians. In the park. I was an innocent bystander. I hit the ground when I heard gunshots." He escorted me to the table by the fireplace.

"Well, you're safe now and you can be sure no Italians will show up. They don't seem to like this place. I don't serve the spaghetti and the meatballs, do I now?"

He winked, then he went away to put in my order for soup and a hot toddy. I was suddenly quite cold and I didn't want to tell any more tales of gunshots. When Devlin returned, I changed the subject.

"Have you seen my show yet?" I asked.

"Been meaning to, but—"

"Would a couple of comp tickets help?" I knew how difficult it could be just to put a few dollars aside for a show.

"Now you're speaking my language. I've been promising Molly a night in the bright lights."

I took a couple of passes from my bag and signed them. My allotment of free tickets was almost gone. "It's going to close soon."

He nodded his big head. "Yes, but word is out it's a hit and I'm betting you'll be moving the production to another theatre."

"Sal is working on it."

"And a new play? With a part for me?" He grinned.

Story of my life. Nobody wants to buy a ticket, everybody wants a part. "I'll let you know. Might be a while."

I repaired what I could in the powder room. My slacks were soaked from the drizzle, so it didn't matter that I took a towel and soap to wipe off most of the mud. I caught a glimpse of my face in the mirror and frightened myself. I washed up, taking care with a scrape on my chin. It stung anyway. I combed my tangled hair. I did what I could with powder and lipstick and a dab of mascara.

When I emerged from the room, Devlin Sullivan approved.

"Better, lass. You looked like you went ten rounds with a wild dog, or a wild leprechaun. I'm told they can be quite nasty." He was making fun, for my sake, but he was clearly concerned.

"You should see the dog." I was grateful none of Marco's blood had splashed on me. I spied the phone booth near the back of the bar. "Need to make a call, Dev. Be right back."

I couldn't alert the police, for fear of reprisals from the mob, but perhaps Chase would be interested. After all, it was his case. The late Dante Scavullo was his client. My information might help somehow. I wasn't opposed to helping someone find a murderer.

The shell casing was cold now, but it still burned in my imagination, and my pocket. If Chase wasn't interested, then forget him. For that matter, Reggie would want to know that another mobster connected to Frank Romeo was involved in a shooting. Maybe later.

I called Chase's and Robbins answered. "Please give this message to Mr. Chaseborn."

"Miss de LaForet, I'll get him."

"No, please just tell him Marco Scavullo was shot in Central Park. A bullet grazed his face. Police were not involved. This is complicated, but I found one of the shell casings. I can send it over tomorrow."

Graydon apparently snatched the phone away from his valet.

"Esmé, what's all this?"

"Someone shot Marco Scavullo. Do you want the shell casing?"

That stopped him cold for a second. "Where are you?"

"Waiting for my potato soup and I don't feel like talking to you."

"You bloody well are talking to me."

"My, my, the language. I'll send it to you tomorrow."

"Esmé—"

I hung up, feeling vexed, and made my way to my favorite table. Devlin handed me my hot buttered rum and a glass of water.

"You're shaking, Rafferty. No wonder, arriving here covered in foliage and muck. You look like a production of *A Mid-Autumn Night's Dream*. Ah, but you mentioned the Italians."

"A tale for another evening, Devlin, when I've had time to embroider it." I slumped in my seat. I was grateful for the fire. I took off my jacket and put my camera around my neck. I didn't want to take any chances on losing it. I decided my sweater was halfway presentable.

"The rum will help. Ah, here's the soup now."

Molly, his lovely wife, red haired and freckled, delivered my meal with a smile, then they left me in peace.

"Come, Devlin darlin', let Miss Rafferty collect herself."

I sipped the hot toddy. It warmed me all the way down. I retrieved my notebook and started making notes before the details faded away. I was halfway through the potato soup when Chaseborn arrived. I uttered the most theatrical sigh I could manage.

"What the hell are you doing here?" I inquired.

"You mentioned potato soup. Where else would you be but here at Lafferty's? Detective, you know."

"The intuitive detective. I'm impressed. Next time I'm going to Delmonico's. Please go away."

"No. What were you doing with Marco Scavullo?" He sat down, too close for comfort.

"I wasn't with him! I was in the park taking photos. He showed up out of nowhere, with Bianca in tow, and he asked me out while her back was turned. The bastard."

I didn't want to say Marco seemed to be following me. I didn't have to. Graydon took my hand. It stung from where I had scraped it. I took it back and reached into my pocket for the crumpled handkerchief with the shell casing. I showed it to him.

"Here, you can have it. There were at least two shots. One hit him, but I only found the one casing."

"How do you know this was from the shooter's gun? It is Central Park, after all."

"I rolled over on it. It was still hot when I picked it up, and it smells like fresh gunpowder. Happy? Now go away."

He sniffed it. He stuffed my handkerchief and the shell in his jacket pocket. I picked up my spoon and ate more of the savory soup. It was warm and creamy, but I wasn't as hungry as I had been. Graydon, who simply could not take a hint, or a direct order, signaled Sullivan.

"Pint of Guinness, please." The Brit accent sounded out of place.

Devlin looked at me for my permission. "Esmé Rafferty?"

"As long as you give him the bill for all this."

"No way, lass. Yours is on the house, in exchange for those tickets." He patted his pocket.

"Those are comps," I said. "Make him pay."

"Whatever you say, Rafferty." Devlin departed to pull the pint for Graydon, who seemed to be thinking about what to say.

"You seem to be angry with me, but you still called me."

"It's your case, isn't it?" I said. "First, someone took out Dante Scavullo, then Guido Moretti, and yet another bootlegger, I don't even know his name, and now an attempt on Marco Scavullo. What do they have in common?"

"You could have been hurt much worse." He lifted his finger to my chin. "You have a scrape."

I thought I had covered it well enough with the powder. It began to throb.

"I'm sorry I offered you the stupid shell casing."

"Don't be. It gives me more information." He sipped his Guinness. "It won't do for you to get shot."

"I don't intend to." At that moment, I wondered whether I should take my Colt Detective Special .38 out of my locked trunk and keep it handy. That had been another little gift from my grandfather, Marshal Rafferty. It was perfectly natural in his world to go about armed. As I was his only granddaughter, it was natural for him to teach me how to shoot and carry a gun.

But here in New York City carrying a gun would feel very different.

Graydon put on a show of concern, but I still didn't trust him. Everyone was lying to me. All I ever did was return a stupid pocket watch!

"What were you doing out on such a miserable day?" he asked.

"It's not miserable. It is raining and delightfully gray. I was taking pictures. The light was perfect. Moody."

He glared at me. "Give me your version of this."

I glared back. "I was strolling through the Ramble and taking photographs. I wanted to use up the film in my Leica. I have pictures of Marco bleeding. At least I think I do. I was taking them from the ground under a bush."

"What were you doing under a bush?"

"When I heard the first shot, I hit the ground and rolled under the bush. That's where I felt the shell casing. So small and yet so hot. I didn't see the shooter. I aimed my camera and took pictures. They didn't hear me because he and Bianca—"

"The one who always has a fresh bruise?"

"Right. They were screaming at each other. They didn't notice me."

"How did you have the presence of mind to use your camera?"

"I'm a reporter! Or used to be. I've always been a reporter, a writer, a photographer."

"Lord help us, Esmé. Elf."

I took another spoonful of the soup. Still tasty, but not as hot. I signaled to Devlin for a cup of coffee.

"Coffee? Do you have a date?" Graydon asked.

"Yes, with a darkroom. I know one where I can rent space."

"Why tonight? You look perfectly raw to the bone."

I ran my fingers through my hair and straightened my clothes.

"Photos of the scene of the crime. A few of Marco. It's hard to say what I got, because I took them from the muck, right next to the trail. He was screaming at Bianca. And Patrick 'Lashes' Dentino showed up too." I lifted my camera to prove my story.

Devlin arrived with the coffee. "Here ya go, Rafferty. Pop the pennies off a dead man's eyelids."

He stared intently at Graydon, as if to warn him to behave. I grinned and thanked him. He was right about the coffee. It was heavyweight-prizefighter strength.

"I also have photos from opening night of *Leaving Alamogordo* that I need to develop." It wasn't late, but it was dark outside and it felt like midnight. "First, I'm going home to change out of these filthy clothes."

"I'm going with you," he insisted.

"No."

"Yes. Don't argue with me, Elf. Not this time."

"If you insist, then you will have to pay me for my work."

"What?" His face registered surprise, which gratified me.

"You're interested in the photos. If I have a good one of Marco clutching his bleeding face, you have to pay."

"You are exasperating, Esmé, but it's true I want that photo."

"If I allow you to come along, it will cost you. After all, I am a witness and an informant." If he had any decency, Graydon would refuse and leave me alone. He didn't. He considered a moment and then he actually chuckled.

"Very well. I'll pay you. As an associate. Mrs. Carter will send you a check. I pay informants weekly. And I can help with the processing."

It helped that Graydon was being businesslike, and it felt like a small victory. It was also a huge annoyance to have him tag along. As for my poison pen pal, he had nothing new.

At least I got to finish my potato soup.

FORTY-THREE

THE CLERK AT THE DARKROOM in the Village, not so cleverly named "The Darkest Room," knew both of us.

We'd both used the facilities. Obviously, never at the same time. There were four small darkrooms on site, open all hours for photographers, detectives, and, no doubt, blackmailers.

Graydon and I spent a couple of hours developing my film, using the enlarger, and making prints. The moment when the pictures came into view always felt like sleight of hand to me. We focused first on the photos I'd taken in the aftermath of the shooting.

The photos of Marco came out better and clearer than I anticipated, although my point of view—shooting from the ground up—didn't lend itself to the most flattering poses. Marco clutched his face in all of them. However, his blood kept flowing, and Bianca stayed by his side, reaching up with her handkerchief to staunch the flow. When Patrick was in the frame, he was all concentration and concern. He seemed to be looking for someone, perhaps me.

I had also taken a couple of shots of the brass shell casing, catching the light, which made it glow like gold against the leaves. Graydon had to take my word for it that it was hot when I retrieved it. What the photos failed to show was any trace of the shooter. The unknown assailant left no mark that I could see.

"These are good, Esmé. Very clear. Unfortunately, they don't tell us who fired the gun."

"We can't have everything all at once, can we."

I hung the prints up to dry and pulled out more photo paper. I enlarged and exposed the photo of Scavullo's watch, hoping I'd be able to see the details later. Then I examined more of the negatives.

"Now what?" he asked.

"Pictures from my opening night, *Leaving Alamogordo.* You can leave. I'll catch a taxi."

"We are not having this argument again." He folded his arms and leaned against the table.

"I don't want to keep you from your fawning females, the Snow Queen, Priss-Pot, Trixie. Are there more?"

"We should get one thing straight right now. There are no other women in my life. I was planning a quiet night at home."

"Just you and your faithful valet. How novel."

I dipped the sheet in the developer. The theatre marquee at the Irv came up, with a crowd of people. In the dim red light, I couldn't make out all the details, but I was pleased there were more photos of me than I expected, showing the details of my gown, and a closeup of my face that was flattering, glowing with happiness. I was aware that not every moment in the theatre would be as sweet, and I was grateful that Reggie Pendleton was no slouch with my camera. He took several beautiful shots in the theatre lights, knowing I'd want them later. He also handed the camera off to Willie, who took a couple of Reggie and me, because we'd want them for our scrapbooks. Although I was at the center of many of the photos, there were also strangers around me. Perhaps some of those society dames that filled Chaseborn's calendar were in the crowd.

"I was going to tell you, Esmé, about me. About being a Chaseborn."

"When, Rupert Graydon? When Hell froze over?"

"I toyed with the idea of telling you a bit at a time. It's not unusual to have a different professional name. You should know, being in the theatre." I didn't say anything. It was just like him to keep talking while I was busy with the photographs and chemicals. I hung up another print to dry. "I didn't count on you running into Priss-Pot, you see."

"Apparently not. New York is a big city. I'm sure you could keep a few willing females in the dark. Or the dark-room." Graydon put another piece of paper under the enlarger. "More?"

"I want copies of these too. Marco Scavullo was in the crowd that night. Perhaps someone was following him. We'll make two of everything."

He paid the entire darkroom tally and we each had a complete set of eight-by-tens. I was calculating a reasona-ble fee for my time and effort as a crime scene photogra-pher. I wasn't about to let him forget.

By the end of the session, we were more casual around each other, but still reserved. We caught a cab back to his apartment, ostensibly to examine the prints in good light and with a quality magnifying glass. At least that's what Graydon said. I made a note to myself to buy a magnifying glass. Every detective should own one.

I hadn't been back to his penthouse in the sky since dragging him there when he was ill. I certainly wasn't dressed for the occasion, but I could run away fast if I needed to.

Graydon took my hand and led me through the front door. The familiar thrill of his touch startled me. Appar-ently, I wasn't over him yet.

"He won't approve of my trousers," I said, indicating the night doorman.

"That is no one's concern except mine, and those pants flatter your delightful bottom."

I had changed them between Lafferty's and The Darkest Room.

"Not your concern either. Really, Graydon, I must go home." I turned around, intending to leave.

"Esmé, this won't take long, and I'll make sure you get home safe. With bullets flying around you today, I am even more concerned for your safety."

We rode the elevator in an uncomfortable silence. Inside his apartment, he steered me into the study and spread the photos on his massive mahogany desk. Graydon turned on many lights and took out two magnifying glasses so we could search for details.

The photos in Central Park were good quality and clear. My Leica saved the day. There was pretty-boy Marco, outraged and in pain, holding his face with blood dripping onto his jacket and shirt. I separated out my own set of pictures.

"Where's Robbins tonight?"

"Out, with your Amelia, the wonder housekeeper. Bowling or some such. They seem taken with each other."

"Maybe someone gets a happy ending here," I muttered. I paced around the room while Graydon was busy with the magnifying glass. I wondered if he was silently grading my camera and darkroom skills. In fact, I was sure of it.

I peered into his studio, expecting to see those paintings of Chaseborn's nude paramours, but they were missing. My eyes were drawn to another entry in his oeuvre. I moved into the room to view it more closely. Curiosity compelled me.

This painting seemed to glow from within and was vibrant with color. While he had depicted the Snow Queen and Priss-Pot against pallid backgrounds as naked as they were, this one was multihued. Those were tall vertical paintings, while this one was horizontal. I gasped without thinking.

In the center, a woman lay on a bed with a green velvet headboard that seemed to grow into a tree with many branches. Her eyes were closed as she rested her head against the lacy white pillows, her long red-gold hair ringleted down her pale shoulders, where the straps of her nightgown had slipped. Drops of perspiration beaded on her forehead, and her expression seemed to linger somewhere between pain and pleasure. A small brass nameplate identified it as "Fever."

I was looking at myself.

The rat had painted me when I was sick and out of my head! When it was my turn to be felled by that ferocious fever. It was a small mercy that he hadn't painted me naked. Not quite. Although I wore my pink nightgown, it was sheerer than the one I recalled wearing. Practically transparent, the negligee in the painting left nothing to the imagination, or rather Chaseborn's imagination. Darker shadows lay beneath the flimsy pink silk gown.

I took a deep breath and considered the rest of it. The green cover and white sheets had been kicked off in disarray during the fever, and he had painted her legs bare from her knees down to her feet, with delicately painted pink toes. I couldn't decide if it was lewd, or lurid, or something else—

If it hadn't been me, I would have said it was beautiful and sensual. But it *was* me and I was appalled. I'd never been the subject of any kind of painting, and here I was in the practically altogether.

He didn't make a sound as he came into the room. I felt him standing behind me.

"It's for you, Esmé, if you want it."

"I didn't give you permission." I refused to look at him.

"No. I didn't give you permission to plunder my history either."

"I didn't need your permission, it was all in the New York Public Library."

"True. I'm sure we could argue the fine points. But I was compelled by your beauty and my fear that you might die and leave me. It reveals more about both the artist and the model than is polite, I realize. And I think this is the best painting I've ever done." He reached out as if to touch it.

"It could be interpreted in a couple of different ways," I pointed out. "One, a fever that nearly killed her. Whoever she is."

"And two, a woman in the throes of passion. I know."

"It was your deliberate choice, Graydon."

"Guilty."

"You are a rat. A rat troll."

"I've been called worse." It was hard to stop staring at the painting. "You may do what you want with it. Destroy it, if you must."

I paused before speaking. "I couldn't do that. It's strange and beautiful, Graydon. It also infuriates me." But it compelled me as well. While it wasn't exactly something I would put over my mantel, I saw the work and the feeling that went into it. I felt shaken.

"I couldn't stop myself, Elf. If I couldn't have you, I wanted your portrait, lovely and vulnerable."

He moved closer and put his hands on my shoulders, which sent a different kind of thrill into me.

"With my eyes closed. I don't like being vulnerable."

"You couldn't see me. I fancied that you needed me and to be honest, I never knew how sick I'd been until I saw how desperately ill you were."

"I've forgotten much of it."

"I felt quite helpless," he said.

"But not so helpless you couldn't sketch me while I was senseless."

"Nurse Jesse ordered me to stop fretting and do something useful. I was making her nervous. So I sketched."

I turned away from the picture and the subject of me.

"Are the photographs satisfactory?"

"They're more than I anticipated. They prove Marco is a target, like his uncle was. But why?"

My stack of photos was lying on the desk next to his. I picked mine up.

"I'm leaving."

"I'll get the car."

"I need to be alone, Graydon. My thoughts are all jumbled. You can call a taxi for me."

He reached for me. I pushed him away. I was on the verge of tears.

"Very well. Let me escort you downstairs. I don't suppose you want to kiss goodbye forever again, do you?"

FORTY-FOUR

FOR ONCE IN MY LIFE, I had secrets I couldn't tell anyone, or even write, which was my usual escape. Graydon Chase was the only person with whom I could discuss these things. And he was out of the question.

I'd witnessed a mob-related shooting in Central Park and, if I didn't keep my mouth shut, I could be next. And then there was the painting. I tried not to think about the woman in the pink nightgown as *me*, but some other woman. Graydon had plundered my most vulnerable moment. Yet in that same moment he had also saved me, and brought in the nurse. The finished painting spoke of many things.

I told myself she was an idealization of a woman, prettier than I was, a different person. I just happened to be there when he had paper and pen. He sketched me and then transferred it to an oil painting. It must have taken hours and hours.

Though lovely, Graydon's painting shocked me. It presumed a great intimacy that was not there. Or was it? Being ill and being exposed while helpless rips a kind of veil away. I worried over a hundred things. Did he paint it to get back at me for my dossier on him? But how could he be angry?

All the things I had found, the stories and the photos, the women he was seen with, they were all, first of all, paraded in the public eye. Then in the newspapers, and finally collected in the library. I merely compiled a list. Graydon knew all of this. I reminded myself to retype my list of his activities—and make a carbon copy. It didn't seem likely that I'd get the original back now.

I tried to forget the whole thing. On the way to the theatre that morning, I bought a newspaper. *The Times* proclaimed NEW DEAL SCORES NATIONWIDE VICTORY. The papers were full of election news, and I was glad to see that a New York woman, Caroline O'Day, had won a seat in Congress.

But I wasn't interested in politics today. I looked for something else. There was nothing about the shooting in the Ramble. Marco and his crew hadn't gone to the police, nor had anyone reported hearing gunshots. I wondered if Marco knew or suspected who shot him. May broke into my thoughts and offered me a cup of coffee. That was unusual. I didn't have any extra goodies to share.

"What's up?" I asked.

"Congratulations. Sal found another stage for *Leaving Alamogordo*. He's pretty proud of himself."

"Another theatre?" I dropped the papers and reached for the coffee. "Really? Where? And thank you."

"He's not going to name it until Friday night, the post-show party."

"I have to wait?"

May laughed. "You playwrights. No other words?"

"They'll come, give me a minute." I sipped May's magical elixir and figured Sal would have a very difficult time keeping a secret. "I am stunned, happy, astonished, thrilled, and very possibly scared to death."

"What? Why?"

Because I could worry about *anything*, especially good luck. My parents had distrusted luck. If I got lucky now, would I ever get lucky again? "The first run has been great, but... Will there be an audience for the next run?"

"We could sell out half another run right now. Esmé, your show is safe and so is your job. *Leaving Alamogordo* will reopen just before Christmas."

"For the holiday season." My head spun. "And I find out Friday where it's going to be? Really?"

"According to Sal." She returned to her roster of reservations for Friday. "Here's an interesting name. Francis Romeo and guest."

"No, it couldn't be." That's what I said, but I worried about why 'Frankie the Cat' Romeo was coming to my show. To see if I could really write? I'm sure my feminist perspective and sassy heroine would not please the very traditional macho Italian male, not to mention the traditional gangster.

"He and Sal are old friends," May said. "He's been to a few of our shows. Seems nice. You never met him?"

"Oh my God. You've got to be kidding." My nerves felt frayed, as if by a cheese grater. "Old friends? How old?"

"High school. And I know he's one of the, you know, *Italian club*, but he's never interfered with a show. He knows they go bust as often as they succeed. And he's always on his best behavior here. Always a gentleman."

"That's supposed to make me feel better?"

"Your feelings are your business. Another cup?"

If that weren't enough of a shock, Nina Ogilvy wanted a few words with me for 'a piece' for the society pages. Slated just before Friday's show. Nina intended to break the news that it was definite, that the run of *Leaving Alamogordo* would be extended in another theatre. She was bringing a photographer.

Me, in the society section? Irony was afoot and sprinting. My parents would be proud and horrified. I had relatives who believed decent people didn't belong in the newspapers, or even writing for them. Well, that train had left the station.

"Look glamorous, doll. It sells papers. And tickets," Nina said before hanging up.

As it turned out, most of my comp tickets were coming home to roost, as most of them had reserved for Friday night's performance. Patrick Dentino was taking his mother. Nurse Jesse and guest were on the list. Even Lady Jane Chaseborn had managed to convince the box office to seat her and a companion for that evening.

And my housekeeper, the skeptical Amelia Applewood, had finally consented to attend the show, with Robbins, but I'm sure it was her interest in him and not me that spurred her out of the movie theatres and over to Broadway.

&

Sal Rossi proved he could keep a secret, increasing the anticipation and nerves of everyone connected to the show. By Friday, the theatre was a madhouse. I fled early to prepare. I hadn't heard from Graydon since our last parting. Perhaps he was abiding by my wishes. Marco hadn't turned up either. Maybe his face was really damaged. I didn't know, but I took the respite as a gift.

Amelia decided she'd come over Friday and stay the night in the maid's room, because her mother was driving her crazy.

"She for sure is going to come up with some crazy nonsense to delay me. It's her special genius. Besides, you need me to help you get ready. And did you say something about a photographer? You should look like a glamour girl. Like a movie star. I can do that."

However, first we had to deal with another crisis. Amelia swore she had nothing to wear. She had her eye on an older evening gown of mine, and I was happy to give it to her. The simple pink satin gown complemented her coloring perfectly and I hadn't realized we wore the same size. It was the first evening gown I had bought, before the navy one, and it too had seen its share of plays. While it was pretty, the shade never quite suited me or my coloring, not the way my theatre costumes did.

"Wouldn't you prefer something new?" I asked her.

"Why? This is new to me. And it's in perfect shape, not like you played baseball in it. I could just borrow it. Honest, I'll treat it like gold."

"It's yours, Amelia. I have enough."

Amelia squealed, actually *squealed* with delight. She tried it on and looked like Jean Harlow, though prettier and softer than Harlow. She took it off and concentrated on me.

"Don't forget you need me," she said. "Makeup and hair."

"I've been doing all right."

"True, but you're wearing a spectacular new gown, it might need a tweak here and there, and don't forget that newspaper photographer your friend Nina is bringing."

"How could I forget?"

Photos reminded me I wanted to take another gander at the ones I'd taken and developed side by side with Graydon. Something was nagging me about them.

I groaned at Amelia and sat demurely in front of my dressing table in my robe while she suggested things for me to do, starting with a face massage and a mask and lying down for a half hour. She peppered me with suggestions.

Amelia had taken a long time working on her own makeup and hair, which seemed a tad blonder and shinier than usual. She wore a smock to protect herself before donning the pink frock.

"Black velvet ribbons with pearls entwined in your hair," Amelia ordained. "We can braid it over the crown and tuck the rest under in the back. You sure you don't want me to cut your hair? Just a quick trim? Remember, Esmé, photos are forever."

I shook my head. She made do with pulling some curls around my face and securing them with her special hair-setting concoction.

"Photos are forever. I remember. Clearly." I leafed through my crime photos from the Ramble as she continued improving me.

I submitted to her ministrations like the utterly cowed employer that I was. I closed my eyes while she performed her little makeup miracles. When I opened my eyes, I was surprised to see a wash of silver eyeshadow on my lids and a hint of dark green higher up. My eyebrows were darkened. Lips, a bright red. She dotted my cheeks with the lipstick and commenced rubbing to blend it.

"What the hell is that?" She screeched at a close-up of Marco holding his face. Blood dripping through his fingers, Bianca next to him, all anguish and love. "They look like gangsters, real-life gangsters. And what is up with her and that baggy coat?" I looked closer. Baggy coats were the style that season.

"Um, these are from the theatre," I lied. "Rehearsal for another show. Just a little stagecraft."

She didn't believe a word I said. "Sure, stagecraft. That is so ugly! I don't care how handsome he is. Or was. Did he really get shot in the face?"

There was something about the three of them in the next photo. Was it the composition, or Marco or Bianca, or Patrick looking over his shoulder? I let my thoughts simmer. Amelia grabbed the photos away and set them face down where I couldn't see them.

"Concentrate, Esmé."

Amelia and I together defused my anxiety by making me look my best for Friday night's show and after-party. You never know who you might meet. Hopefully, someone to make me forget Graydon Chase. Someone handsome, and honest. Without that English accent. But preferably with that same electric touch in his fingertips.

I chose the one evening dress I'd been holding back from *Afternoon Tea with Nigel,* a glorious creation with a sleeveless black velvet bodice and a deep V in the back with silver lamé straps, and silver lamé gores set into the black velvet skirt that flared out dramatically (stiffened with horsehair in the hem). If I spun, I'd look like a very expensive and glamorous top.

This black velvet and silver lamé creation was yet another testament to Willie's talent and alteration skills. The bias-cut gown slipped over my head and shimmied down my body. It was tight fitting over the bust, with cleverly concealed snaps under the left arm. It created a beautiful geometric pattern as I waltzed around my living room. Amelia whistled. No last-minute tweaks were needed.

"Yeah, I know you're glamorous, Esmé, but you got to go. I'll be along with Robbins."

Amelia handed me my evening coat and tiny silver bag, barely big enough for a miniature lipstick and compact, cab fare, and my housekey—and shoved me out the door.

❧

"Another shot over there, under the chandelier."

Nina Ogilvy was ordering her photographer around. Her pen was stuck behind her ear and her notebook was tucked into the décolletage of her copper satin gown. Dressed up and ready to take on the world, her rings and bracelets sparkled as she pointed this way and that. She had a genius for making me laugh during almost every photo.

"Be fair, Nina," I begged. "I don't want to look like a laughing hyena in all of them."

I was positioned on the red carpeted stairs with the skirt of my dress sprayed out, thinking it was a shame the pictures would be black-and-white. "I can get copies, right?"

"Right. And maybe you could get one tinted. Dramatic."

At that moment, Rupert Graydon Chaseborn opened the heavy glass door in the lobby for his mother. I froze, staring at him. He stared back. I heard the flashbulbs pop.

"That's it. We've got the shots," Nina said. "Good stuff, Esmé."

"What?" I swiveled her way.

"We're done. Enjoy the show. I'll write this up in the back row. Don't worry, it's puff. This one's going to be cotton candy, sweet as sugar, and I hope not too sticky." Nina lowered her voice. "But here, I got something to tell you."

Nina gestured and I met her on the stair landing. The photographer fell away and Graydon was taking care of Lady Jane's coat and things.

"Listen, I got a request from our mutual pal, Reginald Pendleton the Third, to help head off some scurrilous rumor about you. Naming no names, of course. But we both of us don't like this rumor."

"Me? Rumors?"

"Yeah, you and some millionaire playboy." She lifted her head toward Graydon. "Rupert Chaseborn, aka Graydon Chase. Isn't that him over there? Don't worry, I know it's just a crazy rumor." She winked.

FORTY–FIVE

I THREW HER A *DON'T-GO-THERE* look. "Tell me what you've got, Nina, and I'll tell you the truth."

"Some floozy's trying to pawn off this rumor, wanted it planted as a 'blind' item."

"No names, but everyone would know who you're talking about?"

"Exactly. Not generally the sort of trash we peddle. Well, sometimes. She alleges you spent the night with him."

No good deed ever goes unpunished. When would I ever learn?

"The God's honest truth is that I was at a gentleman's apartment right after he was struck with that virus that's killing people. We were going to meet for lunch, but one look and I knew it was a no-go. I took him home. You know how fast it's hitting everyone."

"Yeah, they're dropping like flies. My editor had it. And no fooling?"

She pulled the pencil from behind her ear. It was heading toward her notebook.

"I was there, but I wasn't alone. There was a doctor, a valet, and a nurse. The nurse was there all night. The gentleman in question was deathly ill and I couldn't leave him until I was sure he was going to live."

Nina paused and looked at me. We'd known each other long enough that she knew my life story.

"Reminded you of watching your parents die, didn't it? And then poor old Roger."

"Poor old Roger." Funny thing that when I nursed my fiancé for days on end, no one cared. No one ever thought my honor had been compromised. "If it makes any difference, the gentleman's place was pretty crowded, with the doctor, the night nurse, the valet."

"And the floozy? How did she find out?"

I doubted if Tricia Dunlop really was a floozy, but I wasn't going to correct Nina.

"She showed up early in the morning, after getting a hot tip from the doorman or someone. Tried to make me believe she was the gentleman's fiancé. She never was, by the way. Word has it she's a gold digger. Out of cash and out of luck. Just a rumor."

Nina chewed her pencil as she calculated how she'd handle the item, if it had to go in. "So, we don't have a Scarlet Woman tale, not that I'd believe it anyway, or blame you if it was true. We gotta take our shots in this life." Her eyes drifted over to Graydon.

"You were saying?" I prompted. I could see her writing the lede in her head. It wouldn't be more than a couple of paragraphs in a lengthy column packed with juicy gossip.

"Right. This isn't a tale of scarlet shame, but a Florence Nightingale, ministering all night at the risk of her own health and reputation. No names. What do you think? Maybe 'lady of the theatre' would be better than 'playwright'?" she suggested.

"Agreed. I hope it's nipped in the editorial bud."

"I don't know, depends on my editor. But it's juicy. And there are witnesses?"

"Like I said, doctor, nurse, valet. And thank Reggie for me, for wanting to protect my reputation." I wasn't going to top off this item with information on my own battle with the virus. That would hardly lend any glamour to it.

Nina's pencil danced in the air. "What if I want to check this info with the millionaire himself?"

"He's right over there, and we're not an item."

"Great. Don't worry, Esmé, you're going to come off smelling like the proverbial rose."

I didn't feel like a rose. Nina was at Graydon's side in a flash, asking him for confirmation. He lifted his eyes with a question for me. I nodded that I was good with Nina. He spoke with her briefly, but I could sense he was threatening to sue her newspaper. I saw Nina smile. That kind of talk would never scare off Nina. I reflected that if this item made it to print, I could add it to my Chaseborn dossier.

Lady Jane managed to scoot across the lobby and waved to me. "My dear Esmé! I am so looking forward to your play."

Could this be the same woman I'd met? She was positively animated. She seemed years younger.

"Do be kind," I said.

"No need, I know I'm going to love it. And let me tell you, I am several chapters into my novel. Why, it seems to be writing itself! With me at the helm, of course."

I told her how impressed I was with her progress, and she should keep at it. I suspected she'd been writing it in her head for years. I knew how that worked.

"Oh yes, and I've decided to put in the grisliest murder. It's delicious."

Over her shoulder, I spotted Robbins and Amelia. They headed our way to greet Lady Jane and take care of her. Amelia winked at me. Meanwhile, Graydon dispensed with Nina and headed my way. Several long-legged strides and he was by my side.

"This not-seeing-each-other isn't working very well," I said.

"You arranged for the tickets for my mother. I can't imagine why."

"I have a weird sense of humor."

"I should have known. She asked me to come with her and she's been quite decent lately, since she met you. I couldn't say no and I am beyond chagrined."

I simply shook my head. "What did you tell Nina?"

He stood closer to me, ostensibly so no one else could hear us. I assumed it was to make my heart beat faster and throw off my equilibrium. He leaned down to whisper to me.

"I may have mentioned my eternal gratitude to you. I did threaten to sue if either of our names got out. If your name is dragged down? There'll be hell to pay."

"What did she say?"

"I believe she put a stick of gum in her mouth and started to chew."

"Some people will be able to figure it out. It will tickle her to paint me as Joan of Arc."

"This thing has got to be the work of Tricia. It's monstrous."

"She'll regret it after Nina gets through painting her as an anonymous trickster who's merely a jealous gold digger trying to destroy me." I felt a little sick about the whole thing.

"Did you tell her we were friends?" Graydon asked.

"What else could I say?"

He lifted my hand to kiss it, making sure Nina, and everyone else, could see us.

Patrick Dentino walked into view in the lobby with a handsome redheaded woman who had to be his mother. I could see where his long lashes came from. He pointed me out to her and she strutted right over. They both looked spit-polished, he in a suit, she dressed to the nines, her hair in a cloud of ginger curls.

"Sure, and you must be Esmé Rafferty de LaForet."

"Mrs. Dentino." We shook hands.

"I'm indebted to you for this wonderful night and the tickets to your play. I was at a Broadway show once, before I married Patrick's father. And loved every minute of it. And to think you're a woman writer! But of course you are, aren't women always the smart ones? My son Patrick is a smart one too, don't you know, when he's not listening to the siren song of sin."

"Ma, knock it off," Pat said, and I pictured him with a gun in his hand.

"Won every academic prize in school, and a way with the words, he has. And you encouraging him to go to school gladdens my heart."

I could see that 'Lashes' Dentino was in pain, but I was enjoying it. "Then it would be a sin not to at least try it out. Even for a year. You'll like it, Pat. It will challenge you."

His mother smacked Pat in the arm. "Isn't that what I always say?" She stopped and looked off behind me, narrowing her eyes. "What is that monster doing here?"

I turned and saw Frank Romeo watching us.

"Maybe he bought a ticket," Patrick said. He steered her away into the crowd. "Maybe he likes the theatre. Let it go, Ma."

"Don't look at the devil, lest we invite him in."

I took a deep breath. "Enjoy the show," I said and moved on.

A perfectly matched couple caught my eye next. Nell and Evan Williams from the jewelry shop were dressed to the nines, he in a tuxedo and she in a silver gown, which she wore with silver chains and amethyst bracelets. They weren't lying about enjoying the theatre. They greeted people like old friends. I stepped over to say hello.

"Many thanks for the tickets," Nell said. "It's a grand night for the theatre."

"Did you puzzle out any more about the pocket watch?" Mr. Williams asked.

"Sadly, no." I didn't need to be reminded of that gold trinket.

"Some secrets we take to the grave. It's the way of the world."

"And pocket watches?"

"Sometimes that too."

Nell Williams squeezed my hand and nodded to her husband that it was time to take their seats.

Sal sped by in his best tuxedo, and in his glory. He spotted Frankie the Cat and the two men embraced like old friends. I hoped Romeo had nothing to do with financing my play. Sal had often said he wanted no mob money. It was a bad bet, he said, because plays were so unpredictable. And in his experience, he said, mobsters weren't usually interested in losing their money, or in roughing up actors or producers, or even playwrights. But the mob could be unpredictable too. Sal was much more interested in rich angels who knew the theatre and knew that a play was always a gamble.

Still, I was nervous. Frank Romeo turned my way. He smiled and nodded when he saw me.

I almost stumbled into Jesse O'Banyon, the nurse who had helped both me and Graydon. "Jesse! I'm so glad you're here. I may have a heart attack," I declared.

"You're being dramatic," she laughed. "You'll live." Jesse was a down-to-earth tonic.

"You look spectacular in that dress." The hand-me-down navy blue flattered her figure, the sparkling trim was just enough, and she was pleased to have it.

"I'm keeping this dress for the rest of my life. This here is Hal."

She introduced the man she was with. He was a tall, thin intern at one of the Upper East Side hospitals, and he was very attentive to this suddenly very glamorous version of Night Nurse Jesse. The bells chimed and they walked into the theatre holding hands.

I wished I had a hand to hold on to, myself.

FORTY-SIX

I KNEW WHY GUIDO MORETTI *was killed.*

The thought suddenly hit me the way thoughts do, coming at you sideways, surprising you. It sneaked into my head while I was watching my play, following the actors click through their lines like clockwork, listening to the audience laugh on cue. My brain apparently had the spare time to work out a motive for Guido's "senseless" murder.

I peered around as if someone had whispered it in my ear. I wanted to run this thought past Graydon after the show. Not because I was in love with him, but because he was a professional detective, or so his business card said: *VERUM SEQUOR. I chase the truth.* A professional detective might have some other answer, or another theory. And strangely enough, because having broken it off with him, I felt safe with Graydon.

I still didn't know *who* exactly killed Guido 'Ratty' Moretti or Dante Scavullo, but the reasons were becoming clearer. Guido would do anything for anybody. He looked like a rat, but he was true blue, with a few flaws. Everyone said so.

This time, he had done a favor for a friend, probably without even knowing why. He was happy to do it.

Guido drove the getaway car for the killer who dispatched Scavullo.

He must have. Frank Romeo had praised Guido's talent behind the wheel and his loyalty. And Scavullo got in the way of someone's ambition.

I remembered my experience on Columbus Day, talking to witnesses in the school parking lot right after the bullets flew. Scavullo was shot, the assailant fled the scene from a second-floor window to the fire escape, then dropped down to the street and flung open the door of the waiting getaway car. The vehicle sped away before the killer shut the passenger side door.

The car itself looked like hundreds of other four-door black sedans. The cops weren't investigating. As Graydon told me, they were happy to let 'the scum' take care of each other and save them the trouble. Unless the public started to complain or someone walked into a police station and confessed, they would do the most cursory of investigations.

As far as I knew, Graydon's cop friends who were on the scene were nonplussed that Scavullo was killed and the killer got away. But not terribly troubled.

Guido may not have known what the assailant was up to in that moment, that the guy was at the school to kill Scavullo, but he certainly did later. Maybe he knew he would be in trouble and he wanted to confess to Romeo—unless the mob boss had a hand in it. Guido was both an accessory and a witness. The killer decided he couldn't leave any witnesses alive.

I looked for Graydon after the show, but he'd left with Lady Chaseborn. I hoped my insight would keep. Well, it wasn't like it was fresh information. Just a fresh angle.

Sal's after-show party was held in the lobby of the Washington Irving. The chandeliers were dimmed, their crystals glistening a little more softly. Round tables were graced with white linen cloths and candles, which made the space seem intimate, yet grand. The champagne flowed freely at the bar and waiters passed trays of hors d'oeuvres.

Finally, with a flourish, Sal made the announcement that *Leaving Alamogordo* would be extending its run. And moving about five blocks away, to the Nathaniel Hawthorne Theatre. A very respectable choice, though not quite as large as the Irv. A roar of pleasure erupted from the party and the applause went on and on.

Robbins and Amelia held court with new friends at one of the tables. And though many men circled around her, she leaned in close to the tall valet, who looked even more distinguished in his evening clothes. Patrick Dentino and his mother had one glass of champagne before wishing me adieu, and Jesse and her tall intern were already gone. The crowd was thinning, and it was time for me to make my exit.

Before I left, I asked Robbins to please inform Mr. Chaseborn I was heading to Bonaparte's, the small restaurant where Graydon and I had eaten after Scavullo's viewing. I was sure they'd let me in.

"I have some information for him. I'll be at the restaurant for at least an hour." I realized I didn't have any proof. It was just a theory about Guido, but that theory was knocking at my brain, and I knew it was true. Perhaps it was an Irish thing, the gift of "the knowing." Maybe I could get a bite to eat before private detective Chase ruined my appetite. I didn't know if Graydon would show up or agree with my theory about the deaths. No matter. I wanted his opinion. "Please tell me if he doesn't want to see me, Robbins."

"I doubt very much if that's the case, Miss Esmé. I'll phone Mr. Rupert from here, or from your flat, with your permission."

"Of course."

"Mr. Robbins is escorting me to your place," Amelia put in, "on account of I'm staying there and he wants me to be safe."

Had Amelia found out his first name? Would I ever find out? She was glowing and she threw him a worshipful look.

"I'll return home directly afterward, Miss Esmé. Mr. Rupert will receive the message. You have my word on it." He paused then added, "We both enjoyed the play, greatly."

He was already speaking for her as if they were a couple. That was interesting.

"Yeah, what he said." Amelia grinned.

I thanked him, grabbed my wrap from the coat check, and wove my way through the remaining groups of people and out the lobby doors. The air was brisk and smelled of woodsmoke. There were no cabs to be had.

I took a deep breath and strode briskly the few blocks towards Bonaparte's.

I had nearly reached my goal when Marco Scavullo emerged from the shadows of an unlit alley blocks away from the theatre. He startled me, and I was tired of it. Why was he always following me, waiting for me? I jumped away when I saw him. He reached out his arms to me.

"Hey, pretty lady. I think tonight you come out with me, yes? Let me charm you."

Impossible, I thought. "No, Marco. I'm not going anywhere with you." I picked up my pace and aimed for Bonaparte's. It was in sight, but it felt miles away. Marco easily caught up to me.

"Hey, do you not know me? I do not scare you, do I? I look the same, Esmé." He reached up and touched his new scar resulting from that day in the park. "Maybe I look a little more dangerous, my Aunt Juliette says. But I won't be dangerous with you."

Marco's scar wasn't that large. When he was shot, I thought it would be much more dramatic, because it bled so furiously. The bullet's mark was puffy and red, leaving a two-inch gouge on his cheek to always remind him of the day he was shot. The wound would calm down in time, but now it looked angry, and so did he. His handsome face was intact, but the scar underscored a hardness I hadn't seen before.

"I said no." I turned around to see if anyone else was near us.

"What's the matter? You afraid of the dark? Don't worry, Marco will take care of you." That was exactly what I was afraid of. "You've been ignoring me," he complained.

If I had, it wasn't working. "I'm not writing a play for you. I'm never writing a play for you. I have other things to do."

He wasn't listening to me. He moved closer, putting his arm around my shoulder and drawing me close. I shook him off, wondering how many women fell for this act. He backed away, but it wasn't far enough. New Jersey wouldn't be far enough.

"I got it all figured out, Esmé," he whispered in my ear. "You and me, we are meant to be together."

"What!" Bonaparte's lights twinkled for me. I practically ran for it.

"Wait, where are you going? You don't want to go in there." He looked with dismay at the restaurant.

'Yes, I do!" I yelled and he seemed surprised. "Don't tell me what I want."

Marco stopped and stared at me. "All right, all right. You got some fire in you. We go here. Together."

"I'm going in alone."

"I say no!"

I barged ahead through the doors. I could smell fresh bread baking and a hint of wine. I practically bumped into the waiter I'd met before. He remembered me.

"I'm waiting for Mr. Chase."

The waiter smiled. "Ah, the romance is still on."

His face fell when Marco entered through the door with a sullen scowl on his face.

Marco slowed, staring at the elegant room full of diners and taking note of the people at the bar. I tried to signal the waiter that things weren't right. He nodded briefly and addressed Marco.

"What can I do for you, sir?"

"A table, away from everyone. I want my lady to myself." Marco led with his chest.

"I'm not your lady," I said, through gritted teeth.

"That room." Marco seemed familiar with the layout. The waiter brought us into a small private dining space, separated by a red velvet curtain, but left open a few inches so we could see a slice of the larger room. Marco held my wrist with an iron grip. I was afraid he'd leave bruises, like the ones on Bianca's face.

"No." I glared at him.

Marco dragged me to the table and pulled out my chair. "When I tell you what we gonna do, you won't be mad." He said it like a little boy very proud of himself.

"I have no interest in you, Marco. You have Bianca Lombardi. Remember? She's crazy about you."

"Bianca! She's a little crazy, but she's nothing to me. You, Esmé. I'm thinking, you and me— We get married."

I gasped. "You're insane." I was horrified. It was possible that my morbid curiosity kept me frozen. Exactly how crazy was he?

"Is a good plan," he said. "I drive for Frank Romeo! I move up in the organization, like my uncle. You are famous playwright, you make lots of money. We have a good life."

"I'm not famous! You can't count on playwriting and I'm tired of people jumping to conclusions about me and what I might have and don't have. And I'm not having you!"

He waved away all my objections. "You have big apartment. We will live there. You are beautiful woman. I am handsome man." Briefly his hand brushed his cheek. "This scratch doesn't matter. Badge of honor."

Marco had no problem with his ego. It was massive. I wondered if he would tell me why he had killed his uncle—he had to have been the one who pulled the trigger. He convinced his pal Ratty Moretti to drive him to the school that day, though I wasn't sure whether Guido knew what he was doing there until it was all over.

The waiter brought a bottle of their cheaper wine. Did Marco expect me to pay for it? I had to escape.

"I need to use the ladies' room."

"What, right now?"

"Yes, right now." I stood up and grabbed my purse.

He stood and took my hand. "You come back. Leave your coat, I keep it safe." His other hand nestled on it, as if holding it for ransom.

I grabbed my coat, but he grabbed it back. There was no sign of Chase or the waiter. The pay phone was across the restaurant, and Marco opened the curtain to watch me as I headed for the powder room.

Inside the ladies' there was a blonde, a little tipsy, making a show of combing her hair and fixing her makeup, taking great care with her lipstick, though it would soon be worn off, leaving traces on her glass, her napkin, and her man.

"Excuse me, miss," I said, "I'm in a jam."

She squinted at me in the mirror. "Aren't we all, sister?"

"There's a crazy guy out there." I needed to get through to her. "He's after me."

"Story of my life," she agreed.

"Pease listen to me. I'm in trouble. Serious trouble."

Something in my tone changed her. "No kidding, sister? Real trouble?"

I scrawled on a piece of paper and handed it to her. "Call this number and tell them that Marco Scavullo is here and I need help. I'm Esmé."

"I'm Linda. Pleased to meet you. Got a nickel for the phone?"

I dug in my purse and handed her a fistful of change.

"Gee, thanks. I'll do it. Scavullo sounds Italian." She screwed up her face as if trying to remember where she heard that name before.

"He is. But you'll be talking to Robbins. He sounds like that actor, Ronald Colman."

"Oh, I adore Ronald Colman! 'Bulldog Drummond'!" Linda said. "You leave first, I'll make the call. Promise."

Marco was waiting for me outside the door, right in my face. "You sick or something?"

"Maybe. Could be that virus that's going around killing people. It could kill you."

That didn't faze him, and he steered me back to the table in the private dining room. I looked for Chase in vain. I felt abandoned. I knew Marco couldn't force me to marry him, not tonight. He couldn't force me out of this restaurant. I would make one hell of a scene and someone would call the cops. First, however, I wanted answers. What prompted this fresh insanity?

"Drink. Drink some wine, we celebrate. I drive us to Maryland tonight and we get married. Is legal there." There was a mad, excited gleam in his eyes.

"Maryland?" I'd heard stories about Maryland.

"Yeah, I'm smart guy, see. We get married in Maryland same day, no problem, no wait."

"You don't want to marry me, Marco." I willed myself to think of some way out of this. Maybe just screaming? I couldn't bear the thought of him touching me, this brutal handsome moron.

"You change your mind. You good Catholic girl." He poured me a glass of the cheap red wine.

"Do you want me to pray for you?" I set the wine down. "Catholic women get married in the church. Not in Maryland."

"Good idea, we do that too, big church wedding, after legal marriage tonight. After I make sweet love to you." He thought that was funny. I inched away from him. "You will like it. I take you to the beach, like Dante takes Juliette."

"The beach?"

"My uncle, he loves—" He caught himself. "He loved the beach, swimming through the waves."

Bells were ringing in my brain, like the waves that were etched into Dante Scavullo's pocket watch.

"What beach?" *The numbers!* The numbers in the waves. Maybe the numbers were an address at a beach?

"He liked that boring beach. Cape May. Too quiet. All families, full of old people. But I take you to Atlantic City, lots of action there." He flashed his best smile. The scar wrinkled.

"I would never marry a murderer. But do tell me, Marco. Why did you kill your uncle?"

Forty-Seven

"WHAT YOU TALKING? WHERE YOU get this stupid idea?" Marco was suddenly angry and wary.

"Is it stupid, Marco? Convince me you didn't kill your uncle."

"Not me! Some other mob killed Dante." He gulped some wine. "A little gang war. Why would I kill my uncle?"

"You didn't want him to leave the mob. It embarrassed you that he had a mob connection, a connection *you* wanted, and he was giving it up."

"I liked my uncle. But he wanted to be a nobody. I am somebody. You, you need a strong man to keep you in line."

Marco needed a woman with a whip, but hopefully he'd be behind bars first. Where the hell was Chase?

"You don't want a wife who knows your secrets."

"You know nothing." His eyes darted around.

"And Guido?" I pressed. "Why was he killed?"

Marco shrugged elaborately. "Was very sad, but why would I know?"

Little Bianca Lombardi barged in, leaving the red curtains rippling in her wake. While he'd been following me, she'd been following him. She pointed her red fingernails at Marco and he jumped to his feet. I recognized the baggy brown coat she'd worn in the Ramble, now over a red dress. Her lipstick was smeared and both her eyes and her rouge were too bright. Her black hair was tangled and wild.

"I told you to stay away from her, Marco." Now she pointed at me. "She is no good. That bitch will never have you." She reached for him, her nails right in his face. He swatted her hands away.

"Bianca, I will never want him," I broke in, but they were paying no attention to me.

It was odd, I'd never seen the small, furious, and often bruised Bianca Lombardi as a pink-notepaper kind of gal, though it was perfectly obvious now that it was she, not Trixie Dunlop, who wrote that anonymous note. I thought Bianca could read my disdain of Marco and the mob at every turn. I was no threat to her. But she refused to see it. Why? Because Marco was such a prize?

"Go away, Bianca," Marco said. "Leave me alone."

She stretched up to bring them face to face. "You are mine, Marco. We share our secrets."

I was willing to bet there was one secret he didn't know.

"How about this one?" I said. "Bianca is the one who shot you, Marco."

They both stared at me in horror. He stood and towered over her. "What is she saying? You shoot at me? Bianca, you shot my beautiful face?" He paused in disbelief. "Why would you shoot me?"

I was pretty sure everyone in the restaurant could hear them. Outside the curtain, the low hum of conversation stopped, no dishes clattered, all glasses were stilled. I could feel the crowd listening, breathing, attentive as a Broadway audience. Someone please call the police, I begged silently. But was I running for the door? No, I had to see the end of this scene.

"It's a lie," Bianca lied. "I love you, Marco, I would never hurt you."

"Except when you miss your real target," I said. They turned to me. "You were both busy, but I have photos from that day in the Ramble. I was lucky I turned away from you for just a moment, Marco. Or it would have been me. I heard something in the bushes. Bianca was waiting. She had the pistol in her pocket. You can see the fabric of her coat sag in my pictures. There was no one else around, except me and Patrick Dentino. It had to be her." I had finally worked it out. Bianca would never deliberately hurt the man she adored. "She was aiming at me, Marco."

"You should have died," she screamed at me.

What do you know? I was right. Marco looked confused. He was not quick on the uptake, proving Frankie the Cat Romeo right.

"It can't be true! She always loved me," he said. "Bianca? You were going to kill my Esmé?"

"The question is who killed Guido?" I asked, now that I knew I was on the right track.

An anguished Marco raised his fist to Bianca and she cowered away from him. "Guido didn't need to die," he said. "You did that."

I thought I heard whispers from the other side of the curtain. Marco and Bianca were too busy to notice. I backed away. This was getting messier and messier.

"Guido needed to die," she hissed. "He was going to tell Romeo you killed your uncle."

"You told me to kill Dante! You said I would take his place, move up in the organization. Be a big man. You said Mr. Romeo always hated Dante, but he couldn't do nothing about it!"

"Yeah, yeah, like I said, you just have to be smart, Marco," she pleaded with him. I have found that pleading with someone to be smarter never really works. If only it did.

Marco shook his head. "You gotta get out of my life, Bianca, or I tell Mr. Romeo you hid in the back of his car and shot Guido in the head. It was wrong. Guido was a sweet boy, he'd never tell nobody."

"Guido had to go! And now she has to go." She reached for her purse—her gun must have been in it.

I slapped it out of her hands, it landed with a loud thud, and I kicked it under the table. She was torn between hanging on to Marco and going after her gun. He grabbed her and kept her from flying at me, her pointed red nails clawing the air.

"And what about the other bootlegger?" I shouted at Bianca. "You killed him to throw Romeo off the track, to make it look like a gang war."

"You think you're a genius or something?" Bianca sneered. "Maybe you are, but nobody's going to know, because you ain't leaving here alive, Miss Esmé de LaForet. That guy was like Dante, he was a nobody. But he was handy, and he had so much cash on him. I never had no money. I never had nothing till I found Marco."

Marco gawked first at Bianca and then at me. "Nobody's hurting Esmé. See, she's better than you, Bianca. She figured all this out. She is prettier, richer, smarter." He looked at me with some alarm at that realization. "She will love me, she will be my wife."

"No. She is not prettier and she's not smarter." Bianca lunged for me. "And she ain't gonna marry you."

He held Bianca back and she may have spat something, but to my ears it sounded like snarling and hissing.

"Listen to me, you idiots. I do not love Marco. I don't even like Marco. I am in love with somebody else." I hated to admit that even to myself. I was backing away, almost to the curtain, where I could flee.

"Who?" Marco demanded.

"Stupido, who do you think?" Bianca said. "You don't know? She loves that Englishman. Chase."

Did everybody believe I was in love with Chase before I did? God, how embarrassing. It didn't matter, maybe I was in love with him, but there was no future for us. We were too different. He had yachting parties and country clubs in his future, while I looked forward—I hoped—to dusty theatres, opening nights, and ghost lights.

"Is it true?" Marco demanded. "I will kill this man Graydon Chase."

I backed away and bumped into something large behind the curtains. Two men with guns drawn, and they burst past me into the private dining room. Behind them uniformed police officers rushed in.

"You won't be killing anyone anymore, either of you rats." Frank Romeo pointed his gun from Marco to Bianca. "Traitors."

Next to him was Graydon, gun in hand. They'd arrived at the same time. Later I learned that Romeo had seen Marco following me and Bianca following him, and he followed the pair of them. It was a regular pied piper moment. And then both he and Graydon had listened behind the curtain, along with all the diners, while I spelled out what I had deduced about the murders.

In my opinion, they could have acted a little sooner. They missed several crucial cues. Someone had called the police. The diners seemed paralyzed in their seats. It was a full house, at full attention. What were they waiting for? Gunshots? Chekhov's Law?

Graydon held me close, and I didn't protest. My legs felt like rubber, and when I slumped, he lifted me.

"You can collapse later, Esmé," he whispered. "You're doing wonderfully."

Frankie the Cat was terrifying in his wrath. He emanated a freezing sort of rage. Dante's nephew was a rogue killer, that was bad enough—but he'd also betrayed his Aunt Juliette, the woman Romeo would never stop loving.

"What are you going to do to me?" Marco squeaked, trying for defiance.

Romeo pulled a pair of leather gloves out of the pocket of his famous camel hair coat, and the young killer flinched. Frankie the Cat took the gloves and slapped Marco across his face with them, as if he couldn't bear to touch the man barehanded.

"We got a system of justice in this country," Romeo said. "You killed your own uncle, who was leaving the business, leaving clean. You had no cause. Dante and me, we were both satisfied with the arrangement. It breaks my heart that Juliette needs to know the truth, you stupid punk. She gotta know she was living with a snake from Sicily. She was feeding a traitor, a killer. You."

"You can't turn me over to the cops! We don't do that, Boss. Not people like us. We don't turn in our own kind."

"People like us? You got no idea. You and me, kid, we ain't the same kind." Romeo gestured and the cops pushed in and handcuffed Marco, roughly. Now he advanced on the wailing Bianca. She was shaking on the floor, curled up in a ball, as if to hide, scratching vainly for her purse, far under the table.

"We did this for you," she screamed at Romeo. She scooted away from him on her bottom, tears streaking her face.

"You shut up, you little witch. You killed my boy, Guido. How could anyone do that? You should have listened to your father and stayed away from Marco, and from Guido, and most of all, me." The cops hauled her to her feet and cuffed her. Bianca Lombardi was small, but she fought ferociously, harder than Marco, like a fierce little badger. "Now, you gonna pay," Romeo said. "They put women in the electric chair now, you know that? Sing Sing, nineteen twenty eight, and again this past summer. On the front page. They say you can smell your skin burning when they pull the switch. Maybe you make the front page too."

Bianca screamed loud and long. "Nooooo!" Romeo slapped her face with the same pair of gloves, which finally silenced her.

"This is your fault, Bianca." Marco's shoulders moved as if to hit her, but his hands were cuffed. "I got plans! I had a future with Esmé de LaForet, her apartment, her plays, her bed! You ruined everything."

"I love you, Marco," Bianca sobbed. He turned his face away from her. His scar seemed to glow.

Without Bianca pushing him, I realized, Marco would never have pulled the trigger on his uncle. Marco's big talk about taking Dante's place in the mob might have remained just that—talk. Miss Lombardi was the murder mastermind, the one who had whispered in his ear. Bianca wanted to be with a big man, she wanted to call the shots, and finally she killed poor Ratty Moretti to get what she wanted. And then she killed a local bootlegger, simply to throw everyone off the trail.

"There are ways of taking care of the two of you, the old family ways. But out of respect for Juliette, I hand you over to the City of New York. And the loving arms of the electric chair. You make me sick." Frankie the Cat spun on his heels and stomped away to the bar.

The cops dragged off their prisoners, the private dining room emptied, the other diners resumed dining, and I found myself alone with Graydon Chase.

"I didn't think you were coming." I blinked back my tears so they wouldn't fall. *Damn it, I am not going to cry.*

"Esmé, darling, I was delayed escorting Mother home. I phoned Robbins. He told me an inebriated woman called to relay that you were in danger, and Marco Scavullo was with you here at Bonaparte's. Then I learned Romeo was headed this way too."

"Did you learn anything else?" His smile affected me down to my toes and the scent of him filled my head. His blue stare was altogether too beautiful.

"Apparently, Robbins sounds just like Ronald Colman. I had no idea. And I also learned that you're in love with me."

Forty-Eight

I WAS MORTIFIED. EVERYONE KNOWS the man is supposed to say it first. Every playwright knows this. That I didn't say it to him directly made no difference, no difference at all. My saying it first meant that he had all the power. Worse, he didn't say it back to me, and I had no way of knowing what his feelings were. Heartless playboy. Who wrote this terrible play?

In the meantime, Bonaparte's had become a scene of utter confusion. Police stomping in and out, waiters and the maître d' talking all at once, diners chattering. None of the diners left their seats, they seemed riveted by tonight's entertainment, but the noise level was rising.

I saw my tipsy friend Linda from the ladies' room, peeking through the curtains. She raised her glass to me. "Thank you for the phone call," I said.

"I didn't know whether to believe you, but what do you know? I make a phone call. Ronald Colman answers! Wow. Then all hell breaks loose. Quite a show."

"You helped save my life."

"All in a day's work." She giggled and signaled the waiter for another drink. I reached for my purse to pay for Linda's bar tab, but she shook her head. It was taken care of. Romeo? Graydon? She returned to the bar.

Graydon tucked his gun away in his shoulder holster under his tuxedo jacket. Marco and Bianca were being shuffled through the restaurant's front door by the cops, minus her purse and gun. She was sobbing. Marco was stoic, radiating a silent fury. Bianca should have been grateful to have the police guarding her, or the younger Scavullo might have killed her with his bare hands.

Frank Romeo watched them go. He returned to the private dining room with a glass of wine in his hand. He nodded to Bones and another man, standing by the door. The two men visibly relaxed.

Romeo, Graydon, and I stared at each other in silence for a moment. Finally, Romeo addressed me.

"So you figured this out, Miss de LaForet. I knew Dante's killer had to be someone close, someone in the organization. But Scavullo's own nephew? I never figured him for this. Too stupid."

"Bianca had the backbone," I said. "She pushed Marco into it and she pulled the trigger on Guido, probably because he was going to confess to you."

"That explains it, Romeo," Graydon said. "The female is deadlier than the male. And no one understands that better than a female. We underestimate them at our peril. It took Esmé to realize what was going on. And now we know Bianca was our pink-paper pen pal."

Frank Romeo looked puzzled. At least Graydon understood. However, I wish he'd simply said the female is *smarter* than the male.

"She wrote you a letter? This is a hell of a thing," Romeo added. "That little frail threatened you?"

"Anonymous letter. Even I didn't think it was her." I took a breath.

"Bianca's so little she fooled a lot of people. Like me." The mob boss lifted his glass to me. "I owe you, Miss de LaForet."

I was alarmed at the very thought. I could feel Graydon's hand in mine now, squeezing it in warning.

"You don't owe me anything, Mr. Romeo. Really."

"I pay my debts. Point of honor. I don't forget. Not ever." I gulped. It wouldn't be a good thing for anyone to associate us. "What can I do for you?" I thought fast.

"Come to my next play."

"I will. And don't worry, I won't invest in the show." Romeo smirked. "I hear the theatre is usually a bad bet. But what can I do for *you*?"

"If you feel you have to do something, why not let Patrick Dentino go to college? You know, 'Lashes' Dentino?"

"The half-Irish? Good kid. But why college?"

"Because his mother wants him to go. Because he has a hankering to write, and I think he might be good at it."

"His mother? She thinks I'm the devil incarnate."

"I take it he might never rise all the way in your organization," Graydon said.

Romeo shrugged elaborately. "It's the family thing. If he was full Italian, maybe. Nothing for yourself, Esmé de LaForet?"

"The world needs good writers, ones who've seen a bit of the world, the rough and tumble of it. And I'm half Irish myself."

"You think he'd leave Frankie the Cat?"

"I think he could be persuaded it's a good thing. If he can leave clean. Who knows, maybe he'd be the one to write that play. The one with the handsome leading man?"

Frank Romeo laughed and clapped his hands. "Done. Dentino, the college boy. We'll give him a scholarship. No strings. Esmé da LaForet, you and me, we are square. We owe each other nothing. The slate is clean. But if you ever need a favor—"

"Thank you." A favor that would never be called in.

He turned to Graydon. "Chase, tell Juliette for me. Tell her—everything."

"I'll do that," Graydon agreed.

"Give it to her straight. It's gonna hurt, but it's the best way. And the two of youse. Don't let these little problems get in the way of true love, *capisce?* No need to protest. It's written all over you. See you in church."

Frank Romeo left. Graydon and I stared at each other before slipping through the curtains into the general dining room. There was applause. Shouts and questions rang out throughout the room. Tonight, they'd had a free show thrown in with dinner.

There was also a wall of reporters and photographers, notebooks in hand, cameras raised. Police holding them back. Flashbulbs popped on big four-by-five news cameras, blinding us momentarily. It was interesting and a little frightening to be on the other side of the Fourth Estate. I tried not to show any fear.

The reporters focused their questions on me, because they knew me. I had been one of their own. I'm not sure they recognized Graydon Chase/Rupert Chaseborn. These weren't society reporters. I pasted a smile on my face so I wouldn't look terrified. I lifted my hand and waited until everything was quiet.

Then the questions began.

"How'd you meet Marco Scavullo?"

I sidestepped that question. "Anyone can buy a ticket to my play. And I hope they do."

"Is it true Marco killed his uncle Dante Scavullo and you figured it out?" another one shouted. Yet another answered, "That's one for our team." I may have nodded. More questions.

"How did you tumble to Bianca Lombardi as the mastermind?"

"I was a reporter," I replied. "I can't give out trade secrets. I'm sure the police will have more answers for you."

"We heard the mob boss's nephew was in love with you."

"Any woman can tell you about unwanted attention. It was all in his head."

After a few more questions, I held up my hands. "It's been a very long day, boys. Thank you all." I smiled as more flashbulbs popped.

Graydon pulled down his hat, shading his eyes, as he efficiently rushed me through the restaurant and outside to the street.

"You've had experience with this," I said.

"I've escorted a society deb or two. Boring assignment, compared to you, Elf."

❧

Graydon and I talked late into the night, but we spoke no more of love, or even of the reporters and the police, or what the future held for the murderers. Instead, we talked about the beach, Scavullo's pocket watch, and its recent engraving.

He accompanied me home, where I retrieved my hand-written description and my poorly drawn image of Scavullo's pocket watch, and the numbers I had seen among the waves. I showed him the photo I'd taken of Scavullo's pocket watch, which was considerably better than my sketch. At first, Graydon was skeptical, but curious about the watch. I'd refused to turn it over to him the first time we met. In that supply closet. When he pulled a gun on me. When he kissed me.

Now I offered my idea of where Juliette's nest egg might be, the money that Dante said he would leave her so she would never have to worry.

"Why didn't you tell me about the watch earlier?" he asked. "You actually found the watchmaker? Yet you said nothing. It's possible we could have answered some of these little mysteries before now."

"The watchmaker, Mr. Williams, didn't know what the numbers meant either. They simply supplied the engraving. I didn't take a good look at the watch until later anyway. It was a hot potato, one I didn't want. And you had this picture in your stack of photos all along, after we developed them."

"Let's not argue, Esmé."

A couple of brandies gave us something to hold on to. "How can we figure out now what the engraving means?"

"How could anyone? Scavullo turns out to be a pretty cryptic character. Unexplored depths, it seems. Romeo said he was just a numbers guy. Now it turns out Dante may have hidden his secrets in numbers." He picked up the photo of the engraving and stared at it. "Possibly."

"What if the waves represent the beach?" I said. "The numbers could be an address, or a safety deposit box, or something."

"There are a lot of beaches, Esmé. Not to mention safety deposit boxes."

"I'm talking about the beach he loved, according to Marco anyway. My guess is Cape May, New Jersey."

"Cape May?" Graydon tilted my terrible drawing this way and that, catching the Roman numerals. He compared it to the photo, then wrote the numbers down in a small notebook.

"After Marco said he would marry me in Maryland, he'd take me to Atlantic City." I shivered at the thought.

"Steady, darling. You're safe."

I may have misheard the *darling*. A sip of the brandy helped my nerves. "He said he would skip that 'boring' beach that Dante and Juliette loved. If these waves meant something to Dante, it would be that boring beach, where families go."

"Cryptic, yet typical. Cape May. Pretty place."

I hadn't been there. "I can't be sure the engraving is a message. I only knew he picked up the timepiece the day he died. Afterwards, he was so distracted by a phone call, he left it on the counter."

"I've been thinking about that," Graydon said.

"Do you recall the pictures of Scavullo in the newspapers, with his pockets turned inside out? Were they looking for the watch, as well as his cash?"

"The alleged hidden stash? Who knows? You could have mentioned you were out sleuthing on your own."

"Could I? I didn't know whether you really were some kind of private investigator, or some rogue mobster. Or a gigolo. Second, I didn't know the watch was the key to all of this. I still don't. Three, I didn't know what you were up to with Juliette."

He leveled that blue gaze on me. "I thought you were merely a debutante, a dilettante, a playwright. As for Scavullo, he left very few hints as to where that money might be. The engraving may be a false clue. Juliette has had the watch all this time and never suggested it meant anything. So far, I've turned up nothing. Banks? As you can imagine, people of their ilk don't really believe in banks."

"Marco thought he was boring."

"So did his wife, but she regarded him highly. Families can be a terrible burden."

I yawned. "I can't keep my eyes open much longer, Graydon."

If I was looking for some kind of declaration, I didn't get it. Instead, he squeezed my hand.

"Get some sleep, you'll feel better tomorrow."

He checked the windows and doors to make sure they were secure. I opened the front door for him. He kissed me gently as if I might break. "We have things to discuss, my dear. However, tonight it's much too late."

"When will I see you?" Famous last words of women who never see men again. I could have bitten my tongue.

"Soon, Elf Queen. First, I need to visit a widow, and possibly a beach. Such a shame you have to work."

FORTY-NINE

"I CAN'T BELIEVE THIS HAPPENED on my night off!" Reggie blasted me on the phone the next day. He was aggrieved over missing the mobster murder story and not being at Bonaparte's. And he seemed upset with me personally for some reason, until I mollified him with an exclusive.

I had Amelia to thank for reviving me and pouring coffee into me so I could make that date. She greeted me in the early afternoon with a stack of newspapers and far too many questions.

"You solved the whole murder thing. I can't believe it. And your play was okay too."

I fled to the shower and managed to dress myself, but not without criticism.

"Are you wearing that?" Amelia demanded. "How are people going to know you without the glamour and gloss? And a copy of the *Post*?"

"I'm incognito." I needed the comfort of a warm sweater and the mobility of slacks. I grabbed a shawl and a hat that hid most of my face.

"If you insist. Don't worry, I won't miss anything," Amelia promised. She seemed ridiculously pleased with herself. "I'll work on your scrapbook today."

On the way out the door, she promised to clip all the news articles about the murder and me and Chaseborn and paste them in my scrapbook. She pointed out that Nina's soft society story—THE PLAY'S THE THING FOR ESMÉ DE LAFORET—made the front page and was linked to another article about the murders. Amelia also flashed some other paper headlines:

NEPHEW AND GIRLFRIEND FINGERED IN BOOTLEGGER DEATHS

BROADWAY SCRIBE AND PRIVATE EYE SOLVE MOBSTER MURDER MYSTERY

PLAYWRIGHT AND PLAYBOY UNRAVEL SCAVULLO MURDER: COMBINING DETECTING AND ROMANCE?

Reggie kept watch at the diner window and waved me in. He immediately started demanding answers, but first I hit him up for a roast beef sandwich and some milk.

"I couldn't know that Marco was developing an obsession with me," I said. "Besides, he was only after my royalties and a part in a play, and what he thought was my glamorous life. Nothing personal."

Reggie pouted. "You were in the middle of the whole Frank Romeo murder drama and you never told me, your oldest friend in New York City?"

"That's Nina. And you know I don't say things until I'm sure of them. Especially when Sir Reginald Archibald Pendleton the Third has a pencil in his hands."

"I expected more loyalty from my future wife." He stirred his coffee for a long time.

"I know, it's awful. Grounds for a future divorce?"

"Better be more awful than this. This Marco creep wanted you, wanted to marry you? Makes my skin crawl."

I waved that thought away, mentally gagging. "But not for my charming self. Like you do."

"That was the guy following you the night we went to Sardi's?" He shook his head in disbelief. "Hopefully, he's on ice until they fry him. Start talking, Esmé. Or else I make it all up."

"You won't, because I'm giving you an exclusive."

"An exclusive? I'm listening."

"It's a story of obsession, Reggie. Bianca's obsession with Marco, and his obsession with me. Or rather, my things. He thought I had money, he wanted it. He wanted my apartment, my life, and he wanted me to write him into my plays. Bianca Lombardi wanted him. They thought the solution was murder."

Reggie pulled his slim notebook out of his jacket pocket. I didn't object. "A double obsession turned deadly. Interesting."

"I dismissed Bianca because she was tiny, her father beat her, and she clearly was besotted with the younger Scavullo. I didn't recognize the madness beneath the bruises." I fiddled with my coffee while Reggie scribbled notes.

"Madness beneath the bruises. Good line," he said.

"By the way, thanks for heading that blind item off at the pass." I remembered Trixie was part of the mix of misdirection. "I owe you."

"We couldn't let your reputation be tarnished by some nobody with a crush on the elusive Chaseborn." He set his pen down for a moment. "And Esmé, I wouldn't blame you if you had spent the night with Chaseborn, without the supporting cast of characters, the butler, the nurse, the entire medical profession."

"You're just trying to salve your own conscience." I dabbed my eye with a hankie. "Thank you."

"Don't go sentimental on me now, Rafferty."

"But anyone with a brain's going to be able to figure out it's me and Chase," I complained.

"That's why we love blind items." He grinned broadly. "So how is it with you and Chase? Big romance?"

"No." I stared out the window. The leaves were falling. Soon they'd be gone.

Reggie flipped a page in his reporter's notebook.

"Says here you declared your love for Detective Chase while the madman threatened to drive you across state lines and forcibly marry you. Many witnesses. Apparently, everyone in Bonaparte's dining room heard you, not to mention the press dogs." Reggie could look very superior when he wanted to. "I am so sorry I missed all this."

"I think I'll have a whiskey."

"Now you're talking."

FIFTY

TELEGRAM FROM CHASE CAME to my office on Monday.

CAPE MAY SUCCESS. YOUR LEGWORK ESSENTIAL. BACK TONIGHT. PICK YOU UP AT EIGHT. GRAYDON.

He didn't give me any hints about where we were going, but Amelia had laid out my emerald-green chiffon gown. Unusual choice for a theatre dark night. I gathered that the dress was a hint and Amelia had been in touch with Robbins. She knew I hadn't worn it yet. She also knew that clothes would help keep my mind off this guessing game. I had half a mind to wear slacks. I hadn't actually said yes to his invite. What if I'd had plans? But the dress won.

The glorious gown felt like a dream, with its lovely layers of skirt flowing almost to the floor. Reaching my elbows, the sleeves were anchored to dark green straps studded with faux jewels, which danced like angel wings around my shoulders. The color made my eyes look greener.

Who knows, I thought, maybe Graydon wanted to take me to Delmonico's or the Rainbow Room. We were going to dinner to celebrate a job well done.

Mr. Chaseborn picked me up and escorted me to the Pierce-Arrow. It was his car, of course, and not a friend's. He told me I looked wonderful in my Willie-designed frock. Yet I felt he was holding the "love" word over my head, just like the newspapers did. I was surprised when we drove to his apartment building. He stopped at the entrance and handed the keys to the doorman to park the car.

"Here?" I asked.

"Here. We can go dancing later, if you like."

Chase being mysterious made me crazy. When we were alone in the elevator, I noted his pressed evening wear, but I said, "Tell me about your trip to the beach, to Cape May."

He smiled his slow, satisfied smile. "Quite successful."

"Is there more?"

"You're so impatient."

We strolled from the elevator to the apartment, where Robbins opened the door and took my coat. I saw fresh flowers and glowing candles all around the room. It looked ready for a party.

Two caterers bustled about, and one offered us champagne on a silver tray.

"Perrier-Jouët?" I looked to Graydon as I picked it up.

"I understand you like champagne for special occasions."

"Yes. Is this a party?"

"I hope so, for two."

Even though I'd slept most of the weekend, I was miffed that he hadn't bothered to call. Puzzled, I let the scene play out. We seated ourselves on the elegant silver-blue silk-covered sofa. The fireplace was lit, and we enjoyed a view of Central Park. Lights twinkled in other windows in other buildings.

He touched his glass to mine. We sipped the luscious liquid. It was, after all, Perrier-Jouët.

"I am sorry, Esmé, but there was so much to deal with— the police, and Romeo— I had to make absolutely sure he knows I am finished with any business relating to his organization or personnel. Our meetings took most of Saturday. We parted amicably. But I never stopped thinking of you."

"And yesterday?"

"Yesterday I met with Juliette Scavullo. About this Cape May business."

"You thought it was a long shot."

"Don't be ridiculous. I thought it was impossible. Wild goose chase."

I moved to the window to admire the view. "I often wish I'd never picked up that watch. Let Ray at the diner steal it. Pawn it for five bucks. Who cares."

He followed me and put a hand on my back, shooting hot feelings of lust through me.

"Funny thing about that, Esmé. Scavullo may have had some kind of premonition of disaster. When he saw you at the diner, I think he decided you of all people would retrieve his prized watch, with its ambiguous clues, and keep it safe. As you say, you knew him from church."

I don't know why that made me sad. "But what about Juliette and the money?"

"She said they always spoke of retiring to the beach, in Cape May. They stayed there in the summers so often, Dante even opened a bank account, representing his move toward becoming legitimate. She thought he was just spinning dreams."

"He wasn't though, was he? He may have been a bit dull, but methodical. Maybe a little bit creative?"

"Her son Anthony let me see the watch, and they were there, as you said. The numbers and the waves. We were all duly amazed."

"Cut to the chase, Chase."

"I lit out early today for the beach. There were a couple of safety deposit boxes at the bank under both their names. I had the keys and a notarized letter from Juliette Scavullo granting me access. All very tedious stuff."

"You're killing me! And in the box?"

"A deed to a house there. A set of keys. The street address was the same number as the safety deposit box. So they couldn't forget, I presume. Also, a healthy amount of gold and cash. Silver dollars, paper. A pearl necklace he was going to give her for their anniversary. Juliette's very grateful to us both. She thinks we're good together, by the way, but she said she'll tell you Sunday next."

"I need to find a new church." I put the French Catholic place of worship at the top of my list. He laughed.

"Sir, Miss Esmé?" Robbins escorted us to a windowed corner of the living room where a small round table had been arranged with candles, roses, and orchids in a vase. There was also a silver bucket filled with ice and our bottle of champagne.

"This is gorgeous." I wanted to breathe it all in. Graydon was full of high spirits. He held the chair for me.

"Robbins said you found the dining room a bit imposing and impersonal." Not really, it was merely large enough for a dance hall. With a full orchestra.

"It doesn't have the same view." I was puzzled at all this ceremony. Did Graydon dine like this all the time? Did rich people? "I told Robbins I'd never come back."

"He's very glad you did. It's been a good day, Esmé, my dearest Elf."

The lights of Manhattan glittered outside and surrounded a dark swath of Central Park. I was dazzled. I had no words; the next move would have to be Graydon's. He filled my glass again and cleared his throat. "I had thought of taking you to someplace like Delmonico's, but I wanted this moment to be between us, quiet and glorious."

"Glorious?" I asked.

"You are all things to me, Esmé. I love you."

What did he say? "You let me say it first."

"You didn't exactly say it to *me*. You declared it to two killers."

"You were listening, along with a Mafia boss and everyone at Bonaparte's."

"But you said it," he said. "You're blushing. You can't back out of it now, my dear."

"The man is supposed to say it first." I was still aggrieved by that.

"You didn't know? I've loved you almost from that first moment."

That was a little embarrassing. "The first moment, in the broom closet?"

"Yes. I love you for so many reasons, because you are intelligent, and tenacious, and you always have a ready reply."

Except now. I seemed quite mute. I felt my eyes go wide and my pulse race. "Me?"

'You're willing to help people, even when they are the wrong people. I even love you, Elf, when you annoy me."

"I annoy you?"

"Don't interrupt, darling. I have things to say."

This was so out of character. Was he about to have a stroke? "Are you all right, Graydon? Feeling well?" Did someone dope his drink? Certainly not I. He swallowed most of his champagne.

"This is hard for me, Esmé, as you know quite well, I am British. It is hard for us to declare our feelings, but I am declaring myself for you."

"Declaring?" I couldn't stop staring at him.

"Perhaps it has something to do with being an American now, with that American freedom to speak out. I love your beauty and the expression you get when you are about to puncture someone's ego, when you are amused and about to skewer someone when they deserve it. I love it when you hold back and catch my eye so we can share the joke. I love that you express yourself, whether it's in your work or merely by throwing a martini in someone else's face."

"I haven't done that yet, but it is a lifelong goal," I admitted. "For the pure drama of it."

"I love you. And you love me. Don't you, Esmé Elf?"

I paused. I made him wait.

"Yes, I seem to love you. Far too much."

He kissed me. Even my toes felt the tingle. I wondered briefly if this was it, the only time I would hear Rupert Graydon Chase Chaseborn express himself so thoroughly.

"I want to marry you, Esmé." He paused, reached into his jacket, and withdrew a ring box. I choked up completely. I found it hard to breathe. "Speechless, my love? We can work out all the issues. I promise not to stifle your independence. You have the soul of a suffragette."

"That's a pretty big promise, Graydon. I am the daughter of a suffragette. I'll never quit writing."

"I wouldn't ask you to. And certainly not now that you've infected my mother." He gestured around the apartment. "We can trade this in for a brownstone, a townhouse, a hovel, or any place you wish, if you like."

"I have my own place."

"And it's adorable. For the record. I'll never ask you to give up your flat. It will make a charming love nest, or you can make it your office, where you spin your tales. Or whatever you wish. I would insist we live together."

"I'd never agree to separate bedrooms, the way the English are rumored to do."

"Neither would I. You would be stuck with me," he said, nuzzling my cheek.

"What if I want to work with you? On detective things?"

I watched his eyebrows rise and his brain calculating.

"My detective work will never be this exciting or dangerous again. My work will be too boring for words. But if I ever need your help, I'll ask for it. And you can always supply the drama. On stage."

I was silent for several moments. I had so many problems with the idea of *us*, with us being married. Married to Graydon Chase, aka Rupert Graydon Chaseborn. It wasn't how I saw myself. Still, I didn't feel the panic I'd had with Roger. I felt warm and oddly safe, and still that electric current flowed between us.

"You know I believe in long, very long, engagements?"

He flashed his wolf grin. "I know you believe engagements are for getting to know each other better. Biblically."

As often as possible. "A woman wouldn't want to make a big mistake."

"So you have said." He took my hand. "Nor would a man want to make a mistake."

"What about all those society debutantes?"

"They could never hold a candle to you. Will you marry me, Esmé Rafferty de LaForet? Please."

He opened the box and presented it to me. This was no trifle of a ring and it had the look of an heirloom. It was a very substantial diamond with small rubies set around it in filigreed gold. I don't know how to count carats, but it was stunning.

"It's so beautiful." I blinked tears away as he slipped it on my finger. A perfect fit. "Where did you find it?"

"If you don't like it, we can get something else."

"I adore it."

"She said you would. Mother, of all people. She said you would prefer an heirloom, a family piece, with sentimental value."

"But she— I don't understand. I don't suit you at all. Or her."

"She changed her mind about you the day she met you. Scones, tea, and sherry worked wonders. Said we had some sort of fever for each other, nursed each other through the plague, or some such nonsense, and it's such a rare thing, it would be a tragedy to let you slip through my fingers."

"Lady Jane is writing a gothic romance. I fear she might be writing us into it."

"Yes. She approves, but Esmé, darling, do you? You haven't said yes." His bravado was slipping. The man who always seemed so in control was nervous and waiting on me. "I only gained the courage to ask when I overheard you say you loved someone else and Bianca shouted out that it was me, at the restaurant with that idiot Marco. I've been debating how to ask you all weekend. With help from Robbins, who knows all manner of things."

I took a deep breath and sipped the champagne. Did I love him? I did, desperately, madly, to my utter surprise. That was the problem. I could almost hear my late parents objecting.

You've got yourself into quite a pickle, Esmé, but do you love him? Love smooths the rockiest seas.

Graydon and I were a complete mismatch, weren't we? But hadn't we worked well together? And wasn't it exciting?

"Yes, Rupert Graydon Chaseborn Chase. I will marry you. But be warned—it will be a very long engagement."

He kissed me and kissed me and kissed me again, the electrical current pouring through me like lightning through a kite on a string.

I even forgot to ask what was for dinner.

Author's Notes

CROOK TALES FOR TWO EMERGED during the recent pandemic, which is fast fading from our consciousness. Now it's hard to imagine that we were sequestered in our homes for so long, wearing masks, sanitizing our mail, and washing our vegetables. I was longing to rejoin the world, and in the midst of it all, I had a dream that was set in 1934 in New York City, shortly after Prohibition was repealed. How did I know? I simply did, the way you do when you awake. That dream was so real and so vivid and so dramatic that it became the first chapter of *Crook Tales*.

Although I was finishing a couple of other works at the time, I would wake up in the middle of the night with general pandemic anxiety and for the next hour or so I'd pen the next scene in *Crook Tales*. I craved glamour and excitement and this tale of a playwright, a playboy, mobsters, society folk, and the Broadway theatre world kept me going.

Once I started writing this, I seemed to be surrounded by happenings in, you guessed it, 1934. I wondered, when did the Tavern on the Green open? And the Rainbow Room? Answer: 1934. It was a bad year for mobsters. Bonnie and Clyde, Pretty Boy Floyd, John Dillinger, and Baby Face Nelson all met their violent ends in 1934. Jazz was sweeping the land and it seemed that everyone was dancing. Pre-Code movies were at their zenith, handling adult subject matter with wit and a wink; at least until halfway through the year 1934, when the infamous Hollywood Production Code kicked in, and the pre-Code era ended.

I was reading vintage magazines from the 1930s, for the fashions, the vernacular, the current events, and pure enjoyment. I also found *The New York Times* online archives invaluable for the same reasons, and I could track every day in which the book takes place. The only problem with *The Times* archives is that they are addictive, from the ads to the society news to the crimes. There were multiple kidnappings, robberies, and news of people hiding money beneath the floorboards. Writing and researching this book were so much fun that at times I didn't want to let go of my *Crook Tales* story. But I did, and finally it is here.

However, a book is not simply the words and story, there is also the cover to consider. I wanted a cover that would entice readers into the world of the story and give them a hint of the action. Let me offer many kudos to Kate Lamoure, whom I approached after seeing her YouTube video on the great American illustrator of that era, J. C. Leyendecker. I wanted the feeling that Leyendecker created of sumptuousness and glamour, but adding an extra touch of danger and romance. Kate was the artist for the job. We discussed the color palette, the Art Deco feeling of the piece, and the plot. She created this gorgeous cover image and even set in an Easter egg or two. Thank you, Kate.

I can't forget to laud Robert A. Williams, who designed the overall cover, with the type treatment and placement. Bob also designed the book, edited it, and kept me going. Always, my gratitude.

About the Author

MYSTERY AND THRILLER WRITER Ellen Byerrum is a former journalist in Washington, D.C., as well as a produced and published playwright. She also received her private investigator's registration in the Commonwealth of Virginia. Her latest book, *Crook Tales for Two,* is a departure from her previous books in terms of setting and time. Yet it is still *screwball noir*, incorporating mystery, comedy, and romance.

Byerrum's Crime of Fashion Mysteries feature D.C. fashion reporter Lacey Smithsonian, whose talent for solving crimes with fashion clues leads her to bodies dyed blue, haunted shawls, and the lost jewel-filled corset of a Romanov princess. Two books, *Killer Hair* and *Hostile Makeover*, were filmed for Lifetime. The *Brief Luminous Flight of the Firefly* is the 1940s prequel to her Crime of Fashion series, and features a very young Mimi Smith, the "Great-aunt Mimi" mentioned throughout the series. *Firefly* takes place during WWII in Washington, D.C.

Beyond the traditional mystery form, Byerrum has written a stand-alone psychological thriller, *The Woman in the Dollhouse*, which Best Thrillers says, "bewitches on page one and continues to mesmerize until its shocking conclusion." She has also penned a middle grade mystery, *The Children Didn't See Anything*. More recently, she published a children's rhyming picture book, *Sherlocktopus Holmes: Eight Arms of the Law*. In addition, two of her plays (under her pen name "Eliot Byerrum") have been published by Samuel French, Inc., and are available through Concord Theatricals.

KILLER HAIR
The First Crime of Fashion Mystery

"AND THEY SAY a bad haircut can't kill you…" In *Killer Hair*, set decades after *The Brief Luminous Flight of the Firefly*, OPA investigator Mimi Smith's great-niece Lacey Smithsonian arrives in D.C. as a young journalist. Lacey was a hard news reporter out West. But in Our Nation's Capital, "The City That Fashion Forgot," she gets saddled with her newspaper's despised fashion beat. Lacey grumbles, but she's the only one in the newsroom who dresses with style—and can decode what our clothes really say about us. Her friends call this talent her "Extra-Fashionary Perception."

When a young hairstylist is found slashed to death and nearly scalped with a straight razor, the D.C. cops call it suicide. But Lacey's EFP tells her no stylist would be caught dead with *that haircut!* She plunges headlong into a (nearly) one-woman murder investigation, armed only with her nose for nuance, her sense of style, her talent for trouble, her passion for a good story, and her friends. And her fabulous vintage wardrobe. Meanwhile, an unknown slasher's bloody razor seeks yet another victim with a beautiful head of hair. Can Lacey cut short this serial killer's career—before the killer cuts *her?*

Lacey Smithsonian's adventures in murder, romance, fashion, and comedy begin with *Killer Hair*, the first in Ellen Byerrum's bestselling Crime of Fashion Mysteries. Discover the whole series at your favorite bookseller.